Enthusiastic reviews for Lior Samson's novels –

The Rosen Singularity

"The plotting is ingenious and the characters come through strongly. It succeeds marvelously on the thriller level, but it also delivers a substantial intellectual and emotional kick."
— *Rebecca Goldstein, MacArthur Fellow, author*

"Vibrant and distinctive characters and thoughtful, yet engaging narratives and conversations, . . . an exciting, pulse-pounding story."
— *Laurie Jenkins, book blogger*

Bashert (The Homeland Connection)

"Samson writes with a crisp elegance, like John Le Carré, and weaves his plot magically, sustaining suspense throughout."
— *James A. Anderson, author*

"An ambitious novel, . . . moving with the speed of light between interconnected events, three continents, and a group of unique and memorable characters."
- *Avraham Azrieli, author*

The Dome (The Homeland Connection)

"Suspenseful and timely, . . . I cannot say enough good things about this novel."
— *Alan Caruba, critic, BookViews*

"An excellent read, and very highly recommended."
— *Midwest Book Review*

Web Games (The Homeland Connection)

"An outstanding tech thriller—better than Tom Clancy. . . . This ranks up there as one of the best [thrillers] I've read in 2011."
— *James A. Anderson, author*

"This extraordinary author has the ability to anticipate events. . . . You will not put it down."
— *Alan Caruba, critic, BookViews*

Chipset (The Homeland Connection)

"[A] multi-dimensional thriller that will satisfy discriminating readers who crave realistic stories populated by flesh-and-blood characters."
— Avraham Azrieli, author

"Lior Samson hits another one out of the park. ... Few thriller writers can match Samson's ability to deliver a gripping story."
— James A. Anderson, author

Gasline (The Homeland Connection)

"Samson turns up the heat with a high-energy plot and ... a perfect mix of techno thrill and human conflict. ... a rip-roaring ride. Excellent!"
— Avraham Azrieli, author

"[A] great novel ... high concept, flesh-and-blood protagonist, and realistic action. ... [It] will raise your blood pressure and make you think."
— Columbia Review of Books and Film

Flight Track (The Homeland Connection)

"Well plotted ... compelling and entertaining. ... The characters are developed with dialog that provides insight ... kept me turning pages."
— Harrison Jones, airline pilot, author

"Stunning, compelling, thought-provoking. To the book's broad scope and expert pacing, add three-dimensional, engaging characters."
— M. Thornburg

The Four-Color Puzzle

"[A]n authentic thinking person's ideal mystery; an eloquent feast of words and an excellent story. ... [M]ay be the best [book] I have read this year."
— Jeanie B. Clemmons, author

"[A] fast-paced crime story that had me rooting for the hero while also feeling conflicted by his choices. The story challenges the reader."
— Patricia O'Sullivan, author

THE
ROSEN
SINGULARITY

THE
MILLICENT
FACTOR

Two Novels

THE ROSEN SINGULARITY

THE MILLICENT FACTOR

by Lior Samson

GESHER PRESS
Rowley, Massachusetts

Gesher Press
Rowley, MA 01969
Author site: www.liorsamson.com

Printed in the United States of America.

5 4 3 2 1

ISBN 978-0-9885275-8-4

Cover and book design: Larry Constantine
Set in Alegreya and Alegreya Sans
Cover painting: "Passages" copyright © 2015, Dianna Daly
DiannaDaly@gmail.com

To the memory of my father and of my brother, who both died too young but whose gifts live on within me

Death is very likely the single best invention of Life. It is Life's change agent. It clears out the old to make way for the new.
— Steve Jobs

Contents

Author's Preface

Two novels follow, but they are one story told with an unbroken narrative. I did not set out with that agenda when I first penned *The Rosen Singularity*. My developmental editor, who doubles as life partner and best friend, told me that my early drafts of that novel were all wrong. In particular, she insisted that I had completely bollixed the ending. After extensive rewrites and several more revisions, the story made sense and finished with an open-ended epilogue that left room for something more to come. She was happy, and so were my readers.

I had originally intended that those readers would fill in the blanks of the aftermath however they wanted or imagined, but I continued to be nagged by the voice of one of my characters. In *Singularity* I had given Rosen David center stage to tell his story and allowed his wife, Millicent Geller, to remain in the supporting role she had chosen. But now Millicent was tugging at my mental sleeve, insisting there was more to her story and asking for the chance to finish it.

In many ways, Millicent was, from the beginning, more enigmatic to me than Rosen, and it took quiet listening to her voice along with many discussions with my editor before I understood who she was, what she was trying to tell me, and how I should share it with readers. Whereas Rosen was a researcher, a man in many ways more comfortable with numbers and abstractions than with real people and emotions, Millicent was a teacher for whom teaching and her relationships with students were as important as the subject matter. Although their journeys were complexly linked, each would have to follow a different path in wrestling with their demons and the demons of the world. Each would have to confront their own mortality and decide what was personally at stake in those struggles. Although their stories can be read independently, the second begins where the first leaves off, and they belong together.

THE
ROSEN
SINGULARITY

Singularity: the state or quality of being singular, unique,
particular; a discontinuity in space or time; a point, such as a
black hole, where the normal laws of nature cease to operate; an
event of such complete and abrupt alteration that history is
changed qualitatively and fundamentally.

Prologue

The keys slipped from Janella's shaking hand. She did a perfect grand-plié to retrieve them, then struggled to guide the front-door key into the lock.

She was chilled to the core of her small frame. The forty-minute hike down Mass Avenue from Bram's apartment near the West Somerville line to the icy porch of the white Victorian in Cambridge had left her sobered but shivering. She opened the front door, sending a swirl of powdery snow onto the mat inside. She stepped cautiously, but the old wide-board flooring creaked as she entered the darkened house. She paused, listening, trying to control her shaking as she removed her wool tam and placed it with her keys and purse on the stand by the door. The house was silent.

She jumped suddenly.

"Oh, shit!" she whispered. She had forgotten the manila envelope with the research paper at Bram's apartment. "Douglas will kill me if he finds out."

Douglas was even more possessive of the paper and the work it represented than he was of her. He did not approve of her involvement with Bram Dekker but had said nothing. He had, however, stated clearly that their work was strictly confidential and no longer to be discussed with anyone. Not only had she shown the paper to Bram, but Bram had been the one to confirm her sense of its singular importance.

They had spent the first part of the evening at the kitchen table, washing down pepperoni pizza with cheap Chianti and talking their way through the highly technical research results. They had spent the rest of the evening in bed with Dutch beer from Bram's stock, arguing about the grim developments in the war in Vietnam, about the proper care and feeding of laboratory rats, and about the correct way to write

DO loops in FORTRAN programs. Between debating the implications of Gödel's Theorem and disagreeing about Chomsky's notions of deep-structure grammar in natural language, they had managed to squeeze in two rounds of lovemaking.

Janella, realizing she would have to retrieve the paper, replaced her tam over her dark hair, grabbed her keys from the table, and slipped back out. A dusting of new snow was already beginning to obscure her tracks on the sidewalk. She crossed her arms and set off at a jog in hopes of warming herself. Like a member of the corps de ballet crossing a darkened stage, she ran through the night with sure-footed steps, her long plaid scarf a pink-and-purple banner streaming behind her.

It was long after midnight on a winter weekday, and she ran alone, unnoticed on the deserted streets. Gradually, her pace warmed her, the heat starting in her thighs, then rising and spreading until she had to loosen her fur-trimmed jacket to keep from overheating.

She was almost within sight of Bram's basement apartment when she finally slowed to catch her breath. As her breathing quieted, the winter stillness deepened. Through the muting curtain of falling snow, she could hear the sound of hurried steps behind her.

With a dancer's heightened sense of place and position, she waited until the unseen follower was nearly upon her before planting her left foot, kicking off with her right, and spinning around with determined precision.

1

The world tilted sharply as the Gulfstream 650 banked and angled down toward pebbly cloud cover that revealed a teasing mosaic of the bronze and blue-green African landscape below. Veteran traveler though he was, Ferguson felt his stomach lurch as the plane started its sudden steep descent. The co-pilot, who had left the flight deck to chat with the two minders seated at the front of the near-empty plane, stumbled and ended up in the lap of one of them. He struggled to pull himself erect and up through the open doorway to the flight deck while the pilot shouted to him in rapid-fire Portuguese. Ferguson caught only one word of it. *Merde!* Shit.

The plane suddenly rolled left and into a precipitous dive, followed immediately by a sharp right turn again and a gut-wrenching climb that pressed Ferguson deep into the glove-soft leather of his seat. The plane continued to climb so steeply that Ferguson wondered if they were on the verge of stalling out. For a moment, they seemed to hang suspended before the plane rolled again into a plunge nearly straight toward the center of the earth, the twin engines screaming as the fuselage shuddered in protest.

Not this way, Ferguson thought, not like this. The obvious question sprang into his always analytical mind: what way, then? What way, good doctor, what way and when? Sooner or later, someway, somehow death had to come. Even he had to die—a painful reality that he preferred to postpone as long as possible.

The plane shook violently as the pilot struggled to pull it out of the steep dive. A bright flash, like a stab of sunlight, filled the window beside Ferguson, and the plane seemed to hop to one side. The thud of an explosion and thump of a compression wave left his ears ringing. Slowly the plane settled back into what seemed to be a normal flight, and his hearing returned. The pilots and the two men up front were laughing, shouting something about Matata and his people.

"Can somebody tell me what that was all about?" Ferguson called up toward the front of the plane.

"Matata, the troublemaker," the pilot said. "He lives up to his name. Matata Sabri and the EUN." His accented English mixed Portuguese overtones with the rhythm of the Lusanyu dialect, the language of the Busanyu majority. "They must have gotten their hands on a surface-to-air missile, but these Gulfstreams are pretty maneuverable if you know how to handle them, and we can out-fly that outdated Russian crap. That's all they can afford, those poor peasant bastards. Now the army will hunt them down and cut out their hearts." He snorted as if enjoying the prospect. "If we can't catch the traitors, our soldiers will go to the villages of their families and kill everyone with machetes. Matata will not try this again."

Ferguson was not reassured. The *Exército de Unidade Nacional*, the Army of National Unity, which government forces referred to as the Army of National Disunity, was only the most visible evidence of many hidden enemies. That President Mbutsu had enemies was not unexpected, given his totalitarian regime and long history of human rights violations.

It was always a risk coming to Busanyu, but there was no choice. They needed Edgar Jabari Mbutsu as an underwriter. And, of course, he needed them. He could not come to the clinic outside Moscow any more than he could drive through the streets of downtown Mbutsu City unless in an armored vehicle with heavily armed escorts. Indeed, Ferguson knew the truth, that Mbutsu rarely stepped foot outside the grounds of the Presidential Palace. There were even rumors that he had actually died back in 2010, and that his third son, Edgar Abimbola Mbutsu, was secretly running the country. Ferguson knew the rumors were just that—without substance but nevertheless convenient. It could be a comfortable fiction for a country that hated and feared its leader in equal measure.

Ferguson wondered whether the insurgents would have fired the missile had he arrived on one of the regular commercial flights. Now that Busanyu had finally gained U.N. recognition, there were two flights a week from Lisbon and one from the Canary Islands. No, the insurgents knew nothing of Ferguson's travels. The attack was targeted for Mbutsu; it was his private plane, his ostentatious display of wealth and power, like a sleek, subsonic peacock, the orange and blue livery of its tail proudly defiant—and inviting. Ferguson much preferred the anonymity of commercial travel to the luxury—and uncertainty—of private accommodations. But this was not one of Ferguson's regular visits to Africa; it was a command performance at the request of Mbutsu to jump the queue of Ferguson's short list of patients. The charter flight from London in his own jet had been Mbutsu's idea, a gesture of hospitality, he claimed, one that he knew could not be turned down.

The whole trip was also a power play, a claim to equal standing in the long stalemate between the underwriters and the organization. Ferguson, for one, regretted they had ever entered into the devil's deal with the underwriters, although it had seemed they had little choice at the time, a time when there was so much research still ahead and so little in capital behind them. Now—or soon—there might be alternatives, but a transition would not be straightforward.

Ferguson stretched, hitched himself fully upright in the spacious leather seat, and massaged his aching neck. The scare from the rebel forces had abruptly brought him out of the semi-conscious trance in which he had passed the last hours of the nine-hour flight from London. He was slipping his unused e-book reader back into the medical bag beneath his feet when he looked up to find the co-pilot standing next to his seat.

"We're coming into Mbutsu International, Dr. Ferguson," the man said. "We'll be starting our final approach in a few minutes." Though he wore the insignia of a lieutenant colonel in the Busanyu Air Force, he spoke with quiet deference that evidenced how keenly he was aware of the high status and importance of his only passenger. Although the cabin of the Gulfstream could be configured to carry as many as eighteen, in this one, luxuriously finished in soft beige and camel tones offset by the bright blue-and-orange signature of its owner, the plane had been appointed to carry only eight in spacious comfort. The other two men, seated at the front of the near-empty plane, did not count as passengers. Though they were out of uniform, Ferguson knew they were military police, minders charged with keeping an eye on himself and the pilots. He had been entrusted to top officers in the Air Force, but the current regime in Busanyu was not one built on trust, and Ferguson imagined that the minders, too, were somehow being monitored in turn.

Dr. Charles Ferguson was a real doctor of medicine, but his medical credentials, like his passport, his name, and his entire personal history, were fictitious. The transformation had become necessary more than two decades earlier when colleagues had begun voicing suspicions and resentment—all in good humor, of course—about his excessively long tenure as head of the Cancer Biology and Genetics program that he had created at the Dana-Farber Institute outside Boston. The program was largely a cover for the real work that he directed elsewhere, but the handwriting was on the wall and clearly writ. When glossing over the good-natured graffiti of his detractors with humorous brush-offs no longer quelled their suspicions or quieted their envy, one leading Welsh oncologist based in Boston "disappeared" while on holidays in South America, and the unassuming Dr. Ferguson was born, created by the magic of money and resources that knew few limits.

Ferguson stared out the window past his own reflection. He was Hollywood handsome in the classic mold of generic good looks and appealing but forgettable faces. The translucent image that interposed itself atop the shifting scenery softened the lines in his face, lines that spoke less of mere years than of years of responsibility. His medical practice, and the peripatetic life it demanded, both aged him and kept him young. It was not the life he would have imagined when he graduated from medical school and began his research career. It was not the life he had imagined when he married Ruth Pincus in Newton. He missed Ruth. He missed having someone to come back to other than his housekeeper in London. But housekeepers kept their places and stayed in role and could be replaced every few years—not so wives.

There were compensations, of course, in the life he had chosen, and not merely the obvious one. He had learned that companionship comes in many costumes, and impermanence has its intrinsic charms. He smiled as he thought ahead to his next visit to Russia and to Sveta, the bright young lab technician who found talk of telomeres and oncogenes and nucleotide polymorphisms to be such a turn-on. She was as talented in bed as she was in the lab, and she had dark Russian eyes and thick Slavic thighs that reminded him of Ruth as a young woman. But, where Ruth had regarded sex as a wifely duty, Sveta was a screamer who approached bedroom antics with the same enthusiasm with which she attacked the ski slopes or maneuvered her Mercedes along the narrow country roads that led to the unnamed and all-but-invisible artificial village where she worked on projects for Ferguson and The General. The differences between Sveta and Ruth, including the half-century difference in birthdates, were not enough to completely erase the small reminders that sometimes brought back sweet and painful memories. Ferguson had come to believe that we live with our first loves for all our lives; the later ones all come with an expiration date. He was not sure whether Sveta qualified as a love or merely as a current love interest, but he knew that it would not last, could not last. The organization would never approve extending her expiration date—she was too unstable, too unimportant, too ordinary, too obvious. Too bad.

Ferguson would not have counted himself as either jaded or a cynic, but he went about the complex business of maintaining his life and those of his few patients with a well-modulated sense of resignation. As a doctor, he had lived too long not to have distanced himself somewhat from the melodrama of life and death that played out on the human stage. He had finally become, somewhat unexpectedly, more a part of the audience and less and less a participant in the on-stage story.

The final fifteen minutes of the approach into Mbutsu International Airport kept Ferguson's attention focused on the immediate present. Even in the nimble Gulfstream and with no more missiles to dodge, it was a white-knuckle landing, with a steep, banking descent to avoid Kinyetu, the next peak in the chain of mountains, followed by hard braking to avoid going off the edge of the flattened top of Mount Durban. Sir Anthony Durban, nineteenth-century explorer and raconteur, would have been appalled had he lived to the twenty-first century to see what had become of the dramatic summit of his namesake. Ferguson supposed it could be called progress of a fickle but effective sort, since the mountain had first been beheaded by strip mining to recover its mineral wealth only a few years before the overburden had been recycled as backfill to transform it into an airfield.

Ferguson remembered the early days of his involvement with Edgar Mbutsu, when his transportation into Busanyu was a chartered C-130 and the runway was hard-packed red clay. Now, at the edge of the modern airport, surrounded by a moat seething with the pulse of submerged fountains, a white-winged terminal building sailed like a graceful giant of a water bird taking flight from a wind-roiled African lake. The stunning design, one of the first commissions by Paolo Pereira de Canha, student of the Brazilian architect Oscar Niemeyer, was typical of the extravagance with which the Mbutsu government displayed its public face.

Niemeyer, never one to have obsessed over human proportion or efficient use of space in his monumental architecture, had trained his protégé well. Pereira de Canha had created a terminal building as impressive inside as out. One wall of windows, sprinkled with rhomboid panels of yellow and magenta glass and thin stripes of the Busanyu blue and orange, looked back at the tarmac; another of clear glass faced out over a precipice, across the verdant jungle that carpeted the region, and through a cleft in the mountains offering a glimpse into a patch of sun-browned savannah beyond.

Inside the cavernous building, security guards with Kalashnikovs outnumbered the few scattered passengers. When the afternoon flights for other African cities departed, only the footsteps of the guards would echo in the terminal.

Ferguson was efficiently ushered through the terminal by his minders, speeded without ceremony past security guards and passengers and customs officers and into a waiting limousine where there was a long delay while all his baggage caught up with him and was loaded into a panel truck, unloaded again, rearranged, then reloaded amidst much arguing and gesturing. Ferguson was used to such mixes of speed and inefficiency, so he was not surprised when he was told by the driver that there would be another delay while the road ahead was patrolled and cleared.

Finally, it seemed they were ready to move when they were joined by two armored personnel carriers, fore and aft. But the gathering convoy remained idling outside the terminal for another twenty minutes until a motorcycle escort arrived to lead the procession. Through darkened windows, Ferguson watched the bare beauty of the airport surrounds gradually give way to tin and cardboard shanties erected on the slopes just beyond a deep roadside ditch that carried raw sewage.

It took nearly an hour of trailing red dust clouds down the switch-back road from the sheared-off mountain and on through the crowded outskirts of Mbutsu City before they reached the far side and an isolated stretch of paved highway with no other traffic and only one destination: the Presidential Palace.

The Palace, a sprawling complex of mismatched buildings, was no Niemeyer-inspired creation. More military than monumental, it was a small city unto itself. The main gate, a massive sliding panel of gray-painted armor plate with red-brick guard towers on either side and walls topped with razor wire, would have done justice to a maximum-security prison. To the right of the heavily guarded entrance were the military barracks, complete with their own helipad; to the left was a school for those children of the President who lived with him as well as the children of permanently stationed military families and others in a small inner circle who lived at the site. Beyond was the stark steel-and-tinted-glass façade of the fully equipped hospital, and behind the hospital, an unseen electric power station grumbled quietly. Atop an incongruous rise in the otherwise flat landscape stood a small stucco cube with a heavy, vault-like door, the above-ground entrance to an underground communication center, a complex of satellite-linked computers that might have been the envy of some of the smaller of the European intelligence services. Straight ahead, down a broad avenue lined with exotic and stately eucalypts, loomed the polished Italian marble columns of the palace proper, home to the President, three of his four wives, and some twenty-odd of his unnumbered children. Several of his closest advisors also lived with their families in the palace proper, along with an unknown number of relatives and other hangers-on.

The convoy pulled up beside the massive concrete security bollards lining the circular driveway that fronted the palace. The ugly cylinders were an architectural addendum installed in response to an earlier assassination attempt when a bomb-loaded delivery van had been driven all the way up the palace steps. The driver died in a hailstorm of automatic weapons fire, and the bomb had failed to detonate, adding yet another chapter in the myth of a President who some claimed was indestructible, who seemed to lead a charmed life protected by potent magic.

Now, as Ferguson stepped out of the limousine, stopped a safe distance from the palace entrance, a cheer went up. "Not for me, I would hope," he said, with a concerned look on his face.

"Oh, no, good Doctor," the chauffer holding the door said. "It is for the pilots who so skillfully evaded the missile and who also spotted the dust of a fleeing vehicle on the road through Samputu. An army patrol in the area immediately intercepted and captured them. I am afraid that you already missed the trial, but you are still in time for the execution, if you make for the courtyard with some haste."

"Well, no one can say that Busanyu justice is slow," Ferguson said, shaking his head. "But I think not. I am tired and still have much to do to be ready for the President's appointments this week."

"Are you sure? I could escort you there."

"I am sure. I will go inspect my suite at the hospital and make sure everything arrived in good order. I can find my way. Please have my bags taken to my usual room."

Ferguson took a few steps toward the hospital, then cringed involuntarily as the crackle of nearby gunfire interrupted the afternoon quiet.

"Not to worry, Doctor," the driver called out. "It is just the firing squad." Another ragged burst split the air. "Special justice," the driver said, retreating and leaving Ferguson standing there with a puzzled look. There was another round of gunfire.

2

The stark skeletons of winter were now peppered with the pale green and deep pink buds of spring along tree-lined Argilla Road. The trees cast pulsing shadows as Rosen sped past. He was eager this morning, eager to get back to the intriguing lead he was following. He slowed, but not enough to prevent his tires from letting out a brief squeal as he made the switch-back corner and headed up the undistinguished long driveway leading to the Ipswich Labs. A sea-blue sign, less than a foot high and located halfway up the curving drive, was the only indication that the former mansion was now the North Shore Laboratories of Biontolics Research, LLC.

Rosen's lime-green Honda Prius was the first car in the lot, yet, despite his hurry, he parked farthest from the building. He extracted his tall and well-muscled frame from the small car, grabbed his thermos and briefcase, and started to jog across the parking lot. Rosen considered everything in life as amenable to optimization. His preferred parking spot would be shaded from the afternoon sun by the adjacent trees, and the modest trot from the far corner of the lot, around the house, and up the broad steps into the front entrance of the building counted in his mental ledgers as exercise. Others might simply use their keycards to enter by the convenient parking-lot entrance, but Rosen's everyday life operated on the accumulation of small tweaks that he believed added up to noticeable effects, even as in his work, where minute patterns were magnified into visibility by his arcane arithmetic arts.

The Labs' many-gabled house and its outbuildings had once been a rich industrialist's North Shore retreat, replete with a gentleman's farm and a widow's-walk balcony that overlooked the salt marshes stretching toward the sea. In recent years, the marsh lands had become dotted by little black boxes, traps for the biting flies that had long plagued the residents of the area. Biontolics Research had quietly acquired the neglected property—and radically expanded the number of little black boxes—not long after the arrival in Ipswich of New

England Biolabs, their much larger and better known neighbors just to the south. Both labs had begun tapping into the deepening pool of science and engineering talent migrating northward from the universities and older high-tech institutions inside and along Route 128, Boston's fabled Technology Highway. Biontolics had refurbished the interior of the main house to create office suites, turned a barn into a world-class microbiology research laboratory, and made a guest house into a computer center. With its long driveway and the buildings painted to match the dark New England slate on the footpaths, the compound was all but invisible from the road.

At the front desk in what had once been a sitting room, the white-haired guard greeted Rosen with a sleepy smile. "Good morning, Dr. Rosen," he said, as he ticked off an entry in an on-screen log. Rosen had long ago given up correcting the man. He was Dr. Rosen David, no middle name, because Michael David, his father, emotionally traumatized by a childhood filled with teasing for having two first names, had flipped the bird at the world by giving his first-born son a surname for a first name. Of course, Michael David insisted on telling everyone that Rosen was a perfectly fine given name, that it was of Hebrew origin, with the correct accent on the final syllable, although no one pronounced it that way, and that it meant that his son was an honored person. After growing up taunted by new variations on old schoolyard themes, the college-bound Rosen David had finally embraced fate and learned to turn the memorable distinctiveness of his offbeat name to his advantage. As David Rosen, he would have been one of hundreds on Facebook, thousands of hits on Google, but as Rosen David, he was singular, unique.

Rosen took the stairs two-at-a-time up to his second-floor office. He hip-checked his posture chair, sending it skidding across the room from where he had left it next to the small circular conference table, then booted up his computer while still standing. He was impatient to get back to the work that his promise to meet Millie for dinner the night before had interrupted. His wife, knowing that it was one of the few ways to guarantee that Rosen would return from work at a reasonable hour, insisted on a dinner date every Thursday.

Other nights, he was apt to find her already in bed when he arrived home, usually curled up with a book—usually about nature—but sometimes already asleep, her cheek creased by the edge of the book she had been reading. And tonight he would have to leave work early again because it was Shabbat, the beginning of the Jewish Sabbath, and, although neither he nor Millie were observant and both were scientists and devout non-believers, they never failed to mark Friday evening with candles and with blessings over the bread and wine.

Rosen sat down at his desk and ran a hand through his curly hair as he made a perfunctory scan of the subject lines of his email before closing the in-box without reading any of it. He was notorious for missing important memos and not responding to urgent inquiries from management, but it was not so much by any rebellion against authority or an uncooperative nature as by the tendency for his attention to be always elsewhere. Elsewhere was usually the analysis of the last batch of numbers to arrive at his desk.

He unzipped his jacket without taking it off and, at the same time, finished logging in to retrieve results from an overnight computation he had run on the supercomputer at Biontolics Southland, the company headquarters and computing center in Research Triangle Park, North Carolina. An array of unintelligible numbers swept over his screen. While the numbers continued streaming in, he pipelined the array over to his newly devised data visualization program that would turn digits into colorful graphics, abstract paintings that could more easily be eyeballed for elusive patterns. At the same time, he started another program on his local workstation that took the results of the overnight computation as input and generated yet another set of numbers.

This was how he did biology. His work was all about looking for patterns, identifying results in experiments that even the experimenters had missed, the subtle and unintended consequences of science scaled up. His specialty was known as meta-analysis, a discipline that looked at dozens or hundreds, sometimes even thousands of old studies, and mixed them all together into one statistical stew to see if any newer or clearer results bubbled to the surface.

He was correcting a formula in an internal memo about a previous project, when his computer chimed and the big 26-inch LCD monitor to his right started painting the tinted shapes generated by his visualization program. He stared in eager anticipation as the high-resolution display filled in successively refined levels of detail, sharpening the boundaries between contrasting colors in the patchwork. To the uninitiated, it might have resembled a nightmare painted by Chagall or the false-color x-ray images generated by airport security scanners, another form of visualization that used sharp contrasts in color to highlight tiny differences.

Rosen's heart started pounding as a small but distinctive, red-hued patch began taking shape amidst a field of blues and greens and yellows. His reaction was not unlike what a TSA agent staring at a screen in an airport might feel, an agent who had suddenly spotted a pistol-shaped shadow in the x-ray of someone's carry-on bag. The patch of red was a signal amidst the noise of irrelevant blue and green, a sign of success, an indication that some small numbers among many thousands of measurements had been ever so slightly different than expected.

Rosen lived for such moments. Most of his work, most days, meant telling researchers and funding sources the bad news that the drugs they were trying didn't work or the traces of chemicals they sought simply were not there or that the theory they were espousing didn't prove out. Some days, like this particular Friday, he caught the scent of significance, the glimpse of real results, and he was like a bloodhound on the trail.

The patch in the picture was only a flag, drawing attention to buried possibilities. The real work would be teasing out exactly what the connections were in a collection of spurious results from diverse publications, and more importantly, deciphering what they meant. Behind the numbers were words, and behind the words were poetry, the poetry of new science and undiscovered truths for which Rosen rose in the morning and which still spun in his head as he drifted into sleep late at night.

Rosen became so absorbed in scanning summaries of studies and setting up another analysis on a subset of the data that he did not even notice when his officemate, Jeannine Carsten, arrived for work or when she left for lunch. He finally looked up from his keyboard and screens when he realized his thermos of tea was cold and his bladder was uncomfortably full. The clock told him it was nearly one-thirty.

When he returned from the bathroom, Jeannine was back at her desk, chin resting on one hand as she entered data on her numeric keypad with the other. "Oh, hi," she said, her husky voice filled with good-humored sarcasm. "Nice to see you, too."

He gave her a lopsided grin. "Sorry," he said, "I was really into it, I guess. I think I am onto something. A lot of checks and counter-checks to run, still, plus some new tests, but this is looking good. Something subtle is going on in this mess of research that my new program has flagged. I'm not sure what exactly it is yet, but I'm going to pull in all that old work on telomeres from Bischoff and Muybridge, you know, the studies of rat longevity, plus, well, a bunch of stuff." He had to remind himself that Jeannine was a statistician—simply that, a pure mathematician, competent in her work but largely uninterested in the science behind the numbers she manipulated. Despite his frequent disclaimers, Rosen actually was a real biologist in that he understood the meaning of the numbers on his screen and the significance of the experiments he analyzed. In a string of papers published while he was still a student at Tufts University, he had broken new ground by combining deep scientific insights, particularly in genetics, with original and powerful mathematical techniques.

Jeannine smiled at him and twirled a finger in the air. "Well, ride 'em cowboy. Corral all them stray numbers and line them up in neat rows." She turned back to her screen and started tapping out strings of numbers again.

"No, really, this could be something big," he said. "I am going to have to go back and re-read all the papers from this collection." He waved a finger at the reddish patch still displayed on his screen. Jeannine swiveled in her chair and nodded but immediately turned back to her own work and otherwise ignored him for the rest of the day. They were two number-crunching introverts who had long since worked out their quiet pas-de-deux for sharing the small office. If Rosen were to be asked how tall Jeannine was or the color of her hair, he might make something up that he believed was an acceptable approximation, but, in truth, he hardly noticed her, certainly not the way she watched him when he was not looking.

She was still tapping away behind him when, late in the afternoon, his cell phone rang. It was Millie. "Do you know what time it is, Rosen? Do you even know what day it is?" she asked, the casual lilt of her voice salted with irritation.

"I know I'm in trouble. Does that help?"

"Not unless you get your distractible self home real darn fast. The sun is setting, my love, and I should be lighting the candles."

"My *eshet chayil*, my woman of valor, thank you for reminding your clueless love that the world keeps turning even when his computer slows to a crawl. I'll leave right now. I just have one more text clustering to do, then I'll shut down for the weekend."

"No."

"No? No what?"

"No, you do not have one more analysis or one more test or one more anything to do. I know you, Rosen. One becomes two and two become a dozen, and I won't see you before midnight."

"Okay. I'm really quitting. I'm logging off and shutting down," he said, even as he typed a new command to run another long job at the Research Triangle computing center. "Hear that? I'm on my way." He grabbed his jacket off the back of the chair as he continued to reassure Millie that he really was leaving work. Jeannine watched as he scowled at the long error message that popped up on his screen. Her IM to him popped up beside it. "I can correct that. You go home," it read.

Rosen nodded to Jeannine, told Millie once more that he really was leaving, and headed out the door.

Jeannine sat down at his desk and corrected the error in his remote job command before resubmitting it. Unlike Rosen, she had no one waiting for her; like Rosen, the work was an addiction. It was more than an hour until she reluctantly returned to her own desk where she finished the data entry job before logging onto a remote facility in Europe to post her weekly report.

~ ~ ~

It was well past seven o'clock that night when Rosen got home to the small, white, black-trimmed Cape Cod colonial on the far edge of Essex, a modest little house on a small lot that had been bargain-basement priced when they bought it but was more than enough for the two of them. Millie welcomed Rosen warmly but let him know her displeasure with his late arrival by heading for bed immediately after dinner. Rosen did his usual perfunctory job of cleaning up before heading down the short hall to join her.

Their so-called master bedroom was tiny by modern standards, having been carved up by the previous owner to create an equally tiny *en suite* bathroom. Millie sat propped up in the queen-size bed that nearly filled the room. The current issue of *Edutopia* was in her hand, and an assortment of Audubon field guides were spread around her.

Rosen belly-flopped down beside her, bouncing the field guides a few inches into the air and sending one handbook onto the floor.

"Thanks a heap," she said, as she stretched to retrieve the book.

"Anytime," he answered. "So, tell me Millie, how would you like to be married to a Nobel Laureate?"

"Depends which Laureate you mean. I always thought Krugman was kind of ruggedly handsome, you know, in a classic Ashkenazic mold. And Kornberg, in chemistry—balding, yes, but still kind of cute."

"Krugman? Paul Krugman, the economist? You think he's handsome? Brilliant, yes, but. . . Anyway, I meant me. How would you like that?"

"Being married to you? Hmmm?" She paused for a three-beat. "Could take some getting used to." She was teasing, of course, but there was also a tautness to the tease that Rosen in his excitement missed completely.

"I'm serious. I am that good!" he said, gesturing with his highly controlled version of a fist pump. "I think I am onto something at the Lab that is big, really big."

"It's all really big to you, Rosen, always has been. The first day we met you were already telling me that you were going places. A plumped up ego can be charming in an undergraduate, but it can wear with time." She spread her magazine in her lap, turned the page, and frowned in concentration as she bent toward it.

"Millie, listen. I mean it. This might be the most important work I've ever done. I wish I could tell you all about it, but you know, it's, like, top secret and all. If I'm right, though, this really is potential Nobel material. As soon as I can confirm it, I'm going to see if I can negotiate a release and get a paper accepted by *PLoS Medicine* to get it out before somebody scoops me." PLoS, the Public Library of Science, was an open-access, online collection of publications that made it possible to disseminate scientific findings much faster and more widely than in traditional bound journals.

"You don't seem all that happy at the thought of being married to a world famous mathematical biologist," Rosen added, his voice filled with unspoken hurt.

Millie forced a smile and gave him a wet kiss on the cheek. "I'm happy for you, sweetheart." She was not happy for him, though. The very thought of their settled life being disrupted by fame terrified her.

Rosen, straight-tacking Rosen, had been the safe, easy choice for her, her Mr. Spock, relentlessly rational, his cool logic protecting her from facing inner fears. "Send me an email when the Nobel Committee announces," she said.

She gathered her books and stacked them on the nightstand before turning out the lamp on her side of the bed. As she closed her eyes, she was thinking about being married to Rosen and about being married; as he watched her feign sleep, he was thinking about signal-to-noise ratio in research results and about the optimal place to publish his blockbuster journal article. He drifted into sleep while mentally composing the draft of his Nobel acceptance speech.

~ ~ ~

The weekend, having started late, ended early for Rosen and Millie. By Sunday afternoon they were facing each other across their laptops on the kitchen table, logged into different systems and working in different worlds.

Millicent Geller David was a biologist, like Rosen. But unlike Rosen, she was what he referred to as a real biologist, one who picked up insects and could name trees by their leaves. Rosen had long ago given up trying to explain his obscure profession of mathematical biology to dinner guests or to new acquaintances at school functions. Millie, on the other hand, taught middle school, which was easy to explain and meant that she was up before the sun to be in her classroom by seven and spent weekends planning lessons that would challenge her students, the easily bored teenage and pre-teen children of the iPod generation.

Rosen and Millie were, by every measure, an odd couple. She was short and slight, with wispy honey-blond hair; he was six-two and somewhat beefy, with a head of thick, kinky hair the color of fresh asphalt. Despite her waifish physique and a long list of allergies, Millie loved the outdoors, hikes in the woods, swimming at Crane Beach, and kayaking on the Ipswich River. Hers was a passionate, visceral, and immediate involvement with Nature, which she had always spelled and spoken with a capital N, even as a small child. Rosen, who never liked to sweat without purpose, had a mechanically mediated approach to the natural world. His version of staying in shape in- volved mowing the lawn or ferrying groceries from the neighborhood store on his bicycle or, on rare occasion, weather permitting, cycling to work. His three bicycles, work stand, and tools took up most of their small garage, relegating his Prius and Millie's bright yellow VW to their short driveway. Millie had tried for years to get him to go backpacking with her, but his idea of camping out was a half-opened bedroom window in the dog days of August.

They had met in college, accidental lab partners in an organic chemistry class, and were instantly connected by their shared love of science—and of sex. "I'm someone who is going someplace," he had told her, as they walked across campus after class. "How would you like to come along for the ride?" She was drawn to his soft-spoken arrogance and said, "Sure. Where are we headed?" That afternoon, someplace turned out to be his dorm room. By the end of the semester, they had moved in together, and they were married in the summer before starting graduate school. But Millie had her heart set on a career as a biologist doing field research, and Rosen was beginning to discover that the real fun for him lay not in preparing specimens for electron microscopy or in discovering new species of soil bacteria but in crunching numbers.

Rosen had slalomed from specialty to specialty, taking courses in biochemistry, genetics, and even bioengineering before settling down to pursue a doctorate in mathematical biology, a field of applied statistics that was more math than bio. That suited Rosen, who had come to dislike chemicals and animals and plants in equal measure. He took his time on an ambitiously original doctoral dissertation while Millie doggedly searched for field research jobs before giving up and going back to college for her master's in education. She was already settled into teaching at the Nock Middle School in Newburyport before he finally finished his dissertation. That work, on the application of an obscure branch of information theory to the analysis of experiments, had attracted the attention of Biontolics, which had pursued him aggressively and put him under contract the week before he defended his dissertation. He had been working at the same desk in Ipswich ever since, doing an interesting job that, until now, had seemed to be an end in itself, a journey without a destination other than the completion of one project and the launching of the next.

Sitting at his own kitchen table, Rosen called up another research paper from the remote server, read the abstract, and saved it off in one of a dozen folders he had created. He was a biologist again, following a trail, sorting species unearthed along the way, immersing himself in the experience of discovery. As he waited for the next paper to download over the sluggish connection, he looked up from the screen to find that Millie was no longer across from him and her laptop was closed.

Orange and blue bunting draped the semicircular dining hall of the Presidential Palace in honor of what the government spin-doctors were describing as a major victory over opposition forces of the EUN. Ferguson, among the last few to enter the hall, spotted Raul Gomes, Minister of the Interior and former Angolan smuggler of blood diamonds, motioning toward an empty chair to his left. "I hear you had some fun coming into the airport yesterday," Gomes said to him, as Ferguson seated himself. "You must fill me in. I want to hear all the details."

Ferguson was about to answer when a slim giant of a man, his nearly blue-black skin set off by a bright yellow traditional tribal wrap, entered from the doorway to the far left and ceremoniously thumped his carved wooden staff on the floor twice. He held his staff aloft and called out in rhythmic Portuguese a phrase that Ferguson knew by heart: "His Excellency, the Doctor Edgar Jabari Mbutsu o Basanya, President for Life and Supreme Commander of the Armed Liberation Forces of the Sovereign State of Busanyu." The herald repeated the announcement in Lusanyu, the language of the Basanya people, the dominant tribal group of the region for whom the country had been named. The hundred or so guests in the hall rose in unison as the President for Life took a step into the room and the opening bars of the national anthem sounded. *"Basanya kyahm ngala,"* they sang— Basanya people now unite.

Edgar Mbutsu did not look like a man born in 1922, although he did look like one who had fought in wars and insurrections in half the countries of sub-Saharan Africa. His knobbled face, red-brown and mottled like the earth of the land around, bore the irregular pink line of a poorly stitched gash from a machete that had nearly severed his left ear, and his chin sported an off-center dimple from a bullet wound. He was proud of his scars and even of the slight limp that spoiled his gait when he hurried, so he had a tendency to stroll when he wanted to appear dignified, stride when he wanted to draw attention to his long service and humbler origins.

He was a military man turned politician in the old style of twentieth-century Africa. He had been leader of a successful secessionist movement and survivor of more coup attempts than anyone had counted. He was a man of unmeasured personal wealth, fueled by his country's oil, diamonds, and newly discovered minerals, as well as by his percentage off the top of an extensive trade in contraband that went largely unreported. He was ruthless and fearless in defending what was his, but relentless in his pursuit of stability in the region, which made him a friend to Western governments and the latest in a long history of brutal dictators tolerated or supported because they were good for business. Except to encourage trade and honor treaties, Mbutsu was without personal or political ambitions beyond Busanyu's borders. He had everything he wanted and more, and the time to enjoy it. He would proudly declare his simple foreign and domestic policy positions in a single statement, that Busanyu was enough for Mbutsu—and Mbutsu was enough for Busanyu.

As the anthem ended, Mbutsu, tall and imposing, unbent by age, strolled with dignity toward the focus of the semicircle, where his immediate family waited for him at the head table. Just short of the table, he turned his head and looked straight at Ferguson, then picked up his pace to walk past his family and approach Ferguson instead. Grasping Ferguson's hand in both of his, the President for Life of Busanyu nodded gravely, then grinned and administered a crushing bear-hug and a thumping back-pounding.

"You are looking better than ever, old friend, my doctor." He, stepped back. "The medicine man's medicine keeps you well."

Ferguson frowned at Mbutsu, then covered by smiling and looking around the room at the many faces turned their way. "We are both well," he told Mbutsu. "That is what counts."

"I do have much to thank you for, Doctor, particularly yesterday. If you had not accepted my invitation and drawn the fire of the criminal scum that follow Matata, who knows what might have happened. Why, I might have been killed." He said the last without irony or humor. "I must apologize, though, for the humble transportation that was not of the class that you deserve and have earned. You know, I am sure, that the Gulfstream 750 is still in such regrettably short supply and orders can take years before they are filled. So, in the meantime, while I await delivery, my guests must all resign themselves to transport in my humble G6." Mbutsu was bragging rather than apologizing, as Ferguson knew. The false modesty of a man who personally owned a G6 and had a G7 on order fooled no one.

Mbutsu continued. "The skill and bravery of our pilots and troops were not quite enough, alas, because that bastard coward Matata got away, leaving behind eight of his men, including two of his top aides and one of his grown sons, all for us to capture. Convenient. We gave them a speedy trial and special justice. This is a country of laws and of swift application."

"Emphasis on the swift."

"Thank you," Mbutsu said, acknowledging the remark as if it were a compliment. "I have been at this business of building and running a country for a very long time, Doctor, as you know. One gets good at something when one does it long enough. But in this case it was not all that difficult. The criminals were caught red-handed. They had the launcher still in the back of the Land Rover, the one that was spotted from the air by your most able pilot. You really should have come into the courtyard to see how effectively special justice is carried out here in Busanyu." He patted Ferguson on the shoulder before leaving to join his family at the head table. There he raised his glass in a traditional toast that Ferguson already knew: *Franda bmeli ontani!* May we outlive our enemies.

~ ~ ~

As the thick after-dinner coffee was being served, Ferguson turned to the Minister seated next to him. "What is meant by this term, 'special justice,' Raul?" he asked. "I am not sure whether I have heard it used before."

"Special justice is the term we now use when the crime is very bad, like this one, since theirs was really, in effect, an attempt on the life of the President. It was the President's personal plane they tried to shoot down, thus it was an attack not only on the State but on the Head of State as well. In such cases, the entire village of the criminals is brought to watch, or as many as can be rounded up in time, so the lesson can be learned by the neighbors and relatives as well. Because the evil that is in these men is in their blood, we must be sure also that the evil is not carried on, so first we take care of the children of the criminals. His Excellency, our President, graciously gave the rebels a choice: they could kill their children themselves or the Presidential Guard could do it for them."

Fergusson tried not to look too shocked. "You ask the accused to shoot their own children?"

"Oh, no! For children, a firing squad is unnecessary. A machete works just fine."

"But why? Why would anyone ever choose to kill their own children?"

"Because they can do it quickly, perhaps with a single blow. When the Presidential Guard does it. . .well, they are trained as soldiers not marauders or field workers. In the hands of one who does not wield the machete that often, it can be somewhat clumsy and slow, taking sometimes many blows, especially if the child runs or tries to fend off the blows." The Minister demonstrated by raising his arm as if to shield his face. "You can see the problem, of course."

Ferguson lowered his head and covered his eyes. He told himself that he had always known who he was dealing with, although it made the present circumstances no easier. He wondered what it said of him that the man known to the world as The Butcher of Busanyu was his patient. Aloud, he said, "And then the firing squad for the rebels themselves."

"Yes, of course, but first we bind them to posts and gag them so they cannot scream."

"Scream?" he asked, but quickly wished he had said nothing.

"Well, yes, because the first volley is for their feet, the second for the kneecaps, the third for the navel. We wait between. For effect. And then for the heart. That usually is enough."

"Yes, I would imagine," Ferguson said, rising from his chair and steadying himself on the edge of the table. "You will have to excuse me. It was a long flight, and I still have much to do in the morning."

Minister Gomes rose with him, determined to finish the story. "We also take care of the women," he said. "The firing squad get the first chance for the wives and daughters. Then the others. But that is more a matter of tradition than of law. At least this way they do not go to waste, the women and girls, before they are gone. But all that comes first, so the criminals can watch their women raped by their enemies. I do not know exactly what the legal status of that is, but it is custom sanctioned by the President. It is not only good for morale in the forces, but it discourages rebellion. That is the theory, at least."

Ferguson nodded slowly and left without saying any more. In his room, he reminded himself that Mbutsu had, in his unprecedented long reign, brought stability to the region, that African nations like his were, relatively speaking, enjoying prosperity and strong growth, lifting their citizens out of poverty—or at least helping those who survived, the ones who kept their heads down and their mouths shut. He reminded himself of the ongoing mutual dependence between them, that both their very lives depended on maintaining that relationship.

Still, he slept fitfully, awakened several times by gunfire and screams that were only in his dreams.

~ ~ ~

In the morning, he was a doctor again, carrying his incongruously battered black bag across the compound to the hospital where he had an appointment with the Butcher of Busanyu. Mbutsu casually entered the special suite of the clinic forty minutes late, flanked by his personal bodyguards and accompanied by an old man. "This is Fallu," Mbutsu told him. "He is to be my tester today."

"I don't understand," Ferguson said. "What do you mean, tester?"

"It is a new procedure that we have thought of, a security measure. We trust you, of course, but we do not know who else might have had access to your drugs, your equipment. Everything you do to me, you will first do to him; everything you give to me, you will first give to him. That way, we will know it is safe, just as when my tasters try my food before I do."

"That is crazy, Mbutsu, madness. You have become paranoid."

"I have enemies. They stalk me and fire missiles at my plane. That is not paranoid."

"In any case, Mbutsu, the organization will not allow this plan of yours. What if it works? You know what that would mean. We cannot risk a . . ." He stopped without finishing.

"There is no risk, my shortsighted doctor. He will not live long at any rate; we will see to that. He is old and has served his purpose already. Now he is to become a defensive weapon, a single-use weapon. Do not concern yourself for him. Just give him the injections before you give them to me."

"Mbutsu, you know full well that the effects can take hours, days, months in some cases. Are you going to watch this man for ill effects while you become ill yourself, waiting for the medication you depend on? Besides, I have no extra with me, none to spare. You know how difficult the treatments are to produce. This is. . .this is simply stupid!"

Mbutsu slammed his palm on the examining table, causing his guards to jump and to reach reflexively toward their weapons. "You! You do not call me stupid!" he shouted. "No one ever. Not even you. You will die here, today, and the organization will send someone else in your place."

Ferguson, his heart pounding, struggled to control his voice. "They will send no one. You know that. You may not be stupid, but that does not save you from stupid ideas. What you want of this man will not work. Send him back to his village."

Mbutsu glared at Ferguson for long moments before nodding. One of his bodyguards opened the door, said something in Lusanyu, and shoved the old man in the back.

Mbutsu laughed and signaled his bodyguards, who followed the man out. Mbutsu placed his hands on Ferguson's shoulders. "It is not wise for men such as you to live dangerously. I have a lifetime of practice at it, and you are still just a novice.

"But, you are correct; it would not have worked. It was a stupid idea, and my head of security, the one who first suggested it to me, will find himself working the yam fields again. Now, let us begin this uncomfortable ritual that will take us days to complete and leave us both tired. Yes, tired but rejuvenated, is it not so?"

Ferguson shrugged but said nothing.

"Not to worry. We will, my doctor friend, outlive our enemies. All of them. And most of our friends as well." He started to undo the buttons of the midnight-blue military dress uniform that was his everyday attire. "Remember this, that stability requires continuity. The revolutions that swept the Arab world north of us reminded everyone of that lesson. Mubarak and Gadhafi were growing old and were no longer able to hold on, to provide that continuity for themselves or their countries. The outcome might have been different had they the arrangement we have. Is that not so, Dr. Cass? Oh, forgive me, Dr. Ferguson, I must have been thinking of someone else, someone from the past."

Ferguson ignored him while he busied himself smearing the EKG leads with electrode jelly. There were no assistants when he treated one of the underwriters. Fortunately, there were only a handful, which meant he had time—time for research, time for reflection, time to figure it all out.

4

Monday mornings tended to mean a late start for Rosen, but finding Jeannine already in the office when he arrived was unexpected. He was also surprised to see that his system was on and the big monitor was displaying the work that had now obsessed him for several weeks. Jeannine turned quickly from where she was standing by his desk and crossed over to the conference table, where she casually picked up a copy of a Biontolics internal publication and carried it to her own desk as if it were an important document and not a piece of company puffery.

"Are you interested in my work? Or are you trying to cut in on my territory, now?" Rosen said, his sarcasm sprinkled with seriousness. "Would you like a demo? I didn't think data visualization was exactly your thing, but maybe some of the information theory behind these new techniques I've been working on might be of interest."

"Maybe, later," she said. "I've got a presentation to deliver to the Foundation that I need to polish before heading downtown." The Foundation was the Boston-based Gerard and Hannah Berkowitz Charitable Foundation, one of the major funding sources supporting the Ipswich lab. Catering to representatives of the Foundation was a necessary, but largely resented, part of their jobs. Biontolics carried out the sort of obscure basic research, long-haul programs or long-shot gambles, that was difficult to fund from ordinary sources. Occasional contract work for drug companies was the exception, but most of their research was supported by a handful of American and European private foundations. Rosen had never figured out precisely why the Berkowitz Foundation or any other private group would fund their sort of research nor what was in it for their contributors, but the money and the requests kept coming, and that meant that Rosen had a job he loved at a time when the economy was still on the long, slow slope up from what had been a prolonged recession, even though most economists had been reluctant to use the term and had declared its end on multiple occasions.

Rosen sat down at his desk and did his ritual scan of the email in his in-box. One message, leapt out at him. The subject line read:

FW: RE: IP release request.

The body was mostly boilerplate reminding him that all his research was proprietary work-for-hire and all Intellectual Property belonged to Biontolics Research, LLC, and/or the sponsors of its research projects. The final paragraphs delivered the real message.

> Your request to publish a paper with the working title of "Role of selected oncogenes in regulation of telomere activity in genetic chimeras: a multi-factor meta-analysis," has been denied by the funding source. It was felt that the work does not merit publication at this time. It does not represent original research and is of limited scientific significance. In any case, further work would be required to develop and refine the research sufficiently.
> We appreciate your excellent contributions to the research agenda of Biontolics and its partners and look forward to more in the future.

"Can you believe this?" he said, waggling his finger at the screen. Jeannine gave him a quizzical look. "They turned down my request to publish. They have never turned down any of my requests before. The first time I do something really good, and they reject it. 'Does not represent original research.' Quote-unquote. It's a meta-analysis, for God's sake. Of course, it doesn't represent original research. Who are these clowns? 'Limited scientific significance.' Didn't they even read the abstract. The conclusions are a game changer. Then this: 'Further work would be required.' It's a meta-analysis of completed research, you idiots. What further work do they have in mind?"

Jeannine shrugged. "It's just one paper, Rosen. You already have dozens in print. You're one of the most productive people in our section."

"But this is the one that matters!" he snapped, surprised at his own rising anger.

"Don't bite my head off. I didn't reject your request. Blame Widmark in the Intellectual Property group. IP can be bull-headed at times."

Rosen scrolled down to the signature block on the email: J. Thomas Widmark.

"How did you know it was Widmark?"

"Er, I guessed. I suppose he's always the one to deliver the bad news. Well, anyway, he turned down my paper last month."

"I didn't know you were working on a paper."

"Yeah, well, one of many things you didn't know." She tilted her head to one side letting her short brown hair fall across her face. "Like, for one thing, I think you are good, but also too serious for your own good. Let this one pass and propose another project. There are a lot of good ideas waiting to be studied.

"Oh, yes, and another thing. I like sushi but not wasabi," she added with a quick laugh.

Rosen wondered whether she was flirting with him but decided against commenting. He did not want to prolong the conversation at a time when what he really wanted to do was fire off a long email to Mr. J. Thomas Widmark. That, however, was not Rosen's style. His style was to line up all his ducks in a row, polish his arguments, and methodically build his case, then deliver the whole thing in one surprise attack that left the opposition dumbstruck. He turned back to his desk and started building his intellectual roadside bomb.

It turned out to be a dud. They turned down his second request.

And his third.

~ ~ ~

Two weeks later, he was working on a fourth submission when the email arrived. WE NEED TO TALK, its subject line shouted all in caps, as if some junk email had snuck past the corporate spam filters. It was the return address, however, that really grabbed his attention. It was internal, from Atchison Dougherty, CEO of Biontolics, a man whom neither he nor anyone else at the Ipswich offices had ever seen, but who was a legend. A summons from the man known to his far-flung troops as "The General" was unprecedented. Rosen opened the message. The body was an Outlook appointment: Monday, 15:30-16:00, Suite 1100, Berkowitz Building, Boston.

"I have until Monday to figure this out," he said aloud. "I have to puzzle out what is going on before I go in there." He reached for the phone, called Millie's school, and left a message for her at the school office. It was only the second time he had ever canceled a date with her. The first time was when they were still in college, after which she had broken up with him and refused to see him for a month. He wondered what the consequences would be this time around.

~ ~ ~

Suite 1100 in the Berkowitz Building consisted of a mahogany-paneled reception area, a large corner office with views out over Boston's financial district, and a small conference room furnished with a walnut table that barely left space for the chairs around it. The suite was hardly more than a drop-box, a luxuryous but little-used serviced facility that supplied an address and a place for meetings. When Rosen introduced himself to the receptionist, a plump woman in her fifties with an Eastern European accent, she ushered him into the conference room, told him to have a seat, then left and closed the door behind her. Rosen flipped open the portfolio that he carried and tried to concentrate on rereading the synopses of the two reports he had prepared. He cringed when he spotted a misspelled word in the second paragraph. So much for trying to impress the big boss, he told himself.

Atchison Dougherty kept him waiting, but not for long. A few minutes after the hour, he opened the conference room door several inches and announced that it would be a few minutes more before they could meet.

"Not a problem," Rosen said to a door that was already closing again. Dougherty returned twenty minutes later and motioned Rosen to follow. He wordlessly waved Rosen toward the large office on the far side of the reception area, paused and accepted a stack of papers from the receptionist, then entered the office himself and closed the door behind him.

"Well!" he announced. "You are a determined young man, Dr. David. Determination is a meritorious quality so long as it is not one's only quality. Please, take a seat." The General remained standing, his legs slightly apart as if at parade rest. He had slate blue eyes topped by untamed eyebrows. His mouth was a thin-lipped stroke across his square face. He looked like a man who had earned every letter of his nickname, one who might have launched a military career pacifying villages in Viet Nam.

"To get right to the point, your excellent work on a number of projects has not gone unnoticed. We want to put you in charge of an important line of investigation funded by a rather sizable new grant. I have already spoken with your supervisor, and you are to be reassigned to the Nutrition Sciences Group. This is a promotion. You will have three junior staff working for you, your own office, and a not inconsequential increase in salary. Oh, yes, and we have upped your allocation on the North Carolina facilities. We expect you to make good use of our supercomputer down there."

"What about the research that I have been trying to publish? I'd like to see that through to some resolution."

"I don't think you understand, Dr. David. Your paper is not going to be published. It has already been decided not to pursue further research and not to publish. I brought you here to tell you about your promotion but also to impress something on you. To put it bluntly, no matter how many times you submit a request and no matter how many pages of appendices you attach to your application, the answer will always be the same: a plain and simple no. So, you can cease wasting your own good time and that of our overworked Mr. Widmark in the IP Group. It is a dead end, and we will be doing no further research in that area. None whatsoever.

"So, if there are no questions, please accept my congratulations. And don't forget to have the receptionist validate your parking ticket." He reached out for a handshake but Rosen remained seated, with his hands in his lap. The General's expression darkened with a mixture of annoyance and puzzlement.

"I do have a question," Rosen said.

"Certainly. Anything."

"Why are you here, Dr. Dougherty? I mean here in Boston. Corporate headquarters is in Research Triangle, and you live in London, at least according to the company magazine piece about you. When I rang our London office, they said you had flown over for a meeting in Boston. Why am I so important?"

"Well, I would not want to deflate your ego too much, but perhaps you are not that important. I just happened to have had business here with the Berkowitz Foundation and thought I would take the opportunity to deliver the good news to you in person."

"I am yet to be convinced that it is good news you are delivering."

Dougherty turned away for a moment, then sat casually on the edge of the desk. "Trust me, it is definitely good. We think you have a bright future with us and that it will be brighter if we focus your considerable talents in an area of more value to us and our underwriters."

"That is difficult for me to believe. Just let me try to explain my paper and its significance."

"I read your paper, son. I did molecular biology at university," he said, with rising impatience. "I am telling you that we are not going to publish it. Period."

"Why?"

Dougherty's face took on an expression that suggested he was not accustomed to being asked to supply reasons for his actions. He grunted. "Let us just say that our underwriters do not think it serves their interests. They pay the piper, hence they call the tune. In this case, that tune is a dirge for your research. Finis. I would not want it to turn into a tragic grand-opera finale for you. You are too valuable. And I would remind you that, should you leave, you would still be bound by non-disclosure and non-compete agreements."

Rosen raised his eyebrows. "Perhaps, then, you could answer a different question. Why were all my other earlier publication requests approved?"

"Because they were better, I suppose, more appropriate. I don't involve myself in that level of detail. I can't afford to indulge in micromanagement or in second-guessing my people."

"Might I suggest a possible explanation?" Rosen said. "Perhaps they were less important. Over the weekend, I completed a small-scale study of my own, an impact analysis. Did you know, sir, that out of a random sample of 1000 papers published by Biontolics people over the last decade, only two appeared in so-called first-tier journals? Two-thirds appeared in journals ranking in the bottom quartile on Impact Factor, the accepted measure of influence in scientific publications. And the vast majority of our papers were cited once or not at all."

Dougherty shook his head slowly from side to side. "I've always believed that Biontolics has an enviable publication record. I am told that, for our size, we are one of the most productive research enter-prises in the world."

"With all due respect, sir, we are purveyors of mass mediocrity. My analysis shows we are publishing material that nobody cares about. With few exceptions, it's mediocre and irrelevant."

"Now wait one minute, I don't have to listen to this sort of talk."

"Bear with me, please. As you probably already know, my specialty is meta-analysis, the art and science of sifting through other people's work, mining the discarded detritus of research to reveal trends or patterns, the forest overlooked by others too busy examining all the trees. The science is statistics, but the art is spotting patterns. When I finished the analysis for my last paper, the one I can't publish, I went back and read through all 54 papers in the core cluster of studies. You know what I noticed that wasn't in the tables or the statistics? Not one of those papers was written or co-authored by anyone from Biontolics, not one. That is amazing, sir, because those papers, those important papers, are all in areas that fall within our primary mission: oncology, genetics, epigenetics, gene expression, apoptosis, and cellular growth and longevity. These are our bread and butter, yet not one of our people were represented by a paper in that group."

Dougherty shrugged and spread his hands. "Do you have a point?"

"That was my point. But I also have another question. It struck me as strange that no one from Biontolics was publishing in that area, so I went back into our own archives, reran my earlier analysis, and found more than thirty internal, unpublished papers that would have fallen into the same cluster and lent even greater strength to my conclusions, yet none of these studies had ever been published. Why do you think that is?"

"Because they were not good enough to be accepted by the journals, perhaps?"

"No!" Rosen said, lightly tapping his clenched fist on his thigh for emphasis. "They were unpublished because Biontolics would not allow them to be published. I cross-referenced with the IP Group's database and found that Biontolics had turned down every publication release request for every one of those papers. What do you make of that, sir?"

Dougherty clenched his teeth as he mulled it over, trying to decide what tack to take with a conversation that was lurching out of control. "I don't know, exactly. I think it is a matter that someone will have to look into, but I am certain we will find an explanation, one that will satisfy you. At least I hope we can, since I would hate to have us lose someone as resourceful as you seem to be." He tried to modulate the level of threat in his voice. "So," he pronounced as he stood, signaling that the meeting was at an end.

Rosen ignored the hint. "If you are going to have someone look into the matter, sir, perhaps they will find this useful. Several of the earliest unpublished papers in our own archives cited this one as an unpublished research report, but it was not in our database, so I tracked it down on the internet. It was never published, that much I confirmed. From the references it cites, it would seem to date from the 1970s. Apparently, someone had once scanned it into a .PDF document and left it forgotten on a server at their university. It took some real digging, but I have learned that if you are clever and persistent enough, you can track down almost anything on the Web."

He slipped a stapled document from his portfolio. The cover sheet was darkened toward the edges and peppered with a telltale accumulation of speckles from too many generations of successive photocopying. It was a typewritten manuscript with the word "CONFIDENTIAL" repeated across the top and bottom of the page. The title, "Cancer expression, cell longevity, and mosaicism in Rattus norvegicus," was succinct testimony to close parallels with the research integrated in Rosen's own meta-analysis, except this paper reported experimental results from decades earlier. The authors were listed on the cover sheet as Atchison D. Dougherty, Ph.D., Llewellyn A. Cass, M.D., Emile Aubuchon, Ph.D., and Janella Kai.

When Dougherty didn't take the paper from his hand, Rosen stood up to leave and laid it on the desk. "I guess you were barely more than a grad student then, and now you are the last man standing, it would seem."

Dougherty's face remained placid save for a double crease that subtly deepened between his eyebrows. "Meaning?"

"Well, all the other authors are either dead or disappeared."

"All? How do you. . .," he stopped himself and locked eyes with Rosen.

After an uncomfortable few seconds, Rosen broke the silence. "You have someone look into that. And I trust you will let me know what this is all about." He walked out and strode past the receptionist without remembering to get his parking ticket validated.

The General sat down again on the edge of his desk, rocking back and forth ever so slightly as he thought through the scenarios. He picked up the phone on the desk, punched a long series of digits, and waited. After a half-dozen warbling rings, the voice on the other end said, "What?"

"Andras, it's Dougherty."

"I know who it is, but do you know what time it is?"

"Sorry. Where are you?"

"Moscow, the clinic."

"We have a problem. We have to meet."

"Do I know about this problem?"

"Not yet. I'll see you at the Center tomorrow night."

"No, you come here. I just got in from Africa. Are you certain this can't wait? At least give me a hint over the phone."

"No, it can't wait, but, on second thought, I can take care of it, or at least engineer a short-term solution. So, until we next meet in Zurich. The chemist. I have to go. I have to make some arrangements here." He set down the phone and picked up the mottled paper from his desk. He had not known that a copy still existed outside the safe in his London townhouse. Who had made it? They had shown the draft to almost no one once they had decided what to do about it. But someone among the handful they had trusted had given a copy to someone else who had passed on another copy. This version looked like it might have been scanned from a sixth or seventh generation copy. It wasn't possible to go much further than that in those early days of photocopying.

Dougherty made another phone call. "Holzinger, it's Dougherty here. I want you to track down something on the internet and make it disappear, completely, even on the Internet Wayback Machine. Every copy, every reference, every link. I don't want a trace left behind. Can you do that?"

"I know the team that can do it, but it will not be instantaneous if the distribution is wide. And if there is anyone on the other end trying to preserve it, we can get into a put-and-take game that can drag on and on."

"We'll head that one off by starting with every system inside Biontolics. Begin with the Ipswich Lab and work outward from there. I'll send you particulars by secure email. Start scrambling the moment you get it. And put a tail on a Dr. Rosen David in the Ipswich Lab, infect his workstation, and get into his home system if he has one. You report back to me directly. Understand?

"*Ich verstehe!* I understand. *Tchüss.*" The line went dead.

5

Rosen knew he should have gone straight home after the meeting in Boston, but he had been driving on automatic pilot and had continued on directly to the Lab instead. Once there, he had gotten caught up in tracking down new references cited in a fresh batch of unpublished papers that he had retrieved from the internal archives. Millie would not be happy. In the weeks since his discoveries began, a murky shadow had descended on their relationship, and the distance between them had been growing. It would have worried Rosen had he been given to worry, but in their division of roles and responsibilities, worry was Millie's department, just as taking out the garbage and mowing the lawn were his.

The house was dark when he arrived, but he could see a light on in the bedroom. When Rosen rattled his fingers on the half-closed door there was no response. He pushed it open enough to see Millie lying with her back to him and her arm cantilevered straight out over the side of the bed. The coverlet was heaped like a tent over her, leaving only the top of her head exposed. A pocket guide to edible weeds lay on the pillow beside her.

He whispered, "Sorry," in hopes that he hadn't awakened her but in fear that he had. He tiptoed out again, gently pulled the door to, and quietly walked back down the hall to pour himself a drink and watch something from the TiVo. The tension of the meeting was still with him, though, and he found it impossible to concentrate, so eventually he poured himself a second single-malt scotch and headed back to the bedroom.

Millie hadn't moved.

Rosen froze, a wooden totem pole standing watch over the fragile figure of his wife lying still on the bed. A breeze from the open window stirred her hair where it peeked from beneath the covers, but there was no other movement. His heart hammered in his chest as he forced himself to edge around to her side of the bed. His knees cracked as he slowly lowered himself until he was eye-level with her motionless face.

He had no a label for the feeling that gripped him as he reached out to touch her shoulder.

"Millie," he whispered. There was no response. He gently shook her. "Millie, I am sorry. Please."

Her eyes fluttered half open and she looked into his. "Are you all right, Rosen?"

"Yes. No. I thought,...for a moment I thought maybe...You didn't move."

"I'm exhausted, Rosen. These nights when you have been working so late, I try to stay up to see you, to talk, but then I have to leave so early in the morning. It...I...I just can't do it. It's not working."

"I'm sorry, Millie." He lifted her gently and pulled her to him. "I was," he searched for a word, a synonym for the fear he had felt. "I thought," he said, choosing a safe and neutral verb, "I thought that maybe, maybe I had lost you. That's crazy, I know, but ..." Her head lay deliciously against his chest and a wisp of her hair tickled his lip. "I love you, Millie."

"I love you, too. Come to bed my future Nobelist, my noblest of biologists. And please come home earlier more often." His tenderness and concern had touched her. She started kissing him with the little popping kisses that were her way of inviting him in.

He drifted in and out of their lovemaking as Millie's sudden passion and his dark thoughts of conspiracies warred for his attention. Millie, on the other hand, mounted and rode him with undivided concentration. She climaxed astride him, then bent to whisper in his ear. "We have to talk. I'm taking a sick day tomorrow and so are you. We have to talk."

It was a litany that he had heard before, and his discomfort rose as he lay beside her. Whether in whispers in bed or shouted in capital letters in an email, the message did not usually mean that what followed would be easy for Rosen to manage.

Rosen's wide-ranging intelligence did not extend to insight into the subtleties of human emotion. He interpreted the feelings of those around him by formula and only with some difficulty. His own emotional experience was largely one-dimensional, ranging from moderately good to moderately bad. Good could be anything from simple satiety to his own carefully modulated version of elation; bad could mean anxious or angry, discouraged or disappointed. Feelings, he had once written in a note to a friend, were like numbers: they could be positive or negative, real, or imaginary, but mostly complex. It was a mathematician's play on words that brought a groan and a grin from his friend, an excitable electrical engineer who wore his feelings up front, next to his pocket protector. To Rosen, though, numbers, including the so-called complex numbers, made simple sense in a direct way that feelings never did.

Ask Rosen how he felt, and he might say "I don't know." Press him on it, and he might elaborate. "Good, I guess," he would add, or, "Not good, but okay." Millie accepted his handicap as she accepted the tin ear that rendered him incapable of carrying a tune. His muted emotions often served as a convenient counterbalance to her many anxieties, but acceptance did nothing for her need for engagement and intensity, which periodically rose to the point of crisis between them.

~ ~ ~

The day spent playing hooky with Millie had proven to be a good idea and not nearly as taxing for Rosen as he had anticipated. She told him she was unhappy and becoming unsure whether they should stay married. She missed him and wanted more time with him. She wanted more independence and more togetherness. She felt the pulls of their very different careers and wondered if they might just slowly drift apart. She was proud of him but also felt diminished by his glamorous job in cutting-edge research that contrasted so critically with her own position teaching biology and health science to adolescents.

They had been holding hands as they walked in silence along the harbor front in Gloucester with freshets of the fishy Atlantic breeze tossing Millie's silk-fine hair. Then her small hand tightened on his, and the core of her perennial pain poured out. They had just reached the Morgan Faulds Pike sculpture of a young woman and her two children gazing out over the sea.

"I wish we made love more often," Millie said.

Rosen nodded, but it was a nod of agreement not of understanding. They stood silently for several minutes, each appreciating in their own very different ways the beauty of the three figures in bronze. Rosen, having completed his visual survey, spoke first. "Isn't it extraordinary, such lifelike detail," he said. "Look at the drape of the dress seeming to blow in the wind as if it were thin cotton rather than solid metal. I read somewhere that the artist had her models pose nude for the initial sculpture. That way she could build up the clothes more realistically in the original from which the bronze was cast."

Millie looked at him with sad eyes then turned her gaze to the young child in the woman's arms as the tears began to flow. "I wish we made love more often," she repeated, "even though . . ."

Even Rosen understood this for the trope it was. She regretted that they couldn't have children. The regret, which was deep, real, and recurring, surfaced someway in every such talk. It was most painful to both of them—painful to Millie because she saw it as her failing, painful to Rosen because he knew how much it meant to her.

He liked the idea of children but had always found the reality less interesting than the idea. He was willing to adopt—emphasis on the willing—but the issue to her was as much about bearing the children as raising them. As she saw it, her career gave her abundant opportunities to mother-hen a young brood. What she couldn't do was conceive and give birth.

She had all but convinced herself that it was a blessing not to be having children. The biologist in her said that it was Nature's way of keeping reproductive handicaps from being passed on to another generation. She worried about the growing number of couples who bore children only with the help of expensive and elaborate medical technology. Their investment would only ensure that future generations would be even more dependent on intervention. She took secret comfort in the fact that she had persuaded Rosen when they were in graduate school to donate to a sperm bank. At least one of them might continue to contribute to the human gene pool, but she said nothing of any of this in their day-long talk.

Later, he had stood, stroking Millie's hair as she sat on a rock, knees tucked under her chin, hugging herself as she cried and the incoming tide washed the gravel beach. Back home, they had made love in the afternoon with the late sun streaming in the bedroom window.

It had been a day filled with conversation and without conclusion, a day that Rosen could replay in his head but without insight. He knew these times transformed, that even without resolution, even without change, they made life better between them, but he had no idea how. He only knew that it felt good to have Millie's head on his shoulder and the scent of her hair in his nostrils and her breath warm against his neck.

6

Mbutsu glanced quickly around the long ebony table, its highly polished surface dancing with reflections from the chandelier above, and realized that it was good to be dining alone again. Alone was only a relative concept for the President for Life of Busanyu. Both of his newest wives were across the table from him, but the children had already dined separately and been paraded before the table, then herded off to studies and to bed. Tabansi Faruq, Busanyu Minister of Defense and the youngest son of one of Mbutsu's old school chums, was on one side with his wife, Daib. On the other side was the mayor of Mbutsu City who had arrived with a petition at the palace and managed to invite himself to dinner, along with his pudgy teenage daughter. An aide had quietly informed the President that the Mayor was shopping his daughter to high-placed officials and might even have in mind her becoming number five in the President's household. Mbutsu, who had seen the daughter before, had laughed.

Mbutsu pushed his plate away and leaned back in his chair. The plate was immediately swept up by a server, a young girl who shyly stole a glance at Mbutsu as she retrieved his cutlery.

Mbutsu raised a finger, bringing the butler to his side. "That one," Mbutsu said, nodding toward the rapidly retreating serving girl. "Who is that one? I do not recognize her."

"She just returned from Angola where she was studying. One of the drivers recommended her. She is a hard worker and a quick learner."

"And very pretty."

"And very young." The almost inaudible remark came from across the table, but it was not clear who had spoken. Mbutsu shot a glance at his wives, who both stared straight ahead, grim faced.

"I like them young," he said. "You should both be glad of that, or you would not be here, now, eating like the queen of Egypt."

Boipelo, the older of the two sisters and mother of three of his children, sniffed in reproach before wiping her mouth slowly and deliberately with her brocaded napkin. "And the older you get, Edgar, the younger you like them. Is it not so, husband?" She drew out the last word for emphasis.

"It is not so, wife number three," he said, putting her firmly in her place. "I simply never lost the tastes of my youth." The tastes of his youth were legend. As a soldier, he had encouraged the men under his command to rape the women of the villages they overran, and he was said to have saved for himself the prettiest among those who were barely more than girls.

While locking eyes with Boipelo, Mbutsu signaled again to his butler.

"Excellency," the butler said, leaning slightly forward in anticipation of the request to come.

"Have her brought to my room in an hour," Mbutsu said, speaking quietly but loud enough to be heard by those across the table. He did not shift his gaze from Boipelo.

"The serving girl," the butler said in confirmation, but with a subtle hint of question. Mbutsu nodded and dismissed the man. Boipelo held her husband's eyes as she rose from the table, made a show of straightening her chair, and backed away without turning, as if she were leaving the presence of royalty. Her mouth remained fixed and unexpressive, but her eyes flashed anger.

"Wives," Mbutsu said, leaning forward and speaking to the Defense Minister who was seated just past his own wife. "It is probably that time again, when they get moody and jealous. At least eventually that monthly inconvenience stops, although then they are not that desirable, either, as you know."

The Minister squirmed with visible discomfort, but neither he nor his wife spoke, and the rest of the dinner proceeded in silence until Mbutsu suddenly rose. Everyone still at the table stood.

"I think I shall be off to bed, then. I have meetings early in the morning," he announced in a quiet voice, before walking slowly from the room.

~ ~ ~

Mbutsu ignored the soldier from his personal guard who stood at attention outside the door to his bedroom suite. He entered the room and found the girl already waiting for him, standing beside the bed, barefoot, wearing the simple, light-blue shirtwaist dress of a schoolgirl.

"You are early," he said.

She kept her head bowed slightly in respect. "I asked them to bring me here so that I would be ready."

He looked surprised and pleased. "You are eager, then?"

"You are Mbutsu. I am only one who serves. That is why I am here: because you are Mbutsu."

"Does the one who serves have a name?"

"Afya." She didn't offer a family name.

"And how old is Afya?"

"Nineteen."

"You do not look even fifteen."

"Is that a good thing or not," she asked, "to look younger than you are?"

"In a woman, it is a good thing, and in your case a very good thing. In a man, it is another matter, and in a President, it can be a definite problem."

"It is said that our President is more than ninety years old. My grandfather told me that he saw you on the television when he was a boy in school, and you were already a grown man, a soldier fighting against the government. But that is impossible. You do not look to be ninety."

"No, I do not," he said, dismissing the subject.

He crossed over to her and started undoing the buttons of her shirtwaist. Her breathing deepened and picked up in pace as he proceeded. He placed a finger on either side of her neck and traced the lines of her collarbone, slowly spreading his hands, pushing the top of her dress apart until it slipped from her shoulders. She was wearing nothing underneath. Mbutsu trembled slightly as he slowly lowered both hands until his fingers rested lightly on her large nipples, as dark as espresso against the light cocoa of her skin.

He pushed her gently but eagerly down on the bed and started to undress himself. She lay there, atop the covers, legs slightly spread in invitation, arms raised and hands beneath the pillow behind her head. She opened her mouth as if to speak.

Mbutsu climbed onto the bed, spreading her legs still farther as he lowered himself.

He screamed.

The pain, at first a mere stitch in his side, shot through him, ripping him apart like lightening through an old tree in a storm. Her arm had come around suddenly, catching him low in his left side. He grabbed the arm and twisted it with such desperate violence that he heard a snap as a bone in her wrist gave way. She screamed as the guard, already at the bedside with his gun drawn, jerked her erect.

The knife had done real damage, but Mbutsu knew he would heal. He was an old soldier who had survived worse. He calmly grabbed a pillow from the bed and jammed it against his side to staunch the rush of blood. A pistol lay there on the bed where it had been hidden under the pillow.

"Pity she decided to use the knife instead of finishing me off with a single shot," he said, laughing with grim humor.

"You deserve more than a single shot!" she spat. "Special justice, like you gave my father. I will cut off your balls and feed them to you."

Mbutsu laughed and winced in pain. "I think you will do no such thing. I think it is you who will get special justice."

Three soldiers suddenly entered the room. "Get the doctor. Now!" he barked at the last of them. "And take her away," he said to the other two, as his personal guard helped steady him. There was a traffic jam at the door as the three soldiers all took the same moment to try to exit.

"Wait, leave her." The soldiers hesitated a second but then threw the girl to the floor and stood over her with their side arms drawn. She lay there, her hand wrapped around her broken wrist, and glared up at Mbutsu.

"Who is your father, Afya? What is your family."

"My father was Ntansi, Matata's half-brother. And you are nothing beside either of them. Matata will eat your eyes after he is through with you. You will beg for him to be through. They will butcher the Butcher of Busanyu. The people will win in the end. Bastard! Pig!" She spat again.

Mbutsu looked down at her and grew thoughtful. The sound of running feet reached them from the hall. Mbutsu scanned the soldiers in the room and reached for the pistol on the bed.

His personal guard flinched and took a step back. Mbutsu calmly shot him in the head and the man fell to the floor beside the girl. The Captain of the Presidential Guard, rushing into the room, shouted, "What happened? Are you all right, Excellency?

Mbutsu gestured with the pistol. "Take these men away. This girl had help. There was a gun and knife in here with her. I want you to find out how they got here, who all was involved."

"Look out!" the Captain shouted. Before anyone else could react, Mbutsu kicked at the girl's good arm, sending the gun she had retrieved from the dead guard skittering across the polished wood floor.

Mbutsu, his face turning scarlet, lowered the pistol he held, turned it sideways, and pressed the barrel to the bridge of her nose. He waited until she raised her eyes to meet his in defiance, then pulled the trigger.

"Get this mess cleaned up, Captain. And I mean more than just the mess in this room. And where the fuck is my doctor?"

"Your doctor left this morning, on your jet, Excellency. You said your goodbyes."

"Yes, of course. Then the other one, the clumsy butcher from South America. Just get him." Mbutsu staggered and pressed harder on the blood-soaked pillow at his side. "And I said to get this mess cleaned up—before I slip on someone's brains and take a fall. Unless you want it to be your blood that I next wash my feet in."

He stood there, naked, badly wounded, but still very much the feared Butcher of Busanyu.

Rosen had spent the entire week trying to be a good boy, trying to behave himself while getting used to a new position in which he was quickly learning that his main responsibility was keeping three junior analysts busy believing they were doing real science when they were actually only pursuing make-work assignments handed down to Rosen from unknown sources in Research Triangle Park. He was not succeeding very well in his new job and was finding that more and more of his time was spent sending emails of protest to North Carolina or London or trying to persuade the local Lab Director to take yet another meeting with him.

Millie actually liked the new regime at first. Rosen's lack of real responsibility and the absence of any engaging challenge that might keep him at the lab meant that he was coming home at seven or even six most evenings. But his sullen disposition and growing unease, muted though it might be, was beginning to worry her.

Rosen, however, remained worry free but impatient as he glanced at the clock gadget on his monitor screen and wondered how much longer it might take him to wrap up the last of the many routine electronic forms for which he was now responsible. He was watching the animated second hand slowly circle for the third time when he had a flash of inspiration to take another look at the author names on some of the unpublished papers. He realized that he could define a query and pull them off the server again, but there was a folder and a database with everything he needed already sitting on his old machine. He typed in its address on the network, but instead of getting a login dialog got an error message. He double-checked his spelling, tried again, but got another message that the address was invalid. He did a search for the computer by name and this time got a response that no computer named SULTANA1 could be found. Rosen, figuring it must be a network or local search glitch, switched to a global search and tried again to connect to his old computer. No luck.

It seemed unlikely, but it was possible that the machine was turned off, since no one had moved into his old office yet. Rosen took the back stairway to the second floor and rapped on the closed door. There was no answer. He pushed the door open. The room had been cleaned out except for the desks, chairs, and conference table.

Jeannine, who seemed perpetually present wherever Rosen was, poked her head around the corner from the hallway. "Looking for something?" she asked.

"Yeah, my old system. I wanted to pull some files from it."

"Oh, I guess when they moved my stuff over to Nutrition Sciences they must have grabbed it, too. Must be around someplace."

"Well it doesn't show up on the network, so if it's around it's not connected. And you've been sent to join Nut Science, too?"

"Please, I prefer to use the official name, even though 'Nut Science' might be the favored terminology in the hallways."

"No, I tell you, it really is Nut Science. Haven't you heard the latest findings from my group that 500 grams of walnut meats a day cuts your risk of cardiovascular disease and colon cancer in half?" He paused, waiting for a laugh or a rabbit punch that didn't come. "Which team have you been assigned to?"

"Yours. You're my new boss." She grinned at him and mimed a curtsy. "I want to keep an eye on you, see how you do it, so I can become a rising star, too."

"Rising, falling, who can tell the difference? Right now I'm headed down—to check with the IITS people to see what happened to my computer."

Information and Infrastructure Technologies and Services was located in the converted guest house, which was itself larger than most single-family homes in the area. One had to go outside to get there from the labs or the offices. There had been talk of building a tunnel or covered walkway, but IITS had always vetoed the idea. They liked the separation. Those in Technical Services, the "help desk," particularly preferred to be able to put people on hold or stack them in a message queue rather than have to face them across a counter.

Rosen now leaned on the Technical Services counter and looked down at the chunky nebbish in a flowered dress standing on the other side. "You are saying that the computer—my computer—was scrubbed and rebuilt?"

"That's what it says here on my Equipment Disposition Log," she answered, with more than a hint of impatience. "The hard drive was reformatted and the OS was reinstalled on Tuesday."

"Why?"

"Security policy. We sent you an email last week, but you didn't respond."

Rosen fluttered the fingers of his left hand against his jeans, his version of getting steamed. "You wiped the hard drive."

"Yes, Dr. David, multi-pass random overwrite to DoD standards. Even the Pentagon would approve of our procedures."

The pace of Rosen's fluttering fingers picked up. "Right, I guess that's it, then. Thanks. Carry on."

Rosen left and shifted gears into his determined problem-solving mode. Back in his new office, he accessed the backup share for SULTANA1. The Lab automatically maintained a backup copy of everything from its many scattered computers. More than once Rosen had been saved from redoing work after accidentally overwriting the wrong file.

He let out a sigh of relief and a quiet "Yes!" The backup share was still there. He opened it to scan through folders. It was empty.

Rosen stared at the screen, thinking of his next move. The report and project archives might have a copy of his data if he had attached them at the time of filing. It was worth a try. He accessed the archival database and once again sighed in relief. Everything was there. He scanned down the list until he came to Project Zoetrope, his last assignment, and opened the folder. It, too, was empty.

Rosen could feel his heart speed up, but he calmly switched to a corporate directory, located the listing for Chief Librarian of Libraries and Archival Storage, and sent off a message to Enid Amundsen. The reply came within minutes.

> The files you were attempting to access have been removed
> from the Libraries and Archival Storage databases.
>   —Enid Amundsen, Chief Librarian, LAS

He typed a reply and got another quick response.

> I am not in a position to say the reason except that the
> removal was made at the direction of Corporate Security.
> And, yes, removal means expunged completely. We have

no backup copy or any other means to restore the
information removed.
  —Enid Amundsen, Chief Librarian, LAS

~ ~ ~

It was over take-out pizza for a late dinner that Millie brought up the
matter of his mood. "Tell me what's going on with you, Rosen," she
said. "Something is really eating you."

"No, I'm okay. Anyway, I really shouldn't talk about this stuff," he
said, which Millie recognized as his coded declaration that he could
and would talk about it in his own good time.

"You have to trust me," she said, reaching across the table to take his
hand. "I can keep a secret, you know."

"I know, it's not that. I trust you, but it's complicated. I'm under
contract; they could go after me for talking out of school."

Millie said nothing but waited patiently for him to decide to talk.

"You know what happened today?" he began at last. "I went to suck
over some files from my old system, and the computer didn't show up
on the network. I went over to the other building, and they told me the
system had been scrubbed and rebuilt. I asked why. Actually, I
insisted. They said it was a security issue, that they had nothing to do
with it. Corporate Security had told them to retrieve my machine and
all my media and scrub them clean. I stormed out of there. Back at my
office, my nice, new, antiseptic office—it's on the back corner with a
view out over the picnic tables—I figured I would just pull what I was
looking for out of the archives. Nothing. Gone. I searched the backup
servers and found zip. I called the head of IT and asked her what had
happened, and she gave me the same song and dance about security.
Corporate had directed that everything be deleted. Everything.

"It's as if the last months never happened. My old reports and my
published and internal papers are still in the reference database
except for my last project, Zoetrope, which has vanished completely."

"What do you think is going on?"

"It doesn't make sense, but I'm becoming convinced that the company might be actually suppressing research. From what I can tell,
they are giving away dreck and censoring the good stuff."

"That could make perfect sense. Don't corporations usually keep the
best ideas to themselves?"

"Sure, if they are building cars or developing drugs or manufacturing computers, but Biontolics doesn't make anything real. Their only product is research; they manufacture and distribute knowledge."

"What about your clients? You do research for clients, right? Keeping important stuff proprietary would make sense for them."

"Yes, for the drug companies that we do stuff for, but that's less than maybe ten percent of our business. Most of what we do is for foundations funding pure research. There is nothing to be gained by not publishing and everything by publishing, particularly in this area that I've been working on. It's really important research that needs to be put out there so that others can followed up on it."

"What's it all about? Just tell me in general terms if you can't be specific."

Rosen took a deep breath and another bite of pizza before answering. "It's about what causes cells to age and die and the genetic and other factors that regulate that. On the one hand, you have ordinary cells that only live so long and can only go through so many cell divisions before they give up the ghost."

"Apoptosis, cellular suicide," she offered.

"Right, and without that you end up with cells that go on living and multiplying forever. Cancer. Like the immortal HeLa cancer-cell culture so widely used in research. There doesn't seem to be anything in between, not in nature, but researchers have been trying to figure out an end run around nature, to regulate cell aging and longevity and, ultimately, to extend the lifespan of the organism."

"You mean like calorie restriction, anti-oxidants, that stuff?"

"Not exactly. Some of that more superficial stuff may eventually be proved out to be useful, but most of what passes for life extension is just snake oil and pseudoscience. Besides, who wants to live to a hundred and twenty if the price is to spend your life being cold and hungry or eating nothing but wheat grass? No, what I am talking about are more fundamental mechanisms, like telomeres."

"The little strings at the ends of DNA that protect the DNA but gradually wear away with each cell division. At least that's how I explain it to my students."

"Right, except that it turns out there are a bunch of studies with small samples and inconclusive or incomplete results that happened to have included chimeras."

"You mean animals with a mosaic of genetically distinct cells from more than one set of parents. And?"

"And, I can't yet tease out all the details, but the presence of certain oncogenes, genes that would normally lead to or increase the likelihood of cancer, have a modulated effect on normal cell aging and longevity when they are part of a genetic mosaic in a chimeric organism."

"You're saying a chimera, like a rat that has cells with the genetics of different sets of parents, one with mosaicism, could live longer?"

"Maybe. The problem is that most of the experiments were investigating cancer and cancer treatment, so the animals were 'sacrificed' at a certain stage in the experiment. Somebody would have to do a whole new series of studies solely with chimeras in which they were allowed to reach natural death."

"And?"

"And this is an extremely promising line of research toward a possible mechanism for life extension."

"If you're a chimeric lab rat."

"It's not limited to rats, remember. Chimerism turns out to be fairly widespread in nature and not all that rare in humans. Non-identical twins have been found to have swapped genetic material in the womb. And most women who have had children end up incorporating cells from their offspring in their bloodstream."

"Are you suggesting that if I could have children, I could live longer?"

"Well, you can reduce your chances of breast cancer. That's been shown." He stopped and looked at his hands before reaching out to her. "Sorry. I didn't mean anything by it, just. . .well, it's true.

"Anyway, the point is, there has been a lot of good research that adds new pieces to the puzzle, some of the best within Biontolics, and all the Biontolics work has been censored. They put a lid on good science and smothered my work." He told her about the direct orders not to pursue his previous line of inquiry.

"The kicker is that Dougherty himself was lead author on a paper that anticipated my findings on a small scale by maybe thirty or forty years; there's no date on the paper, so I'm guessing about when it was written. Something is not right with this picture." He stood up suddenly. "I think I'll go log into my account at the Lab and try another tack. The company contracts with an off-site firm out in Colorado to keep ultimate backups in some underground bunker or something. I think I may be able to find a way to retrieve my stuff from there.

"Here, you can finish the pizza," he said, crumpling his paper napkin into a small ball and snapping it across the room into the sink.

"Don't do that. Put it in the trash, dummy." She walked over and retrieved a soggy wad from the sink and gingerly transferred it to the upright bin in the corner.

"I could have done that," he said.

"Yeah, I know. But you're you, and I'm me, and this is how I do it. Go analyze your whatever, my messy mathematician."

"Biologist," he corrected, as he blew her a kiss. "Mathematical biologist. Soon to be famous mathematical biologist. Either that or unemployed."

~ ~ ~

Millie, deciding to check in with him before she headed for bed, found him still working in the den. He was uncharacteristically agitated, shaking his head and muttering under his breath as he alternated between short bursts of typing and almost savage clicking on his mouse. "Well it seems to be gone from the data archiving company, too. It took a while, but I finally managed to tunnel in through the lab and back out again using my new credentials to get read-access privileges in Colorado, but my paper, the raw data, even the .PDF that I pulled off the internet, are all gone. I don't know how they did it." He pulled up a browser. "One more shot; I'll try going back to the Web. Let's see, what the fudge was that URL where I found the old paper in the first place? It was something like trollhouse dot some university dot some country. The Netherlands, I think." He tried several guesses before switching to Google, where he entered the first five words of the title in quotes. Google dutifully reported back in 0.13 seconds: No results found.

"It's gone," he said.

"Are you sure about that? Things don't just disappear from the Web. Quite the opposite. They hang around forever, even when you want them to go away—like those pictures of us skinny dipping at the lake that your dear little cousin posted. I am sure they are out there, someplace, still, if not on the Web itself, then on some pervert's hard drive."

"Shush, Millie. I have to think. Where could there be another copy of any of my stuff."

"I thought companies had to keep copies of everything."

"Millie, I told you," he said, with growing impatience. "I already checked the share server. My backup files have also been purged. This is so crude. Somebody must be real scared—or real stupid."

"What about your laptop? Don't you sometimes work on this at the kitchen table? Could there still be copies there?"

He was already heading for the closet to retrieve his laptop bag.

~ ~ ~

Millie awoke at 5:30, as usual, to find no one in the bed beside her. Rosen was at the kitchen table where she had left him at 10:30 the night before. "Don't tell me you pulled an all-nighter."

"I did. Call me in sick again. I'm going to see Steven," he said, pushing back his chair and closing the laptop.

She knew immediately who Rosen meant. Steven King was one of his few heroes, a man of broad interests and deep intellect who had taken the young Rosen David under his wing and coached and coaxed and cajoled him through his disillusionment and his dissertation. Professor Steven King held an endowed chair at Tufts and had appointments in three departments. He would start every semester by writing his name on the whiteboard, underlining the V in his first name and announcing, "I'm the Steven with a V; I write journal articles. The Stephen with a PH writes novels. One of us is rich, the other is not. I'll leave it to you to hypothesize which is which." It was lame, college-lecture humor, but it always got a laugh, and none of his students ever misspelled his name.

8

Rosen finally located his former advisor in Halligan Hall, a brick building removed from the heart of the Tufts campus. It housed an odd mix of disciplines and activities, and the office Rosen had been directed to was sandwiched between a supply room for the athletics department and the locked double doors of the Intelligent Robotics Project, its title spelled out in Legos cemented to the door. A standard-issue plastic plaque below declared it to be for Authorized Personnel Only.

Rosen walked past the closed robotics lab and peeked through the open door of a tiny, windowless office. It was not what one might expect, not the typical academic abode lined with bookshelves, littered with boxes, and festooned with piles of papers. The walls displayed a few framed posters, the largest for a Marc Chagall exhibition from a generation earlier, and the modest desk held a single neat stack of student essays alongside a keyboard and a small computer display screen. Professor King believed that books and bound journals were of little value in his profession, particularly in an era when nearly everything of consequence could be accessed online.

"You're a hard one to find these days," Rosen announced, as he tapped on the doorjamb and entered. "Is this how the University now treats the Shmuel Pfeffer Distinguished Professor of Mathematics and Medicine?"

Steven King looked up from the stack of papers he had been grading and smiled broadly. "I'm Emeritus now, just plain old Professor King. They put me wherever they can find an empty closet. But look at you, Rosen David! What an unexpected pleasure." He stood and took Rosen's hand, pumping it enthusiastically. "Please make yourself comfortable in my little den."

"You will never be plain old anything to me, you know," Rosen said. He remembered Dr. Steven King as a giant, a man who went nowhere on campus without at least one attentive student in attendance, a man whose most casual comment could trigger a flurry of note-taking among his graduate students. It was hard to reconcile the memories with the man in front of him, a smallish gentleman in a gray Van Dyke beard who now squeezed himself back into a squeaky secretary's chair behind a battered metal desk in an office the size of a large janitorial closet. "What's up? What are you doing," Rosen said, gesturing, then adding, "here?"

"I'm retired. I still teach pro bono, one course a term, usually alternating Experimental and Quasi-Experimental Design with Non-Parametric Statistics, which let's me meet the new students and mess with their minds before the younger faculty completely corrupts them. Besides, nobody wants to teach that stuff anymore, certainly not to students who come from a half-dozen different departments and might have to be told how to pronounce 'chi-square.' I'm yesterday. 'Let the old guys teach the old stuff.' That's what they say when I am not at the meetings, which is almost always, because I never liked meetings or departmental politics, and now I am simply too old to waste time on that crap."

"You don't seem old to me. I didn't even think you had reached retirement age."

"I took early retirement a few years ago when the University was desperately trying to cut expenses while clearing out the deadwood to make room for new growth. The payoff they offered was modest compared to the parachute my older brother got when he left Burroughs-Welcome, but Miriam and I are comfortable. Both kids are grown, off on their own, happily married—or at least married—so it doesn't take a lot for us. Did you know that we're going to be grandparents? Elspeth is pregnant. You remember Elspeth? She had a crush on you, you know, when she was in middle school. She married a WASP, a musician, and moved to San Francisco. Somehow Keith manages to make a living in this so-called indie music scene—even has his own label and a studio in their attic. It's amazing what these kids can do these days with a Mac, a few mikes, and some software.

"Speaking of kids, what about you?"

"No, not in the cards. But back to your retirement," he said, quickly changing the subject. "That blows my mind. I had no idea. I mean, you're still publishing and all. I read your last paper in the *Journal of Neuroscience and Cognitive Studies*. It was good."

"That was all Jacobson's work. I just helped fix his statistical analysis."

"You're too modest. That was a clever technique you applied to test for the significance of volumetric differences in functional MRI scans."

"Clever, maybe, but hardly groundbreaking. Jacobson and his neuroscience whiz kids are the ones exploring new territory. I'm just tilling old soil, replanting the same old crops in Latin Square plots."

Rosen smiled at the play on words that only someone who knew experimental design would get. It was a coded message in the private language between them, an acknowledgement of their connectedness. Like Rosen, Steven King was not given to much in the way of open emotional expression, but both of them knew that their affection was mutual and deep.

"Frankly," Steven continued, "I think the neuroscience people are straying too far afield, getting too full of themselves. Take Jacobson's work. It's interesting, incremental science, but I am not sure it proves anything, certainly not that consciousness is an epiphenomenon, a side-effect of complexity, as he claims. If consciousness is merely an illusion, then the question I ask is who or what is experiencing the illusion? Jacobson and his cronies are convinced that's all it is. They speak as if the debate were concluded. Awareness is illusory, they write in uppercase, which may well be true for them, I grant. Frankly, I think the whole lot of them exhibit certain deficits in self-awareness, particularly at conferences when they are dealing with those whom they regards as lesser beings, meaning anyone who does not share their views.

"As for me, my own consciousness is self-evidently no illusion, therefore, with a single counterexample their thesis is disproven." He snorted disdainfully, then leaned forward and dropped his voice into a conspiratorial tone. "Besides, that magnetic imaging stuff is over-rated, a research fad that became popular in large part because of the pretty pictures you get to publish—that and the fact that the equipment is massive and expensive and makes for good demonstrations when taking prospective benefactors on laboratory tours. This," he tapped the side of his head, "and this," he added, patting the top of his computer monitor, "are less dramatic, but that's where the real stuff happens.

"So, tell me what brings you here, Rosen? You didn't drive into

Medford and search all over campus just to pass the time listening to me pontificate. You've certainly heard all my sermons before."

Rosen laid two papers on the desk and turned them to face the right way. Steven bent toward them and tilted his head back to study them through his reading glasses.

"So, I see you are forcing me to wear both my hats in order to understand these. Oh, my poor head. It's been such a long time." He was referring to his double degrees in medicine and mathematics. Like Rosen, who had gradually moved from straight biology to applied math, Steven had found out during his early work as an internist on the cancer ward at Dana-Farber that he was more interested in the experiments in treatment than in treating the patients. He had completed a Ph.D. in statistics in record time and was immediately snapped up by Tufts to fill a joint appointment created especially for him in the Medical School and in the Department of Mathematics. His Biology appointment was a later addition.

Steven swiveled in his noisy chair as he read the abstract of Rosen's meta-analysis, then flipped through the pages of the blotchy older paper. "So, what do you make of it?" he asked.

"That's what I'm asking you. But let me fill you in on the background, first." He outlined what had been happening at Biontolics up to and including the point where his files had disappeared. "Do you think I'm paranoid? Paranoia is so,. . .so illogiccal."

"I was an oncologist not a psychiatrist, Rosen—cancer not gray matter—and I never put much stock in nosology, anyway. Just because you can classify and label something doesn't mean you understand it. Modern psychiatry, when it isn't all about drugging patients into submission, is preoccupied with putting them in a box with a name on it. Back in the 1960s, the radicals used to say that what the establishment called paranoia was merely a heightened sense of reality. Of course, the APA, the Ancient Psychological Association, as I like to call it, keeps changing the definitions of the boxes and renaming them with each release of their *Diagnostic and Statistical Manual*. But I would say that the reality is pretty much the same as it always was. Just because something sounds paranoid doesn't mean it might not be real. End of today's second sermon.

"So, Rosen, stop beating around the bush trying to get me to say something. What's your best guess? Do you think there is some kind of cabal controlling research in this area?"

Rosen took a long time to answer. "Look, Biontolics has research programs in many different areas—in geriatrics, pharmaceuticals and biochemistry, genetics, nutrition, oncology, cell biology, neuroscience—but there is a single subtext running through all of them. Everything we do is tied somehow into the issue of longevity. And it is becoming clear to me that the best of what we have been creating is being buried. I want you to help me make sense of it, to get to the bottom of it, to figure out why."

"I can think of several possible reasons, most of them having to do with money. A real life-extension technology, one that actually worked, that could be packaged and sold, would be worth billions. No, I take that back. As it is, the long-life industry with their pills and supplements, their diets and treatments, must be worth many billions—and that's all big bucks for little or no difference. The real deal would be worth trillions and would change the game."

Rosen shook his head. "Doesn't quite ring true, because they are making it harder for even their own people to see the whole picture. It's like they want us to keep working on little pieces but not know how the pieces fit together."

"That might be exactly what they want, like the Soviets and the Americans during the Cold War, each with their secret chemical and biological weapons research and no one but a handful at the top knowing what was really going on. Maybe what your people are working on now is just improving techniques, streamlining a process that is already worked out but perhaps is still too crude, complicated, and expensive. Have you considered that, Rosen?"

"You mean, they may have already succeeded but don't want the world to know, at least not until they are ready."

Steven looked over the top of his reading glasses and stared into Rosen's eyes. "It just might be possible, you know. I would have to study these papers more carefully, of course. Still, from my own, somewhat casual, reading in the area of life extension, I'd say we are a very long way from figuring this one out. There are a lot of very bright people going full tilt at the problem, and a lot of big money is being poured into it, not only by the usual bunch of foundations but also by super-rich individuals who want to use money to cheat death. So far, though, all we have is hints and hopes and hype. Maybe in a few decades we will be able to add another ten years or so to the average lifespan, but I simply do not see the Ray Kurzweils or the Craig Venters of the world getting their wishes granted and living forever. Like everyone else, whether they admit it or not, the life-extension lobbyists are afraid of death."

Rosen gave him a look that said he wasn't buying it.

Steven continued. "Hey, some people make up stories of an eternity in heaven, others fantasize about reincarnation, and still others invent scenarios in which science rescues them from the abyss of a personal end. But it all comes down to one thing: death, coming to terms with it. Do these people think it will be any easier to face the void after living another twenty or even two hundred years? The end is the end."

He shuffled the two articles on his desk before continuing. "I'm no expert in this area, but I just don't see us as being on the verge of a singularity where medical science will suddenly enable people to live for hundreds of years—much less indefinitely.

"It is wishful thinking by a few rich men with enormous egos who would like to believe that their wealth will enable them to survive, even thrive, until this singularity is upon us. It is the wishful thinking of people of lesser means but equally exaggerated senses of self-importance who hope that, if only they are disciplined enough, if only they work out every day and eat enough buckwheat bran or drink enough carrot and banana-peel smoothies, they, too, will be able to reach the ripe age of 150, to live until the singularity when they can join the immortals. It is the fantasy of other poor deluded souls who grasp onto isolated and widely misinterpreted experiments and then choose to go through life perpetually hungry, shivering in the July sun, because they think by eating little they will live long. Modern science and pseudoscience aside, that is symbolically and physically straight out of the thirteenth century: the denial of the flesh in pursuit of immortality.

"But there I go, mounting my soapbox again, while you sit there, polite but pained. Let's see." He looked down again at the papers on his desk. "This one," he said, tapping the mottled front of the older paper. "I know some of these authors. Well, everyone knew Llewellyn Cass, or Andras, as he preferred to be called. He was a force on the Boston cancer scene for decades before he disappeared on some kind of expedition in South America. Soft-spoken but with boundless energy. He gave a series of lectures here at Tufts that were later published as a monograph, something about slow-growing cancers, varieties like certain prostate cancers that are best left untreated because they never become life-threatening during the patient's life."

Steven became suddenly thoughtful, staring at the Chagall poster on his wall for several seconds. "I was going to say that Cass must have been in his mid-to-late seventies when he went on that ill-fated eco-tour to Patagonia, although he looked and acted more like a man in his fifties. Funny, that, wouldn't you say?"

There was a long silence between them. Rosen started to say something, but Steven interrupted him. "I remember this Janella Kai, too. A biochemistry major, I think, very bright, wanted to start her own drug company and retire rich, if I remember right. Petite, athletic, very pretty, too. Mixed race, from Mexico or something. More than one of the Assistant Professors in her department would have loved to become her mentor in more than one manner of speaking. She came to me a few times for consultations on experimental design." He noticed Rosen smiling at him. "Just consultation," he added. "I don't know what happened to her. Probably married a CEO in big pharma, with a ranch in California and two beautiful teenagers away at private school in Europe."

"Isn't that a bit sexist?"

"Sexist? Me? Talk to Miriam about that. I'm a devout realist. Had I been born female—and observant Jewish men thank God every day that they were not—with Janella Kai's brains and good looks, I could imagine the appeal of such a career path. But, like I said, I don't know what path she took."

"Neither do I, which is interesting, because it is so easy to track down people on the Internet. Everyone leaves footprints on the Web, but Janella Kai is the only one of those four authors who doesn't exist, except in Tufts alumni records and on Reunion.com, where her high-school classmates at Cambridge Rindge and Latin have her on a 'does anyone know what happened to' list. I even checked marriage records through two genealogy sites but couldn't find anything. Who knows.

"The interesting thing is that two of the authors are dead, according to the records, Kai is missing-in-action, and only the lead author is still around. I've met him and I've done the math. He's in his nineties, if it's the same Atchison Dougherty, but he doesn't look a day over fifty. Interesting, I'd say."

"Yes, interesting. Maybe it's his son. Or maybe the father has joined the gods. Maybe this line of research does lead—or already has led—to life eternal. That doesn't make it a good idea."

Rosen cocked his head in question as Steven continued. "Cells die to enable the individual to live on. Individuals die to enable the human enterprise to survive and thrive. Death is a curse to the person but a gift to the race. I once read a science fiction story called 'Death's Children.' I remember the title and the story vividly, although I've forgotten the author. It's about a race that had solved the mystery of life and death, that had found a way to live for many hundreds of years, but they threw it away, took a pass on immortality—or its approximation."

"Why?"

"It's in the title of the story. At one point, one of these aliens is speaking with a visitor from earth and draws attention to the sound of children laughing in a courtyard below. Such music, he tells his guest, the sound of youthful joy, of renewal and unending rediscovery, that is Death's greatest gift. If everyone lives forever, that's all gone. Children are the gift made possible by Death."

"Not everyone has children," Rosen said, with an edge in his voice.

"Not their own, perhaps, but ours, humanity's. Remember when you were my teaching assistant? Remember the incoming freshmen, their naïve energy, their unbounded belief in themselves and what they could and would do in life?"

Rosen shook his head vigorously. "I remember them sleeping through lectures and saying 'Yeah, duh!' and 'So?' I remember lame stories to justify missing assignments."

"That, too. But you and I were no different in our own times and ways. We could sleep through classes and skip assignments because we already knew it, already knew everything, knew that what we were being taught was bullshit that we could ignore and transcend. The future *does* belong to the young, and with good reason. They do things the old would never do, because we already know it couldn't be done. They don't know what's impossible, so they just go ahead and do it. They are ignorant, so they see with fresh eyes. One can only see something for the first time once.

"Caution and conservatism are the coin of advancing years, and the cost is creativity. That applies to me as much as to anyone else." Rosen started to protest but Steven held up his index finger and continued. "Do you think it's some kind of a fluke that the important developments in our field, in mathematics, have always been the work of younger people? It's been said that a mathematician who hasn't done something important by the age of 35 will never contribute anything of significance."

"Now you've gone from sexism to ageism," Rosen chided.

"Realism, my son, simple realism. I'm not saying geezers are worthless. As long as you can move and speak, you can contribute. Why do you think I'm here? I can still teach introductory classes in statistics. I've done it enough times that I could probably do it in my sleep, and some of my students would probably say that I sometimes do. I don't believe in retirement in any form, Rosen. I don't care how much you worked or how much wealth you've amassed, my view is that as long as you are consuming you ought to be producing—at least doing something useful.

"My Miriam once told me about her family stopping at a farm stand selling nuts. Her parents bought a small bag of walnut meats from a girl of twelve or so, who proudly told them that her grandfather had cracked all the nuts on the table. She nodded toward an old man with gnarled hands and a weather-ravaged face hunched over one of those big old long-handled affairs, cracking walnuts one at a time, very, very slowly. Miriam said he looked like he was a hundred to her girlish eyes, but there he was, doing his part to keep the family orchards going. Maybe he read to his young grandchildren in the evening when he was too tired to crack any more nuts. Maybe he entertained the family with stories from the old days, polished and embellished by years of retelling and by flagging memory. Who knows? But that man was not off playing golf or mahjongg in some retirement community or taking up bed space in a nursing home while waiting to die."

"That's a bit harsh. Not everyone gets the gift of vigorous golden years. Don't we eventually earn the right to take some time to ourselves, to do what we please, or at least not to have to get up every morning and drag ourselves off to some stupid job?"

Steven jabbed his finger at Rosen. "I'd say no. Everyone contributes, everyone adds something, whatever they can. It's what Miriam and I call TANSTAAFL economics: There Aint No Such Thing As A Free

Lunch. Everybody pays part of the bill, each according to their means."

"I never would have taken you for such a communist at heart, Steven."

"Communist, hell, that's chapter and verse from an icon of right-wing libertarianism, Robert Anson Heinlein."

"I always thought he was an icon of the flakey free-love left."

"That, too. And he started out as an active socialist. He was an icon of more things than the ubiquitous Apple logo. And, like the others of his strange species, *homo sapiens*, he was a messy mix, an inconsistent collage."

"Wait, didn't Heinlein continue to write well into his seventies?" Rosen said, smiling in smug triumph.

"Yeah, but the later novels just kept getting longer and more discursive," Steven countered. "The best of his oeuvre were all in his earlier works."

"Look, Steven, we have gotten off into literary criticism, which I remind you that I dropped in college even though you insisted it would be good for me, that it would help to sharpen my critical thinking skills. Plus, frankly, I never did care for science fiction."

"You darned well better care for it, since you may soon be living it, if the crew at Biontolics are on the trajectory we are extrapolating. And you need to figure out what you're going to do next."

Rosen looked lost in thought, his eyes focused on some point a meter beyond the top of Steven's head. "I'm going to do what any good academic would do, Steven," he said at last, pushing his chair back and standing to leave. "Thanks for the inspiration."

Steven broke into a broad smile. "You're welcome, Rosen," he said, nodding slowly and repeatedly. "Anytime. And thanks for the papers. Keep me posted."

Steven listened to the sound of Rosen's retreating footsteps, then spent the next several minutes in thoughtful concentration before waking up his computer and launching a browser. He was suddenly excited at the thought of beginning a fresh line of investigation. He whistled to himself, a soft and breathy tune, as he started digging into the University's archives.

9

"Fuck!"

Ferguson jumped. "What is it, Douglas?" he asked, closing his laptop with a soft click. The only other sounds in the third-floor conference room were the soft buzz of the overhead fluorescents and the almost inaudible thud of Atchison Douglas Dougherty knocking his fists together as he made faces at the screen of his computer.

It was past midnight, and they were alone in the building, except for the security guard down in the lobby who had recognized them but still insisted on seeing their ID cards and passports before letting them in. Revic AG was a tiny Swiss pharmaceutical firm with offices on the picturesque but business-like Talstrasse in Zurich and its plant in its own building in an industrial park nearer the airport. Revic carried out small production runs on rare and hard-to-manufacture drugs for selected customers. Only one of their customers mattered: the owners. The owners used the company for many purposes, including quiet meetings on important matters.

After filling in Ferguson about events at Biontolics and the meeting with Rosen David, Dougherty had logged into Revic's Wi-Fi to collect his email only to find that an RSS feed had delivered bad news unbidden to his desktop.

"Our boy has published," announced Dougherty. "He didn't even wait to go through an accelerated peer review on *PLoS Genetics* or *Medicine*. He obviously just wanted to get it out there, post it as fast as possible. It's an e-print in, of all places, arXiv Quantitative Biology." ArXiv, pronounced 'archive' as if the X were the Greek letter chi, was a repository of pre-publication manuscripts maintained by Cornell University. Dougherty fussed with the touchpad on his laptop and clicked on something. "It's a .PDF file, and judging by the size, the little bastard has expanded his paper. I'm downloading a copy now."

"Do you really think anybody is going to find it there? I mean, arXiv is basically just a database, a listing."

"All it takes is one, one reader who recognizes what they are reading. This is not like all the other little near-miss studies we've let go by in the past. This is a meta-analysis. Rosen references our paper. Our paper, Andras. Besides this is an important database. The arXiv q-bio listing is closely watched by anyone who has an interest in computational biology, genomics, cell behavior. Needless to say, we follow it closely ourselves. It's where precedent is set and early claims are made. The people who read in these areas are not ignoramuses. Our boy's piece won't be hard to spot among the 25 or so papers a month that are usually posted. We may already be too late. If it popped up on my feed, you can bet that others are probably having a look-see right now."

"Then let's take it down," Ferguson said, looking at his watch. "The IP Group in North Carolina might still be on the job if we act quickly. Or we can get our crew in San Diego to get on it."

"All either group can do would be to lodge an objection requesting that the paper be taken off the site. The thing is administered at Cornell where it is also the end of the day. Best case scenario, with extraordinary luck, is that it will take hours; more likely, it could be late tomorrow before any action is taken. We need to act fast."

Ferguson smiled triumphantly. "Ah, but the original poster can withdraw the paper at any time."

"You think Rosen can be persuaded to kill his own work? He's already gone renegade on us."

"No, of course not. I was thinking of Holzinger. You told me he has access to Rosen's computer and files; how long can it take him to hack into Cornell under Rosen's login credentials?"

Dougherty picked up the cell phone from beside his computer and placed a call. It took a dozen rings before he got an answer. "Holzinger. Get on your computer and Skype me. Now!" He thumbed the phone off and fiddled with his computer again. Skype was their preferred mode of communication for sensitive subjects and to keep the phone records relatively sparse and clean. With its built-in encryption and fragmentation of conversations into small packets that caromed around the Internet along varied paths before rejoining at the other end, it was the closest thing to truly secure communication available to the ordinary citizen. The organization had looked into getting its own encrypting telephones, but when they learned that even the clandestine services of a number of countries used Skype, they stuck with the cheaper alternative.

A German-accented voice, gravelly from sleep and distorted by the tiny speaker on the laptop, announced, "Okay, I'm here. *Was ist los?*"

"What is the matter? What is the matter is that I need you to do something immediately. I want you to retrieve Rosen David's login credentials for arXiv Quantitative Biology hosted at Cornell, then use them to withdraw his recently posted paper. After you've confirmed the paper is gone, change the password to keep him off the system for a while. Can you do that?"

"It's as easy as cooking bratwurst," he said. "I'm already working on it." The connection dropped.

"How long do you think it will take him?"

"I don't know. Ten minutes maybe?" he glanced at the time on his cell phone. "We'll see. Holzinger is the best." Gus Holzinger had been one of Germany's leading security consultants before Biontolics had hired him. He was now part of an inner circle that knew at least some of the scope of interlocking companies and foundations and captive professional societies that made up the organization. He was not a true insider, so he did not know exactly what they did, but he was aware that the annual reports and the scattered websites did not tell the story. He was paid very well not to ask questions. Ferguson, who had met with him in Germany on several occasions, sometimes wondered just what Holzinger thought the organization did. The man was the quintessential security type, someone who did whatever he was asked and never talked of anything but the technical elements of his work, even after several rounds of good German beer.

It was an hour before Dougherty's laptop trilled with an in-coming Skype call.

"He's not using our system, and he's not using his home computer," Holzinger began without introduction. "So, I was not able to recover his user name and password from our logs."

"What are we going to do, then."

"It's already done. Go look at the site."

Dougherty and Ferguson both switched to browsers and accessed the page at the same time. The paper was gone.

"How did you do it?"

"I hacked into Cornell and disappeared the paper plus a couple of others to throw people off the scent. Then I changed the email address on the system so that we get any notices from the arXiv that would otherwise go to Dr. David's Gmail account. It will likely be a while before he even learns that the paper is gone."

"Excellent work."

"That's what you pay me for. But the fix is only a temporary. Once he finds out, he can always post someplace else. You are going to have to deal directly with this Dr. David." He disconnected without saying more.

Dougherty picked up his phone, thumbed it off, and carefully set it down beside his computer, squaring it up perfectly with the laptop. Ferguson had seen this before in Dougherty, whose compulsive rigidity grew with increasing agitation. Dougherty realigned his phone once more. "Holzinger is right. It's not enough to kill the paper," he said quietly. "We have to take care of Rosen, too. I just don't see him as the sort who will keep quiet."

Ferguson was reluctant to follow the implications of Dougherty's announcement, but he knew better than to argue, particularly when Dougherty dug in his heels. Still, he did not want an impulsive move to jeopardize what they had managed so well for so many years. "Douglas, this guy is not some unknown little research assistant, like Janella was." Dougherty bristled at the mention of Janella but said nothing. Ferguson continued, "This one has an established career, a reputation, his own bio in the Wikipedia. It is going to be tricky."

"That's why we are going to have to go outside the organization. Maybe we should have given more consideration at the outset to using mafia money. At least that way we might now have a trail we could follow to some talent. Aside from Mbutsu, maybe we have depended too much on altar boys."

"I would hardly call Xander Quarry an altar boy."

"True, but different sins than what I had in mind. Actually, that might be the germ of an idea. I think you should pay a call on Xander and Bernice. They might have some ideas of their own or some useful names from their days of wheeling and dealing in Las Vegas real estate. After all, they also have a stake in the outcome of our current crisis."

"Why me?"

"Because you have better excuses ready at hand. You're the doctor— an early checkup, perhaps? You can pump them for information without tipping the entire hand. If I showed up at Quarry Ranch, their radar would be sounding alarms like it was a raid from the DEA. They've only ever met me once, whereas you're a regular at their little retreat."

"Retreat, maybe, little, no." Ferguson sighed forcefully. "Okay, I'll do it. California, here I come! You know, you think I live in London, like you do, but that shows how much you know about your oldest friend— and I do mean oldest. I do not live in London, I live in planes: Boeing 787s, Airbus 340s and 380s, and the occasional Gulfstream G650. That's my residential address: goddamned airplanes."

"First class, though, Andras. You always go first class."

"True. But you know, you shouldn't call me Andras. Makes for habits that might lead to a slip up in public sometime. Llewellyn Andras Cass has been dead for decades. You know, it's funny, but I'm not even sure I remember him anymore."

Dougherty gave him a concerned look. Ferguson reacted with a reassuring shake of his head. "No, don't fret. I retested just last month and the cognitive, new trace, and recall scores are all fine. I'm not starting to go senile on you. I just find that Dr. Cass seems so distant, as if he were somebody else instead of me. It's hard to explain. You didn't have to go through that; I did."

"Sooner or later I will, too. And you will do it again, when it becomes necessary. It's a small price, wouldn't you say?"

10

It had been years since Steven King had last made the trek into downtown Boston to attend one of the brown-bag lunch-time seminars on the Med School campus. He had little interest in the topic of the day, a presentation on a new class of immunosuppressant drugs for organ transplant patients, but he was confident that he would intercept Dr. Edwards there.

The ride on the T and the short walk from Charles Station had taken longer than he expected, so he arrived just as the session was letting out. His old friend's bald head was easily spotted bobbing above a knot of shorter colleagues exiting the auditorium. "Marcus, wait up," he called out, as he hurried down the hall. He caught up just as Edwards was entering an elevator.

"Steven King! It has been a while. How are you doing?"

"As well as can be expected at my age. And you?"

"Bored. But what can you expect after yet another big pharma pitch disguised as continuing ed. What brings you downtown? I thought you retired."

"You know how it is, you can't stop an old professor from lecturing—not even at a cocktail party. So, I still teach a couple of courses and consult for some of the young turks who are too busy to learn how to analyze their own bloody brilliant, ever-so-important experiments. I—"

Marcus interrupted him. "This is my floor," he said, stepping out of the elevator and blocking the door open with his arm while Steven followed him out. "My office is just down the hall."

"Are you still active in immunology?" Steven asked, hurrying to keep up with the taller man's long strides.

"I suppose you could call it active," Marcus said. "I have three doctoral students doing their own thing. It's not like the old days where you could shape a long-term agenda. These kids have minds of their own, and it's really hard to steer them." He unlocked the door to his office and ushered Steven in.

"You know who still drives research the old-fashioned way?" he said, gesturing toward the only extra chair in the small office. "The genetics people just up the river, that's who. They have things under control with old Gabriel Costa still at the helm, hanging on forever and dominating his department as if he had invented biology. The man is pushing 80, and they can't seem to be able to get rid of him. He's the Energizer Bunny of biology. Brings in grants, honchos conferences, serves on the editorial board of more journals than you can count. He is the ultimate gatekeeper. No one enters the kingdom—or the phylum—save by him. Stubborn as ever and convinced that the new paradigm, epigenetics, is garbage. Nothing will persuade him. He calls it the return of the rancid residue of Lamarckism—his exact words. He says it's the last gasp of long discredited Soviet science invading America. The younger faculty are just waiting for the day when they can dance on his grave." He paused and pulled a battered paperback book from the shelf beside his desk. "You've read Kuhn, haven't you? *The Structure of Scientific Revolution?*" he said, sliding the book across the desk.

"Of course."

"I mean actually read it through. Everybody but everybody cites it, and it's probably almost as common as *Gray's Anatomy* in offices around campus, but I'll lay odds that not one in ten of our colleagues has actually read it, and fewer still remember what Kuhn really had to say about scientific paradigms."

"I think I know where you are going with this, Marcus."

"Maybe. My point, the point Thomas Kuhn made and that so many conveniently forget, is that the old paradigm is ultimately overthrown and replaced by a new one not because of better experiments or the accumulation of superior evidence or the perfection of persuasive arguments but because the adherents and advocates of the old paradigm eventually die.

"That's us, too," he said, tapping the book for emphasis. "So, what do you want to talk about, Steven. You obviously came here to ask me for something. I hope it's not another one of those damned committees for the preservation of whoop-dee-something. The only thing I give a flying fig about preserving anymore is the equity in my retirement accounts." He knuckled the desk top. "Knock on wood that I last long enough to see retirement. You remember Jamison, Hanny Jamison, the molecular biologist? Retired last year and croaked on the plane on the way to his retirement digs in Miami. Sixty-six. Young guy.

"So, are you looking to sign me up for something?"

"No, I have a puzzle for you, Marcus. I'm interested in the immunology of chimeric organisms, and I wanted to get the opinion of a real expert."

"It doesn't take an expert. In a chimera, two or more distinct tissue types are combined, but, being present from before birth, often from the blastula, their surface proteins are recognized by the organism as self rather than other. There's no rejection, no problematic response from the immune system. The immunology is really straightforward."

"What about chimerism in adults, I mean where the genetic mosaic was not present from birth but originated later."

"Sure. Microchimerism. It happens all the time in multiparous women. They incorporate small populations of fetal cells during each pregnancy. We had long known that the fetus can get DNA directly from the mother through the placenta, but then in the late 1970s it was discovered that it can work the other way. A woman was found to have cells with Y chromosomes in her bloodstream. They obviously had to have come from her son *in utero*.

"You know, Steven, maternal microchimerism is an interesting case for a couple of reasons. One could say that the relationship between mother and fetus is immunologically privileged, otherwise you'd see graft-versus-host and host-versus-graft disease all the time in pregnancy; the mother's immune system would reject the fetus or the fetus would kill the mother. Obviously, evolution selected against those outcomes. The other interesting thing here is that the incorporated cells in maternal microchimerism are very often stem cells. They even have been found to take on a tissue repair role in mothers with certain maladies: thyroid or liver damage, things of that sort. The cells and the effects can linger for decades. The incorporated fetal cells can reproduce indefinitely and remain pluripotent if not totipotent; they can become almost any tissue.

"Does that answer your question?"

"Yeah. That's more or less what I figured. But one more question. If you wanted to generate chimerism in an adult organism, how might you go about it?"

"Not sure why I would want to in the first place, but let's say I did, for some reason, such as to create some really exotic version of a lab rat. Okay, embryonic stem cells would be one promising line, if it weren't that research in that arena is so tightly restricted by the residue of a religious-right agenda. Of course, all along, pregnant women have already been benefitting from natural fetal stem cell transplants. Ironic, wouldn't you say?"

He gave the paperback on his desk a spin. "Okay, back to your question," he said, picking up the book and gesturing with it. "Maybe you could find a way to engineer retroviruses that could be used as a vector to introduce new DNA. Or one might directly manipulate the nuclei of cells. It would be damned tedious and expensive, but might be worth a try. That's off the top of my head. I would imagine that if you wanted to badly enough and were backed by generous enough research grants, you could probably find a way to pull it off eventually. Why do you ask?"

"Acute curiosity, an intellectual puzzle, that's all."

"You know, the issue of chimerism takes on a whole new twist in light of the new paradigm in genetics. Epigenetics has really brought to the fore the influence of environment and the experience of the organism on gene expression. Not so long ago our colleagues in genetics were convinced that genes were genes, that genetically controlled traits were inherited and fixed. Now they are learning that the environment and experience of the individual can influence gene expression through methylation, maybe other mechanisms, and the effects can be passed on to succeeding generations. So, what and how you ate as a child can end up affecting whether your children and grandchildren are prone to obesity or vulnerable to diabetes. Old Gabriel Costa is right in his labels but wrong in his conclusions. I really do not understand why he is always trying to quash any interest in this area among his students."

Marcus was obviously on a roll and Steven just let him continue. "With a chimera, when you factor in epigenetics and gene expression, the whole picture becomes enormously more complicated. Cells from one genotype could influence gene expression in another. The history of one cell population could regulate the expression of some genes in cells from another genotype. Intriguing. I wonder if anyone has done any work on that."

"Probably," Steven said. "Look, I must go back to the more boring work of preparing my next statistics lecture. Cheers." He stood to leave.

"Well, I will say this, Steven. You've gotten me to thinking. There are some promising lines of research in this discussion. Thanks."

"Anytime. Give my regards to Phoebe and the boys," Steven said.

"Oh, Phoebe and I are history. We split years ago."

"Oh, I'm sorry."

"I'm not. I remarried. Janet is fifteen years my junior and really good for me. Keeps me young. Are you still married? I mean, to the same woman?"

"No," Steven said, smiling. "Miriam has never been the same woman. Not for more than a few months in a row. Keeps me young."

11

Ferguson gunned his rented yellow-and-black Mustang up the zigzags of the unpaved road leading to Quarry Ranch Retreat, a 47-acre estate perched in the hills roughly an hour-and-a-half's drive south from the San Francisco airport. It had become notorious for its free-wheeling, week-long parties in the 1970s but in recent years had managed to stay mostly out of the spotlight. None of the underwriters were without original sin, although compared to Edgar Mbutsu, Alexander and Bernice Quarry would seem almost angelic. They had made their money, first in insurance and then in Las Vegas real estate, with only intermittent suggestions of impropriety that never blossomed into full-flowered investigations. Ferguson knew that the improprieties were real but well buried.

Bernice, always the cannier of the two, accounted for the bulk of the couple's assets, which was a constant irritant to Xander, who would have to turn to his wife whenever he needed real money for some of the more grandiose of his idiosyncratic improvements at the Ranch. The Quarrys had well-earned reputations as sybarites. Aside from their involvement with the organization in its earliest days, the Ranch and its self-indulgent, laidback lifestyle were their life.

Xander may have been envious of his wife's wealth or her gift for financial manipulation, both above and below the table, but he was not jealous of the younger men who lounged naked by the Olympic-sized pool and fetched drinks for her. He had no need to be jealous, having his own clutch of forest nymphs happy to consort with him at poolside or to cavort in the sun playing nude volleyball on a man-made beach while beside them, high in the hills and miles from the ocean, his custom-engineered wave machine generated artificial surf. Ten years earlier, a *Sacramento Bee* exposé had dubbed them the last of the swingers, painting Bernice as an anorexic, sex-crazed septuagenarian and Xander as a dirty old man whose wealth and reputation kept a rotating retinue of well-endowed young hopefuls eager to show him what they had learned in school.

Ferguson was only glad that the private parties with under-age participants seemed to have stopped—or at least gone so deeply underground that there had been no fresh scandals for years. The organization had worked long and hard on a quiet campaign to place sympathetic or indifferent officials in positions of authority throughout the county. The DEA was still a problem, but in recent years they seemed to have turned their drug-enforcement attention farther north to the medical-marijuana outlaws of the Bay area and to raids on cannabis plantations in the hinterlands. The sophisticated psychotropics and designer drugs that were *au courant* with the Quarrys and the rest of the retreat's residents and visitors were probably not yet even on any government list.

Ferguson pulled into the circular drive and left his car parked in front of the glass-paneled building that housed the Ranch's second Olympic-sized swimming pool, an indoor pool kept at body heat for the experiments in sensory deprivation that had first made the Ranch famous. With nothing left to learn about or from sensory deprivation, the pool was now just an extravagant curiosity that held the attention of newcomers only briefly before they discovered that mindlessly floating in tepid water was not as interesting an aquatic activity as screwing in a hot tub or doing laps in the sun-warmed outdoor pool.

Bernie Quarry waved to Ferguson from the 24-foot redwood hot tub that had once been cited in the *Guinness Book of World Records*. "Chas, come on in and join us!" she called. Bernie, who had always had a thing for Ferguson, insisted on using the nickname that he preferred to reserve for a tiny circle of real friends. He had always cultivated her erotic interest without ever allowing it to blossom beyond flirtation. It was useful in sustaining the complex relationship between the Quarrys and the organization. They had been the first underwriters, and though there had been other bigger donors since, their initial investment had made the whole operation possible. They had been the angel investors, and Ferguson had always found that term more than a tad ironic.

Ferguson blew Bernie a kiss. "Thanks," he called out, "but I'll sit this one out. Later maybe?" He tried to keep a small residue of promise in his voice, but there would not be any 'later.' Meeting in the hot tub was about neither hygiene nor good clean fun; at Quarry Ranch it was tantamount to an invitation to group sex. Ferguson had tried that once—not at the Ranch but long before, in his college days—and found it not to his liking.

Xander Quarry, wearing only a Hawaiian shirt that hung like a tent over his ample form, came out of the Conference Center, the main spread of buildings facing onto the tennis courts, the pool, and the surf machine. Xander Quarry had silver hair that hung to his shoulders when it wasn't tied back in a pony tail as it was now. He was shaped like a wine barrel, and the joke was that it was obvious what he had consumed to acquire his figure. In truth, it was Bernie who was the lush. Xander was rarely far from a glass of expensive California white, sauvignon blanc preferred, that he would nurse until it was too warm to drink, but Bernie was the one who could start drinking heavily before noon and not let up until she passed out after midnight.

It was a lifestyle whose rhythm was not lost on the young sycophants who surrounded her. The more observant among them— particularly the ones who found her dyed hair, sun-leathered skin, and silicone breasts less than a turn-on—would aim their erotic attentions toward her at the end of the day, accompanying her to bed knowing full well that unconsciousness was not far off. In the morning, they would score points for still being in bed with her and would flatter her with tales of how wonderful she had been the night before. Then they would rush off to their own daytime dalliances in other of the many suites in the sprawling ranch.

Xander grinned as he emerged from the building. He had one hand holding his ubiquitous glass of wine and the other around the waist of a girl in a hot-pink bikini. She looked to be not a day over twelve, and Ferguson gritted his teeth as they approached. Xander removed his hand from her waist and extended it to Ferguson. "Welcome, Doc. Again. Seems like it was only a month or so since you were last here."

"Seems like it because it was. I have some extra tests I want to run."

The girl steadied herself on Xander's arm while she stood on one foot and extracted something from her flip-flop. Ferguson made sure that Xander was looking his way as he raised one eyebrow, an unspoken inquiry with a subtext of silent criticism. Xander laughed. "This is Nadia, my daughter. Her mother dumped her here with us for the summer."

"I didn't know you had a daughter."

"Neither did I. All these years I thought I was shooting blanks. Low sperm count and very low motility, so they say, right? Anyway, I have the DNA profiles that prove that Nadia is mine, so I guess it's all just probabilities, right? Fuck enough women enough times and sooner or later..."

Nadia screwed up her face and turned it toward Xander. "Dad!" she said between clenched teeth.

"She doesn't like me saying fuck."

"Dad!" she growled, drawing out the single vowel into two syllables.

"I think she is trying to civilize me, which my friends all tell me is about time, and which she just might succeed at. It's been days since I've been drunk, weeks since I've done any drugs, and I can't remember the last cluster-fu..."

Nadia gave him another fierce look.

"The last orgy, I was going to say. Anyway, her mother is not the most reliable and together person on the planet, so this is probably a righteous thing that she got dumped here. I think the Ranch is good for her."

Ferguson shot him a skeptical look. "I'm not sure this is exactly a child-friendly environment, Xander."

"Oh, there are those who would say it can be a mighty child-friendly place. No, no!" He ducked and feinted in mock defense. "Just kidding. Actually everybody knows that if they even think any thoughts about Nadia, I'll shoot off their ..." He paused and glanced down at her. "Their *cojones*."

"I know what that means, Dad." She elbowed him in his blubbery stomach, and he doubled over in faked pain.

"See what I mean, Doc?" he said.

"I do see. I don't know about how good the Ranch is for her, but I do suspect that Nadia will be a positive influence on you."

"So, Doc, what really brings you here?" He noticed Ferguson's eyes shift to Nadia, who was once again standing like a stork while she worried at something between her toes. "Nadia, sweetie, why don't you go have a swim. Your tutor will be here this afternoon and then it's your sax lesson with Jeremy, so there won't be time later."

"I understand, Dad. You want to talk without me. I'll get lost." She did a high kick, sending her remaining flip-flop soaring into the air, and took off at a run for the pool.

"Cute," Ferguson said. "And savvy, too, I can see. She really is your daughter?"

"Yeah. Mind blowing, isn't it? Do you know how old I am? Yes, of course you do. This is so wild. I don't think I've found it so interesting to get up in the morning in a very long time. Years. Decades. Every day it's something new. Last month she was listening to an old Coltrane cut and announced that she wanted to do that. I found someone from town who could give her lessons, and she is really starting to sound like something. Amazing. The tenor sax is almost as big as she is. She is more fun to talk with than," he waved his hand, "than any of these fuckers—excuse my French—who hang out here to entertain Bernie or to be entertained."

"No French, no excuses," Ferguson teased. "You're the father of a preteen girl now, and you are going to have to watch your words." There was a girlish screech from the pool. Ferguson glanced over and grinned.

"What?" Xander asked.

"Just thinking, how odd. She's the only one in the pool wearing a suit."

"Yeah, well, that's new. When she first came here, she was just like everyone else at the Ranch. I mean, you know that these hills are caught in some kind of time warp, that it never stopped being the 1960s here. At the Ranch, we wear clothes when we eat, because hot soup in the lap can be a pain. The rest of the time, unless it's too cold, we are pretty casual about what's covered and what's not. And I have always argued that swimming suits are the stupidest invention in the history of civilization. But, well, Nadia, she's skinny but cute, and there was one of Bernie's Boys, as we refer to them, who found her little titties quite appealing. He's long gone, and she now wears clothes, including in the pool. We have this deal. I don't get falling down drunk, and she doesn't run around naked.

"Last week she asked me if I would make an exception for her when her boyfriend shows up. I freaked, I tell you. So I started asking about this boyfriend. They start so goddamned young these days. She's not going to be thirteen until December. But she was kidding. Her quote boyfriend lives in Switzerland. They met once, and he kissed her. It was a big deal to her. She told me about what she likes in men—boys—what she thinks makes for a good relationship. She thinks a lot about that, owing in part to the fine example her mother set with a long string of good-time lovers and fair-weather friends.

"But look, Doc, Nadia is off swimming, Bernie is about to climax noisily in the hot tub, and you still haven't started telling me what this is really about." Ferguson shrugged and looked around. "Okay, Doc, I get the message, a private conversation. Let me grab a pair of trousers and then let's go for a hike. There are too many people around today. Today? Hell, there are always too many people around here, period."

~ ~ ~

An ambitious and lonely young man who had frequented the Ranch in its heyday had carved out a meandering trail through the brush that led to several notable vistas before looping back to the main facilities. As they walked along the narrow and neglected path, Ferguson gave Xander a condensed-book version of recent events. Xander was puffing from exertion by the time they rounded the corner of the pool house on the return leg. Ferguson had been on his case for years advising him to lose weight, but Xander Quarry was a giver of advice and not one to listen to others.

"Take my advice, Doc," he said. "Don't dick around on this one. We need to take care of this guy. I know some people who know some people, Doc, from Vegas. I think this thing can be fixed." He stopped in the middle of the driveway, frowning. "Where's Bernie?" He scanned the compound and noticed that her MG was no longer parked in its usual spot. "Hey, where's Bernie?" he yelled.

One of her Boys, a dark-skinned Schwarzenegger-type wearing a torn tee-shirt declaring, 'I'm Tad and I'm Bad,' called out from the pool. "She and Annie drove into town to get something or other. I don't remember."

"She and Annie? Annie doesn't drive. Was Bernie . . ." He didn't have to finish the sentence.

"No more than usual," Tad answered. "I mean, how can you tell with Bernie. I don't know if I've ever seen her sober. With the way she takes it in you'd think she would have succumbed years ago to. . .what's that stuff called, sir something?"

"Cirrhosis," Ferguson said.

"Yeah, that stuff. Anyway, they left fifteen or twenty minutes ago—I don't know—in kind of a hurry. Got some kind of bee up her ass to get something at the farmer's market, I think she said. Annie, did. Bernie said she'd take her, so they hopped in that little car of hers and off they go, down the road." He made a flying gesture with his hand.

Ferguson and Xander looked at each other. Ferguson put his hand on Xander's sweaty shoulder. "She'll be fine. She could probably fly a triple-seven drunk. Inebriated has become the norm for her neurons. Her brain wouldn't know how to function without ethanol for fuel."

Xander did not look convinced, but he spread his hands in a gesture of helplessness and said, "Sure, Doc."

They were headed inside for some ice water when they heard the sound of a car traveling fast on the gravel switchback not far below the ranch.

"That's probably them," Ferguson said, reassuring Xander with a pat on the back just as the car rounded the last curve and shot into the driveway. It was the County Sheriff in his black-and-white.

"Xander," the sheriff shouted, leaning out of the door. "It's Bernice. A motorist spotted her and her friend at the bottom of Fitts Canyon and called it in. We got a rescue team and an ambulance on the way. My deputy, who arrived first, said she's alive but looks like she's lost a lot of blood. He doesn't think her friend made it. She ended up under the car. Hop in, I'll drive you down to County General; that's where they'll take her."

Ferguson grabbed Xander's arm. "We can't let them take her there," he said, turning his head so that the others gathering around the sheriff's car couldn't hear.

"Why? I don't understand."

"Because they'll type her and check her blood, and then it gets complicated, real complicated."

Xander stood open-mouthed for a second.

"You coming, Xander?" the sheriff called out.

"A minute, give me a minute," he answered. He gave Ferguson a pleading look.

"Has the ambulance arrived from County General yet, Sheriff?" Ferguson asked.

"Don't know. Let me check with the dispatcher." He ducked back into the car, then popped back out a minute later. "No, not there yet, but the driver says they'll be there in ten minutes, twelve tops."

Ferguson walked over to the Sheriff and pulled him aside. "I'm Mrs. Quarry's doctor. She has an extremely rare blood type and an even rarer blood disease that can make a transfusion fatal. We have to get her up to University Hospital where they are equipped to deal with this kind of thing."

"We'll have to get a helicopter down here."

Ferguson looked at his watch. "Can you patch me through to the EMT in the ambulance?"

"Sure thing."

Ferguson said who he was to the woman who answered from the ambulance and tried to explain the situation without telling her any more than necessary. She told him there was nothing that she could do without orders from her supervising doctor at the hospital. "And who's that?" Ferguson asked?

"Dr. Morrison is on duty now."

Ferguson coughed. He had met Abel Morrison once, and the two had taken an instant dislike to each other. He had to figure out another way. He clicked off the radio mike and leaned to within inches of the Sheriff's face. It was a gamble, but he had to chance it. "I think you can guess who I am with, Sheriff. And I think you know that we have done an awful lot to help this County, to help you." He paused for effect. "I need you to do something for me, now. I'm going to get a medical chopper to fly directly to Fitts Canyon and to take Mrs. Quarry from there to University Hospital."

"You can do that?"

"I can do that. What I need you to do is tell your deputy that he is not to let the ambulance leave with Mrs. Quarry. The EMTs can stabilize her and ready her for the life-flight, but they are to wait for the chopper. Your deputy can tell them to call in for instructions if need be, but his orders are to wait for the helicopter. Can you do that?"

The Sheriff looked grim but nodded. "Let me get on the radio before the ambulance arrives."

Ferguson pulled back, scanned the compound, and turned to Xander again. "Do you still keep up your license?" he said, nodding in the direction of the tennis courts. Just beyond, a little Robinson Raven four-seater was tied down on the helipad but looked serviced and ready.

"Yeah. I usually let Frank fly, though. What's your plan?"

"My plan is to get us up to University Hospital about the same time as the other chopper, so I can talk face-to-face with the people I know there and can take charge of Bernie's treatment. If we are not there before she arrives or within scant minutes after, all this will have been for nothing."

"Okay, but it will take me a few minutes to ready the Raven, and we'll have to overfly the SFO air space, and . . ."

"Go take care of it. I'll talk with the Sheriff and use his contacts. We'll set things up with the hospital en route."

With the sheriff's help, Ferguson arranged the medical evacuation, then put the organization to work on getting him set up with University Hospital. Xander quickly got clearance for their own emergency routing up to Berkeley, but he was out of practice, and it took him much longer than he had expected to go through the preflight check on the R44. The Sheriff's Department rescue team had retrieved Bernice from the canyon by the time the ambulance arrived, and the deputy spent the next fifteen minutes arguing with the EMTs before the helicopter coming down from San Francisco was spotted. The medical helicopter was already airborne again from Fitts Canyon before Xander had finished warming up the engine of the Raven and lifted off from the Ranch.

Fitts Canyon was to their southeast, a longer run up to Berkeley, but with every passing minute, the gap between them and the much faster Bell aircraft flown by the medical service increased. They were still over ten minutes out when air traffic control told them that the medical flight had already landed at the hospital. Xander kept shaking his head and apologizing to Ferguson over the intercom in the helicopter

When they arrived, they faced another delay, as they had to wait for the other helicopter to leave the helipad before they could land. Ferguson scrambled out of the Raven and ran across the lot toward the emergency entrance of the hospital.

He was met by a surgeon in green scrubs. "You're too late, doctor," the surgeon said. "Your patient was DOA. I'm sorry. You and your foundation went through a lot for this woman. It was quite a scramble here when we got the call."

A part of Ferguson was relieved, and he had to admit that he suspected the same might be true of Xander Quarry when he found out.

"Oh," the surgeon added, "we heard from your county hospital. It seems the other passenger survived. When they lifted the car off her, she was still breathing. The ambulance hadn't left yet, so they transported her to the county hospital."

Xander, just arriving from securing the helicopter, took one look at their faces and could read the truth. "Can I have a minute with her?" he said.

The doctor nodded and pointed toward a cart, its wheels visible below the pale green privacy curtains that already discreetly surrounded it. Xander pulled one curtain aside and exclaimed, "Oh, no!" He grabbed Ferguson and started pulling him toward the exit. "It's Annie. Bernie must be at County General. We have to get down there."

Xander restarted the Raven and had them airborne again as soon as he had clearance. Ferguson tried to use his cell phone to call someone at the organization, but the noise in the cockpit made it impossible. He asked Xander if he could patch him into the hospital or the sheriff. "I can try to raise the sheriff," he said, his voice high-pitched and distorted by the headset intercom. "We'll have to land at the county airport and take a taxi. There's no helipad at the hospital, and I think it would only make matters worse if we pulled some stunt like landing in the parking lot."

"Okay, let's just do it as fast as we can."

"We're doing 110 knots, that's what this baby will do. The shit will be waiting no matter when we arrive."

"Yes, but the longer the shit sits, the more it stinks up the place."

It was getting dark when the taxi from the airport finally dropped them at the small county hospital. They were greeted by Dr. Morrison, who told them that Bernice Quarry was in intensive care.

"You have some explaining to do, doctor," he said to Ferguson, the irritation in his voice evident.

"How is that?" Ferguson answered anxiously.

"Shuffling patients between hospitals, getting the sheriff's deputy to interfere with our emergency medical personnel, raising alarms about non-existent rare blood types, sticking the county with a big fat medical evacuation fee, a wholly unnecessary one, at that. How's that for a few things to answer for?"

"Look, the foundation I work for will pick up all the charges. But what was that you said about non-existent blood types?"

"Your patient, doctor, the one you claimed to be something of a hematological freak. She tested AB positive, we cross-matched her against blood that we had rushed over from the blood bank, and no agglutination, no reaction, no problem. The patient is in serious but stable condition."

Ferguson was puzzled for a moment, then smiled as he realized what had happened. The hospital lab was just not sophisticated enough to detect the abnormalities in Bernice Quarry's blood, and the organization must have already pulled off the modest miracle of getting some of their engineered antigen-neutral supply to the area blood bank. He had years earlier proposed being ready with appropriate supplies in the vicinity of each of his patients, but had forgotten to follow up. Perhaps he actually was beginning to slip in some subtle ways. He grinned broadly at the smug Dr. Morrison and said, "I am so glad to hear it all worked out."

To Morrison's annoyance, within 48 hours Ferguson was able to move Bernice Quarry to the research ward at University Hospital where he could more closely monitor and control her treatment. It was there that she died suddenly two days later. The cause of death was listed as multiple internal injuries sustained in an automobile accident, but Ferguson knew the story was more complicated than that. He knew that the damage to her internal organs was not all from trauma.

After claiming the body, Xander took Ferguson aside and said, "That was way, way too close. Remember what I told you. We need to fix the loose strands before the whole rug unravels right under us. We need to make some calls."

That was the last Xander said on the long drive back to the ranch.

~ ~ ~

Xander Quarry, whose indifference to his wife was legendary, took her death unexpectedly hard. When Ferguson returned to the ranch after a day of cleaning up loose ends, he found Xander slumped in a deck chair beside the surf machine, watching as a young hard-body blonde with big tits tried to stand on her boogie board.

Ferguson was about to make some comment about her sense of balance when Xander looked up at him, head lolling, eyes unfocused, and raised an unsteady arm in a futile attempt to block the sun. "Who? Oh, you. Who?"

"Xander, Xander. You can't do it this way." Ferguson looked around and noted that the dark muscle-builder was still around. "Hey, what's your name again?" he called out.

"Thadeus. They call me Tad."

"Well, Tad, give me a hand here with our friend Xander."

Together they managed to drag Quarry to his feet and steer him into the house. Ferguson had Tad fetch his bag from the car and then gave Xander an injection. Xander sat up, blinked repeatedly, jerked his head and shoulders a few times, and said, "Yes, right. I think I better go take a shower. Maybe a cold one."

Ferguson grabbed him by the shoulders. "You made a deal with Nadia. Remember?"

"Nadia's gone. She left with one of Bernie's Boys when I started drinking."

"Then you better go after her, Dad. Go take your shower, take two of these pills with a caffè latte, then get Nadia back. And be warned: when you crash you are really going to crash. Okay?"

Xander nodded and padded off toward the nearest bathroom.

Tad looked amazed. "You sobered him up just like that?"

"Yup, but it'll only last for ten hours or so, then he'll be out for a day."

"That's amazing. Can I get me some of that?"

"No," Ferguson said, as he left for his car.

He was enjoying the drive down the canyon road when his iPhone beeped. There was no place to pull over, so he just stopped in the middle of the road at a spot where he hoped an approaching driver would have time to react.

It was a text message from Dougherty. "Big M trouble, u back to Africa."

"One bloody mess after another." he said to himself, as he put the car in gear. "One bloody fucking mess after another."

Rosen looked out over a morning sky like buttered toast spread with ripples of marmalade: warm, golden, inviting. It was the first truly warm morning of the spring, cool by the standards of summer in Massachusetts, but warm enough to stir the blood of any New Englander impatient to put mud season behind.

Rosen was inspired. Bike to work, he thought. Perfect! Millie did not like him riding his bicycle to work, a route that took him along well-traveled highways and narrow roads narrowed further by construction and repairs that never seemed to finish. But Millie was already gone, already in her classroom, and what she didn't know couldn't worry her. Rosen checked online. Both Weather Underground and AccuWeather sites promised a sunny day with high, thin clouds and no precipitation in sight.

Rosen dressed, chugged his coffee, and went out to the small detached garage where his bicycles hung from their overhead racks, tires filled, chains oiled, and ready to roll on the long awaited first outing of spring. Rosen owned three bikes, which amused Millie no end, since he spent more time tinkering on them than riding them. The most used, his metallic blue Trek MultiTrack hybrid, might be taken out a few dozen times a year, mostly schlepping groceries or to pick up new parts from the cycle shop down in Gloucester. The hybrid was the only one of the three equipped with a rack to carry his panniers or his briefcase.

Pride of the pack was his carbon-fiber Pinarello, a sleek, banana-yellow drop-handle road racer with a distinctive geometry that always drew attention at meets, allowing Rosen to brag without bragging aloud. Rosen's secret pride was that he had gotten the $6,000 bike for less than wholesale by badgering a cousin who had gotten stuck with it in inventory. Still, Millie had thrown a nutty when she heard what he had paid for it. Her bicycle was a Schwinn off-roader that she had picked up at a garage sale for $30, and she went out cycling three times as often as Rosen.

Rosen avoided anything he regarded as pointless activity or exercise for its own sake. He could allow himself to bike for groceries or to get to work, but he would only race if it was a charity event that would raise money, which meant that the Pinarello saw action only a few times a year at best. The Pan-Mass Challenge two years earlier had been his bragging-rights run, when he had finished on the toughest route. After 190 miles in two long days of hard pedaling, it had taken him nearly a week to recover.

His beloved mountain bike, another Trek, with fat knobby tires and hydraulic suspension, had been his since high-school. He still lovingly cleaned and oiled and adjusted it and had always meticulously repainted every nick and scratch, but these days he almost never rode it except on test runs after each round of routine maintenance.

Oddly, the vernal vitality of the morning drew him toward the Pinarello, but it had no rack on the back. He briefly considered dismounting the rack from the MultiTrack, but quickly recognized that it would be a messy mechanical job even if the rack would fit on the Pinarello, which it probably would not. He thought of stuffing the briefcase into his backpack, but the extra weight, combined with the Pinarello's dropped handlebars, meant risking throwing his back out again.

Somewhat reluctantly, he lifted down the hybrid, strapped his briefcase on the back, and rolled it out of the garage. He removed the reflective strap from where it hung from the right handlebar and wrapped it around the right leg of his jeans. Rosen owned one authentic cycling outfit, which he reserved for meets where proper attire was de rigueur and trousers would be an embarrassment, but the rest of the time he rode in street clothes. There were a couple of serious cyclists at the Lab who regularly rode to work in spandex, then showered and changed, but that degree of fashion-conscious fussiness was not for Rosen.

~ ~ ~

The ride to work had been exhilarating, but the rest of his morning was spent in meetings that left him enervated and longing for the good old days of college classes where one could catch a catnap in the back of the room. By early afternoon he was ready to be anywhere but where he was, doing anything but what he was doing. Without thinking much about what he was doing, he opened a browser and

Googled his own name. The first results were headed by his page on the Biontolics site followed by his Wikipedia bio and an assortment of old miscellany, but nothing new showed up. Rosen clicked on the "More search tools" link, slid his mouse pointer past the selected "Anytime" and clicked "Past month" to repeat and narrow the search. The dozen results were topped by his recent registration for the Essex County Bike-for-Bread to benefit area food pantries and by an item on his appointment to the editorial board of *Bio-Logical: Communications in Computational Biology*. Not a word about his new paper, not even a link to the arXiv q-bio page.

Rosen went to the arXiv quantitative biology home page and scanned down the current month's listing. Nothing. His paper wasn't there. He flipped to the login page, typed his handle and password, and got the little red-framed box at the top of the page saying "Incorrect username or password." He tried again using his email address instead of his screen name and got the same message. About the same time that he realized he was not being smart to be doing this research from the Lab, Jeannine poked her head into his office. "What's up?" she asked, craning her neck to look at his screen.

"Not much," he said, quickly closing the browser. "Just checking some Web resources."

"Well, if you're not busy, what about lunch?"

Rosen was surprised by the invitation but tried to act cool. "Ah, sure. I suppose. What did you have in mind? Who else is going?"

"Nobody, which is why I wanted company. How about The Clam Box to celebrate the real arrival of spring in New England, which, New England always being a bit behind the times, comes a month after the vernal equinox."

The Clam Box was an Ipswich institution, a glorified clam shack shaped like a giant take-out container and famed throughout the area for serving nothing but fried seafood, heavily breaded and dripping with oil. At peak times, the wait in line could be forty minutes or more. For fans of fried clams, The Clam Box rated the equivalent of three Michelin stars. Rosen, however, had never understood the appeal of fried clams and avoided them with the excuse that it was forbidden for Jews to eat shellfish. Lobster, of course, was another matter altogether, and Rosen was not alone among New England Jews ready to forget the laws of *kashrut* when lobster was in the offing.

Jeannine noticed his hesitation. "We could do Chinese. Or Greek?"

Rosen looked thoughtful. "Do you have a car? I biked to work today."

"Sure, where do you want to go?"

"You pick."

"Okay, how about trying that new place up in Rowley? We're less likely to run into the crowd from the Lab there." She smiled broadly. "I'll grab my jacket and keys."

The new restaurant in Rowley turned out to be an old one with a new name. It was the fourth attempt in as many years to launch a restaurant in the same storefront in a small shopping center. Locals always got excited with the announcement of each new arrival, but the eateries never thrived, and most were gone within a year. Rosen commented on the depressing trend.

"Most restaurants don't last more than a year or two," she said. "But the sushi here is pretty good, don't you think? Maybe this time it will work." She leaned forward. "Are you all right, Rosen? I mean, if it's okay for me to ask."

"Yeah, it's okay. I'm okay, just thinking."

"And when aren't you thinking? You are one of the most thinking-est people I've ever known."

"Yeah, well, I'm trying to work out a puzzle," he said, pushing bits of rice around on his plate.

"Is this that rat longevity stuff again? The business that The General told you to back off from? Or have you found an entirely new way to get the High Command coming down on you?"

Rosen carefully lined up his knife and fork and his chopsticks on his plate and slid back in his chair. He said nothing, waiting for Jeannine to fill the gap in the conversation. She didn't, so he took a deep breath and decided to chance it. "Whose side are you on, Jeannine? Are you working for them?"

"Them? Of course, I work for them. We both work for the same company, Rosen, at least last time I checked my employee badge." She lifted it up from where it still hung around her neck. "Yup, it says Biontolics Research, LLC, North Shore Laboratories. What does yours say?"

"That's not what I mean," he said impatiently.

"Then say what you do mean. What are you really asking?"

He shook his head. "Nothing, I guess. Let's get the check and head back. This will be my treat."

"No."

"What? No, I insist."

"No. It doesn't look good. You can pick up the tab when you take the whole team out, but it wouldn't be right to just take me to lunch."

They rode back to the office in silence, and Rosen passed the afternoon impatient to be home so that he could start surfing the Web again without being watched.

~ ~ ~

It was the end of the day when Millie called.

"You biked to work today, didn't you," she said, in a tone that Rosen had not heard since his mother stopped using it on him after his bar mitzvah.

"Yeah, well, it was such a perfect day."

"Was. It's starting to look threatening. You know I don't like you biking after dark."

"It won't be after dark. Besides, I have lights."

"And what are you wearing, darling Rosen? Your black leather jacket? Black jeans? Huh? I know you, Rosen. How do you expect drivers to see you?"

"I don't. I expect to see them," he teased.

"Well, you had better see them, and see them soon. I want you home before sundown. Do you hear? And you're on your own for supper. I have a budget and planning meeting tonight, and I expect it will go long. You had better be waiting for me when I get home."

"I will be. I'm about to leave the office right now."

"Be careful."

He laughed. "No, I will not be careful, darling. I expect to ride recklessly, weaving in and out of traffic, popping wheelies, and grabbing air at every opportunity. Just go to your meeting and stop worrying about me."

"No, I will not stop worrying about you. That's my job. You won't do it, so somebody has to. Love you. Later." She hung up.

Rosen, who was a serious eater but an indifferent cook, did not like the thought of cooking for himself when he got home. He tried to visualize the state of leftovers in the refrigerator and made a face. "Pizza night," he said to no one in particular as he shut down his computer. He stuffed a wad of loose papers and his iPhone into his briefcase, turned out the lights, and headed for the bike racks just outside the back door.

Once underway, instead of turning to cut directly over to Route 133 heading down toward Essex, he continued up Argilla Road and then into the center of Ipswich. At the Ipswich House of Pizza, another small but popular local institution, he picked up a small Mediterranean pizza with extra olives, strapped it on the back of his bike with a spare bungee cord, and headed back down 133. At the turnoff where the highway split from Route 1A, he upshifted and started pedaling hard through the long, lazy curves, past the Corliss Brothers Nursery where Millie was a regular customer and irregular consultant on matters horticultural, and finally into the straightaway at top speed. It felt good to be taking the road flat out. The traffic was already thinning, and, although the sun was down, the twilit sky still provided plenty of light. Rosen reached behind him and turned on his red blinker even though it was mostly blocked by the briefcase and pizza strapped on top of the rack. He switched on his headlight, then flipped it to strobe mode to make himself more visible.

The breakdown lanes in that stretch were wide, but out of habit Rosen rode as far to the right as practical and kept checking his handlebar mirror for traffic from behind. There was a long string of cars doing 50 plus in the 45-mile-an-hour zone, then a break in the traffic, and then the flash of high beams reflecting into his eyes. He shifted his gaze down and to the right in front of him as the blinding lights in his mirror grew bigger and brighter. As the vehicle closed rapidly on him, he steered to steady his front wheel on the very edge of the asphalt and slowed, waiting for it to pass. Instead of passing, it slowed as it approached, as if to make a turn. As it pulled alongside, Rosen, no longer blinded by the headlights in his eyes, could see that it was a white pickup truck, a big 4-by-4. He coasted and downshifted, but the pickup slowed, too, staying beside him and signaling for a right turn. Rosen braked to let the truck pass, but it slowed still more and paced him, all the while edging farther and farther into the breakdown lane.

Rosen crunched hard on both handbrakes, fighting to keep from pitching over the handlebars. The driver in the pickup edged over enough to bump Rosen's mirror. Rosen's front tire hit gravel, and he lost control. At the last second, he spotted the telephone pole flying at him and threw his bike into a skid in front of him. The bike slammed into the pole, wrapped around the backside, and continued, with Rosen sliding and tumbling after. The truck took off down the highway in a squeal of tires and was gone.

Rosen tried to sit up. His arm hurt and wouldn't support him. His whole left side was on fire with pain, and his face was hot and sticky. He reached up and wiped pizza sauce from his cheek.

Another set of lights was approaching. Rosen struggled to try and drag himself farther off the verge as the car slowed and stopped with its lights flooding the area. He waved weakly at the driver. His Trek was a mangled mess just beyond him and his briefcase and its contents were scattered twenty feet up the road. Rosen's vision blurred.

"Are you all right?" Two people got out of the car and stood over him, a couple in their thirties or forties.

"I think so," he said softly. He looked down at the hamburger that was his left leg where his torn slacks exposed the road rash beneath. His vision blurred again, but he gritted his teeth. "Did you see anything? Did you see the pickup?"

"Yeah, hit and run. But they'll catch him."

Rosen groaned in pain. "Better call an ambulance. I think I need to be looked at."

"Heidi already called, and the police—so they can pick up that driver. They'll get him."

"You keep saying that."

"Well, he left this behind." The man held up a passenger-side mirror. "Cut so close to that pole that he knocked it clean off. We saw it land in the field there. Shouldn't be all that hard to spot a white pickup with out-of-state plates and a missing mirror." He grinned in triumph.

Rosen struggled to stay conscious. "Have you got a cell phone on you? Can I call my wife? I seem to have lost mine." He pointed toward the briefcase still lying in the road.

"Sure thing. Just tell me the number and I'll dial it for you."

Rosen had just started to recite the digits when he heard the sirens approaching. It was the last sound he heard.

13

Ferguson looked down at the wound, an oozing, beet-red and cheddar-yellow gash. He gently pressed his gloved fingers around its margins and shook his head. In Portuguese, he told the doctor and nurses what they should have already figured out on their own, that the wound was infected, there was evidence of peritonitis, indications of possible internal bleeding, and absolute certainty of their own incompetence.

"I am from Argentina, not Brazil," the doctor responded in English. "We speak Spanish. You speak too fast, and I do not understand you."

"Well, now you understand me, then. So I will tell you in English that you can take the next plane out of here and wing it right back to Argentina, because you are unfit to call yourself a doctor. I can repeat that in Spanish, if you prefer."

"Who are you to speak to me that way? You just arrived. Do you know who I am? I am the President's personal physician. Who do you think you are?"

"I think that I am the man who is going to save your life by having you deported instead of executed. That's who I think I am." Ferguson signaled to one of the ever-present soldiers, who hustled the protesting doctor out of the room. He turned to the two nurses and spoke to them in Lusanyu. "Prep him and scrub for surgery. Show me that you know what you are doing, and I won't say anything to the President when he awakens."

He left the room to get supplies and scrub for surgery himself.

~ ~ ~

The operation did not go well. Ferguson already knew that would be the case with the first incision. By the time they were ready to close, Ferguson was struggling. Anywhere else he might have let one of the nurses close, but this was not anywhere else, and there was not anyone else he trusted. By the last stitch in the four hours of emergency surgery, Ferguson was on the verge of collapse. He knew that as a young intern he had pulled much longer shifts, but he was not an intern and not young. First Zurich to San Francisco to meet with the Quarrys, then Bernie's death and Xander's collapse, then the ten-and-a-half hour non-stop back to Heathrow with the nine-hour flight to Mbutsu City waiting for him: it had proved too much. Ferguson dragged himself out of the operating theater, then collapsed on a bench. When he awoke in his room the next day, he had coffee and toast delivered before he called Dougherty.

"I operated," he told Dougherty, "but it's just a holding pattern. He needs a real surgeon. He needs Colfax."

"You know Colfax won't go to Africa."

"He has to. I can't do this. I'm an internist not a surgeon, and Colfax has done resections before. I only watched the video on YouTube."

"You're too modest. I've seen you pull off miracles. How bad is it?"

"Bad. I loaded him with antibiotics—our stuff, the latest, not the commercial crap—and pumped a new batch of cells into him, but the damage...The knife wound was bad enough, but Mbutsu apparently did most of the real damage when he wrenched the girl's arm. Then his goddamned personal physician finished the job by botching the surgery. He's out of here—on a plane home or lying by the side of a road somewhere —I don't know. I don't really care anymore. But my patient is in bad shape."

"Maybe it's time."

"Are you crazy, Dougherty? Mbutsu is still a quarter of our budget. Besides, anything happens to him now, and they will never let me out of the country. He dies and I'm a dead man. You read the news, so you already know what his army did after the attack from the girl. They razed an entire region of the country. They leveled it. You could see the fires from all the way across the border. Then the infantry went in and finished off the survivors. Red Cross sources estimate that 25,000 people were killed in a week; the army claims double that. Mbutsu was unconscious most of that week. They don't even need his leadership any more, if leadership is the word you apply to such savagery. He has been around so long that his barbarism has become institutionalized."

"Okay, I'll bring Colfax myself. He's not completely rational, you know, but he's still the best in his field, and he'll come if I go with him."

"I don't think that's a good idea—you, me, and Colfax all in Busanyu at the same time, with the country burning."

"It will be a swap. I'll hold Colfax's hand on the flight down. They'll refuel, board you, and fly right back."

"You're sure Colfax will do it?"

"Yes, I'm sure. I'll have him put under when we get into the limo, and we'll bring him around when he's in the operating room."

"So, we add international kidnapping to our dossiers."

"He's one of ours, so it doesn't count. We'll add it to the collective rap sheet when we kidnap someone outside."

Ferguson laughed despite himself. "Sooner or later, I'm sure we will."

~ ~ ~

By nightfall, Dr. Abraham Colfax was at the Presidential Palace outside of Mbutsu City and scrubbing to operate. He was furious with Dougherty, who had not, in fact, flown with him to Busanyu, but had drugged him and passed him on to the capable hands of a couple of minders. Ferguson had delivered both the shot of sivilac that brought him around and the news that he had been abducted for the greater good. Colfax protested until he saw the MRIs and had examined their patient. Old memories and over-trained responses were stirred. The gifted surgeon in him took charge again over the anxious and unstable recluse he had become, a virtual hermit who could not always hold up a normal conversation. He was transformed by the challenge that was now made even more challenging owing to the population of new cells eagerly trying to repair the damage on their own. He consulted with Ferguson for an hour, then announced his plan.

Ferguson did not announce his own plan. Once he realized that his options had expanded, he abandoned Colfax and left immediately for the airport with a smile on his face. To save time, Colfax had been brought down on a flight chartered by the organization instead of on Mbutsu's G6, which would have required further delay while it was flown up from Busanyu. Instead, the chartered Gulfstream waiting for Ferguson at Mbutsu International was now his to command. He intended to command it to file a flight plan for Moscow. He would get a full night's sleep on the plane and meet Sveta for brunch.

~ ~ ~

Spindly trees flickered past like pickets in a fence as Ferguson pushed his black Mercedes along the forested road in an effort to break his previous record of an hour and fifty-three minutes from the airport at

Sheremetsavo to the *Nichevo* clinic. It was not, strictly speaking, a clinic, and the town was not named *Nichevo*. In fact, the town referred to by Ferguson and his colleagues as *Nichevo*, Russian for nothing, had once had a postal code for a name and could be found on no map. One of a number of secret cities and towns created by the Soviets during the autumn of the cold war to manufacture weapons and carry out secret and forbidden military research, this one had been spared from becoming a ghost town after *perestroika* only by way of Ferguson's inspired intervention.

The organization had bought the town outright through Russian intermediaries for several million dollars in cash, a price that was proving to have been a bargain. Its captive chemists, biologists, and engineers, who had once labored in obscurity on wholesale death, now worked on its retail defeat. Laboratories and production facilities constructed to churn out chemical and biological weapons had been repurposed to make pharmaceuticals and synthetic versions and variants of proteins, enzymes, and neurotransmitters. Some of the transition was less a leap than naïve outsiders might imagine, owing to overlaps in the basic science needed. While others of the nameless towns were now crumbling and weed-choked, *Nichevo* thrived, and its resident professionals enjoyed a good, if somewhat isolated, life. In that, for them, nothing had changed.

The setup was perfect for the new purposes: isolation and anonymity, established security, and a pool of highly educated talent eager to work on interesting challenges with no competitive employers on the tree-peppered horizon. *Nichevo* was the centerpiece of the organization's research strategy, the place where they could do precisely the experiments they wanted, even on human subjects, without having to create a cover of legitimacy. It was the gateway that gave them easy access to the supply of embryonic stem cells that were essential to their techniques and that were all but impossible to obtain through legitimate channels. The new Russian leaders, each in turn, had gladly accepted the cash compensation of regular fees, and they willingly turned a blind eye to the details of operation. Even with the surcharge of obligatory payments to the Russian mafia for protection, *Nichevo* was providing a stunning return-on-investment.

The guards at the gate in the chain-link fence, armed with Kalashnikovs and accompanied by dogs who looked as bored as their handlers, no longer wore the old soviet-style uniforms from the early days of the conversion, but they were the same guards, some now grizzled and bent, but all smiling at their benefactor, the Brit who had let them keep their jobs and who paid them both more—and more reliably—than the Red Army ever had. Like their neighbors, their silence and loyalty were easily bought. They were the lucky ones at a time when so many of their cousins or former officers were starving on half-rations or running to stay a meter or two in front of the police or the Russian mafia.

Old Konstantinov, who by rights should outlive Ferguson but almost certainly would not, greeted him warmly in his Bulgarian-accented Russian. "We are so glad to have you back again so soon, Comrade Doctor. I will telephone ahead to the House in case they are not yet fully ready for you."

To Konstantinov, caught in a closed, time-like loop that perpetually returned him to the days of his youth, everyone was *tovarisch*, comrade, as if he were still in the same secret unit of the Soviet security machine. He raised his hand to signal his juniors to slide open the gate, which had once been powered by a motor that no one had bothered to replace. Ferguson made a mental note to bring it to the attention of Colonel Markov, who now handled security at *Nichevo*.

~ ~ ~

Sveta couldn't meet him for brunch but at the end of her shift met him in the lobby with his marching orders for the evening. "You are going to a concert. Andropova is leading our chamber orchestra in two works by Gaiyden." Sveta's English was pitch-perfect in most areas, but names she had grown up with seemed resistant to correction, and in Russian, the prolific baroque composer's name was spelled with the letter *geh* and pronounced like guide-in.

Ferguson faked disappointment. "I had in mind more impro-visational music," he chided. "But, Andropova is very good," he said, switching to Russian. "Maybe she will want to go back to my suite with me to make for an encore."

Sveta shoved at his shoulders. "You are always the dreamer, my mysterious doctor, but Andropova likes her lovers with more curves than you possess. Perhaps she will come instead to my apartment after the concert."

Ferguson patted her behind as he grabbed a quick kiss. He liked

Sveta's sass, but did not always know what to do with it. She was too young for him, he knew, but then, nearly every woman in the world was too young for him—or soon would be.

"A good Gaiyden concerto followed by a private duet would be wonderful," he teased.

~ ~ ~

If she had been one to smoke, Sveta would be smoking, filling the empty minutes after intercourse with ritual distraction. Instead, she picked at something imagined or real on her left index finger while she coughed little chirps that signaled Ferguson to wait until she was ready to speak.

"I know what we are researching, what you are doing," she announced, fixing him with her walnut-brown eyes. "I have figured it out. On my own. I want to be one of your subjects."

Ferguson took a breath and let it out slowly. "What is it that you think we do, exactly? In what research do you want to become a subject?"

"You want me to say it because you do not think I am that smart, but I am, and I want to live to be two hundred and fifty. That is the experiment I want you to include me in—the immortality experiment. You will do this for me because you are in love with me."

"And who is it who said that I am in love with you?"

"I said it, because it is true, just like my analysis and conclusions regarding the research we are doing. We, here, at what you call the clinic when you are not here—see, I know more than you think—we are working on the next generation, aren't we. We are designing the simpler, cheaper ways to regulate the balance so there is not this perpetual race between metastasis and cellular cascade, so you do not have to monitor so closely and have treatments every few months. This is what we are doing for you. And what you will be doing for me is making me to keep young."

Ferguson shook his head slowly, again and again.

"No, I am wrong? Or no, you will not? That is not the right answer, my doctor, my love. The right answer is yes: yes I am right, and yes you will keep me young."

"It is not that easy. You are too young."

"I am 36, which for a Russian woman, is already of a certain age. That cannot be too young. I do not want to get any older."

"No, you should be in your forties, preferably in your fifties. It took a long time for us to figure that one out. I lost a friend because we didn't realize that an older, less vigilant, more complicated immune system is needed to start with. The sledgehammer approach of completely knocking out the immune system is too aggressive and brings on its own problems. Besides, I do not make these decisions."

"That is okay, because then I will make the decision for you. Otherwise, I will decide that it is time to talk to an ex-lover, a journalist in Moscow, who will be so very glad to see me again and so very glad to have a story that will see publication beyond the miserable little rag he now writes for."

"You are not a foolish woman, Sveta, and that would be a foolish move that would only guarantee you would never get anything more from us, not even another paycheck." Ferguson studied her face, the sweeping brush strokes of her eyebrows that said so little of the inferno of intelligence behind them, the thick lips that could pull him in like a vortex. He was thinking of those lips and those eyes and the woman behind them and seeing the relationship with her stretching out far into the future. It left a sweet-sour taste in his mouth, and he wondered if there would ever be anyone who could sustain his interest the way his attention was held by the film festival of women parading through his life. Even now, there was Sveta with this year's *palm d'or*, but there were also the runners-up—Brigit in London and Alicia in California—as well as the not infrequent short subjects of young women met on a Virgin Atlantic flight or in a tony London club for those who have arrived and those looking to arrive by way of some wealthy and well-toned older gentleman.

"I will talk to my employers," he said, "but I can promise nothing."

"Ah, my elusive doctor, we both know that you are the employers; there is no one else to talk with."

"And there you would be wrong again. There are many discussions to be started, and many others who must weigh in on the matter before anything could happen. And, as I said, there is time, some years' worth of it."

Her face pinched into a pout, and her thick brows lowered as she considered him. She decided to drop the matter for the time being, to enjoy the moment, confident that she could eventually wear down his resistance. She pushed him over onto his back and started the physical persuasion, running her big hands down over his belly and to his inner thighs.

Ferguson let out a groan of pleasure and surrendered—for the moment.

14

Rosen attempted a smile at Millie as she entered the hospital room, but his face didn't seem to be responding right. "I'll be ready in a few minutes," he said, pushing the words out with a tongue still thickened by sleep.

The nurse at his side turned and spoke to Millie in a tone of professional impatience. "I'm just changing his dressings. Why don't you wait outside until I'm through here. This might take more than a few minutes."

Rosen gathered his strength again and said, "They're almost ready to discharge me."

"Discharge you? Wait just one minute! You're injured, Rosen. You've had a serious accident. They can't possibly be ready to send you home."

"We're not ready to send him home," announced a wide, dark-skinned Indian woman standing in the doorway. She wore an unbuttoned doctor's coat like a vest over her rose and saffron sari. "But we cannot keep him if he insists on being released." She walked over to Millie. "I'm Doctor Ramachandran. You must be his wife. I wasn't on duty last night, so I just met your husband, who's convinced he'll be better off recuperating at home."

Rosen raised his head and leaned as far as he could to talk around the nurse, who had advanced up to changing the bandages on his hip. "You know what I think of hospitals, Millie. No offence, doctor."

"Oh, none would be taken. It is not my hospital. I just work here. And my job at the moment is to try and persuade you to stay here at Beverly Hospital for at least another day."

"No luck, Doc," he said, just beginning to hit his stride. "Just shoot me full of methicillin, give me a prescription for oxycodone or your favorite morphine analog, and send me on my way."

"Oh, are you in medicine?" she said, looking down at his chart. "Mr. David? Or is it Mr. Rosen? These night admissions people can make a mess of names."

"No, it's Dr. David, but not your kind of doctor. I work in," he stopped, reminding himself of his recent reassignment. "I work in Nutrition Sciences at Biontolics up in Ipswich."

"Ah, yes, Biontolics. My sister-in-law works at New England Biolabs. Adhi Kandiyar. Do you know her? No? Well, I will give you a prescription for oxacillin, Dr. David, but ibuprofen will be the pain reliever of choice for you, I'm afraid."

"Damn. I was looking forward to feeling better—much better." Millie shot him a disapproving look. "Just kidding, of course. Working at the Labs I have access to all the opiates I need."

"Rosen, stop it. Doctor, he is just like this—doesn't know when it's not appropriate to kid around."

"Oh, it is not a problem. We consider it very appropriate. It makes it easier to fill out the police report." She looked down at her chart, made a couple of check marks, and looked back up at Millie. "Just kidding, of course."

The nurse at Rosen's side gathered her things and stood up. "I'm through here, doctor, if you don't need me."

"No, that will be fine. Are you new on this ward? I don't remember seeing you around."

"I'm part-time staff," she said over her shoulder as she wheeled her cart out into the hall.

The doctor flipped through the chart in her hand. "Nothing broken, Mrs. David. It looks a lot worse than it is," she said, trying to reassure her. "Just have him take it easy for a few days. He'll be stiff for a while. And have him see his regular doctor within the week, sooner if anything starts really hurting or he starts running a fever or shows any reaction to the antibiotic." Millie did not look convinced.

"It's just road rash, honey," Rosen said. "I'll heal. You know me. My poor bike took the real beating. Aren't you glad I wasn't riding the Pinarello?"

She gave him a withering look of disapproval. "What about your dislocated shoulder?"

"I've located it. See?" He twisted his right arm, now in a sling, toward her. "There it is, right where it's always been."

"Not funny, Rosen," she said, just as an orderly showed up with a wheelchair to escort them out. He smiled down at Millie, then helped Rosen into the chair and expertly swiveled it around the end of the bed and out into the hallway.

"I was worried sick all night," Millie said, walking alongside and continuing her monologue as Rosen was wheeled toward the entrance. Rosen kept looking up at her and nodding. "I'll bring the car around," she told the orderly. "Don't let him move!" she admonished.

Rosen looked up at the orderly, who rolled his eyes sympathetically but stood in silence as they waited several minutes for Millie to arrive with Rosen's Prius.

"I told you not to ride your bike to work," Millie started in again, as the orderly helped Rosen into the passenger seat and buckled him in. "The traffic on 133 can be something else. There are so many accidents."

Rosen waited until the door was closed and the orderly was headed back into the hospital before he spoke. "It wasn't traffic and it wasn't an accident. Someone tried to kill me, Millie. The man ran me off the road. He was signaling for a turn and there was no road there to turn onto."

Millie let out a puff of breath. "Don't talk that way. That's crazy. Who would try to kill you?"

"The same people who do not want my paper to get out."

"Biontolics? Are you losing it, Rosen? This is not like you, Rosen. I don't like you scaring me that way."

"My paper is gone. It's been removed from the quantitative biology arXiv, and I can't log in anymore."

"Rosen, stuff like that happens all the time. That's why they have those lost-password links."

"It's part of a pattern, surely you can see that, Millie. And there's something I didn't tell the officer who took my statement last night. Just before the guy steered me into a telephone pole, the pickup bumped my handlebar mirror and I looked over as I went down. I saw the guy, he was looking straight at me. It was no accident, I tell you."

Millie fought down anxiety that threatened to overwhelm her. She wanted to support Rosen but couldn't let herself accept the implications of his story. "Are you sure, Rosen? You didn't, like, imagine this? Because your head hit the pavement pretty hard. You said that your vision blurred." She was reaching for straws and Rosen was beginning to see it.

"Yeah, but I didn't pass out then, and I didn't hallucinate, Millie."

"Why didn't you tell this to the police?"

"Tell me, have the police found the truck yet? A white pickup with out-of-state plates and a missing passenger-side mirror, speeding down Route 133. So easy to miss something like that," he said, with vitriolic sarcasm.

Millie pressed her forehead to the steering wheel. "What are you saying, Rosen."

"You know perfectly well what I am saying."

"What are you going to do?"

"I'm going to go home, get on the computer, do some research, and post my paper again. That's what I'm going to do." He closed his eyes for a minute. "And I'm going to get Dr. Jervis at the Peabody Clinic to prescribe me something stronger than ibuprofen. My God, everything hurts."

~ ~ ~

Rosen spent the next two days recuperating and doing research. He created new login credentials, posted his paper on three sites, and followed up on his citation studies. His leg hurt like hell, and he was beginning to think it was getting hot to the touch, but he decided to tough it out and say nothing to Millie, who was already fussing anxiously over him. On the third day, Millie came home from school to find him stretched out on the sofa in his undershorts, delirious and burning with fever. His left leg was badly inflamed and peppered with patches of discoloration.

Dr. Jervis returned Millie's call right away and told her to call an ambulance.

~ ~ ~

Rosen's head rang with the dissonant warble of a siren as the ambulance wove in and out of the traffic coming down Interstate 95. He was not sure what the emergency was, but he could see that the paramedic had started a drip and had him hooked up to monitors. His leg felt like it was being scalded with steam, and he raised his head just enough to get a glimpse of it. There was a terrain map in red and purple, brown and gray painted over his left leg. He started to say something about it to whomever was holding his hand, but passed out again before he could get the words out.

He was just coming around once more about the time they wheeled him into the Beth Israel Deaconess Medical Center through the emergency entrance.

"That was my second time in a week," he said to the lights flying by overhead. "Ambulances sway a lot more than I would have expected. Not fun." He drifted off again before he could finish his thought.

On Dr. Jervis's direction, Rosen was taken directly into Isolation, where the doctor's suspicions were fairly quickly confirmed: MRSA, methicillin-resistant staph. They started him immediately on vancomycin, but within a few hours, as the patches of discoloration on his leg continued to spread, they realized they were dealing with something even more dangerous. Without waiting for the rest of the lab results that could take hours, Jervis switched him to an intra-venous cocktail of powerful antibiotics that included linezolid and daptomycin, relatively new drugs that had proven effective against multidrug-resistant bacterial strains. Then they waited and watched.

It was early evening when Dr. Jervis met Millie in the waiting room. She looked at him questioningly and held her breath.

"I want you to know," he said, speaking slowly, "we brought him down here to Boston because this way we have the best facilities and resources at our disposal. He is getting the very best treatment available anywhere, but I also want you to know that we are fighting a real battle now. I told you over the phone that I suspected it might be MRSA."

Millie nodded, letting her breath out in little pulses.

"Well, it is, a particularly nasty strain, one we've seen before but not often, but it's more than that. We're also dealing with necrotizing fasciitis."

"You mean the so-called flesh-eating bacteria."

"Right, in this case the lab now confirms it's a polymicrobial infection, several bacterial strains, not all of which have been identified unequivocally yet. He was not responding to intravenous vancomycin, so we switched to a more powerful cocktail of antibiotics. He's also now getting intravenous immunoglobulin. It's too early to tell, but we are hopeful. I have to ask you some questions, though, because this sort of fierce polymicrobial invasion is extremely rare, and usually would only be associated with a compromised immune system. Is there anything that might account for that."

"If you mean is he gay or bisexual or an intravenous drug user, the answer is no, no, and no. I would know."

"Well, it's very puzzling, then, because the timing would suggest he contracted these infections in the hospital, but Beverly has not had any outbreaks of MRSA, and they got a clean bill of health from the team that just got back from there."

"Can these be soil dwelling? I mean, could he have picked them up from the accident."

"Both the strep and staph bacteria are endemic. We live with them, constantly. It is theoretically possible that they were present on his skin and got access through the wounds, but I have never seen anything like this before. The onset and progression are so fast. Oops, there's my pager. Gotta go."

"Can I see him?"

"He's in isolation, but I'll see about it. I'll be back." He took off down the hall in the hurried walk of someone trying not to appear to be running.

15

In the morning, anxious despair turned to hesitant hope when Dr. Jervis told Millie that he had good news, that he had just learned about a drug research program looking for subjects between the ages of forty and fifty with MDR-MRSA and/or necrotizing fasciitis. The research protocol seemed almost as if it had been written with Rosen in mind.

"Do you have power of attorney for Rosen?" he asked her. "Did Rosen ever give you medical authority?"

"Yes, I have the papers filed at home somewhere. Do I need to get them?"

"I'll take your word for it. I think if you bring them in tomorrow for the Human Subjects Office here, that will be okay. For now, just sign on the lines marked with an X on all these forms."

After Millie signed the informed-consent papers, Rosen was accepted as a subject in the study and was administered an experimental series of treatments. Over the course of the next week, he made what was being described as a miraculous recovery. The doctors were saying they had never seen such rapid healing after necrotizing fasciitis. His leg was looking dramatically better, and it was even beginning to appear that he might not need skin grafts. As suddenly as he had been admitted, Rosen found himself being discharged.

Millie drove him home in the Prius and waited until they were home before telling him what had happened. "You haven't asked about my car," she said, out of the blue as they were finishing dinner.

He twisted in his chair to look out the kitchen window. "I hadn't noticed. It's gone. Where is it? Is it in the shop?"

"I totaled it. Well, the VW is totaled, anyway."

"What happened? You didn't say anything."

"You were fighting for your life. I didn't want to add to your problems."

"Yeah, bad car karma can interfere with antibiotics."

"Rosen, be serious. I was just looking out for you. Still am."

Rosen knew it was his turn to say something meaningful, but his mind only offered up more wisecracks, so he just looked at her and kept silent.

"It was on my way home from school," she said, suddenly very solemn. "I was driving down Route 1A, giving Henry Armand a ride home—his Saab was in the shop. Just before the turnoff for his house, I noted a pickup truck at a stop sign on the right. Without warning, it shot across the road, coming right at us, broadside, tires smoking. It shoved us all the way across the road and sideways into a fieldstone wall, then backed up, looking like it might ram us again, but it took off when a minivan came around the curve."

"Oh, my God. You could have been killed."

"Yeah. But all I had was a few scratches, nothing serious—'treated and released' as they say." There was a long silence. "Henry...Henry died in the ambulance on the way to Anna Jacques. He didn't have a chance. The entire passenger side of the VW was stove in."

"What about the truck? The driver? Did they catch him?"

"No." She closed her eyes. "They didn't catch him, and they haven't found the white pickup. Rosen, when he rammed us, he was looking right at us, just like with you. It was no accident. I told the police. I also told them that it looked like the truck had a new mirror on the passenger side. It didn't quite match."

Rosen put a hand over his eyes for a moment. "What are we going to do?" he said, at last.

"It's like you have been sucked into a minor war, Rosen. I don't know. You realize that some people have said that Henry Armond looks a little like you. Cynthia, the secretary at the middle school, even though you two might be related."

"It's dangerous to be around me—is that what you are saying?"

"Yeah, I guess. I don't know. I don't understand what's happening, except that ever since you got into that Nobel-grade research, things have been going wrong. Maybe the universe is trying to tell us something. Maybe messing with Nature is not such a good idea. This...this whole thing is beginning to really scare me. I just want to run away. I shouldn't, but I do. Intense stuff like this is easier for you. You've always been so logical and controlled, but it gets to me. I didn't sign up for this."

"You could maybe stay with your mother for a while? Until this is sorted out."

"I thought of that. I don't want to abandon you."

"No, you should. You should go. In fact, I insist."

"My mom's place is too far, and I still have eight weeks of school in the term."

Rosen wanted to make everything all right, to reassure her and reassure himself, but he could think of nothing convincing.

"The police said they would be looking into it," she added, a footnote to her frustration.

"There you go. I'm sure they'll figure it out."

"Rosen, I can't tell anymore whether you are serious or trying to be cute. This is reality, not reality TV. I'm not hopeful." She held his eyes. "I don't want to die, Rosen."

Rosen thought of many ways to answer, but just said, "Me neither. We'll think of something."

"I feel guilty for feeling this way," she continued, "but I don't think I can handle this. I'm really getting scared. You were always the unflappable Mister Cool. Nothing really penetrates, nothing rattles you. I'm not that way. I feel things. The world churns inside me."

Rosen watched as the image of his wife sitting across the table from him turned watery and blurred into visual static. He blinked and felt a warm, wet spot on his cheek. "It's not really like that, Millie. I just have trouble figuring out feelings—my own, too. But," he began, but then left the entire thought unspoken. He was already shutting down, lowering the internal pressure, sliding the safety rods into place in his mental reactor. "You do what you have to do, Millie," he said at long last. "I don't want anything to happen to you."

She reached across the table to rest her hand on his. He stared down at their hands, recording a high-contrast image of them against the bright spring colors of the table cloth, freezing the frame until he realized that Millie's hand was no longer there and she had left the room.

Ferguson and Dougherty faced each other across the conference table in the London office of Selian Atlantic. Ferguson had his Drambuie and Dougherty had his Irish whiskey, and both of them were tired.

"It wasn't me, Douglas."

"Nor me. So, who has been trying to do bodily harm to our boy in a very visible, very public way."

Ferguson stiffened defensively. "The only person I have talked with about Dr. David is Xander Quarry, but we made no plans and didn't initiate any action. Bernie's accident put everything on hold, and we never got back to discussing the matter. You don't think. . .?"

"I do. Look, somebody tried to run the guy off the road, and then we learn through a contact in the Ipswich Lab that he was taken by ambulance to the hospital where he was fighting for his life against an onslaught of infectious agents that had 'prescription cocktail' stamped all over them. Luckily, we had our informant in place and were able to concoct a cockamamie research protocol that would enable us to administer some of our private-stock antibiotics.

"It is a good thing that we had the foresight years ago to keep pushing development of a deep reserve of never-released drugs and the discipline to use them selectively and rarely enough so that nothing out there has had a chance to develop resistance. Fortunately. If our Doctor David had died and there had been an investigation, who knows how far the probe could have reached. We are talking about Boston, here, not some country clinic in rural California run by rubes. These people know what they are doing."

"Well, for the moment, Douglas, all is quiet on the eastern front, but we better quickly find out who unleashed the assault troops so we can get them to sound retreat."

"You know what I'm thinking, Andras?"

"Chas, please."

"Okay. You know what I'm thinking, Chas?"

"No, but I can guess. Whatever, it probably involves a plane ride."

Dougherty nodded and took another sip of whiskey. "I hate it every time it comes to this, have from the beginning."

Ferguson swirled his drink. "And it has been coming to this from the beginning."

Dougherty sucked air. "You never let it go, do you? It was so long ago, and you are still holding onto it, as if you had been the one, as if it were your story."

"It's all of our stories. And Janella's." He could picture her still, feel her energy, her determination. She had been unstoppable.

Janella Kai was the copper-skinned daughter of a Japanese-American businessman with a taste for Hispanic women and a Brazilian housekeeper who was determined to rise above poverty. Janella's mother saw her as a window of opportunity, and her father had added an extra L to the Portuguese word for window to make her name easier for Americans to know how to pronounce. Always one to look for ways to make things easier, particularly for himself, Haruto "Harry" Kai had departed when Janella was still in diapers and had never bothered to return from South America.

Raised by her mother to be their two-for-one ticket up from the Cambridge projects, Janella had twice skipped a grade, then soldiered her way into Rindge and Latin High School and finally into a full scholarship at Tufts, where she had maintained a straight-A average until her mother had died suddenly. Janella, on her own at nineteen and with no promises left to keep, dropped out of school one semester short of a degree.

The pint-sized ballerina had danced into the newly opened cancer research lab at Harvard, trailing her long scarf like a young Isadora Duncan. When she spotted Emile, she snaked her way through the labyrinth of partially unpacked boxes and miscellaneous equipment disgorged on the floor to plant herself, splay-footed, right in front of him. "I'm Janella Kai," she announced, slapping a folded and marked-up copy of the *Harvard Crimson* onto the granite top of the workbench. "I'm your new lab assistant."

"Well, hi! I'm Emile Aubuchon. I didn't realize that Dr. Dougherty had hired somebody already."

"Yeah, well, here I am. Where do I start?"

Emile, a post-doc and youngest of the recently assembled research group, was not only taken aback by her entrance but was also hypnotized by her exotic looks: her skin the color of a newly minted penny, her long hair like dark-roast coffee, and her eyes, improbably bright, like polished brass. He stared, then looked around and shrugged, momentarily tongue-tied by being in the presence of a goddess.

"Well, then," she said, whipping off her scarf and coiling it atop the newspaper, "Why don't I start over there with organizing the glassware. This place is messier than a freshman dorm room during midterms."

~ ~ ~

In truth, Dougherty had not yet hired anyone, but when he checked in at the lab the next morning, Janella was already there, feeding the Norway rats and making notes on the clipboards hanging from each cage.

"This pup is off its feed," she told him. "You might not want to include her—or him, hard to tell when they're this little—in the study. It may just have a little rat-sized tummy ache, but maybe more. Why start out with an outlier? I figure, we'll get enough outliers later for reasons we'll never decipher. Right? Oh yes, you also have a whole litter of chimeric rats in cage number eight. Shouldn't make a difference, but I thought you should know.

"And I was looking over your research protocol. Emile gave me copies of everything. I think you are going about the synthesis of some of the experimental drugs all wrong. I sketched out an alternative scheme that cuts out two steps on one and three on another sequence. Of course, you'll need to use some different reagents. I can order them for you."

Dougherty scowled and tilted his head back. "And you are who?" he said, in confused annoyance.

"Janella Kai, your new lab assistant. I'd shake hands, but I've been handling the lab residents, you know. Say, you wouldn't happen to know where I might rent an apartment, like real cheap? I'm still sleeping at West Hall, but I'm not actually a Tufts student anymore." She emphasized the word *actually* as if it were ironic or ambiguous or both. "It's one of the quads and my roomies are cool about it, but it's getting sticky sneaking in and out. Pretty soon the residence police will figure out they have a spare bed and move a new student in on top of me. Personally, I prefer to pick my bunkmates myself. So, do you know somebody with an extra room?"

Dougherty, realizing the hiring was a fait accompli, offered to let her stay at his house as a temporary solution, one that turned permanent once their affair started. Emile, who remained fixated on Janella and oblivious to her relationship with Dougherty, continued to follow her around the lab like a stray cat looking for a new home. Eventually, it became evident that Janella had a boyfriend, but Aubuchon, a Canadian transplant, was too polite to inquire or even to comment. It would never have occurred to him that the object of her attachment might be the head of the project and the oldest member of the team.

Janella quickly moved from lab flunky to partner in the project, joining in on meetings, contributing design refinements, and eventually helping to write up results. The affection between her and Dougherty grew until it was obvious even to the oblivious Emile.

The real crisis in the team came not from vying for Janella's affections but from the research itself. Once the results had been analyzed and written up in draft form, their unanticipated break-through lay exposed. They were split two-to-one on whether to publish immediately or pursue further research privately. Emile, insisting that he could see both sides, abstained from the vote, but it was evident that he really sided with Janella, who wanted to trumpet their findings to the world.

Dougherty maintained that they could find sources—wealthy individuals or private foundations—that would quietly fund the transformation of research results into clinical technique. "The biggest advantage of staying out of the spotlight," he explained, "is that we can go directly for the big payoff without worrying about irrelevant regulations and bureaucratic barriers."

It was not lost on either Atchison Dougherty or Llewellyn Cass that the vote had split along age lines. At nineteen and twenty-seven respectively, Janella and Emile were still, in their own minds, immortal and invulnerable; Dougherty and Cass were not. The big payoff for Emile and Janella would have been fame, fortune, and a secure future. For Dougherty and Cass, the big payoff they were looking at would be far bigger and much more personal.

With Emile's polite abstention, the matter was settled. Dougherty insisted on the return of all copies of the draft paper, telling the few colleagues who had seen the work that there had been a major error in analysis and a break in protocol and promising an early look at the revised work once the problems were fixed. But Janella would not retreat. She argued. She pleaded. She shouted. And she threatened to take the whole matter to the papers. Dougherty, seeing the battle escalating out of control, backed off and proposed a delay while the group replicated a key part of the research.

~ ~ ~

The Wursthaus in Harvard Square, a local source of hearty German fare and a popular watering hole at the time, was crowded but just noisy enough to make private conversation possible. "Andras," Dougherty said, leaning across the table, "we have to do something about Janella."

"Something. Yes, I suppose. What do you propose, Douglas? You are the one who got us into this with taking her onto the team and into your bed. If she had remained a simple lab assistant, we would not be at this impasse."

Dougherty savored another bite of sauerbraten, then a thumb-sized potato dumpling, before speaking. "You are right. I got us into this, so I suppose it is my problem. I cannot, unfortunately, merely wave my hand and wish her away. Let me think. Let me think."

Andras sipped his dunkelbier and narrowed his eyes in concentration. "If we had the money, we could buy her off, I suppose. She's hungry. It's unclear to me whether her appetite is more for fortune or for fame."

"Well, we're working on the money part, aren't we? Next week I fly to California to meet these wealthy fruitcakes and try to talk them into switching their research funding from mind expansion to expansion of a different sort. I wish you'd take care of it, Andras. I really do not like dealing with pseudo-intellectual flakes, regardless of how many zeroes might be in their bank balance."

"You know I can't, Douglas. Not yet. I still have duties at Dana-Farber. But I am sure some solution will present itself, and when it does, we will act." He sliced off another section of his bauernwurst and wondered what his conservative parents would have said to see him eating pork sausage and savoring every bite. They had never been religious, but they had always taken seriously their responsebility to properly represent the Jewish people and the Jewish way of life to their Welsh neighbors. It was not until he had returned to Boston after his mother's funeral that Andras had tasted bacon and eggs for the first time. He was an instant convert to what in his mind he still thought of as Christian food.

~ ~ ~

When Janella took up with the young computer scientist from the Netherlands, Dougherty had, in truth, been terribly jealous, but he also wondered if happenstance might have delivered a gift in disguise. Several nights a week, Janella would visit the young man's apartment, invariably returning late and oversleeping in the morning. Dougherty began to hope that this would become her new obsession, that genetic oncology and cell longevity would be forgotten in the flush of new love.

He was wrong.

~ ~ ~

Janella was still examining tissue cultures under the microscope when the rest of the crew decided it was time to leave for the day. She promised to lock up, then embarrassed Dougherty by telling him not to wait up for her. Feeling powerless and resentful, he had left the lab in silence. He stopped off at the Wursthaus for a beer and a bratwurst before walking the few blocks to his empty house and an early bedtime.

He awoke with a start at the first sound of a key in the front door. Janella was back, at last. He glanced at the alarm clock on the nightstand: nearly two. He slipped into his bathrobe and tiptoed down the stairs. From the landing, he could just see the bottom edge of the front door as it closed. Janella was not in the entry hall. Her purse was on the stand by the door but her keys were not. She must have gone out again, he thought. He returned to the bedroom and quickly dressed. Outside, a layer of fresh snow was marked by the tracks of her boots leading down the street and onto the porch, then back down again and up toward North Cambridge. Dougherty finished buttoning his coat and started out in the same direction, hurrying, following.

~ ~ ~

He didn't even know the name of her boyfriend, so he was not much help to the police when they questioned him about her disappearance. She had not shown up at the lab in the morning, and it was another two days before he reported her missing. He explained that he simply assumed she was with her boyfriend. "You know how these young kids are these days," he said, with a wink in his voice. Through acquaintances from college, the police eventually identified Bram Dekker as the mysterious boyfriend. Dekker admitted seeing her that night and said that she had headed back to Cambridge about one in the morning. When asked why he hadn't gone with her or called a taxi, he said, "You don't know Janella. She insists on taking care of herself. She does capoeira—Brazilian judo—and told me she could take down any guy, even a guy like me, easy."

The police found nothing suspicious at Dekker's apartment, and with no body or evidence of foul play and no family to press the matter, the case eventually became just another unsolved disappearance. Dekker returned to Europe when his studies in the States were complete, and Dougherty returned to his quiet research with Andras and Emile.

Dougherty set his empty whiskey glass down on the conference table at Selian Atlantic and stared into it for several seconds before raising his eyes to meet Ferguson's. "Do you want to know what happened that night?" he said. He folded his hands in his lap and leaned back in the conference-room chair.

"No," Ferguson said, flatly, "I don't want to know. If you tell me, then I become an accessory after the fact—long after, but still an accessory."

"There is nothing to become accessory to. I did not kill her. I know that's what you have always thought."

"And that is what you have always said. And there we leave it, until the next uncommon occasion when her name enters conversation."

"You don't believe me, do you? You think I'm capable of that."

"I know you're capable of that, even if you yourself do not pull the trigger or push the victim in the back. We both know what we have had to do to keep this enterprise going and its business quiet."

"At least I have never slipped the needle to a patient."

Ferguson's jaw worked as he bit back words. "On whose direction? And who is it who made the phone calls?" He shook his head sadly. "This is getting us nowhere, Douglas. We have real problems to solve. The business with Janella is old business, so old that I am not sure I remember it."

"I do. I remember it as vividly as if it were yesterday. I remember the fight after I caught up with her. I remember her dancing out of reach when I tried to grab her. I remember the fury in me growing as she ran on young legs, and I struggled to keep up with her. And I remember her sudden stop, her spin like a ballerina, and her foot sweeping toward my face like a club. It was a move straight out of a Jackie Chan movie, except it was capoeira, and it was not done with wires. One second she is running away, and the next her foot is meeting the side of my head.

"And that's it. I came to, shivering in that alley, my jaw and my head aching, feeling lucky to have woken up rather than ending up the subject of headlines: 'Harvard researcher found dead from exposure.' There was no sign of her, no longer even tracks in the snow. I knew as much as the police knew, which was nothing. She vanished that night, presumed dead, as they say, but there was no body, no proof, no charges."

Ferguson let out a deep sigh. "I believe you. I guess I have to believe you."

"That spells a very weak belief, Andras. I loved her. Maybe she was the last person I loved. I would have wanted her at my side, even now."

"You would have had to wait many years. Even now it's not reliable for younger patients. Poor Emile. But we learned a lot in the process, didn't we."

It had been ironic. Emile had volunteered to be the guinea pig for the first clinical application of their findings, which made sense to all three of them, since he was the youngest and heartiest, and they knew better than to consider bringing in anyone new at that time. How could they have known that the whole procedure worked better with older subjects, that the very vigor of youth was a barrier, that the gradual and inevitable weakening of the immune system as people aged made it easier to start the process of chimerization, which was the biological key. Emile had died of a self-administered drug overdose when the pain had become too much to bear and when they all worried that the evidence of medical malpractice would soon become too glaringly apparent.

Ferguson pushed his glass away and stood up from the conference table. "Enough reminiscing. Duty calls. I need to get some sleep if I am going to fly out to California tomorrow."

~ ~ ~

Ferguson's approach to flying was to carry little or nothing and buy what he needed on arrival. It was a lifestyle option open to him but not for everyone. Still, although he had no checked luggage, he went down to baggage claim because he figured that would be where Xander Quarry would automatically expect to meet him. He was standing around, acting the part of the impatient traveler, when someone tapped his shoulder. He turned to find Xander, dressed in black pants, a white shirt with bars on the shoulders, and a black necktie reaching only halfway to his waist and held in place by an incongruously large, gold tie bar.

"You, Xander Quarry, look like some goddamned limousine chauffer. Or are we on our way to some costume party?"

"That's me, just looking the part. Let's go."

He led Ferguson outside to the taxi stand.

"I thought you were driving me. Surely we can't be taking a taxi all the way to the ranch. Or have you now obtained your hackney license?"

"No, no, no. But it's too far to walk." He turned to the dispatcher and said that they wanted to go to the Executive Terminal. The dispatcher looked down at the long line of waiting taxis and shook his head. "Here. First cab. This is one cabbie who is going to be thrilled by such a fare."

The driver did not look happy when he heard where they were headed. "You know where that is, right?" Xander asked.

"Yeah, I know. Out to the 101 north, exit at North Access Road, follow the signs." He flipped the meter and pulled out.

"Are you going to tell me what's going on, Xander, or should I just sit back and enjoy the magical mystery tour?"

"I flew up. Had to pull strings with San Francisco Helicopter to be able to land on their helipad here at SFO. It was either that or the Coast Guard, and I figured it would be damned hard to pull enough strings with the Coast Guard."

When the taxi dropped them off at the non-descript Executive Terminal, Xander slipped the driver a fifty and led the way into the building. He greeted the woman working the desk for San Francisco Helicopter with a wink and announced that his client was ready for the Extended Tour. She winked back and waved him through a door marked "Flight Crew Only." Xander held the door for Ferguson, then marched straight through the room to another door that took them out onto the tarmac. There Ferguson spotted Xander's bright red Robinson Raven being readied by the ground crew.

"I had forgotten what fun it was to fly. Ever since that chase to University Hospital, I have been flying every chance I can get. I figured you might enjoy a flight where you can see what you're flying over for a change. Besides, this is a hell of a lot faster and a lot more fun than two hours of fighting traffic at this time of day.

"Come on get in. This trip I've got time to give you a lesson. We'll start with this, which is called the cyclic and controls the tilt of the helicopter, sort of like a joystick. Except on these Robinsons it is this tilting bar, which, if you just tip it up like this," he demonstrated, "makes it a lot easier to slide in and out." He grinned broadly as he walked around to the other side, tilted the cyclic back again, and slid into the pilot's seat.

~ ~ ~

They were at the Ranch and already sitting at poolside in just over half an hour. Ferguson and Xander watched as Nadia tried for the fifth time to execute a clean back flip off the high board. "Arch your back more, honey. Spot the water," Xander coached her, as she sputtered to the surface.

"How long has she been back?" Ferguson asked. "Where did you find her?"

"She was back the day after you left, towing by his earlobe the poor slob who took off with her. She chewed me out for letting it happen— it was all my fault, according to her—and told me to stay sober or stay out of her life. She acts like she owns this place. Someday she could, since she's my only heir." He poured some more San Pellegrino into his glass, swirled it to reduce the bubbles, and took a sip. "See what I am being reduced to?" he said, holding the glass up to the light and swirling it again. "Mineral water." He set the glass down and squinted at Ferguson. "You were pretty quiet on the way down from SFO and, as expected, said nothing over the phone about the purpose of this visit. What's up?"

"The same matter we were discussing on my last visit. Except it seems that you went ahead and hired a contractor without getting the go ahead."

"I did no such thing. I queried an old contact in Vegas, told him that there might be 100K for the right person who could do the job right, and he told me he would get back to me. I never heard anything more."

"Then it sounds like we have a freelancer on the loose. Some 'mechanic' thinks he has a deal and is trying to complete the contract. But whoever it is, he is far too clumsy. Now we have to make this mechanic disappear before he succeeds and brings everything down on top of him—and us."

"I can talk with my man in Vegas again."

"And have this story get around? It's not like your man in Vegas is either a good judge of employees or knows the meaning of discreet inquiries. No, I have a better idea. Do call your man in Vegas, but tell him the job is done and you are ready to make good on the deal. The mechanic just has to come and collect."

"Here? Are you nuts? We want a mafia hit man showing up at the Ranch?"

"Maybe not. Pick a place to meet, some spot he has to drive to. Make him come to us, where we can manage the stage, someplace where there won't be an audience."

"You know, you are beginning to talk like some of the union goodfellas I bumped into when Bernie and I were riding the building boom in Las Vegas."

"Well, I am a man of many talents and many sides. We need to end this episode and bury the evidence."

Xander smiled and nodded. "That gives me an idea."

~ ~ ~

From the air it could have been a children's sandbox filled with bright yellow Tonka Toy construction equipment left scattered after the preschoolers had returned home from their day at play. As the helicopter descended, details betrayed how long the site had been sitting idle. Rust marred the finish of a front loader, and the larger of the two bulldozers at the site had one track spread out in mid-repair, with weeds growing between the treads. Xander circled once to check for fresh tire tracks or footprints, but there were no signs that anyone had been there for years.

"Now we wait," he said over the intercom, as he spun the helicopter around and retreated over the next ridge. "Are you sure you want to do this?"

"It's a two-man job, you said that yourself. And I need to verify that we have the right man. I have never liked loose ends."

"I could have gotten Frank to fly, you know. Frank asks no questions and has no ambitions."

"Xander, you must know by now that I am really an old-fashioned kind of hands-on doctor who still makes house calls. And look, there comes our man, ready to meet the doctor." He pointed toward a dust plume marking a path through the trees and snaking its way toward the clearing. Xander gently pressed down on the collective to drop the helicopter and then deftly held them hovering barely above the treetops, just out of the sightlines from the construction area. Just as the pickup truck pulled into the open at the site, Xander lifted the helicopter well above the trees and smartly brought it in toward the clear ground between the pickup and the smaller bulldozer. He set the helicopter down parallel to the truck amidst a whirlwind of dust, then left the engine idling and ducked quickly out of the far side. Ferguson hopped out on his side and advanced toward the pickup with his arms spread, his left hand holding a thick envelope.

The man coming around the front of the pickup truck from the driver side was a walking cliché in his denim jacket, dusty jeans, and cowboy boots. His hair was slicked back and tied tightly at the back of his head. He held his jacket pushed open just enough to expose the edge of a handgun tucked into his waistband.

Images of *High Noon* flashed in Ferguson's head, and he smiled broadly as he lowered his hands slowly, keeping them in plain sight.

"Are you Quarry?" the man asked.

"No, an associate."

"You fly that thing?" He pointed past Ferguson towards the now empty helicopter, which was partially obscured by the still settling dust.

"I have many talents. And what did you say your name was?"

"I go by Adam Cain, a sort of biblical reference, you know. Mr. Quarry knows who can always get in touch with me, should you ever need my services again. Just ask for Adam Cain. Now, you do have the money, don't you?" he said, reaching for the envelope.

Ferguson lifted it away from the man's outstretched hand but kept smiling. "I need to know what you did to earn it first."

"Yeah, sure. I hit the mark. Made it look like natural causes, an accident. It was a surgical strike, so to speak. Ha, ha, inside joke. Don't let appearances mislead you. I'm a college grad and have been in this business a long time. I know a lot of ways to take care of trouble. First I got him scraped up really bad, then a nurse I hired slipped in and spread him with an unstoppable stew of nasty bugs, stuff that modern medicine has nothing to fight. She just mixed specimens from several really sick patients from the research hospital where she works. It was what the doctors call resistant strains, multiple-drug-resistant bacteria. You know what I mean?"

"I do. But you didn't tell all the story, did you."

"Okay, there were some hiccups. At one point, I thought I saw him, out of the hospital, so I took action. I was wrong. He was still in isolation, so I ended up taking out some dumb duck who looked too much like the target. So? Anyway, I headed home before the local police even knew the accident had happened. They're still looking for a white Ford pickup with front-end damage. I drive a blue job, with custom detailing, clean as a whistle, as you can see. I'm a pro, and the main thing is: I did the job."

"A pro? Are you sure you did the job? How do you know?"

"What do you take me for? It was confirmed. I got a call that said the guy had succumbed to sepsis a few days after he entered the hospital."

"You don't read newspapers, do you?"

Cain looked puzzled. "Hey, do I get my fee or what? I still have to settle with the nurse."

Ferguson handed the envelope over with his left hand and rested his right on Adam Cain's shoulder. "You get your money, Mr. Cain. How much do you owe the nurse?"

Cain pulled a thick stack of used hundreds from the envelope and riffled through it, smiling. "Ten grand," he said, "that's all I promised the bitch, almost nothing."

The spring-loaded syringe plunged into his neck at the same moment as Ferguson grabbed the gun from Cain's waist and stepped back. Cain reached to his neck and struggled to stay standing, then slumped down against the front tire of his pickup. He looked up at Ferguson briefly before rolling his eyes and falling completely to the ground. Ferguson retrieved the packet of bills and the envelope and walked back toward the helicopter.

As Ferguson slipped into the passenger seat, Xander finally succeeded in starting the reluctant engine of the bulldozer. He steered it around the helicopter and straight toward the pickup truck, which he shoved over into the hollow at the edge of the clearing. It rolled once and rested upside down at the bottom of the depression. Xander backed up and sent Cain's body in after it. Then he started methodically reworking the contours of the area, beginning with a huge mound of fill waiting to the side of the hollow. A half hour later, the site looked freshly worked but with no sign whatsoever that there had ever been a pickup or a Mr. Adam Cain there.

Xander returned the bulldozer to where it had started and climbed back into the still idling helicopter. He slipped on the intercom headset and signaled Ferguson to put on the other one.

"Pretty professional work," Ferguson told him. "Where'd you learn how to operate construction equipment?"

"Oh, when we were dealing real estate in Las Vegas, I would sometimes sub in when a development wasn't moving along fast enough. Bernie worked the numbers and the deals, but I've always been good with vehicles—all kinds. Watch this." He advanced the throttle slowly, then edged up on the collective to lift them off the ground. He then worked the controls like a choral conductor, constantly adjusting the cyclic, the anti-torque pedals, and the collective, orchestrating the helicopter in a complicated dance that used the downdraft to sweep the area clean of footprints, tire tracks, and other traces of recent activity.

"That was fun!" he shouted over the intercom. "And you have no idea how hard that is to do when your own dust is blinding you and you're only feet off the ground. Here, take this and dump it out the window." He handed Ferguson a small sack.

"What's in it?" Ferguson said, as he emptied it.

"Weed seeds. We're due for a rain this weekend. In another week, no one will even be able to tell that anyone has been here. Now, let's head home." He pulled up on the collective, sending the helicopter into a sharp climb.

"We have one more loose end. This guy—called himself Adam Cain—mentioned a nurse who he hired to infect Dr. David. We will have to track her down, but I think all we will need to do is settle the account with the agreed fee. I do still worry about somebody stumbling on this site and digging, though."

"Nobody's going to stumble on it, and nobody's going to dig. I bought it through one of Bernie's many shell companies when the owners ran out of cash years ago. The perimeter of the property is posted. I've overflown it now and then just to see if anyone has been poking around. No one is going to uncover our business, and with the business our Mr. Cain was in, no one is going to be inquiring after him. Frankly, one less hit man on the planet seems to me like the makings of a good day's work." He pushed on the cyclic and angled them back toward Quarry Ranch. "I've got a bottle of sparkling Malvasia Bianca from this Hecker Pass winery that will knock your socks off. Lilacs and lime on the nose and mangoes and lemons on the tongue. The perfect way to celebrate. A couple of glasses won't hurt me."

19

Millie moved out on a Saturday amidst tears and hugs, leaving Rosen more confused than ever. She said she would call every week, but refused to tell him where she was going. She argued that if they were still after him, it was better that he not know too much about her plans. He rejected her anxiety as irrational and felt abandoned by her but kept his own unacknowledged anxiety at bay by making plans of his own.

He still did not know who might be after him, other than that they had some connection with Biontolics. Whoever they were, they seemed to be everywhere. They had even been in the house at some point. With no sign of breaking and entry or anything else missing, his laptop had disappeared from the closet where he kept it. He bought himself a slim new netbook at Best Buy for cash and set about meticulously reconstructing his online life from memory—with significant changes. He created new web email and PayPal accounts, new log-in credentials for sites that he needed to access, and a completely fabricated online persona. He knew that he was an amateur but began to teach himself about encryption software that hid files and email from prying eyes, anonymizers that disguised the location of a computer, and safe ways to use public wi-fi. He never worked from the house but began alternating in a random pattern between a Starbucks down in Peabody, one up in Newburyport, and Zumi's Café, his favorite local spot with great coffee and free Wi-Fi.

He delayed returning to Biontolics for an extra week under the pretext of recovering from his accident and the bout with MRSA, but eventually he had to reestablish his office routine, playing the part of the dedicated researcher working on nothing of consequence. He said nothing about Millie at work, but somehow word seemed to get around that she had left him. Jeannine let a decent interval of several more weeks pass before inviting him to dinner. "I hope that's all right. I mean, I heard that you guys had split, but if you don't want to talk, you don't have to. And we don't have to do dinner."

"No, that's all right. It's not what you think. But I suppose we could have dinner, if you like." He could feel his heart pounding but, as usual, was unable to decipher the precise message his guts were sending him. "Do you want to leave from work, or should we meet someplace?"

"I notice you have been leaving kind of early from here since you got back. You used to put in some impressively long hours, but these days . . ." She trailed off. "Maybe we should meet later. I'm not sure I want to have dinner at half-past five."

"Well, yeah. I didn't think my office hours were quite that obvious, but, face it, there's not a lot of real work here anymore, in case you hadn't noticed. So, where do you want to meet?"

"Maybe Michael's in Newburyport, say eight-ish?"

~ ~ ~

The parking lot at Michael's Harborside was packed, and Rosen ended up having to find a space in a municipal lot. By the time he walked back to the restaurant, Jeannine was waiting. She had changed since leaving work, and the sleeveless black dress she wore showed off her graceful neck. Rosen found himself noticing things: how the color of her eyes matched her light brown hair and how her smile filled her face when she spotted him coming across the parking lot.

Michael's was a noisy mess, with the usual Friday-night crowd multiplied by no less than three special parties. "We should have made reservations," he said, coming back from checking inside. "They're saying it will be 45 minutes before we can get a table, and then who knows how long before we are served."

"Then let's not," she said, taking his arm and turning him around. "We can go to my place. I live five minutes from here. If you don't mind me whipping up something while you have a glass of wine or two."

Rosen was aware that if she had asked him over for dinner, it would have seemed too forward, and he would have declined. But this—this was different, unintended, almost innocent. Almost. He nodded and followed her out of the restaurant.

~ ~ ~

Rosen speared the last sliver of chicken on his plate, drew it through the remnants of a mirror of raspberry-cilantro sauce, and savored it with his eyes closed. He washed it down with the rest of the Riesling in his glass. Before he could say anything, Jeannine had refilled it.

"That was amazing. You are quite the chef, you know. There is more to you than meets the eye," he said.

"You, too," she countered.

Emboldened by the wine, Rosen decided to go for broke. "If I asked you whether you have been spying on me, would you answer honestly?"

"If I had been spying on you, I would hardly answer honestly, now would I?" She stared across the table as if waiting for some cue from him, unsure whether or not to say more. "Spying is the wrong word, anyway," she said. "Truth? Okay, if you are ready for it." She took a deep breath before continuing. "Part of my job is to keep an eye on people. I get paid extra to let London know what you have been up to. There's nothing sinister. You are valuable property, Rosen, and I think Biontolics likes to keep an eye on valuable property."

"Nothing sinister? You call stealing computers nothing sinister? How about attempted murder. Is that nothing sinister? Actually, leave off the attempted. A colleague of my wife was killed. Now that's sinister."

"You don't think Biontolics had anything to do with any of that, do you? I mean, that's crazy. You had a traffic accident. Your wife had a traffic accident." She paused, letting her own words sink in.

"Patterns," he said. "Patterns and probabilities: that's what we deal in, Jeannine. First they block my research, then it disappears; then I post a paper anonymously and that disappears; then all the related research disappears, and then my personal laptop at home goes missing." He almost added, "and then my wife," but censored it. "Plus, after I try to get the word out, I land in the hospital and my wife's friend, who looks a little like me, lands in the cemetery. And you are saying this is nothing, nothing sinister."

She turned her head to one side but kept her gaze locked on him. She opened her mouth as if to speak, then closed it again.

"What do you know, Jeannine? Tell me."

"I know I could be fired."

"Maybe. Me, too. Except I've been involved in a lot of independent activity lately, and one thing they have not done is fire me."

"They wouldn't do that because they want to keep you on a short leash. And you just keep chewing it off."

Rosen got up from the table and walked around to squat beside her chair. He rested his hand on her thigh and looked her in the eye. "Please, Jeannine, tell me the truth. Tell me what is going on."

"I don't know. That's the truth. But I do know that all your computers have had loggers installed, that your phone is tapped and your cellphone has been jiggered in some way, and that they know about your latest gambit of trying to contact somebody at *The Boston Globe*. But you said something about other research disappearing."

"Yeah, all the supporting internal studies have also vanished from the project files and archives at work."

"But how would you know that, since I know for a fact that you have not been doing any problematic poking around at the Lab recently. Like I said, everything you do is monitored."

Rosen felt a flash of triumph as he realized that not everything he had been was being tracked. "Alright, then, whose side are you on, Jeannine? Last time I asked, you dodged the question. This time I want to know. When it comes down to hard choices, what would you choose, them or me?"

She leaned slowly toward him and gave him a long, deep kiss, then pulled back. Neither spoke. Rosen looked down at his hand still resting on her thigh then up into her eyes again. "I don't think," he said, but she put a finger to his lips before he could finish and then rose to lead him into the bedroom.

~ ~ ~

Rosen, who had been with no one except Millie since their college days, felt like an uncertain student again—awkward and eager at the same time. He was shy about the scars that painted his leg and embarrassed at how he kept mentally comparing Jeannine to Millie. Jeannine felt wrong and wonderful in his arms. He marveled at her solid body and the way she wrapped her long legs around him, at how their bodies matched so perfectly in proportions. He savored the taste of her tongue and the exotic smell of her breath, ripe with the Riesling they had been drinking but with another note that was just Jeannine and not Millie. And with each unbidden comparison, he was shot through with excitement and with guilt.

They lay in bed afterward, both staring in silence at the stippled ceiling as if it displayed some secret script to be decoded. Jeannine finally spoke, one word, a word of absolute ambiguity: "Well."

Rosen—who would have preferred the word were "Wow!"—propped himself up on an elbow and asked, "What are we going to do?"

"Not this, not again," she answered.

"Why? What's wrong?"

"This. Oh, don't misunderstand me. I loved it. You were sweet and generous, and you gave me something I have wanted from you for a very long time. But we were not alone in the room. You couldn't escape her presence. Even I could feel it. Each time you thought of her it was as if someone standing in the hallway had spoken, and, for a moment, you would leave and go elsewhere."

"I'm sorry."

"No need to be. I should be sorry for having put you in that position. After all, you are still married."

"Neither of us should be sorry. And I am not so sure that this should never happen again. I'm just, well, out of practice."

She ran a finger down his nose and then kissed it. "Well, you did just fine for someone claiming to be out of practice." She grinned at him and shook her head. "Anyway, I hope one thing is settled."

"What's that?"

"Your question about loyalties. I'm on your side, completely. I hope you realize that. And so, we have to decide what is the best way to use the fact that you now have a double agent behind enemy lines."

The Boardroom at Selian Atlantic was being used for actual business, meaning the cover business of a high-roller reinsurance group, so Ferguson and Dougherty arranged to meet at a club in London. The Nights of the Round Table had a silly, tourist-slanted name and a limited menu, but it was a place where a private dining room could be organized on short notice. On this particular night, they ended up not with a round table but with a square one flanked by high-backed wooden benches and lit by a four-branched brass candelabra. Over Yorkshire pudding and a bottle of a private label burgundy that Dougherty had brought with him, they went through their punch list of matters needing review or decisions.

"Oh, yes, we've had to do some shuffling of assignments at the clinic in Russia," Dougherty said, after flicking past several pages on his open iPad.

"Why is that?"

"We lost two of our best technicians there. Really more than technicians. They were working on independent research that now somebody else is going to have to decipher and carry on."

"Who was it? How did we lose them? Certainly there's nobody around who could hire any of our people away, not at what we pay them."

Dougherty looked down at his iPad and read. "Dmitri Boryshkin and Svetlana Petrova. They worked together in the immunology group. Pity. An auto accident. Those Russians, you know how they all drive."

"Hang on, who did you say?"

Dougherty read the names again, pronouncing them slowly and exaggerating the rolled Rs in each: "Dmitri Boryshkin and Svetlana Petrova. You knew them?"

Ferguson blanched. "I know many people at *Nichevo*. That's where I work, in fact. That is, when I am doing my real work instead of chasing around the globe fighting fires."

Dougherty tapped on the table beside the screen. "This Svetlana—isn't that the Sveta you have mentioned a couple of times? Yes, that's right, now I remember, you were seeing her, not so? You know, maybe you need to be more choosy with your liaisons, my friend. From the looks of it, this woman was pretty wild. She wrapped her car around a tree driving to work one morning. And that happened only days after we got a report from one of our informants that she was talking about some sort of exposé if she didn't get what she was after. Whatever that was. You wouldn't have anything to add, would you, Chas?"

Ferguson's faced turned from white to red. "Anything I might add is no doubt already in your reports. Only days, was it? Coincidence or, perhaps, convenient timing one might say. You offed her, didn't you? You arranged a so-called accident for her because she was beginning to look like what you would call a nuisance. 'Shedding resources' in the management-speak you prefer these days. Without even checking with me."

"And you? It would seem that in your pillow talk you may have said too much, perhaps offered her an inside track without first checking with me."

"I did no such thing. She sussed the whole thing out on her own. She was pretty damned smart, but I had her in a holding pattern. There was no need to take precipitous action, certainly not without our going over it together. Douglas, you are acting more and more like this is your show, and the rest of us be damned."

"It is my show. And yours. There are really no others, not any that truly matter—except as experimental subjects or cash cows or both."

Ferguson knew there was no arguing with his partner, who was both right and wrong at the same time. Certainly it was true that the two of them stood atop a vast pyramid that sustained them, but that was not the same as saying no one else mattered. Ferguson wondered if perhaps he was, at an advanced age, developing a conscience and a sense of ethics. Or was he just going soft? As he thought more on the matter, he concluded that, if anything, he was becoming hardened to the demands of being Pharaoh, perched atop a pyramid, a living god with the power of life and death in his staff.

Suddenly, he became aware that Dougherty was still talking.

"So, as you know from the media reports," he was saying, "Mbutsu's forces have quelled yet another uprising, this time hardly more than a small band of poorly armed mercenaries imported from across the border, but once more the retaliation has been brutal."

"I would think that a few more deaths would hardly bother you anymore, Douglas."

"A few. A few may be necessary—*is* necessary. But this man and his machete-armed minions massacre thousands at a stroke. I do wish we didn't still need his money. Oh, yes, and I hate to say it, but you may have to go down there again. It seems even Colfax wasn't enough to put everything back right. And Edgar now claims he is overdue for the next treatment. I don't know. You are the physician, the one who keeps track of the schedules and monitors everything. I hardly even understand the technology I helped to invent—not any more."

"You know, Chas, with all the time you spend in tropical Africa, perhaps you should line up a little black honey to warm your hut on that end of your travels."

"No need to be crude, Douglas. We all know about the extent of your own sainthood." Ferguson knew he had hit home with that remark, a reference to the numerous times the organization had acted to extricate Dougherty from a dalliance gone sour. There had been little on that front in recent years, but still, the stories were a subliminal irritant that remained beneath the surface, ready for use by a friend who was still stinging from the loss of a lover.

Dougherty, always the one to be in control, ignored the remark and continued going down his list. "And last but not least, we have the matter of our dear Dr. Rosen David. It seems as if he may have settled down or given up. Or maybe he is just playing us on his line. Holzinger says he's been clean for weeks, and the reports from our onsite minder are becoming boringly routine. As the pioneers would say in the old American films, it's quiet out there, maybe too quiet."

"I agree. After Africa, it's off to the New World for this weary pioneer. I have nothing pressing in Russia, it would seem. Our trusted Doctor Nevsky will handle the reassignments to cover our losses in personnel. We can let the clinic run itself for a while—or be run by others, whatever expression best fits. Reader's choice."

Dougherty gave Ferguson one of his undecipherable looks, closed his iPad, and rose from the table. There was a moment when each of them seemed about to speak, but it passed, and the dinner ended with a wordless farewell and a silent exit.

21

At first, Millie's untraceable calls on SkypeOut had been an added bit of Friday night ritual, a way of touching base and reaching out through disembodied voices to sustain some semblance of connection. But then she would miss a Friday and call midweek to leave a brief message at a time when Rosen was out. As the intervals between calls slowly increased, the conversations they did have were filled with less and less. The distance that had always periodically inserted itself in their relationship, even when they were together every day, steadily grew into an ocean that mere conversation could not cross. Rosen could feel the winter ice thickening in the sea between them, could sense his own feelings cooling as the words became mere words and the "I love you" at the end of their calls was like the ritual "amen" after recitation of a prayer long outdated by disbelief.

Rosen's world had tilted, and as one pole was freezing over, the other was warming. Rosen knew full well that he was entering uncharted waters, but he kept seeing Jeannine, both hoping and fearing that they would end up in bed together again. She managed to keep the prospect at bay by controlling the venues, making sure that they were unlikely to be spotted by any Biontolics people and lowering the odds that they might end up in bed. Rosen admired her ingenuity and integrity, while being irritated at the same time. Ironically, the more she insisted they stick to words and keep their distance physically, the more Rosen found that he was falling in love with her. It was a novel experience. He was coming to realize that he had never fallen in love with Millie, that they had fallen into bed and into each other's lives so precipitously that it had been an event, a discontinuity and not a process. There was before Millie, and then they were married and making a life together. Rosen knew that he had loved her, but it was a memory, like the way he still knew the address of their first apartment in Somerville. The love was—had been—real, as real as any feeling was for Rosen, but even now, so soon after her departure, he remembered it rather than felt it.

For Jeannine, it was all process, a process that had been underway since the day she was hired by Biontolics and had started sharing an office with an enigma. The special assignment she had accepted was a bonus that had given her an excuse to insert herself into Rosen's life, to study him under the microscope of corporate espionage. And then, on the very verge of fantasies realized, she had pulled back to hold him at arm's length. So it was that they ate dinner in safely unromantic settings and walked the boardwalk in Newburyport without even holding hands, all the time both of them feeling the heat of sublimation radiating, like the glow from a bed of banked coals in a fireplace just waiting for fresh wood to be added.

It was a cloudy-bright day in southern Maine. They were walking a near-empty stretch of shoreline, their hands separated by inches but connected by invisible magnetic lines of force, pulsing in an insubstantial aura that engulfed them. They talked of science and fate and philosophy as the lines of force connecting them intensified.

"Do you believe, Rosen?" she asked abruptly, without offering a context.

"Do I believe? Yes, I believe. I believe in many things."

"No, silly, you know what I mean. Do you believe in God?"

"No."

"Just that? A one word theology? Surely there is more to the story. I know that you don't like going out on Friday night. For a time, I thought it was because of what happened that first time we had dinner together, but then I caught on that you light candles and eat challah at home."

"Yeah, but that has nothing to do with God. I'm Jewish. On Friday nights, we light candles, eat challah, and bless our wine—whether we believe in anything or not." He did not say that his observance had also been about waiting for Millie's calls, even though they no longer came.

"But why? What's that about?"

"Habit. I mean, these customs, these habits, well, it's a deeply rutted road we Jews travel."

"Did you ever believe?"

"Oh, sure, don't we all, when we are children? I went to Hebrew school, learned to read Hebrew and chant Torah, even did a bar mitzvah. But by that time, I had already figured out that men made God and not the other way around. All that stuff is still in me, though.

I haven't been inside a synagogue since my uncle on my mother's side died fifteen years ago, but I can still rattle off the *Sh'ma* and the *V'ahavta*."

She gave him an inquiring look.

"The *Sh'ma*. It's a theological one-liner, the first Hebrew you learn and the last words on the lips of the dying. *Sh'ma yisrael*. Hear, o Israel, the Lord is God, the Lord is One. That's followed by," he took a breath and started chanting in rapid Hebrew. "*V'ahavta et Adonai elohekha, b'khol-l'vav'kha uvkhol-nafsh'kha uvkhol-m'odekha.* And so forth. You never forget it."

"And what is it?"

"'And you shall love the Lord with all of your heart and all of your soul and all of your strength.' I'm sure you've heard it before in some form. And you?"

"Lapsed Catholic. But I know what you are talking about. I know most of the mass by heart and can still sing 'Adeste Fidelis' in Latin." She started to sing in her husky alto voice, then stopped. "But you get the idea. You are right, the grooves are cut pretty deep in the cortex."

"I said ruts in the road—different metaphor. You have grooves, we have ruts. But the end result is much the same, I suppose. We grow up. We leave the mystical mush behind, but the muscle learning remains. You can take the Jew out of the Temple, but you never get the Temple out of the Jew."

"Or the catechism out of the Catholic. Do you think it comes from being smart, I mean figuring out that religion is just ritual, a game we invented to comfort ourselves on stormy nights—or on our deathbeds?"

"Possibly. But there has to be more to it than just intelligence or education. Some people set it aside and others cling to religion as if their life depended on it, which, of course, is what religions want us to believe. Nick Borofski, Rabbi Nick, was one of the smartest men I ever knew. He had a PhD in physics, yet he believed—with all of his heart and all of his soul and all of his strength. It's complicated. Look, I'm a scientist, and I know too much to believe in a simple God of creation. The God I was taught in Hebrew school makes no sense to me, but dig deep enough in any direction, and the science stops making sense, too."

"What do you mean? Science is one of the few things in life that *does* make sense."

"Only as long as you don't look too closely, particularly when it comes to the biggest questions. Consider: Why are we here? Why is anything here? How did it start? Anyone who believes that modern cosmology explains the origins of the universe is kidding themselves. Physics and astronomy have become elaborate shell games, in which problems are shuffled between hidden dimensions and in which enormously complicated mathematics disguises ultimate ignorance. Even if the theories are right, they are just descriptions that explain absolutely nothing. So, what if our universe was, as some theories maintain, the result of the collision of infinite super-dimensional membranes in a hyperspace bulk? What does that explain? Where did these so-called 'branes' come from? What created them? We have just swept the question under a cosmological rug. It's stage magic on a galactic scale, mathematical misdirection.

"We can describe precisely and in minute detail the first nano-seconds of the history of our universe, but what came before the Big Bang? What caused it? Saying that the question is disallowed because time did not exist before the start of the universe or claiming that the universe caused itself or that ours is only one of an infinite number of alternative universes in a manifold multiverse—this 'science' is little more than learned and intricate word play, an infinite regress, matrochka dolls nested inside other matrochka dolls without end. For the big questions, the ones that one might say really matter, science is insufficient. It comes up short—wordy and complicated but still short.

"The bottom line for me, Jeannine, is that God makes no sense, but a world without God, a purely scientific universe, also makes no sense. And if you want to know the whole truth, I just prefer not to puzzle over such imponderables, which is why I do the work I do, where the numbers know their places and the equations behave themselves and the problems are all solvable."

"Kurt Gödel would have had something to say about that," she said.

"Well, yes, there is that, too. I remember how excited I was when I first worked my way through Gödel's Incompleteness Theorems. To learn that one could prove, rigorously, that logic and mathematics were themselves fundamentally flawed and limited—wow! Heady stuff! And then there's Heisenberg and quantum uncertainty. Incompleteness, undecidability, paradox—these are in the very nature of science, its methods of measurement, and the mathematical tools it depends on. So we can never know. We can even prove it, that we can never know, that it is not just us but reason itself that is limited. Which brings us back to where we started."

"It does?"

"Yes. Spinoza—you know about Spinoza? Spinoza, the supreme Jewish heretic, set out to prove, through logic alone, the existence of God. In a sense he succeeded, at least to his own satisfaction and that of his followers, but Spinoza's God turned out to be, in the end, one with the Universe itself, identical with the whole of Nature—capital N, as my wife always spelled it—and that, as I have just reiterated, is demonstrably unknowable by science and reason. We are back to another paradox."

Rosen knew that he was on a roll, and his eyes danced with excitement. "We might as well turn Spinoza on his ear. Take the set of all functions that cannot be computed, all theorems that can neither be proved nor disproved, all measurement that can never be resolved, all statements that are undecidable—and maybe throw in all unreachable, unknowable reaches of the universe—take these sets, which themselves cannot be enumerated nor limned but that we can rigorously prove exist, and call them God."

"I like it: Gödel's God. Very clever, Rosen."

"But not really original. It's the God constructed of whatever we don't know: the unknown, the unexplained, just the venerable God of the Gaps reformulated in modern metamathematics."

"God of the Gaps: which number is that?"

Rosen started to smile broadly. "Number twelve," he said. "Number twelve of *36 Arguments for the Existence of God.*"

"*A work of Fiction,*" she finished with the subtitle. "You read Rebecca Goldstein, too?"

"Of course. I loved it. The characters are a little talky and cerebral, though."

"Rosen, we're a little talky and cerebral. But are you sure it's really number twelve?"

"I don't know, I made that part up. I just remember the God of the Gaps, an argument from ignorance."

"This is more than ignorance. I think you have gone one step further. Your Gödel's God is not the God of the Unknown but the God of the Unknowable, the Unprovable, not merely the Unknown or Unproven. You've upped the ante and given God a permanent residence instead of a desert tabernacle retreating in the ever-changing sands of scientific progress."

"Yes, well, and this has been fun, but not where we started. You asked me about belief. God aside—whether Spinoza's or Gödel's or Rabbi Nick's—what I believe, what I personally believe, is that we are here for a purpose, whether preordained or of our own inventtion, it doesn't matter. It is purpose itself that matters. And I do mean 'we'—all of us, collectively, are part of something that, by its very definition, is bigger than our selves. Perhaps it ultimately comes down to the conundrum of self-awareness: we are the Universe becoming aware of itself.

"At least that's the answer I came up with for a philosophy term paper I wrote as an undergraduate."

"You are, in your own oddball ways, a deep thinker, Rosen. And you gave me so much more than I asked. I'm still just that Catholic girl turned mathematician and amateur spy who is trying to sort out what Biontolics is really about and what to do about it."

"You haven't figured it out yet? You don't know what they are doing and why this is a life-and-death issue? You really are a pure math person, Jeannine. You have to spend less time looking at the numbers and more at what the numbers represent. If the cosmologists did that, they would be more in touch with the absurdity of replacing the simple deity of biblical storytelling with an unimaginably complex narrative of numbers and equations that hover beyond compre-hension."

He spent the next quarter hour going over in detail what he had learned, starting with the first unpublished paper and leading up to the latest conclusions from his off-hours research.

"I'm still intrigued by what happened to the other original re-searchers," he announced at the end. "I've learned that Aubuchon died in 1982 of a drug overdose, Llewellyn Cass died on an expedition in Patagonia, but Janella Kai just vanished. This leaves Atchison Douglas Dougherty the only witness to history, their history, but I've hit a wall. I thought I knew how to do online research, but I'm getting nowhere."

"Maybe that's your problem, Rosen? Like your comical cosmologists, you are caught inside a box of your own making. To you, research means online research. You've rewritten Mackenzie's First Law. 'If it's not written down, it doesn't exist,' has transmogrified into the mantra of modern methods: 'If it's not on the Web, it doesn't exist.' Fail, Rosen.

"My aunt Cecelia does genealogy. If she took your approach, we would still know nothing about the Italian branch of our family. She had to go into the LDS microfilm archives to get anywhere. You need to get real, leave the virtual world behind and get your hands dirty. Go do some digging in the Boston Public Library."

They had reached a point on the shore where they would either have to start climbing over bus-size boulders or turn around. Jeannine started to turn before Rosen did and ended up stumbling as they came face-to-face, leaving only inches of supercharged air between them. Rosen caught her, looked into her eyes, and kissed her lightly, as if he could control the energy that passed between them. He pulled back, but she took his face in her hands and kissed him with all the stored up passion of weeks of pretending, leaving both of them breathless.

"I am still too Catholic," she said after a long silence. "I hear the voice of my priest telling me that you are married, that we simply cannot be involved. It makes no sense. It's not like I'm an innocent virgin. But you being married makes it different at some deeply visceral level."

"Those grooves in the Catholic cortex, again."

She laughed. "I'm sorry. You know how much I want you, and I know it's the same for you. I can feel you against me, and I want to make love right here, now, on the beach."

"On these rocks? You can't want to make love that badly."

"Oh, you might be surprised. But. What about Millie?"

As if on cue, a puff of chill wind passed over and between them. "Millie, Millicent, my wife. Yes. I have not heard from her in nearly three weeks. I don't think she is coming back. I still don't understand what happened. She got scared, but that can hardly be the whole story. There are moments when it almost feels like we were never married, that we were roommates for decades, good friends, even lovers, but certainly not husband and wife. Does that seem strange to you? Or uncaring?"

"No. Knowing you, it makes a lot of sense. I don't think you 'do' love, not the way most people do. There is a distance between you and the rest of humanity. It is not that you are never passionate, but your passion is about things, your work, not people and not a person."

"I'm sorry. Do you think it's curable?"

"Don't be sorry. I don't think it's something needing to be cured. You are who you are, and I love you."

They both froze at the speaking of the unspoken, the line that had been crossed so off-handedly. "Yes, I suppose you do," he said. "I am not there yet, which is an odd way to put it—so dispassionately to speak of passion—but I am falling in love with you, which is new and delicious. I am hoping you can wait for me to catch up."

The moment was spoiled by the muffled sound of an electric organ at a hockey game working its way up a chromatic scale. Jeannine cringed with embarrassment and fished her cell phone out of the pocket of her jeans. She looked at the caller ID but didn't answer. "It's my handler, the guy I report to about you. Should I answer?"

"No, just turn off your phone and let him get your voice mail."

She complied, then slipped the phone back into her pocket. "Where were we before ominous interruptions."

"On our way back down the beach and up to the road, where we are going to drive a few miles farther north until we find a nice little bed-and-breakfast. There we will take their best room and make the best possible use of it until morning, whereupon we will have a late break-fast before driving back to Massachusetts."

She ran her tongue over her teeth as she hesitated, but finally spoke, one husky word, "Yes."

22

The invitation, a handwritten note slipped under Rosen's front door, had come unexpectedly. When Rosen arrived at Steven King's office, the furniture had been rearranged and the Chagall poster had been taken down. A palm-sized projector on Steven's desk was painting a blue rectangle of light on the wall where the poster had been.

"Come in, Rosen. You're just in time for the next show." Steven gestured toward the chair that was now backed up against the wall opposite the blue rectangle.

"What's all this?" Rosen spread his hands as he took his seat.

"I'm a modern-day lecturer, which means I am incapable of speaking without my PowerPoint. I wanted to show you what I've been doing and did not want to send you the slide deck as an email attachment, for reasons that I am sure you can guess yourself. Please, close the door. This is a private showing that I do not want the robotics people to see."

Rosen closed the door and sat down again.

"You are a scientist, Rosen, which is a handicap in situations like this. I am a medical doctor, which carries the right advantages. Despite the oft bandied term 'medical science,' medicine is not science, it is applied technology—or, in many cases, still, applied witchcraft. The standards of evidence and the solidity of the underlying theory are less important than whether the patient gets better or worse. We do not expect or need all patients to respond as predicted, and we certainly do not need to know why something works to make use of it. You scientists, on the other hand, demand that results be reproducible and are dissatisfied with anything less than a complete and consistent explanation. And that is why, Rosen, that you continue to hover around the evidence, accumulating research, still searching for patterns and puzzling over missing pieces, when the complete story has been staring you in the face forever."

Rosen opened his mouth as if to speak, but Steven continued without pause. "Llewellyn Cass was a doctor, a brilliant and aggressively creative one, not a scientist. That is what you needed to focus on. The research you were exploring was suggestive but inconclusive. Even if you had the access and had been able to pull together all the relevant papers, you would still have been talking about patterns and possibilities, because scientifically, that is all that would be there. Medically, it is a different story."

He tapped his keyboard and the first slide appeared with a text cloud full of technical jargon at its center, the size of each term scaled to represent some measure of its importance or frequency. "If we start with the patterns you identified and outlined in your meta-analysis and follow where each lead takes us, we do not get a scientific picture. We get a treatment picture." Spokes appeared extending from the text cloud and terminating in thumbnail pictures of patients or cross sections of human organs or photomicrographs of cell cultures. "We ask ourselves not what does this mean or how does it fit with everything else, but what does it imply as the basis for a possible medical intervention. What would a doctor do with it? Not, what would a scientist make of it?"

He stood and pointed at the wall, now covered with his diagram. "This is what they are doing. It is complicated and messy, but every bit of it is quite doable on the basis of modern medicine. In fact, nearly all of it has been practicable for decades, although the means have improved over the years."

"But," Rosen began.

Steven held up his hand to stop him. "I knew that would be your first word. I can even fill in the rest of the sentence. And the next, and the next. You were going to say that this is speculative, that it jumps to conclusions, that it leaves out chains of scientific inference, that the research does not fully support it. Right?"

"Well, that's all true, isn't it?"

"Yes, and all irrelevant, because the picture I am building here is not scientific. I am painting a picture of medical practice. And let me do just that. Let me show you, for each of these nine treatment implications, what I am confident represents more or less what your colleagues are doing and have been doing for a long time."

He took his time working through the presentation, explaining for each slide what his best guess was about the treatment technique and what some of the alternatives might be, how evolving practice and technology in medicine since the original paper was published would impact how the treatments might be carried out currently.

"And that's it," he said, turning off the projector. "That is what they are doing, even though from a purely scientific perspective, they still don't know what they are doing. My guess is they are still busy trying to figure out why it all works and how it all fits together in order to make it work better or make the patient management simpler."

Rosen put his hand to his forehead. "So, the implication is that they are using costly and complicated medicine to keep themselves—or some people—from aging and dying. This is not a line of scientific inquiry but the basis for actual medical practice. And you put this together on your own?"

"Well, I am brilliant. And I do have access to some of the best facilities and smartest colleagues. But, you really did the work. It is all in your paper. Well, most of it is in your paper. You just didn't take it far enough, but it's all there for anyone with the right mindset and the motivation to figure it out. The old paper is merely a clue, yours is a map of the whole mystery. That is why it is so dangerous to them and why they cannot let you publish. But they must also be impressed with your brilliance, because no one else seems to have put it all together so clearly."

Rosen stood and started pacing in the small space. "Knowing the what makes me all the more curious about who. Who are these people and what happened to the other authors of the original paper. I need to know who I am dealing with."

"Is there nothing in the world that you think you might be better off not knowing?"

"Not much. The hour of my death, perhaps, but I believe in knowing. Knowledge is my religion, I suppose, having lost my faith in faith and then my faith in science."

"Will you tell me what you find?"

"Why?'

"Because, Rosen, I also believe in knowing."

~ ~ ~

Rosen decided to play hooky from work again, having discovered that it was too hard to do his research on weekends, when it seemed that everyone else in the Greater Boston Area was also using the public library. It was slow, frustrating work, requesting microfilm archives, threading the film through the reader, scanning through the images, and finally, finding nothing, exchanging the microfilm for the next in a series. Oddly, the pace of the search made the occasional discoveries all the sweeter. Rosen's eyes were tired, but it had been a sweet morning.

He had started with a date, a reference point from which he could move forward and back in time, the date in mid-February of 1974 when Janella Kai had apparently disappeared. The disappearance was hardly a headline story—there being nothing to report—but one short piece mentioned the police questioning a visiting professor at Harvard who was identified as one Douglas Dougherty. Another, smaller piece in *The Boston Globe* referred to the police bringing a suspect in for questioning. Rosen spun the knob to zoom in on the name of the suspect: Bram Decker. It was more than mere confirmation; it was a new direction. Rosen scanned through later issues and other Boston papers but found no other references to Decker or to suspects in the case.

He switched tactics and used his netbook to go online through the public wi-fi. He turned up nothing useful initially until he accepted Google's offer to search instead for "Bram Dekker" with a double K. Dekker, it seemed, was a common Dutch surname, and, paired with Bram and surrounded with quotes, it still yielded over 8,000 hits. Sorting through the dozens of Bram Dekkers on Facebook and LinkedIn, Rosen narrowed the field down to a handful that were old enough to be the man mentioned in the newspaper article. One, a retired computer scientist whose LinkedIn profile listed a PhD from Tufts in 1976, had a distinguished career. He had spent most of his years at the Technical University of Eindhoven, where he had teamed up with a group of cryptologists to develop new techniques for secure communications and protecting financial transactions. His LinkedIn profile noted that he was retired from the University but still worked as a consultant.

Rosen clicked through to the personal website listed and was greeted by the image of a tall, dignified man with a bushy white mustache, standing, arms folded defiantly, in front of a building that even Rosen recognized as one of Europe's biggest investment banks. Closer examination revealed that the image was a clever PhotoShop composite in which the shadows almost matched.

The contact page of the website gave a telephone number in the Netherlands and an address in The Hague but no email address. Rosen checked his watch, guessed that the time difference was probably six hours, and decided to take a chance on a telephone call.

A female voice answered, *"Hallo. Dekker Consulting is op dit moment gesloten. Laat een berichtje achter na de toon."* Rosen was about to give up when the same voice switched to English, "Hello. Dekker Consulting is closed for the day. Please leave a message after the beep."

Rosen figured he had already paid for an overseas call on his cellphone, so had nothing to lose. "This is a message for Bram Dekker. If the name Janella Kai means anything to you, please contact me by email at rosenkavelier29@gmail.com." He started to spell out the email address when a voice on the line interrupted him.

"This is Dekker. Who is this? What do you want? What do you know about Janella Kai?" The man spoke in a soft baritone, with a pronounced Dutch accent.

"Dr. Dekker, this is Dr. Rosen David here. I am sorry to bother you at this hour, but I am calling from Boston where I am doing some research, trying to find out something about a Janella Kai who lived in the area in the 1970s and did some research that I am interested in." There was a long silence on the line. "Are you still there? I am looking for the Bram Dekker who also lived here in the 1970s and who might know something about her."

"You must forgive me. It has been a very long time since I heard that name, a very long time. I doubt seriously that I can be of any help to you. I really don't know anything about her. What is it exactly that you are interested in?"

Rosen was thinking that two could play this game. "I thought that you might be able to tell me what you know. This newspaper article I was reading said that she had disappeared in 1974 and that you were possibly the last person to see her."

"Why are you interested in such a very old story, Dr. Rosen?"

"It's Dr. David, but you can call me Rosen. I am really interested in a research paper that Kai co-authored: 'Cancer expression, cell longevity, and mosaicism in Rattus Norvegicus'."

"I think you have reached the wrong person, Dr. David. I am not that kind of a doctor. I am a computer consultant."

"Yes, I know. I'm also in computers. Well, mathematics—same difference these days. Look, I just want to talk with you."

There was another silence of several seconds, then, "I am sorry, but you are wasting your time. As I said, you have reached the wrong person. Good luck and goodbye." The call was disconnected.

Rosen stared at his cell phone before closing it. "I don't think so, Dr. Dekker," he said to the silent phone. "I think I have reached the right person. But what next? That's the big question now. What next?"

Rosen continued to dig through newspaper archives looking for more stories, but finally gave up after another hour. Before leaving the library, he logged into his web-mail account. There was a message from info@bramdekker.com.

> I dislike email even more than I dislike telephones, but I feel that I owe you an apology for hanging up on you today. You deserve at least common courtesy. It is true that you reached the wrong person, because I really do know nothing about Janella Kai. But what I do not know is not a matter for discussion in email or by telephone. The question is whether your travels ever bring you to the Netherlands. Perhaps we can sometime share a beer and speak of distant days.

"The question is," Rosen said to the screen of his netbook, "What is the cheapest airfare to The Hague." He started to research the question.

~ ~ ~

It turned out there were no cheap flights directly to Rotterdam-Den Haag airport, so Rosen decided to fly into Amsterdam's Schiphol and take a train. His departure from Boston was delayed by inbound equipment, and after landing in Amsterdam, he managed to become completely confused by the train schedule to Den Haag. The address for Dekker Consulting turned out to be in the beach district of Scheveningen. By the time Rosen figured out the tram system and then walked to the right neighborhood, it was already late afternoon. He had deliberately said nothing about his trip to anyone, least of all to Dr. Dekker, so it was with some trepidation that he pressed the button next to the name plate at the entrance. He recognized the deep voice that sprang from the intercom saying something in Dutch.

"Dr. Dekker, it's Rosen David. I'm here to have that glass of beer with you."

A pulse of laughter pierced the afternoon quiet. "Ha! I should have known that this is the sort of serious fellow you were, having tracked me down in the first place. Well, then, you might as well come on up." The door latch released with a loud clunk and buzz.

The office turned out to be a second-floor walkup studio that seemed to double as computer center and apartment. The main room held a desk, a side table straddling a computer and topped by an all-in-one printer-copier-fax, and several swivel chairs. A foldout sofa bed under the windows on the far wall left little exposed floor space. What might have once been a bedroom off to one side now hosted a round conference table ringed by four executive chairs. A credenza against one wall was arrayed with dozens of assorted glasses, a coffee machine, and a dorm-style cube of a refrigerator. On the opposite side of the main room, a kitchen nook was curtained off by a sheet of ecru lace that might have been intended that way or merely discolored by age.

"Not much of a headquarters for one of Europe's top security consultants, wouldn't you say, but then I am really only an amateur, at least nowadays. Please have a seat." He gestured toward the windows and the sofa bed. The windows looked out over a small inner courtyard crisscrossed by colorful plantings of tulips and greenery. "Let me get you that beer. You have come a long way for a drink; it should be something special." He slipped into the bedroom-conference room and returned a minute later carrying two graceful, gold-rimmed glasses of dark amber beer. "This is a favorite of mine, Hertog Jan, from a little brewery in a small town about 100 kilometers from here. I used to have to drive there to get it, but now they have a webshop, and they ship. And, of course, as is the custom among serious beer drinkers here, it must be sipped from the correct glasses, the official ones from the brewery. So," he handed one tall glass to Rosen, raised his own, smiling. *"Gezondheid!"* His soft but resonant voice filled the small room.

Rosen raised his glass and lightly tapped it against the other. "Cheers!"

"Said like a good Bostonian, Rosen," he declared, as he pulled one of the chairs over nearer the sofa and sat in it. "I did love it there. Such an alive city. And for a student in those days, at least in Somerville where

I was, cheap living. I was there on full scholarship and had a small stipend and wanted for nothing. Never since."

"But your presence should not be an excuse to indulge in nostalgia. You have come too far merely to humor an old man."

"I came here to meet you." He took a second sip of the beer and savored it. "You live here?" He gestured. Bram nodded. "Not married, I take it."

"Not now. But twice. Once to an Indonesian girl here and once, very briefly, to a girl in Barcelona. Neither lasted, but both had lasting consequences. Those are my two daughters," he said, pointing to a pair of small framed photos on the wall. "Catrijn, on the left, married a Japanese-American and now teaches English in Tokyo. Jacinta, on the right, is a pharmacist in Barcelona, not married, not interested."

"You have beautiful children."

"Past tense. I have their pictures, now, but nothing else. I have a long history of short-term success and long-term failure with the females of the species, starting with my beautiful Janella. I knew her for only a few weeks, but they were intense and wonderful weeks, filled with deep discussions that went on through the night. But I am being too personal, and you must have specific questions, hopefully not about forgotten conversations or long-lost love."

"I want to know what happened to Janella Kai. And I want to know about this paper." He pulled the copy of Dougherty, Cass, Aubuchon, and Kai from his backpack.

"Ah yes, looks familiar." Bram crossed the room to the desk, opened a center drawer, and pulled out a duplicate of the paper. "I knew that someday, sooner or later, someone would find it and make sense of it and do something with it or about it. So, I saved it."

"What about Janella Kai? What happened to her?"

"She's dead."

"You know that for certain?"

"Yes, for certain."

"How is that?"

"Simple. If she were alive, we would have known, the world would know. You have to understand about Janella. She was an unstoppable force, a tiny package of pure, unbounded energy. She would never have walked away from this," he waved the paper, "and she could not have been made to keep quiet, either.

"No, she is dead. I killed her. I killed Janella Kai, my first real love and the most beautiful woman I have ever known and possibly the smartest, as well. I killed her."

Rosen said nothing as he stared into his half-empty beer glass.

"I remember that night, Dr. David. It is as real to me now as this paper is. I can still see her as she left me."

23

Janella stood in the small kitchen of Bram's apartment, her future held in her teeth. She sucked air to keep from getting the stapled photo-copy soggy as she used both hands to engage the slide of her fur-trimmed leather jacket. She zipped it with a sharp flip of her hand, then grabbed her gaudy plaid scarf. With a single helicopter gesture above her head, she wrapped its six-foot length twice around her neck, knocking the paper out of her mouth. She retrieved it, brushed a dirty smudge from the paper, then slipped it into a much-used manila envelope.

Nearly a year of her life was in that paper—perhaps more. She had typed the final copy, and much of the wording was hers. It was also her attentive work with the lab rats that had first drawn attention to the anomalous drug interactions. She understood that the findings were significant but had always had a tendency to lose herself in technical detail and the day-to-day operation of experiments, often missing the grander scientific implications of research, even when it was her own work. Now she understood what was really at stake and how much she was risking in bringing the paper.

She pressed closed the metal tabs on the envelope flap and sighed. "I have to go, Bram. Really."

Bram smiled down at her from the height of his slim Dutch frame. "It's not that late. Stay for a little longer," he pleaded, as he slowly unzipped her jacket again and slipped a hand under her sweater. "You are so beautiful, Janella. And you have the most beautiful little tits."

"They're too little," she said. "It's my mother's fault. She told me that Brazilian girls had small breasts and big butts, as if that made it a good thing." Bram laughed as he shook his head, took another sip of beer, and tweaked her nipple.

"Bram, stop it," Janella snapped. "I really do have to go. Douglas wants me in the lab early tomorrow."

"Oh, so now your professor has become Douglas? I don't understand what you see in that old man."

"He's not old. And what I see in him is the same thing I see in you, my young Dutch stallion. I told you, I find that the sexiest thing about a man is his brains."

Bram brushed a splotch of beer foam from his blond mustache and flashed a slightly inebriated grin at her. "So, I am your *smart* Dutch stallion, then, a 'Clever Hans' maybe. I can even compute powers of two with my foot." He started tapping on the floor. "Does he know, this professor of yours? I mean, does he know about us?"

"Sure, I told him after the party." She had met Bram three weeks earlier at a beer blast in a mutual friend's apartment two floors up. She had arrived with girlfriends from Tufts but very shortly left with Bram to come down to his place. They had been like rabbits ever since.

"You told him? And it's okay with him?"

"I told him; I didn't ask for his permission. I don't think he's completely happy with it, but that's his problem. I think he'd be more upset about our discussing the research than about our making love. He is very possessive about this work."

"I don't understand you Americans. Are you saying that you and the professor are still screwing? I don't think I approve."

"Do you think I need your approval, Bram? You don't own me. Besides, love is good. More is better. I would expect that you would agree, my adorable Dutchman."

"Where did you get that speech from? Some peacenik flower children you met when you were at that conference in California?" he said, curling his lip in disdain.

"I went to California to deliver a paper, Bram, not to visit communes."

"You? You delivered a paper? Yourself?"

"Yes, myself. And I told you. And stop that." She pushed him away. "It was based on my thesis."

"Your thesis? But I thought you said you never graduated. What are you talking about?"

"I started an honors thesis before I quit. I told you that the night we met. I finished the work on my own time, wrote it up, and got it accepted at this conference."

"More work with Norwegian rats? Tell me, do Norwegian rats squeal with an accent?"

"No, my Dutch dimwit. Why is it so hard for men to take us seriously. Small women have it doubly hard. Do you know what they did? They actually brought out a telephone book for me to stand on so I could reach the microphone and see over the podium. Oh, that was a big laugh—great start to my fifteen minutes of fame."

"What did you do?"

"I walked around to the front of the podium, twisted the microphone down on its gooseneck, held up the San Francisco Yellow Pages, and said, 'My thesis.' That got another big laugh, but at least this time they were on my side."

"Remind me what that paper was about," he said.

"Drug resistance, drug resistance in S. Aureus."

"I'm against it, you know. We shouldn't resist drugs," he teased, pausing for another chug from the near-empty bottle.

"You are incorrigible, Bram Dekker. That's exactly what I mean. You men take us seriously as long as you are trying to get us into bed. Afterwards, it's back to the little jokes. And, seriously, I need to get home."

"You know, I do not think I approve of your hippy philosophy. It should not be that way. One man, one girl: that's the way of things. Or at least one at a time."

"That's not me. Life's too short," she said, squirming as he circled her nipple with his thumb. "And stop that. You have a one-track mind, Bram Dekker."

"It is not true that I have a one-track mind," Bram said, shifting his hand to her other breast. "See? I have a two-track mind."

"I am serious, I keep telling you. I have to get back to Cambridge."

"I'll drive you. It's too far and too cold."

Janella extracted Bram's hand from under her sweater, zipped up her jacket, and pointedly stared down at the Grolsch in his other hand. "No thanks," she said.

"Ah, but the Nederlanders can hold their alcohol better than Americans. See?" he said, taking two steps backward and stumbling into the refrigerator.

"Yes, I see," she said, grabbing her purse off the table. "I'll call you tomorrow after I finish at the lab." She stood on tiptoes to kiss his chin, then let herself out of the basement apartment.

~ ~ ~

Bram finished his narration with head bowed, then looked at Rosen.

"What I have never told anyone," he said, "is that she came back to the apartment that night, but I was too drunk. By the time I struggled awake and staggered to the door, she was gone. There was a note slipped between the door and the frame. It said to please return the paper, that her professor, her lover, would kill her if he found out that she had showed it to me and left it.

"That's what he did. He killed her, which means that I killed her, because I was too slow and too drunk to let her in and give her the paper. I never told the police about the note or the paper because I was afraid of getting into trouble. I was still more than a year short of finishing my doctorate, and, selfishly, I didn't want to jeopardize that for a lost cause.

"But I have paid for my cowardice. I have felt guilty ever since, and every year, when the Ides of February approach, I go into a depression that I am unable to fight. We Dutch are given to depression, you know. Perhaps it is because so many of us live below sea level and beneath clouded skies. We are low creatures, creatures of the lowlands, the Netherlands. And in the middle of every February, I sink lower still and drink until I pass out on that very couch where you sit, and no one or no thing can arouse me from that drunken stupor, yet I dream. I dream of a young women with golden eyes and lightning behind them, and I know that I have killed her."

"And the paper?" Rosen asked. "The paper that you preserved and ultimately posted on the Web, do you know what it is?"

"Yes, it is a sort of crude treasure map, a way pointer to the true Fountain of Youth. And Janella's professor, Dr. Atchison Dougherty, tried to follow it for the rest of his life. Now his son carries on the search with his Biontolics Research and its far-flung appendages that reach like tentacles into companies around the globe. Oh, yes, I know about his pursuit. I read about his father in the financial press and now I follow the son on the same quixotic quest, but they are both stupid. They did not have Janella nor Janella's brilliance to shine a light in the right direction. Instead, they chase shadows. I read what they publish, at least the abstracts, and they are still missing the mark and getting no closer with time."

"What's this about a son? I didn't know Dougherty had a son."

"Yes, Junior, the man who now heads Biontolics. I have seen his picture."

"You've seen a ghost. That is Atchison Dougherty. That is Janella's professor."

"No, I think you are mistaken. Dougherty would be in his nineties, and the head of Biontolics is half that."

"You misread the literature coming out of Biontolics. It is a diversion to look like great effort and little progress. The real results never get outside. The real research, based on what Janella helped produce, really works. Atchison Dougherty, the one whose picture you have seen, is well over ninety. They found the Fountain, and they are keeping the location secret and saving the waters for themselves."

Bram stood and started pacing, his head nearly brushing the ceiling of the apartment. "For the last few years I have said, knowing what little still lies before me, that were Atchison Dougherty still alive, I would kill him myself, that it would be a good use of my last years, to right the wrong and bring Janella's killer to the end he deserves. And now you are saying that Professor Dougherty, Janella's Professor Dougherty, is still alive and running a company that will keep him alive as long as he wants."

"I am saying that."

"Then you have brought me a great gift—a reason to live—and an end to depression. I will kill this Atchison Dougherty, I will. I am a computer scientist, but I am a cyber-security specialist who has long consorted with people whose work weaves in and out between the light and the dark. I will find a way.

"But, my new friend, there is so much for us to talk about. You must stay. You must have dinner with me. Do you know *rijsttaffel?*" Rosen shook his head. "Then you must learn. Rijsttaffel is Indonesia's contribution to Dutch cooking. Literally, it just means rice table, but in fact it is a near endless parade of spicy delectables. I know a place not fifteen minutes from here, an easy walk, and an eating experience. Come, first another beer, then hours of good food."

24

Atchison Douglas Doherty was approaching one hundred and was not only, arguably, the best looking man his age, but, although never having ever been singled out by *Forbes*, he was the wealthiest. He reveled in both secret ironies, that he was all but invisible, except for his indulgence as CEO of Biontolics, and that he was still around—and young. His time in Aruba under an assumed name and using one of his many passports, had rejuvenated him. The scuba, the sailing, and the lovely and compliant barmaid, had been precisely what his doctor would have ordered, if Andras had ever bothered to be more than a technician. Ten days of diving and dalliance had proven to be just what he had needed to pull himself out of the pool of frustration into which he had plunged.

He was looking forward to a good glass of champagne in his suite. He never drank on airplanes. The wine, even in first class, was never up to his standards, which seemed to rise higher and higher as the years progressed. A thousand-dollar bottle of vintage champagne was routine—and a pittance in the scheme of things. He owned a *négociant* and a winery and large holdings of vines in several of his favorite areas of France and Italy, and the success of those investments only guaranteed a steady expansion of his holdings and an endless supply of the best of the very best. His partner, Andras, on the other hand, was an excellent scientist and skilled physician who lacked all imagination and was limited in initiative. Dougherty knew he would have to replace the man eventually, but eventually was a term that on the scale of Dougherty's calendar could be decades off. The right replacement would come along, of that he was certain. One only needed patience—and the longevity to exercise it fully—to find that, truly, all things come to him who waits. Dougherty was one who waited and one who enjoyed the wait most thoroughly.

He nodded to his men as he reentered his London townhouse. On the stoop, in the entry foyer, and in the lane at the back, there were the men, his men. Security was easy, even if not cheap. But it was merely part of the cost of doing business for Dougherty, part of the business of living indefinitely.

There was a new man at the entry to his suite, a tall, wiry man with jet-black hair who filled his post with dignity and professionalism, almost imperceptibly speaking into his radio link as he opened the door for Dougherty. When he pushed ahead and led the way into the room, Dougherty began to wonder about his professional zeal.

"Let me check the room for you, sir. It's been unattended in your absence," the man offered in explanation. He switched on the lights, did a quick circuit of the room, opening each door to adjoining rooms, and turning on all the lights. "I think we can safely conclude we are alone," he said.

"Yes, well, I assume we can," Dougherty said, with growing irritation. "Thank you, and good night, Mister, er . . ."

"Dekker, Bram Dekker, at your service, Professor."

Dougherty turned and studied the man. In bright light, his lined face betrayed the coloring in his hair. Dougherty, calmly reached into his pocket and fingered his personal alarm as he considered his options for the short moments that remained before his real protectors arrived. "I don't believe we've met, Mister Dekker."

"No, we've never met, but that doesn't mean we have nothing in common. Indeed, we have something rather special in common, both having bedded Janella Kai." He waited for the message to sink in.

Dougherty glanced anxiously toward the door.

"Oh, you can relax, Professor. Your security people are not coming. I took the liberty of disabling the receiver for your wireless panic button. I have had nearly a week to decipher all the details and attend to all the minutiae while you cavorted in Aruba. What was that wench's name? Maria? Yes, that was it. Seemed to take a very quick fancy to you, a man nearly four times her age. One would almost think she had some extra incentive. But then, you were also so generous with your bonuses, too. I am certain she appreciated every pound sterling."

Dougherty, his military demeanor restored, stepped back and reached toward the bar. "I trust you will not be offended, Mr. Dekker, if I pour myself a drink. I would offer one to you if I thought you would accept."

"Oh, I most definitely would accept. A glass of the finest is just the ff naf

thing for a dying man."

Dougherty frowned slightly in uncertainty.

"Oh, I have no illusion that I am going to make it out of here alive after I am finished with you. It's a small price for divine vengeance."

"And you partake of the divine?"

"No, only the vengeance part. As one of the immortals, you would probably be closer to the divine, except that tonight I will conclusively demonstrate that you are not immortal. As to the divine part, that will be between you and your deity. I forget where Dante Alighieri placed the simple murderers. That would be you, were it a simple matter of murder." He noticed Dougherty eyeing the sidearm at his waist. "Ah, yes. The instrument of said divine vengeance. A Glock 29, 9mm, a good choice for your security personnel. With its 'Safe Action' trigger-release safety, even a martial virgin, an inept user such as your humble nemesis here, can be effective without special attention to preparatory steps."

He withdrew the Glock from its polymer holster and aimed it toward Dougherty's chest. "Double tap. That's what it's called in the trade. One to the chest and then one to the head for insurance. Your guards get this drilled into them. There must never be any survivors to offer their own, potentially contradictory version of any 'encounter,' am I right?"

"What do you want, Dekker? I can offer you considerable incentives to walk away from this."

"No, we both know that I would not get to walk very far, and you would still be walking long after I was only a footnote to your history. What do I want? I want you dead. Before that, I want to know what happened to Janella."

"Are you still hung up on some grad-school affair with a teenager? You're a grown man, Dekker, an old man. Get over it." Dougherty started to walk away, reaching the door to the bedroom before turning. There was a Beretta in his hand. "You missed your moment, Dekker, because you wanted to hear me say it more than you wanted to see me dead. The thing to do was to shoot me in the back while you had the chance. Now the chance is gone, the one chance you have been saving up for, waiting and hanging onto for decades—the chance to shoot me and end your own torture.

"You think I don't know about you, Bram Dekker? You, the morose, pathetic alcoholic whose ritual of remembrance is to drink yourself into oblivion, just as you did in 1974. See, I know all about it, the whole story. I have sources—eyes and ears everywhere. I have to, or I would not still be here. Your bright but ignorant new friend thinks it is all about genetics and immunology. No, it is about vigilance. The biology is far simpler than the social engineering of survival. And you still stand there, finger on the trigger, paralyzed by your own ineptitude."

Dougherty fired his Beretta without even taking aim, hitting Dekker in the forearm and sending the Glock tumbling to the floor. "Survival skills, my Dutch dodo. You are extinct. What do you think I do with my weekends? I learn. I practice. At living, I am the professional. You are the amateur. Maybe I am the first, because who before me has had the time and health to get really good at living?"

Dekker held his arm. The pain and the blood running through his fingers were draining the life from him, sucking away the energy that had brought him to London and sustained him through the logistics of his assault. His vision began to blur.

"So, goodbye, Dr. Dekker. You failed. But you will die knowing not only that, but also the bitter truth that makes it such a pathetic failure. You were right all along. I killed Janella. I caught up with her for a second time just after she finished pounding on your door and was leaving. I strangled her from behind with her own pink-and-purple garrote before she could bring any of her graceful Brazilian martial arts into play. There was no one around on that snowy night, no witnesses. I had a lab at Harvard at my disposal. Disposal of a body was no great challenge. I figured you were a setup as an obvious perpetrator, but you were just a little too clever, so you got off and went home. I have followed you—back to Holland, over to Madeira, home again to Eindhoven, jiggity-jig." Dougherty smiled, pleased with himself and this version of that night's events.

"Why? Why would you do it? Why did you have to kill her?"

"Because she stood in the way, because it had become clear to me that she could never be controlled. She was blocking the way to immortality."

"You sold your soul."

"I don't believe in souls, Mr. Dekker."

"You do not have to believe in a soul to sell it. Hell, you don't even have to have one to sell it, and you sold yours."

"Well, then, I guess that is that. I have nothing to sell and you have nothing I am interested in buying. So, goodbye." He fired once, catching Dekker at the bottom of the ribcage. "Oh, I am out of practice. Too low. Ah, well. Double tap, as you said." He expertly put the coup de grace into Dekker's forehead, then reached around the corner to the wired panic button concealed on the door jamb of the bedroom. "There's been an intruder," he announced to the now-active hidden microphone. "Get your men in here. Now!"

"Ah, Edgar, I am glad you are here," Ferguson said, when Mbutsu arrived at the clinic. "We should talk. You have been busy, from what I hear. Now you are sending troops over the border and claiming a wedge of land on the other side of the river, not so? Here, come sit and we will talk while I ready the first injections." Ferguson gestured toward the examining table.

Mbutsu did not look good. Recovery from his wounds and the two rounds of surgery, even with all the medical miracles at his disposal, had taken a toll. The tall and tempered warrior stood stooped in the doorway, one hand on the doorjamb. The young bodyguards who accompanied him seemed to tower over him. Behind him, almost out of sight, waited an old man who looked vaguely familiar to Ferguson.

Mbutsu gestured for the man to come ahead. "You remember Fallu, Doctor. He was to be my tester, but you talked me out of it. I have changed my mind and will not be talked out of it this time. I want you to give him the injections first—all of them. He is, remember, an old man and of another tribe, so we do not need to worry what will become of him."

Ferguson, sensing that there would be no winning the argument a second time, nodded to the man and patted the padded table. "Here. Sit here," he said in the dialect that fitted the man's style of dress.

Fallu's face lit up, and he answered in kind. "I am not afraid."

"Of course not, a brave old warrior such as you, who protects his president. But, you have nothing to fear from this," Ferguson said, holding up a syringe. "This will do nothing to you, and you can return home tonight to your village and tell tales of how you met the Doctor's doctor yourself."

"I am told that I will not return to my village, but still, I am not afraid."

Ferguson looked over to Mbutsu, who was clearly relishing his moment of small triumph over his doctor. "There is one in this room, it would seem, who is not afraid," Ferguson said pointedly. "And there is nothing to fear in any of these, as I am sure you know, Mr. President. So, let us begin."

Feguson, though he thought the entire exercise to be silly and pointless, played along and put Fallu through every procedure and administered every injection before moving on to Mbutsu. The man's brave front wavered only once, when he was being slid into the big magnet of the MRI. When the rapid fire banging began halfway through the imaging, the man jumped involuntarily and struck his head against the top of the enclosure. It ruined the series, but since it was only an empty exercise, Ferguson pretended that there was no problem and continued as soon as the man was calmed.

At the end of the day, having done everything twice, there was still more to do, and Ferguson realized that his fantasy of a quick visit would not be fulfilled. He pulled Mbutsu aside and spoke to him in English, which he suspected neither the guards nor the test subject would understand.

"Let the man go, Edgar. Let him return home. This business is slowing us down, and you need to complete the treatments."

Mbutsu scowled in contempt. "He is a soldier. He fought in the revolution—on the wrong side, yes, but he fought well and was spared. He cannot return to his village. He has seen and heard too much."

Ferguson, sensing an impasse, said nothing.

"You have grown soft, Doctor. Your life has been too easy. You do not seem to realize that living exacts a price, and the price of living is lives. Some must be taken. It is the way of things."

Ferguson, seeing a parade of faces pass through his mind, glowered at Mbutsu. "Trust me, Edgar, I know about the price of living. I understand sacrifice."

"Good. I hope so. Then I will see you at dinner tonight, and we will talk of other matters."

"Thank you, Your Excellency, but I shall not be at dinner tonight. I am tired and will simply dine in my suite, if that is acceptable. We will have extra days because," he paused, picking his words with care, "because of the new procedure. I will join you for dinner on another night."

Mbutsu snorted his disapproval but nodded in agreement. "Tomorrow, then, good Doctor. More tests and a new tester."

As soon as Mbutsu was out of the building, Ferguson hurried

through his chores and slipped into his private office. There was no place on the grounds, probably no place in Mbutsu City, that was truly safe and private, but on this trip, Ferguson had brought with him more than just medical equipment. He pulled the scanner from his medical bag and carefully swept the room before going to the window to open the blinds, count three, and close them again. He poured himself a glass of bourbon from the bottle in his desk, and waited for his meeting.

"That was fantastic, Jeannine. How do you keep doing it?" Her invitation to Sunday morning brunch in her condo had turned out to mean a spread of a potato-leek frittata topped with goat cheese, a fruit compote with rum-soaked melon balls, and fresh-baked sweet rolls with pistachio topping.

"You've got a caramel-pistachio bit clinging to your chin, dear." She mirror-mimed wiping her own chin as he dabbed with his napkin. "You got it. And this, this was nothing. When my dad was alive, he used to put together a buffet of twice as many dishes every Sunday. My mother and sisters and I would return from mass to a house filled with the scent of fresh breads and sausages and honey-lime ham. Even the drinks were special. He used to make this bergamot-infused blood-orange nectar that he would serve slightly warmed with a stemmed cherry hooked over the rim of the glass. My mother was a good but unimaginative cook. My father, on the other hand, was an artist with a sauté pan and a wire whisk. Neither of my sisters go near the kitchen. They were smart; they married men who could cook. I never found the man, so I learned to cook instead."

"Your father would be proud."

"No, he wouldn't. He was proud of my sisters for marrying well, which he maintained was every woman's first obligation. After that, babies were next on the list. He always said I was too smart, too cerebral. I scared the boys. It didn't help that I was taller than every boy in my class and wore glasses that made me look like a librarian. The final blow between us came when I stopped going to mass. He never went himself, but he expected me to go with Mom, Elise, and Angela. He asked me why I didn't go, and I told him. That was the last conversation we ever had. He was dying in the hospital after his heart attack, and he wouldn't talk with me. He was a stubborn, unforgiving hypocrite to his last breath."

"What did you say to him that triggered that?"

"I told him the truth, that I didn't believe in God. He covered his ears and turned away from me. Mom said he was crushed; she never asked me whether I was crushed to find myself instantly demoted from his favorite, his little girl, to the daughter from whom he turned when I entered the room. When he spoke of me at all, it was as if I were not there, as if I had died when I was fourteen.

"Do you know, that single, two-line dialogue was the only mention of God or religion ever between us. 'Why won't you go to mass anymore?' 'Because I don't believe in God anymore.' That was it. We had never talked about it before, and we never talked again, or at least he didn't. I tried on many occasions to talk about many things, but he would walk away as if I wasn't there.

"Angela and Elise were always so much smarter than I was when it came to Dad, when it came to men. They never spoke with him about things that mattered, which proved to be good practice for their marriages. I ought to know, because I am the one they have always confided in, still do.

"I was always the one who wouldn't settle. Now, here I am, thirty-seven and single and in love with a married man who talks with me and listens and never turns away. How lucky and how horrible."

Rosen wiped his fingers before reaching across the table and taking her hand. As he did so, he realized that it was a simple gesture that Millie had done many times but was a first for him, such a small thing and yet so foreign. Jeannine started to cry.

"I don't envy my sisters. They have the house and the three children each and busy lives, but I know how empty their lives are. I decided long ago that I would rather come home to an empty house than to an empty life."

She pulled away from him and stood, wiping her eyes of tears that wouldn't stop. Rosen stood with her and wiped his own eyes of tears that he didn't understand but that kept coming nonetheless. "I love you," she said between sniffles.

"I love you," he said, his own voice and rhythm echoing hers, as his tears and his futile fingers wiping at his cheeks mirrored hers. There was the width of the breakfast bar between them, but Rosen had never felt closer to any human being before. He wanted to pull her to him, and at the same time he wanted to stand where he was, where he could see her and marvel in her, feeling her strength and her vulnerability, the very image of his own. It was vertiginous, to see her seeing him seeing her, to understand and be understood and to know that she also understood and was understood. He broke the magic with a word: "Wow!"

She threw her arms around him. "I love you I love you I love you I love you, Rosen David."

"And I love you, Jeannine Carsten, and I don't know what else to say. I love you I love you I love you. That's it."

She sniffled and wiped her nose on his shoulder and pulled back sheepishly. "I've gotten tears and mucous all over you, and you just keep smiling at me and crying with me."

"Hey, what are friends for? Here,"—he reached for a clean napkin— "give this a try while I clear the dishes."

She sniffled again and started to cough. "That doesn't sound good?" he said. "Are you coming down with a summer cold? Or is this allergies? There's so much I don't know about you. I'm in love with you, and I don't even know what you're allergic to."

"Cats."

"Really?"

"Really, I saw the musical and have never been the same since. Anything by Andrew Lloyd Weber gives me hives."

Rosen stuck his tongue out at her. "Really, I want to know everything about you that I don't already know. Everything."

"That sounds like Gödel's God again. 'Just tell me what you don't know and I'll tell you all about it.'" She laughed and started into a coughing fit again, but she was clearly enjoying teasing him as much as he was enjoying being teased.

Rosen grinned over his shoulder as he scraped the dishes and sorted them into the dishwasher. "It is so easy with you, so easy to understand you." He was thinking of Millie and feeling guilty about the comparison.

"That's because I'm you. We have the same goofy, sarcastic sense of humor; we both prefer probabilities to people; we prefer red wine to white, websites to newspapers, and making love to doing dishes." She tugged at his arm. "And, you are, I know, already making an inventory list of counter-evidence, thinking of all the ways that we are not alike, exactly as I was doing the very moment I opened my mouth. Right?"

"Uncannily true, my insightful darling. So, are you saying that it is the very fact that there are so many ways that we are different that makes us so alike?"

"No, dearest logician, I am saying we are alike in needing the differences, illusory or not. We are alike in our need to catalog and contradict each other back into safe corners where we are not quite so exposed and vulnerable. Now, put down the fuckin' frying pan and come make love to me before we both start coming up with a list of reasons why not to."

~ ~ ~

The afternoon passed in a mist of more tears and teasing and quiet lovemaking. Over a simple dinner of noodles and pan-roasted vegetables topped with toasted black sesame seeds that Jeannine insisted was the simplest thing she knew how to cook, they talked. Rosen filled her in about his research and his surprise trip to Holland.

"I wish you had told me then, had trusted me," she said. "I could have helped with a cover story at work. As it was, I think nobody believed me when I said I didn't know where you were, which probably cast suspicion on both of us."

He scraped at his plate with his fork, rescuing the last bits of sesame seeds. "I would imagine by now that half of Ipswich knows that we are having an affair. It's such a small town and Biontolics is such a small-town company, even if it is part of a multinational hydra."

"That's not what I mean about suspicions. I'm talking about Biontolics, my handler, the German who seems of late to be spending as much time over here as in Europe. He asks a lot of questions about you and why I have nothing useful to report. I imagine he is catching on by now. That's his job, Rosen, catching on to things. I never liked him, but I did like the intrigue. Now I like him even less and the intrigue not at all."

"Remember," Rosen said, "it was your idea for me to dig into real-world records in the first place. I thought I was being smart tracking down Bram Dekker and getting his story. But the man was obsessed with Janella Kai and convinced that Dougherty had killed her. He told me, he was working on a plan to get to Dougherty and take him out. Then nothing: nothing in the news about him or about Dougherty, no replies to my emails to Dekker, and all I get is the answering service when I call his office. We have another disappearance to add to the ledger."

"Maybe we need to get out, Rosen, do what Millie did and get lost."

"I don't think that option is open for us, Jeannine. You are entangled with the enterprise, and I am an established threat. All the best evidence is that these people play for keeps, and I am no good at this game. I don't know the rules and am clueless when it comes to tactics and strategy. I don't even know what our assets are."

"Not to put a corny spin on it, but we have each other. And our brains. And we have something that they don't want us to have."

"I would put that in the liability column," he said. "And it's my brains that got us into trouble in the first place. And when it comes to you, I am a definite liability. So, our spreadsheet is speckled with red cells, and we are so deep underwater that we should be wearing scuba gear right now. Our big problem is that we are swimming with sharks, and they see that we are a threat to them."

"Then we need to stop being a threat to them. Either we have to disappear so deep in the woods that even their millions and minions can't track us, or we have to trick them into thinking we are dead. Or maybe we convince them that we are not a threat."

Rosen nodded slowly, then noticed that she was nodding in the same way.

~ ~ ~

At first, Rosen had no idea how to do it, but Jeannine showed him the way, the simple algorithm that would home in on a solution. All he needed to do was the opposite of what he thought would take him forward, the inverse of what he thought made sense. He started systematically committing professional suicide, championing lost causes, dropping balls and missing deadlines, citing the wrong people and misspelling the names of the right ones. He got himself barred from posting on websites and managed to get posted papers taken down for rules violations.

In the meanwhile, Jeannine started eagerly passing on information that turned out to be true but of no consequence. She let it become obvious to even the deliberately impervious that she and Rosen were involved, and she accidentally left her desk with a confidential page open on her monitor. Both of them were rapidly gaining reputations as well-meaning but inept people who had compounded their incompetence and bad judgment by falling in love with each other.

The ruse began to work with everyone except those who really counted.

27

Rosen missed the first two notices from DHL, but managed to get off work early enough on the third try to be home when the yellow truck with its red markings pulled up outside, almost completely blocking the narrow street. He signed for the envelope, thanked the driver, and pulled the opener strip. The packet was empty. He was about to dismiss it as a joke, but first inverted it while shaking vigorously. A single, small slip of paper fluttered to the floor and landed blank-side up. He turned it over. There was one word written in neat capitals diagonally across the middle: PATAGONIA. A red X chopped through the word, and in tiny, disciplined script at the bottom of the paper, was the signature: Dekker.

The tracking on the packet indicated that it contained documents, had no value, and had originated with the concierge at a London hotel more than a week earlier. Rosen was about to throw it away when, on impulse, he pried it open once more. Clinging to the inside at the bottom was a sticky note. In the same neat hand was written a name: Charles Ferguson.

Rosen did not recognize the name, but it did not take long to start uncovering the footprints of Dr. Charles Henry Ferguson on the Web, although it was some hours before the link to Patagonia became clear. There was a discontinuity in the searchable records. Dr. Ferguson had been born in 1952, but it was not until early 1993 that there were any traces of him, an unpublished conference paper on medical crisis management of hyper-immune response, a subject that was too far afield to have made it into Rosen's previous searches. Then nothing, as if Ferguson, too, had disappeared from the professional scene. Rosen switched screens to his notes and found that Llewellyn Cass had disappeared on expedition in Patagonia in late 1992. He flipped back to the conference reference and clicked through to an abstract for the paper itself. It was co-authored by Abraham Colfax and Charles Ferguson. A note at the bottom acknowledged the debt owed to the late Llewellyn Cass for the use of his case studies.

"Thank you Bram Dekker," Rosen said aloud. "Now it's I who owe you a beer."

There it was, the missing link from Llewellyn Cass to someone else, a Charles Ferguson. What exactly was Bram trying to tell him? He returned to the first note, with the big red X through the word Patagonia. Not Patagonia. No Patagonia? What? Then it hit him. Cass had not died in Patagonia. There were two survivors from the original research team. Cass was still alive; Llewellyn Cass was Charles Ferguson. Now he just needed to track down Ferguson.

He used SkypeOut to call Jeannine's cellphone, then thought better of it. He looked at his watch and figured she would still be up. Better not to use the phone, he thought. He could drive up to Newburyport and be there in 25 minutes. He closed his laptop but not without realizing that, in his enthusiasm, he had been accessing the Web through his home Wi-Fi router.

~ ~ ~

Jeannine was home and awake as expected, but the enthusiasm drained from Rosen when he saw her. She had bags under her eyes and could barely croak out a greeting. "I think I'm really sick, Sweetie. You shouldn't come near me. I've picked up some kind of bronchial infection, and it hurts to breath."

"Then we should get you to a doctor, check this out."

"No, I'll be all right. I just need a day or two off to recuperate."

"Recuperate? What are you recuperating from? No, we need to get you looked at." She wheezed again and grabbed at her chest, wincing in pain.

~ ~ ~

Rosen spent the night with his arms around her. In the morning, she kept insisting that it was nothing, although her painful wheezing had kept both of them awake through much of the night. He had to almost drag her bodily to the doctors' office.

Dr. Jervis was intrigued and puzzled until he got back the chest x-rays. "There's something there, a shadow. We don't know what it is, yet, but I want to admit you overnight for some tests and a biopsy in the morning. It could be nothing, but we need to take a serious look. Okay?

"And you, Rosen, you go home and get some rest, then come into the hospital around noon or so. By that time we should have a better idea what we are dealing with."

Rosen did his best to stay away, spending the last fifteen minutes the next morning sitting in his car outside the hospital, running anxious scenarios in his head. He finally poked into the room at 11:56. Jeannine was sitting up in bed, propped up with pillows, and staring out the window at the parking lot.

"There's good news and bad news, darling," she began. "They've figured out what I have. That's the good news. The bad news is that they've figured out what I have. I have a tumor in my bronchial tubes. Oat cell carcinoma. No, seriously, that's what it's called. Who knew people even had oat cells? But the doc told me that was just what it was called because of the appearance of the cancer under a microscope. Anyway, it's operable—more good news. The bad news is that it has metastasized and can already be found in nearly every organ of my body. It's extremely aggressive and fast growing. That's bad and good. Fast growing cancers are more responsive to chemotherapy, but . . ." Her brave verbal front suddenly collapsed, and Jeannine began to sob, her shoulders heaving, sending her into another round of coughing fits.

Rosen held her and stroked her hair. "It's going to be all right. We'll beat this."

She clenched her teeth and choked back the pain and tears. "No, Rosen, you don't understand. The chemo is just an exercise so the doctors can feel they did everything they could. It's months, Rosen, that's it, maybe only a matter of weeks, that's what we get: a few weeks or months, and the last days will be a mix of fog and agony, mind-wrenching pain mixed with mind-numbing morphine. This is what we have left, all we get."

"Then let's go."

"What did you say?"

"Let's go. We'll get them to dope you up and pump you full of whatever they need to pump, then let's get out of here. If you only get a few weeks, do you want to spend them here in this dingy motel they call a hospital?"

"They're moving me over to Dana-Farber tomorrow."

"Just as bad. Classier, more expensive, but still a goddamn hospital. If that's what you want, okay. I'm with you all the way, but that's not where or how I would want to spend my last days, and I was given to understand that you and I were a lot alike. That's what you claimed. So what will it be?"

Jeannine could not suppress a smile. "My sisters' summer place in Maine, on Keoka Lake. Can you deal with the doctors and the paper work, Rosen? They are going to go apoplectic. I just don't feel up to arguing right now."

"I'll do what I can, but you'll still have to sign by all the Xs. Which makes me think of something. We're going to stop off at my attorney's office before we leave the state and get a Durable Power of Attorney and all that crap. And let's clean out your wine cellar. We can stay just this side of drunk for the whole time on some of the better vintages. How about DVDs? Anything you always wanted to see? And some new clothes. Let's do our honeymoon in style!"

"Romantic comedies."

"What? Oh, right, movies."

"Yes. 'Love, Actually.' And 'Spanglish.' O yeah, 'Lost in Translation.' You get the picture. Ha, ha."

"I do. Now, let me go see if there's anything I can do with the bureaucrats that are the real power in these places."

~ ~ ~

He returned in twenty minutes to find the room was crowded.

"Rosen, darling, come meet the distinguished staff of this hotel. This is Dr. Anschluss, from Dana-Farber. He heads the small-cell cancer program there—which I am assured is no small deal —and he is not sure he believes me when I tell him I have never smoked because the cancer I have is never heard of in non-smokers. And this is the local head honcho, Dr. McKennon, who thinks we are both crazy and that you are uncaring and iresponsible and selfish to want to take me out of here."

McKennon protested, "That's not exactly what I said."

"No, but that's exactly what you meant, which is what counts."

Anschluss shook hands with Rosen, but McKennon only nodded. "She did say it was your idea," McKennon added, petulantly.

"Now you are being inexact, Doctor," Jeannine interjected. "I said that he had the idea first, but it's our idea."

"We can't force treatment on anyone," Anschluss said. "But her chances multiply if we start aggressive chemotherapy immediately."

"He impresses me as a doctor, Rosen, but his math skills suck.

Multiply zero by anything and you still get zip. The six-month survival rate for this particular variant is so small that it might as well be zero."

"But, Miss Carsten, you could be in that non-zero percentage if we get started and get it right."

"At what price? Rosen, you should hear the laundry list of so-called side effects for the cocktail they want to start me on. It's worse than any disease. And, the good doctors here admit that it might only buy us an extra month or two."

Anschluss sighed audibly. "As I said, we can't force treatment on you. The best I can do is give you the information you need to make an informed decision. If you reject treatment and opt only for palliative care, the end will definitely come faster, that is almost certain, and it will not be easy. Breathing will become more and more difficult as the tumor in your chest grows and the cancer spreads through your lungs. The cancer is metastatic, and as the spots on your liver and pancreas grow, the pain will grow, too. A hospice facility will help you manage the pain, of course, but that does not mean it will be an easy departure."

Rosen interrupted. "I don't think we are talking about hospice care anyway. We want to go off on our own, spend the time together."

"That sounds like you, Rosen," Dr. Jervis said, as he bounced into the room and launched into introductions all around. "I couldn't help overhearing; forgive me. So, what about you, young lady?" he said, leaning over the bed and smiling warmly.

"I'm with him." She nodded toward Rosen as she returned the doctor's smile.

"All right, then. Let's strategize and organize to do the best for our patient, eh, doctors?" He gave a quick look around at his colleagues but gave them no time to respond. "To begin with, I recommend we take care of that lump in your throat, Jeannine, otherwise you soon won't be able to breathe, and you will be coughing and cacking around the clock. What would you recommend, Dr. Anschluss?"

"Surgery. It's operable, particularly as we don't have to get it perfect." He looked uncomfortable. "Under the circumstances, that is."

"No, major surgery is itself a big risk and could rob them of what little they have. Plus, recovery from chest surgery is no small matter. We need to kill this thing with as little impact as possible. Get creative, gentlemen."

"It's a short list, Doctor," McKennon said. "Surgery, chemo: both of those are out, apparently. X-rays, radiation: those will require a whole series of treatments and can have pretty substantial side effects, and they typically are combined with chemo. I don't see . . ."

"Brachytherapy," Anschluss announced. "One course of HDR, followed by permanent implanted LDR. Not the usual approach, but under the circumstances, it makes the most sense. No invasive surgery, an outpatient procedure, minimal side effects—simple anti-nausea medication should take care of most of that. She can be out and on her way in a couple of days with the tumor in retreat."

"Do you want to spell that out for the normal people in the room?" Jeannine said.

"Sure. We put some radioactive seeds directly into the tumor using these long, hollow needles. The first treatment is High Dose Radiation, HDR. The seeds go in, stay there for a little time, and are removed. For the second treatment, we implant Low Dose Radiation seeds and leave them there to continue the work. If the aim were a complete guaranteed cure, we might just do several rounds of HDR and combine it with other therapies, but in this case, we are looking for short-term benefits with the fewest side effects."

Jervis nodded enthusiastically, "That's very creative, Dr. Anschluss, genuinely patient-centered medicine. My respect for the oncologists of the world just went up a notch."

28

It was the end of the week before they were ready to take off. The most prominent evidence of her time at Dana-Farber was a dressing over the patchwork of tiny marks on her chest where the array of needles had been inserted.

Dr. Jervis, insisting on seeing them off, showed up at Jeannine's condo at eight in the morning carrying a brown paper bag. "A going away present," he said. "Don't get caught with it, or they will think you are a drug dealer. And the stuff is ultimately traceable to me, so I could lose my license. And here, fill these prescriptions before you leave town, then see this guy up in Bridgeton to write you another script. Gil and I went to medical school together, and he already knows what this is about. Don't be afraid of it; use as much as she needs to keep the pain under control. You don't have to worry about her becoming addicted at this point. I see that you like wine," he said, nodding toward to the rack against the wall. "Do be careful about alcohol. The combination can depress breathing. She can drink, but don't overdo it, especially as you start upping the dosage. There are side effects, so pick up some laxative while you're at the drug store.

"Enjoy each other," he said, gravely but smiling. "It's a gift you've been given." He turned to leave.

"Thanks for the gift," Rosen said, shaking the bag.

"Not what I meant. I was referring to the other gift. I've known you for a long time, Rosen, since before you graduated. You've been handed a lesson; learn it well."

Rosen was about to ask a question, but then, concluding he already knew the answer, simply nodded with the same serious smile he saw on Jervis's lips. Jervis excused himself and left.

"What was that?" Jeannine asked as she entered the living room wrapped in a bright orange towel.

"The good doctor bearing meds." He shook the bag. "We had better finish loading the car and be on our way. You said we would probably have a few hours' work ahead of us to open up the place."

Her smile broadened. "Who said we have to open it today. We can leave here later and grab a motel room for the night. I think we have business here that also needs attention." She untucked her towel and let it drop to the floor. "We haven't made love since I started treatment."

"That's because I don't want to be nuked by close contact with my radioactive lover."

Jeannine scooped up the towel and snapped it at him. "Rosen David, you come with me now, or I will show you what nuking really is."

Rosen grinned, walked over, and dropped to his knees. "Okay, love, but how about if I focus my attention down here where it's sweet and warm and the gamma rays don't reach."

~ ~ ~

The rustic cabin was a dark brown box dwarfed by white pines and surrounded by a carpeting of pine needles that also covered the roof and the open porch that looked out over the lake. Jeannine coached Rosen on how to clear the needles from the roof with a long-handled push-broom and how to undo and store the shutters that blocked the windows. While she got the spring-fed water system operating again, he started a blaze in the fireplace to take the chill out of the cabin. They stood holding hands in front of the fire for several minutes before she led him to the open sleeping loft that looked down over the fireplace. They made love under thick down comforters, then spent the afternoon in bed, talking and dozing off until the dying fire demanded their attention.

The hardest time at the lake was the following weekend when both of Jeannine's sisters arrived. It was, Jeannine had explained, part of the deal to use their lakeside summer place. She and Rosen had agreed to maintain a pretense that the treatment had been a complete success, that Jeannine was cured. Still, it was Elise and Angela who needed the comforting and support. By the time they left on that Sunday night, Jeannine was emotionally and physically exhausted, but she and Rosen quickly settled back into a routine without routine. They watched movies on Rosen's netbook or made love or paddled around the lake as the mood of the moment dictated. The days were languorous but rushed, as they shared the stories and the dreams and confessed inner conflicts that shrunk into insignificance even as the words were formed.

Jeannine worked her gastronomic magic in the small kitchen of the cabin for the first several weeks, but as she weakened and upped the dose of morphine, she had less energy and interest in cooking. They took to eating out until they had worked their way through all eleven restaurants within a twenty-mile radius. Then began the take-out food, alternating among pizzas and subs from a place just down the highway and pretty good Thai from the nearest ethnic café two towns over.

It was the fights that most surprised Rosen: fiery volcanoes of searing words, rivers of resentment, and floods of cold anger. Nothing in his experience had prepared him for the intensity of Jeannine's heat or cold—or his own.

"I think," he started to say, as he pushed his breakfast plate away, "that you are only looking at—"

"I don't give a flying fuck what you think, Rosen," she snapped, interrupting him. "What do you feel?"

Something seethed in him. "I feel, I feel, I ..." He stood up suddenly, sending his chair flying. "I feel cheated. I feel alone. I feel trapped in a storyline I never wrote. That's what I feel, damn it!" he shouted. "And I feel, no, I resent that you ... no, I *hate* that you seem to think that this is only about you, as if you were the only one trapped in this tragedy, as if I weren't dying, too, because when you die, Jeannine, a piece of me as big as Kansas will die with you. And then, damn you, I have to clean up the next day and go back to Massachusetts and somehow plod through days and decades without you.

"And then, like right now," he said, dropping his voice, "I feel guilty, guilty and angry at the same goddamn time. Because, you are the one who is dying, and who am I to complain, and you are just being so goddamn selfish." He threw up his hands. "And self-centered, and ..." The words stuck in his throat, and when he opened his mouth a cry of primal agony escaped. "I don't want to do this, Jeannine, and I have no choice." The millrace opened and tears gushed from his eyes. "I hate it and I am scared and I love you."

"Me, too, Rosen. Me, too." She joined him on the floor where he had dropped to his knees, and another storm had passed.

~ ~ ~

Jeannine had her good days and her not good days, and the fraction shifted inexorably toward the latter despite her increasing medication. Then there was a sudden reversal so dramatic that Rosen secretly wondered whether she might miraculously recover.

Rosen had cooked fresh pasta under Jeannine's direction, a simple penne with fresh local tomatoes and basil, extra virgin olive oil and garlic. They had accompanied it with a Brunello di Montalcino that Rosen declared to be the best Italian wine he had ever experienced.

"It had better be, my dearest of dears, because that was also the single most expensive bottle of wine I ever bought."

"Don't tell me how much it cost. I want to enjoy it for itself." He divided the last of it between their glasses. "You are in fine fettle tonight, darling."

"It's been a good day. My love cooked a wonderful dinner for me, and a peachy, gibbous moon is rising over the lake. Come, bring your glass, and let's sit on the dock."

They sat and sipped without talking, their heads tilted together as they watched the moonrise.

"The trouble with these Italian wines," she said, breaking the silence, "is that the bottles are too small. See." She raised her empty glass until it was silhouetted against the moon, now only a thin crescent short of full.

"You want more? Are you sure? I mean, are you okay?"

"I am okay, and yes, I want more—more wine, more you, more of everything. Start with the wine."

"What wine? I think that was the only Brunello we have."

"There's a bottle of Fragolino chilling in the fridge. Here, how about a fresh glass?"

Rosen returned with two juice tumblers holding a few fingers' worth each. He sat down and they clinked. "L'chaim," he said.

"I like that: to life!" she said. "Thank you for teaching me."

Rosen took a sip. "Strawberries?" he commented.

"That's how the grape got its name, because it tastes like strawberries, but it's grape wine. Pretty nice, huh? And will you look at the moon down there." She pointed toward the reflection in the middle of the lake. "There's no wind and the water is like a mirror. Perfect, absolutely perfect." They both sipped in silence, listening to the syncopated chirp of early crickets.

Jeannine stood suddenly, steadied herself by reaching down to Rosen's shoulder, then straightened. "The perfect night for a canoe ride. Help me put the small canoe in the water. I think I want to take a little paddle around the lake."

"I don't know, Jeannine. Let's use the other one; I can take the stern."

"No, I just want the solitude. I'll do this alone, Rosen. I won't be long."

"Are you sure?" The air was dead still, and his question hung in it for long seconds.

"Yes, I'm sure. I'll be all right."

They slipped the canoe down the bank and alongside the dock. Rosen helped her into the canoe and handed her the paddle. "Here. Smooth sailing." He knew what was expected, but he almost couldn't say the words. "I love you."

"Me, too," she said, the words hardly more than a whisper. He leaned out over the canoe and kissed her lightly, his eyes open, their lips barely brushing. She pushed off and glided soundlessly away over the glassy lake.

~ ~ ~

There was still no wind, and in the predawn stillness, a lightening sky revealed the capsized canoe adrift in the middle of the lake. Rosen busied himself cleaning up, restoring shutters on windows, and burying the remnants of their stash. It was late morning before the local sheriff arrived with the news.

"She was ill," Rosen said. "I probably shouldn't have let her go out alone."

"I know, son. Word had gotten around the lake; it's a pretty small community, you know. I am sorry. Just don't blame yourself. When you feel up to it, drop by to answer some questions."

Rosen watched the patrol car disappear down the dirt road before he started screaming and smashing dishes.

29

The unreality of the retreat at the lake and the reality of Jeannine's death left Rosen numb. He returned to work, but quickly realized that he could no longer sustain the pretense of doing make-work that was made all the more meaningless and unbearable by the solicitous manners of his coworkers. On the third day back, he gave his notice and left the office after lunch. He was now completely adrift, like the canoe on Keoka Lake, in a windless doldrums. There was no Millie in his life, no Jeannine, no work. Before the week was out, he had finished off more than half of the dozen bottles that still remained from Jeannine's wine collection.

The funeral arrangements he had left to the family. He was only the boyfriend, after all, and her sisters had met him only that once in Maine. Still worse, Jeannine had confided in them that he was still married, which would put him in the second circle of Hell.

The funeral was being held at Immaculate Conception in Newburyport, and Rosen figured that showing up would be rude and inappropriate. That, at least, was the rationale he used to convince himself that he had no reason to go. Instead, he opened another bottle of Riesling from the last of Jeannine's wine cellar and drank it for breakfast, toasting her memory until he passed out on the kitchen floor. It was eleven in the morning.

He awoke to the sound of bells and banging. The wall clock said it was three in the afternoon, but it felt like three in the morning. Rosen struggled to orient himself, then looked up to see Dr. Jervis' round face peering in the kitchen window. "Are you all right, Rosen?" he said, rapping on the window. "Are you all right? Let me in."

Rosen staggered to the kitchen door, holding on to chairs as he went. "Not a good time, Dr. Jervis," he said, as he opened the door. "Not a good time."

"I suppose not. I suspected this would be how you might cope. I am sure you were strong as long as she needed you, but none of us can be nonstop grownups; eventually we crash. However, young man, this is not the way. I think there is something you can do about Jeannine."

"Do? Doctor, she's dead. What is there to do?"

"Right now, get some coffee and splash some cold water on your face. That won't solve your problem, but it will help you feel better. Then I have something for you to read."

Rosen blinked, trying to steady his vision. "What do you have for me to read, Doctor? I already read the obit. I wrote it. The least I could do, I figured. Pretty good, too." He continued to babble as he tried to regain his equilibrium. "I don't think her sisters liked it though, and the paper wouldn't let me say 'survived by her lover, Dr. Rosen David of Essex,' so I told them I was her husband, but that she had always called me her lover. Quick thinking. They changed it to 'survived by her loving husband, Dr. Rosen David of Essex.' The sisters must have raised a royal stink, because the next day the paper published a correction. I didn't even know they did that with obituaries."

Dr. Jervis took his shoulders and looked him in the eye. "You get the coffee going, and after the second cup I'll let you read something."

~ ~ ~

The coffee helped, but not enough to stop Rosen's head from throbbing and not enough to make the letters stay anchored on the page. Rosen handed the printout back. "Just tell me what it's about, Doc."

"Jeannine's cancer was a rare type, as you already know, and extremely rare in non-smokers. The pathologists at Dana-Farber had actually never seen anything quite like it before. I started to do some research. Turns out there were references in the literature to this particular variant. They were published some years ago in one of those third-rate commercial catch-all journals with a few hundred subscribers who pay a thousand bucks a year each. Elliot Longtree, M.D., and Barbara Hecht, Ph.D. Names mean anything to you? No? Me neither. But I did recognize where they worked—a lab down in North Carolina by the name of Biontolics Southland, LLC."

Rosen jerked, suddenly fully alert. "What?"

"They were researching virulent human cancers, implanting them in laboratory animals, and studying their progress. This one proved so potent that they didn't even have to inject it to implant it. They would spray the cells down the throats of their subjects, and the poor doomed mice would obediently develop oat cell carcinoma of the bronchia. The strain they were cultivating would metastasize in every case. The authors were excited because it was such a reliable, reproducible research vehicle, but after the first two papers, there's been nothing more."

"And there won't be," Rosen declared, "because it was important work. That's how Biontolics operates, even when it's off-topic from their main interests. They were saving this one against a future need, in this case a need named Jeannine Carsten."

"You really think this was deliberate? I was thinking that maybe it was some kind of accidental exposure at the lab. You know, in connection with her work."

"She was a statistics wonk, Dr. Jervis. She worked with numbers, like I do. Did."

"So you don't think she was exposed to this in a lab accident at Biontolics."

"Oh, she was exposed all right, but it was no accident. Look, not a word about this to anyone, not anyone. Okay?"

~ ~ ~

Rosen knew that the best thing for him to do would be to sleep it off, but his heart was pounding and he was already getting too wired to sleep, so he grabbed his netbook, slipped the paper that Dr. Jervis had left with him into his hip pocket, and headed for Zumi's to do more coffee and more online research.

It was not until late that afternoon in Zumi's that the thunderclap jarred him fully awake. They wanted him alive, because if they had wanted him dead, he would be in a grave, just as Jeannine was. Either they had changed their minds, or he had been wrong that they were out to kill him. This meant that he had time and that he still had some chips to play, even if he did not know what color they were or what they were worth.

It took weeks of dogged work before Rosen finally had enough to go on. Ferguson had been canny, but even a light-footed traveler leaves tracks in the snow. Dig deep enough, dig wide enough, and eventually your shovel hits something. Each hit led to more, each name he uncovered offered another line of research, each company connected with Biontolics was another lead.

Patterns, it was about patterns and connections, and this was what Rosen did, and now, with nothing else in his life, this was all he did.

He lived on coffee and donuts and adrenaline. Bit by byte, he assembled the dossier until he had telephone numbers and addresses and affiliations. Biontolics and Revic AG were part of Averica SA, which was partially owned by Health Sciences and Services Holdings, Limited, whose board included two members of the Board of Directors of the Gerard and Hannah Berkowitz Charitable Foundation, which funded Biontolics and a research unit of PanAfrica Pharmacometrics. There was a consortium, formed out of something called the Exaction Group along with Slavic Estate Enterprises and a German bank, that actually owned an entire city in Russia.

Eventually, the returns on the Web research dwindled, and Rosen turned to hacking. Even there, the Web was his friend. All the tips and techniques he needed to know in order to hack into private networks and encrypted sites were waiting for him and for anyone else interested. Rosen figured he was leaving his own trail behind him but also figured that if he worked fast enough, it wouldn't matter. Still, he started cultivating his paranoid tendencies: randomizing his schedule, glancing in reflections as he passed store windows, checking his street and his rearview mirror for recurring vehicles.

Every time he became discouraged, he would picture Jeannine, feathering her paddle as she followed the trail of the moon into the middle of the lake. Every time he was too tired to try another password or compare another list of corporate officers, he saw her eyes, open like his, reflecting the moon as their lips brushed for the last time. Knowing. Both of them knowing.

It was all about knowing and being known, and as Rosen began to know his adversaries, their movements and actions began to make sense. He still had no idea what he would do if he ever reached his destination. The pursuit itself had become his purpose—to meet and confront them. And then, suddenly, a door opened in front of him, an appointment on the Exchange Server at Biontolics in Ipswich, where he had kept open the hidden access that Jeannine had set up for him: Ferguson, Berkowitz Foundation, Tuesday, 09:30. Now the only question for Rosen was what to do about it, how to bet the chips left to him.

30

First class on the flight from Boston to London Heathrow was full, but Ferguson didn't care; he had his favorite seat, one in the middle, which meant that an aisle separated his partially enclosed, full-flat, mini-suite from his neighbors on either side. After takeoff, he accepted the salad but declined the entrée. He was finishing his coffee—they had a real espresso machine on board, especially engineered to operate at altitude—when the left window-seat passenger in the row behind stood and started toward the lavatory. The man stopped just past Ferguson's seat, turned, and flashed him a broad smile. He wore tinted glasses and sported a fashionably close beard in the style currently favored by the young intelligentsia.

"Doctor, Doctor Llewellyn Cass. How good to see you. On our way to London, are we?"

Ferguson jerked, startled. "I'm afraid you're mistaken, young man. I've never heard of . . ."

The man knelt beside the seat and lowered his voice. "What, never heard of the famous oncologist, the Welsh wunderkind, world traveler, and medical entrepreneur?"

Ferguson held the man's gaze without blinking but shook his head. "I really and truly do not know what or whom you are talking about. I—"

The man interrupted again. "You were born in Swansea, Wales, in 1928 to a prominent Jewish family, taught yourself English at the age of five by listening to the BBC news on the radio, followed your father and grandfather into medicine, finished your studies at 22, then decamped for Boston where you quickly rose to dominate the sarcoma scene. You prefer to be called Andras, drink but never smoked, and you certainly don't look your age."

Ferguson's heart was racing but he kept his voice to his best patient-calming resonance. "This is absolutely preposterous, young man," he said quietly. "My name is Charles Ferguson, as it says on the passenger manifest and on my passport, and the only part you got right is that I am a doctor. Now, please, I would like to get at least some sleep on this all too short hop to Heathrow. I face a day filled with meetings after we land."

"Please forgive me for being so rude, Doctor," the man said, as he reached across to shake hands. "I should have introduced myself. I'm Dr. David, Rosen David. We've never met, but still, we know each other, Andras. May I call you Andras? I do feel I know you as few others might."

Ferguson quickly changed tactics. "You can call me anything you want, Dr. David—after we get to Heathrow where my limousine will meet us. Until then, please, just enjoy the flight." He frowned. "How odd, I wouldn't have thought you could afford first class on Virgin Atlantic on your salary, but . . ."

"I can't afford it, but one has to ante up to enter any high-stakes game. As you should know, if you have kept up on recent personnel changes in Ipswich, I am currently unemployed. There has been such a high turnover on the North Shore in recent months, hasn't there? First, there was the sad and untimely loss of one Jeannine Carsten, statistician and sometime spy, paid by both Biontolics and the Berkowitz Foundation, it seems, so I am sure the name must have come to your attention at some point. Died of small cell carcinoma, a rare type that seems to have been a specialty of some of your colleagues down in North Carolina."

Ferguson blinked and tried to channel his friend, Douglas Dougherty, with his unreadable face, but Rosen, noticing the momentary flash of discomfort, pressed closer. "Yes, right, clearly a matter we will have to discuss further, Dr. Cass."

Ferguson started to protest, but then held his tongue.

"Nothing to say? Well, then later. I do look forward to that limo ride and the chat. So, sleep well. Goodnight, Andras," he said, winking and rising to return to his seat.

Ferguson, too agitated to sleep, finally gave up. He punched the buttons to motor his bed back upright into a seat again, then turned on his reading lamp. Glancing over his shoulder, he noticed Rosen was also awake, flipping through journal articles on his tray table, and munching on an outsized chocolate chip cookie.

At Heathrow, the two men deplaned without exchanging a word, Rosen following Dougherty a half step behind. The limo was waiting at curbside when they exited the terminal. Ferguson greeted the chauffer by name as the door was held for them. As soon as the chauffer was back behind the wheel, he discreetly raised the privacy window at his back.

"So," Ferguson began, as they pulled out, "you think you know something about me, do you?"

"I know a lot about you—and your organization. Or should that word be plural?"

Ferguson snorted with skeptical amusement but said nothing. Rosen reached over and tapped him on the chest, hard enough to hurt and to make an audible thump. "You know what you are, Dr. Cass? You are a professional killer, an assassin. You kill for a living, you and your colleagues. You kill to keep your secret." Ferguson pushed Rosen's hand away from his chest, but Rosen returned it and thumped again with his index finger, relishing Ferguson's discomfort. "You killed Jeannine."

"You know less than you think, Rosen David. I had nothing to do with that. It was somebody else, acting on his own, an unauthorized initiative."

"Ah, yes, the German, your man Holzinger. See, I do know. I had even figured that his last meeting with Jeannine was about the right timing to take advantage of your group's special insights in oncology. But, if you must know the truth, I no longer really care so much about the details of who did what and who said what and whose initiative was involved. I'm not even here for revenge.

"As I said, I've been doing some research. Anyone could do it with the right starting point and enough persistence. I am surprised that no one has ever tried to expose any of your small circle of friends."

Ferguson, emboldened by the safety of his own turf, responded directly. "Oh, they have, but there are so many ways to deal with such matters when you have the resources. And as you say, the circle is small, although I would not call most of them friends. Patients is the word I use."

"You have some interesting patients, Andras."

"Please, among friends I am now called Chas. Charles is too formal, and Chuck has that American abruptness. Chas was started by a Boston colleague. It's got an old money, faux continental ring to it that appeals to me in an amusing way."

Rosen, realizing the momentum was now with him, replied, "Among friends, you can be whomever you please, I imagine. But, Andras," he said, stressing the name, "we were talking about your patients, right? Let's start with one of the rich and famous who was not hard to figure out: Edgar Mbutsu. You've been keeping that bastard alive, haven't you?"

"What can I say?"

"You can tell me why."

"Because we still needed him. He's our oldest surviving patient and has been under treatment the longest, so he has become somewhat of a living laboratory, a look into our own future. And he foots the bills—not all of them, but the biggest share. He was our banker, our insurance policy, and a guinea pig all rolled into one big black package."

"He's a monster."

"The world has known worse."

"Try the slaughter of over a hundred thousand people who happened to belong to the wrong tribe in his fiefdom."

"It's a democratic nation, not a fiefdom. Granted it's a one-party democracy with rigged elections and a president-for-life who seems to be enjoying an exceptionally long life. You know, when their constitution was amended to grant the title for life, I do suspect they had no idea quite how long a president might live. But Mbutsu didn't slaughter the Bunto-speaking minority; the Lusanyu-speaking majority did that for him. Didn't you even read his Wikipedia entry? Besides, as monsters go, he's minor league. What's a few hundred thousand when the Hall of Famers do millions. Try six million."

"Ah, the old Nazi comparison ploy. After Hitler, who can compete in the atrocity sweepstakes? Not very imaginative, Andras. Do bigger monsters make the smaller ones less monstrous or their collaborators less accountable? I don't think so.

"But, let's see, who else is in your circle? In some cases it's hard to tell. Obviously, records can be doctored, but there are still clues in scattered sources. I found that newspaper archives can be particularly useful to establish probable dates of birth for people who just seem to hang around past their welcome. Of course, I'm just guessing in some cases. Atchison Dougherty is a no-brainer, though. Actually, if he were not CEO of Biontolics, I don't think there would be much of a trail for him."

"It's an ego thing," Ferguson said. "I tried to dissuade him, but he likes to see himself as still leading the charge, herding his intrepid little squad of researchers, even though it is no longer little and not really his to lead anymore. An off-scale ego is a common trait among my patients; one might say it's almost a prerequisite for participation in our program."

"Ah yes, so let me guess on another. Julian Costa at Boston University."

Ferguson's expression was one of embarrassed chagrin. "It's Gabriel, Gabriel Costa. And yes, I'm sorry to say, he is one of my patients. We funded some of his genetics research, he sussed us out, and he's had us by the nuts ever since. But he won't last forever; his time is coming, maybe sooner than he thinks."

"From what I could learn, he seems healthy as a horse, one of the old guard who knows how to play all the palace games all too well. I don't see him retiring anytime soon. His faculty hate him and would love to see him go, from what I read."

"No, he won't retire, but he still won't be around all that much longer." Rosen opened his mouth as if to speak, then seemed to change his mind. Finally, Ferguson said, "Yes, Dr. David, to answer the unspoken question, we do that. Not as often, as you think, and not if we can find an effective alternative, but we do what we must to keep the ship sailing smoothly and on course. Remember that. Costa continues because he does not ask for much, and he knows better than to threaten. Mbutsu continued as long as he did because we needed him, and he actually plays on a small stage in a faraway country. Plus, he sends cash. Or diamonds, which are, at times, even better."

"Yes, I do get the idea that it's mostly only the super-rich who get to join your club. There are some who have been vocal about life extension that are ambiguous cases, maybe they're in the club, maybe not.

"Put your mind to rest. Venter and Kurzweil have nothing to do with this. We don't deal with high-profile amateurs no matter how rich they are."

"So I take it de Grey didn't make the cut."

"Poor Professor de Grey. He writes with such passion and tries so hard to be persuasive, but, no, he didn't make the cut. There are scores of others, hundreds. They have the unwarranted sense of self-importance, they see the singularity looming, but they can't swing the ante. It's a costly club, Dr. David, and the price of admission has been going up as the enterprise grows. The principles are relatively simple, but what it takes to sustain it over the long haul is unimaginably complicated.

"We do not, strictly speaking, arrest aging. We do not have some kind of shot that freezes you in time once and for all. But then, you already figured that one out, I imagine. It's like standing still on a unicycle, which is impossible. The unicyclist is always peddling, forward and back, twisting and returning. It's actually more like balancing a unicycle atop a small stool, a balancing act between competing pulls, between cell death and cancer, between organ failure and rejection of new tissue. In the process, the human chimera that is our patient becomes ever more complicated, comprising the genetics of a growing number of individual cell lines, and the balancing act grows in complexity with the passing years. Fortunately, our research and development have kept pace, although not by a very wide margin. We do not yet know where it ends. Our oldest patients are over 100 with a biological age in their fifties and with little or no aging from year to year. Our simulations and projections tell us this game can be played for another two hundred years or so. We think—"

Rosen interrupted him. "Do you believe in God, Dr. Cass?"

"You think we're playing God, right?"

"No, I just wondered whether you believe in God."

There was a thoughtful pause, then a quiet response. "No. I do not believe in God."

"I, too, do not believe in God. But I believe in good and evil. Do you believe in good and evil?"

"I think the universe is intrinsically indifferent. Good and evil are human inventions, and we are the perpetrators of both. Is that how you see it, or did you mean something more mystical?"

"No, that's pretty much how I see it. As I see it, what you and your enterprise are doing is among the greatest evils ever perpetrated in human history. It is the end of progress, the death of childhood, the triumph of ultimate selfishness."

"Oh, please."

"A few hundred years of Mbutsu? Tell me that's not evil in every sense of the term. An aging academic blocking progress in his field?

On another scale, but still evil. A cabal accountable to no one but themselves cornering wealth and secretly pulling strings to one purpose: to perpetuate their own stranglehold on everyone else?"

"Melodramatic, wouldn't you say? I would have expected something more calmly rational from you, Dr. David."

Rosen ignored him and continued. "You would end death, Doctor. What could be worse than that? Do you know what the late Steve Jobs told the 2005 graduating class at Stanford? Do you know? He said that death is very likely the single best invention of life. He called it life's change agent, because it clears out the old to make way for the new."

"Do you think I haven't heard this hogwash before? It's a matter of scale. If everybody lived as long as Methuselah, it would be different. But we are not talking about everybody, we are talking about a handful—someday, some distant day, as many as thousands, maybe—but never millions. The world can't afford more. Our enterprise is a creator and concentrator of wealth, but it is also a consumer on an enormous scale. So we will always just be one small piece of the story, and the story we are writing is innovation itself. We are the true agents of change. Do you have any idea how much basic and applied research we have underwritten? You know only the tip of the iceberg, Dr. David, only the tip."

"Perhaps, but I also know you are shaping a worldwide research agenda to fit your own ends. And what about the research that you have decided does not suit those ends, the countless studies and promising lines of investigation that you've killed."

"You have to understand some of the subtleties, Dr. David. Obviously, we have a vested interest in progress in all these many areas, but at the same time we have to limit exposure. It is another balancing act, like maintaining political and economic stability in a country in order to enable real progress, slow but steady."

"That may be how you see it, but what about Mbutsu, whose personal wants and wishes become the agenda for an entire country? Forever."

"Not forever, Dr. David. Nothing lasts forever. In the case of Edgar Mbutsu, forever may be far shorter than you or President Mbutsu think. In any case, sooner or later somebody would get through his vaunted security and do him in. Even his legendary luck must run out. You can be certain of that."

"They've been saying that for many years, and with every year, his survival skills are sharpened and his opposition dwindles."

"Life has always been a form of gambling, Dr. David. Survival is always a roll of the die. We may have loaded the dice, but they are rolled, nevertheless. Every day is another roll, another spin of the roulette wheel. We can inhibit aging, but we cannot stop a bullet or prevent a plane from crashing or an assassin's blade from slipping between the ribs."

"Or a pickup truck from colliding with a small car."

"That was a mistake, a misunderstanding."

"A misunderstanding that almost got my wife killed and did kill one of her coworkers—a middle-age school teacher with four school-age children."

"I said it was a mistake."

"Yes, a stupid mistake, the kind of mistake that comes all too easily from single-minded dedication to one cause, one purpose, one end. All other priorities and perspectives fade before that one, all-important objective. Jeannine Carsten was no accident, though, no mistake. You sent her to an early, watery grave."

"She took her own life. You and I both know that."

"So, it would seem that you have been following the developments in the New World rather closely. Suicide or not, you killed her."

"I already acknowledged that it was our security man acting on his own. Look, Dr. David, we are not stupid people. We are a small cadre, yes, but we are also diverse. We have political scientists working for us, and there is even a politician among our small circle of friends—I am coming to like that term of yours—who not only serves the agenda but also helps shape it."

"My God, I just put it together. Senator Thurstone, right? He's rich and he's been around forever."

"You are rather fond of that word, forever, aren't you? Yes, but he will have to retire from politics before too long and find another career. At some point it becomes unseemly and raises suspicions. We prefer our membership to be out of the public spotlight. Like many an old club, we prefer a low profile."

The limousine slowed and pulled into a circular driveway in front of a large brick-and-stone building.

"Wait a minute," Rosen said, reaching for the door. "Where are we?"

"A small private clinic outside of London. You are almost overdue for your second treatment, so you might as well get your money's worth out of your airline ticket."

"Second treatment? What the hell are you talking about?"

"In the hospital, in Boston, the experimental course of antibiotics. There were, shall we say, some extra ingredients in the formulation. And who do you think developed the new drugs that fought off your infection? It was all Biontolics or some other unit of our enterprise. Is that your evil? If we are cut, do we not bleed? If we are infected, do we not fall ill? Much of the most innovative medical research in the world today is directly or indirectly funded by us."

"You said second treatment. You mean . . ."

"Yes, you are one of us, a chimera, one of that small circle of friends. Your application for membership was approved—expedited, I should say. It was my idea, and now we have every intention of keeping you around."

Rosen looked pale and felt sick. Suddenly he was catapulted from thinking he might soon be killed to seeing now the years stretched out before him without any end that he could see. He swayed with the sudden knowledge as he stared into the gulf.

Ferguson noticed Rosen's discomfort. "You'll get used to it. You'll have lots of time," he said, as he stepped from the limousine.

Rosen got out slowly, stood next to the limousine for a moment, looking around as if trying to get his bearings. "I'll have to think about this," he said, then started walking back down the drive.

Ferguson waited until Rosen was nearly out to the road before calling out after him. "If you want time to think about it, I suggest you return and accept our hospitality. Otherwise, you might find that time has run out."

The marshes were studded with mounds of salt hay heaped high to dry in the early autumn sun after the harvest, a practice only recently resumed in this part of Ipswich. Rosen turned reluctantly from the view to find a young woman standing in the doorway of his new office.

"I'm sorry to interrupt," she said. "I can come back another time."

He smiled, shrugged, and motioned for her to come in.

"I'm working on productizing your visualization program so that others can use it. I had some questions about some of the parameters."

"Have we met?"

"No, I don't think so. I was hired when I finished up at Stanford. It was after... after you left. I'm Alana Grossman. Software Engineering."

Rosen studied her face, a face that was pretty because she was young but might become ordinary as the years added up. A nervous smile flickered and fled her face before she looked down at the notepad she was carrying.

"I'm rewriting your visualization program as a Web app," she began again. "I've reverse engineered most of it, but there are some parameters that...well, I'm not sure what they mean. I know what they do in the program, but I meant...I, well, what is the significance to the user? What are they about?" She was clearly becoming uncomfortable under his unflinching gaze, but Rosen kept looking at her, as he might ponder a painting at the Peabody Essex Museum. She swallowed. "Look, I'll come back another time. Or maybe I can email you. I was just thinking . . ."

Rosen was thinking about her dying, this young woman, barely old enough to buy booze in Massachusetts, this young professional just starting out her career, and he was looking at her as if she were already at the edge of death. She was more than twenty years his junior and she would die before he did. Her face would turn pudgy as she put on weight; the breasts that now proudly filled her tee-shirt would wrinkle and sag; her professional skills would grow rusty, and her mind would become less nimble; the vertebrae in her back would compress, and she would gradually go from short to shrunken. And she would die. Rosen would still be much as he was today, and this young woman would be dead.

The thought, strange though it was, did not trouble Rosen. What troubled him was that he could look at her this way, look at her pretty young face and see her dying—and feel nothing. It was like looking at a cell culture under a microscope. She was life, but alien life, a different species. He continued to stare in silence, dispassionately.

Annoyance spread across her face, and she stood suddenly. "Look, this is getting a little too weird. I don't know what your problem is, but I'm just trying to do my job. I'll find some other way to figure this out." She backed away from his desk without turning.

"The parameters link the oblique factor rotation to the distribution of terms in the corpus," he said. "I'm sorry. I was ... trying to remember. It seems like a lifetime ago that I wrote that program. Well, it was, in a sense, another life. Please forgive me. I was lost in ... lost in thought. Sorry."

"Okay, no problem. That makes sense. That's why they feed into the color map, right?"

"Right. See, you probably would have figured it out without me. And, again, forgive me for being 'weird.' I've only been back for a few weeks, and I am still not used to my new life, my new job."

"Sure, I understand." She smiled broadly at him, turning on a megawatt smile that Rosen realized would take her far and get her many things. She turned and bounced out of his office.

His new job, a senior position created especially for him and justifying regular trips to London, was part of the deal of his new life. So were the surges of energy and debilitating bouts of nausea that followed his last series of treatments. He was in process, becoming somebody else, something else, a new species, dependent on medications and on medication for the medications. His briefcase carried a new laptop and a half-dozen bottles of pills. His Outlook calendar was stippled with asterisks that kept him to his complicated schedule and would remind him each time he had to book another flight to London, a redundant reminder, since he now had his own secretary who handled all his appointments and travel bookings. She, too, was young; she, too, was dying. Everywhere Rosen looked, he saw people dying, even the children who laughed in the playground adjacent to his new apartment. Everyone was dying, everyone except him. And Ferguson. And Dougherty. And Mbutsu. And Gabriel Costa.

Rosen did not know the whole list. He wondered if he would recognize other immortals when he met them, if there would be a shock of mutual awareness. I am one of you and you are one of us. We are the watchers. We watch the world, the world of the dying, a world that is not ours.

Of course, that was not quite true. Gabriel Costa was not immortal, because Gabriel Costa was becoming an annoyance and was no longer useful. Stay useful, do useful things, that was the mantra of immortality in the world into which Rosen had been admitted. The mantra was a perversion of Steven King's TANSTAAFL economics. Everyone contributes. Contribute, and you get to live.

The briefing at the London clinic and the earlier presentation from Steven King had prepared him for most of the physical effects, but not for these changes in the world around him, a world that was losing its color as it pulled away from him, becoming monochrome through the wide-angle lens of his extended life. Of course, it was he who was retreating, panning back, zooming out from the people he would have to watch die, making them smaller and smaller in his worldview. It was a radical refocusing of his experience, ironically made necessary by the very feelings to which he had become more open. A younger Rosen David, already detached, would not have had to undergo this surgical separation that removed him from himself and from humanity.

He had acquiesced to their trickery in London to buy himself time, thinking that the purchase price had been his soul. Now he was coming to realize that it was not an outright sale but a mortgage with high interest and regular payments.

He looked at the clock on his desk, its second hand frozen. He looked at the calendar beside it, the date unchanged since he had returned. He looked at his face reflected in the glass top of his new desk, the eyes unblinking, the nostrils not even flaring with each breath. In his mind, the world had stopped, and time stretched out before him, a line of lonely isolation, an infinite arrow, a vector rather than a line segment. He laughed at his own metaphor. Only a mathematician would see it that way.

"I am not a mathematician," he said to his reflection, which sprang into life as he spoke. "I am a mathematical biologist. And I have a soul, still."

He started thinking about what it would be like to be celebrating the next turn of the century—or the one after. He was neither elated nor depressed by the staggering number of years that might lay before him, the things and places he might do and see.

He got up and walked past his secretary in the outer office. "I'm going for a walk," he said, without looking at her face, which was unlined and attractive and would remind him that she was dying. He walked out the front door without signing out, which would have been unnecessary now anyway, since the new guard, along with everyone else at the Labs, knew him on sight, the Lazarus who had returned from the lost to win a cushy new position. How little they knew.

He turned left out of the driveway, heading toward the Crane Estate and the beach. Although he had worked for years within an easy stroll of the Estate, and the beach had always been one of Millie's favorite local haunts, the seashore had never meant much to him. Now he would often hike to the end of Argilla Road and walk the sands and stare out across the visual infinity of the Atlantic, sometimes until the autumn sun set and the beach patrol chased him off. Late, on weekdays after Labor Day, the beach was sometimes all but deserted.

Today, he looked out across the whitecaps churned by a fresh wind out of the northeast, hypnotized by the visual music that was regular and chaotic at the same time. He could look at this non-human beauty and be moved by it, the unending beauty of Nature with a capital N.

His reverie was interrupted by the sound of the beach patrol approaching, and he realized that he had walked far from the entry and that the sun was a red-orange blob sunk almost to the horizon. The patrol had begun to recognize him and would joke about his taking up residence on the beach. He knew the names of the two regulars, Fred and Julio, and waved when he saw them approaching. Usually they talked, mostly about the ups and downs of the Red Sox, but sometimes about bits in the news or local gossip. Tonight they brought news of a different sort.

"You used to work down the road, didn't you, Doc? At that lab?" Fred said, talking through his soup-strainer moustache.

Rosen smiled and nodded. "Still do," he said.

"Well, then, you probably already know. It was in the news this afternoon. Bionholics, right?"

"Yeah, Biontolics," he gently corrected.

"Right, that's what I meant. Well, the CEO, this limey from London, was in the headlines today."

"What was it? What did he do?"

"Not what he did but what somebody did to him. A crazy from Europe somewhere broke into his apartment and shot him. He died in the ambulance."

"Who died in the ambulance?"

"The CEO. The security guards got the guy from wherever, but not before he had gotten off a couple of shots at your boss."

"Was the guy, the shooter, from The Netherlands, from Holland?"

"Yeah, that's right. So you already knew the story, huh?"

"Yeah, I already knew the story."

Julio leaned toward his partner. "See, I told you. And you still gotta get off the beach, Doc. Rules. We close at sunset, you know."

"I know. Give me a couple of minutes, and I'll be out of your hair."

"Better start hiking back, Doc, there's a lot of sand between you and the entrance."

Rosen grinned broadly and reassured them that he was on his way. The tide was coming in, anyway, and with the erosion from the heavy winter storms of the past several years, there were places where the water would soon be lapping against the fencing that separated the beach from the protected dunes.

"So, you finally succeeded, Bram," he said, talking to himself as he watched the patrol roll out of sight down the beach. "Good for you. You found a purpose and you filled it." The thought gave him comfort, but only for the brief moment before his mind started searching through scenarios and highlighted one labeled Patagonia. Was The General really dead or had they faked his death as they had with Llewellyn Cass? "It's hard to know what's real," he said to the wind. "Death, now that's real, at least for most of the human race. Beyond that, it is hard to tell anymore."

~ ~ ~

News of the second death reached him later in the week. It was impossible to miss, what with all the special features and retrospectives, the file footage and the talking heads of the analysts. "Brutal Dictator Dies." "Butcher of Busanyu Dead." "Future Uncertain in West African Country." "Busanyu Military Assumes Control, Promises Early Elections." "Cause of Death Uncertain for African Leader."

When the follow-on stories began flooding the cable channels and the Internet, Rosen realized that he had gotten his answer about what was real. The President for Life of Busanyu had succumbed to a rare tropical disease that had recently made its reappearance in West Africa. Rosen didn't need to read on; he already knew the name of the invariably fatal disease: Charles Ferguson, once known as Llewellyn Andras Cass.

The commentators made much of the two faces of the late President: the stability he had brought to the whole region and the brutal violence that had been the instrument of his pacification. The old question about whether ends justified the means was displayed on text crawls at the bottom of screens and posed in interviews with political pundits.

Rosen walked the sands at Crane Beach that day, posing his own questions, talking aloud like some displaced denizen of the streets of New York City.

"What is the point? What does it matter that any of us were here. Immortality? For Mbutsu, it turned out to be little more than a century. Who will remember him in another hundred years? Who will remember me?"

His secretary had reminded him on his way out of the office that she had booked him on an overnight to London for the following week. He didn't need the reminder. He had already postponed it more than a week and was beginning to feel the effects of the delay, but he still needed time, time to think. He found it easier to think aloud, so he talked with Jeannine, walking barefoot on the beach with her, feeling the electricity between them again even as their hands did not touch. He was aware that his mind was becoming affected, but it didn't worry him. He never worried. That was someone else's job. His job was to figure it out. There were moments when it seemed clearer, moments like now. It helped to say the words aloud, where he could hear them clearly. At least his hearing was still good, he thought.

"Why are we here?" he said, looking first to the clouds and then to the sea that reflected them. "No, the question is why am I here? That is the question every man must answer for himself." He started mumbling, then merely mouthing the words, then there were only the thoughts. And Jeannine. If there is no God, he said to her, then we must choose our own purpose. If there is a God, then perhaps it had been chosen for us, but still, there is the personal choice to be made. Do we meet destiny or run from it? Do we make our point or leave only an ellipsis?

And what is the point? Bram Dekker may or may not have lived with a purpose, but certainly he had died with one. What had been the purpose of Edgar Jabari Mbutsu's life? Of his death? What had been the point of your ever so much shorter life, Jeannine? To teach me, he thought. To teach me how to understand imaginary and complex numbers, to teach me about mystery and miracles. He smiled at the thought of her smiling when he told her what he meant.

"And what of me?" he said, once more speaking to the waves. "What will be my point, and when will I make it?" He looked down at his feet, noticing the packed sand scribbled with the tracks of the darting shore birds. Millie would know what they were, who had made the tracks, but Rosen had forgotten—if he ever knew. Plovers. Or was it rovers? But now he noticed that among the bird footprints there were what looked to him like Hebrew letters. Rosen knelt on the damp sand and started to scan the tracks with his hand as if reading an ancient text: *Im ein ani li, mi li? U'k'sheh ani l'atzmi, ma ani?* Questions. They were questions that he recognized. If I am not for myself, and if I am only for myself, then what? But there was one more, one more of those pointed questions from Hillel the Elder, questions that were themselves answers.

"If not now, when?" he shouted above the susurration of the retreating tide.

"Indeed," he answered himself. If we are all headed for the same destination, better to make a point on arrival. Jeannine had made her point, even if the only one to hear it in the still of the night had been Rosen. Now it was up to him to make his point in a way that could not be ignored, that would be heard everywhere. It would be tricky. He would have to buy still more time, and the cost could prove to be too high. But he knew he would have to delay his final move until the very last.

Suddenly, completely rational again, his mind sharpened by his resolute choice, he fished out his cellphone and dialed his own office, knowing that his secretary was working late on her regular weekly report to London.

"Marti, it's me. I need you to book another trip. I really need to get away from the office for a few days, change the scenery, get some really good food and some fine French wine. Get me on a morning flight to Montreal and book me into a good hotel for a long weekend. I want to fly back in time to change and catch my flight to London, that way you won't have to rebook that trip. Okay? And get me a car so I can get around a bit."

"Consider it done," she said. "And say hello to Quebec for me."

"Will do. I'll see you after I get back from London." He thumbed the phone off. He would need to use cash, and even then he would not be able to stay off the radar for long, but he only needed an extra week or so. They would know as soon as he missed his return flight from Canada, but they wouldn't be certain until he was a no-show for London. He knew there were still ways to cross back into the U.S. without passing through Customs: logging roads or fire roads without gates or patrols. Jeannine had told him and pointed out the general area to him on the wall map up at Keoka Lake. Keoka itself was not an option for him, much as it appealed to his sense of symmetry. It would be tricky guessing when to resurface, but there was now no doubt in his mind of where and how to do it.

"I will not retreat in silence," he said, as he turned toward the water, the opening lines of a long forgotten poem rising, unbidden, to his lips:

> I will not retreat in silence.
> Let the shofar sound at last
>   its plangent call, both sweet and shrill,
>   one long and final blast, *tekkiah gadolah*.
> Remind the echoing hills
>   that we were here and passed before,
> And left our footprints in the winding streets and dusty stalls,
>   and scratched our marks, still incomplete,
> Upon the city's sun-hued walls.

32

Salt-laden wind swept the deserted beach. Ferguson's new partner turned toward him with quiet fury, snapping his words off between clenched teeth, twisting the rolled newspaper as if it were a snake to be strangled. "You did what? Do you want to spell that out again, just in case I misheard or misunderstood you?"

"I gave him saline. He started feeling much better immediately and sent me on my way. The placebo effect works. Even for the likes of Edgar Mbutsu, it works. Or maybe especially for the likes of the Butcher of Busanyu, a man who long needed to believe in magic and in medical miracles. Given the delay in treatment and his already deteriorating condition, it didn't take long for the cellular cascade to set in."

"And now what? Where does this leave us?"

"Right here, on holidays in the Cayman Islands, carrying on business as usual."

"Are you out of your mind, Andras? You think they won't figure this one out and go after you, after us? It must be obvious what happened."

"No, it is not. They will not. The President's new personal physician was handpicked. He has diagnosed idiopathic hemorrhagic fever, of which there have been a growing number of unexplained cases in West Africa. He has, as expected, done everything in his power, including obtaining shipments of powerful medicines dispatched from the Swiss Institute for Tropical and Uncommon Diseases and from its commercial partner, Revic AG. But, as you know, IHF is unresponsive to even the best antibiotics and is almost invariably fatal. I knew that the fear factor would insure that there would be no autopsy. This is Busanyu we are talking about, not Boston. And, of course, there is no such medical diagnosis as cellular cascade, anyway. We are in the clear."

"And en route to bankruptcy. We cannot operate without the flow of funds from Busanyu. You know that. How could you be so stupid? And how could you be so arrogant, to take action like this without first consulting with me?"

"Is that the procedure, Bertrand?" He pronounced the name in the French style, with a guttural R, an accented long A, and a nasalized N. "We need not consult before, say, shedding resources in Russia, but Africa is different and requires consultation?"

"Is that what this is about, Andras? About your Slavic slut with the soulful eyes and the big mouth?"

Ferguson grimaced. "No, this is about an African dictator who was diverting funds for a new initiative to take over half the territory of his neighbor to the north. It was about our supposedly peaceful and unambitious President-for-Life deciding that his safety and security required pushing back the borders, plunging Busanyu into open warfare that would have been fatal for our relationship. Mbutsu was already talking about scaling back his support for the organization. What would the outbreak of war in the region do to the economy?"

"But now the money stops anyway, Andras."

"For God's sake, Bertrand. How many years does it take before you remember my name is Charles, Chas to you. It took me all of two days to master Bertrand Francoise Lyon, never called Bert. And what do you take me for? The payments have been made automatic. The Secretary of the Treasurer and the executor of Mbutsu's estate are both on the take. Each thinks they know the story and each knows a different one. They both think the funds being siphoned off will be there for their own enrichment when the need arises. But there are many layers to the onion. And, after many years more, when they finally peel it back, they will learn how little remains in the center waiting for them.

"In the meantime, there are those who were interested in seeing an imminent end to a long-running regime. They have a very large stake in seeing to it that there is a peaceful and orderly transition. A death by simple if uncommon disease, rather than at the hands of rebel forces or infiltrators, has improved their chances. And you and I have been paid bonuses by special-interest groups and individuals who gladly hastened the end to the reign of their dear departed dictator. They think they simply paid to keep me away, to guarantee that I would not come in and rescue him at the last minute after he fell seriously ill."

"And who will they suspect, when the inquiries become heated?"

"Each other, enemy agents, the gods, fate—but not us. We are now out of the picture, and a few extra millions richer for everyone having bribed us to stay out of that picture. I would say that we can count on the spigot to stay open for at least several years more, maybe longer. It will depend on how the Busanyu economy continues to grow, how well the country is run after the elections that they don't yet know they will be having soon, and how well our friends connect their self-interests with ours. In any case, there will be time to adjust our investment strategies and identify new revenue streams. In Busanyu, I have been cultivating talent for some years, so things there should go rather smoothly now that the President for Life is no longer President."

Dougherty's name may have changed, but his expression was, as usual, unreadable. "I suppose it makes sense. Mbutsu was always a bit of an embarrassment, even if nobody knew the connection. It had to end eventually, of course. He was too visible, too prominent. Another ten or twenty years and it would have been evident to anyone with eyes that he had some inside track on staying alive. I think I might have chosen different timing and different methods, but this will work."

"I am so glad you concur, Bertrand." It struck Ferguson as odd that the end of their relationship with the brutal Mbutsu had finally been reached, not because of his brutality but because of his insecurity. Economics trumped ethics and pragmatism triumphed over political values, as always. "I am also relieved," Ferguson continued, "that you finally listened to reason about Atchison Dougherty, who was also well past his use-by date. It did not take an orthodontist to see that he was becoming rather long in the tooth. The CEO of Biontolics had a long, rewarding run, but it was time to pass the torch to the protégés that he had so carefully cultivated over the years. I trust that you, Bertrand, will learn from his mistakes and stay out of the spotlight."

"We were lucky, that's all, lucky that a ghost from the past gave us a story."

"I still don't know the whole story or the complete rationale for the timing of our friend Douglas Dougherty's demise."

"It was Dekker. Do you remember the name, Bram Dekker?"

"It sounds familiar, but I am not sure."

"He was Janella's boyfriend. Turns out he had been following my career, as it were. He blamed me for Janella's death. Or disappearance. In any case, he blamed me and decided as his last act to get his revenge. He was a security consultant of sorts and somehow slipped in under our radar. I have had Holzinger taking our security organization apart and putting it back together right. His review uncovered some surprising holes and lapses, including a trusted asset in Ipswich who seemed to have been less than trustworthy, but it turns out Holzinger had already taken care of that.

"Fortunately, in my case, Dekker was a bad shot and I was not. I tell you, Andras, you should take the hand-gun training, too. You never know."

Ferguson scratched his ear. "I don't know. I've always believed the demographics that people who carry guns are more likely to die by them."

"Don't confuse cause and effect, Andras. Oh, all right, Chas. Why do you think people arm themselves in the first place? I'm surrounded by armed men for a reason, and this deranged lowlander was one of the reasons, proof that fortune favors the prepared. Unfortunately, Dekker acted with less preparation, so we had to put him on ice while we figured out how best to make use of his sacrifice. It took a little time to finish my new papers and fill in the blanks in the revisionist historical record."

Ferguson picked up a flattened stone and sent it skipping out over the blue-green waters. "Does it ever bother you, Bertrand?"

"You mean taking on a new identity? I don't think I've had enough time to notice much about it."

"No, I mean the cost, the lives, so many lives over the years."

"People die, Chas, at least most people. Some die so that others might live. It's always been that way. A soldier is killed on the battlefield in keeping the war from reaching his home. A research subject dies in the course of a study that finds a cure for a disease. That's life."

"But this is different. We are choosing who dies in order that we can live."

"Don't lose sleep over it; I don't. They choose themselves. Every one of them made a choice. They nominated themselves for the roles they played." He looked down at his iPad. "Have we covered everything?"

"Do you carry that gadget everywhere? We are on the beach, for God's sake. You don't see me with a phone or a computer. You need to develop some new habits to go with your new hair and name. Save the damned technology until we are back at work, which will be good for both of us. I have one more trip to the States, and then I can get back to basic research, back to the clinic where I belong."

"The Boston problem? Still?"

"He is a single-minded, chap, our boy. He skipped out on the last treatment, a no-show."

Bertrand shook his head in disbelief. "Keep me informed, Chas."

"I will, Bertrand. I will."

33

The nurse taking Rosen's pulse seemed small and lost amidst the spider-web of cables and tubes enmeshing him. Her uniform was ill-fitting, and she was taking his pulse. Rosen was puzzled. He could hear the slow, steady beep from a monitor. He knew that his every heartbeat, every breath, every change in blood chemistry was tracked, recorded, checked, and analyzed. But she was taking his pulse. No, she was only holding his hand in the light, little-girl grip that he remembered from Millie. He looked into the blue-gray eyes above the nurse's surgical mask, eyes that watched him, studied him, and he saw the lines at the edges deepen as if she were suddenly smiling.

"What are you doing, Rosen?" she said.

"I'm dying."

"But why? Why here, why now?"

"If not now, when?" He squeezed at her hand, a bare twitch of pressure. "Millie?"

"Yes?"

He closed his eyes. Minutes passed before he reopened them. "You came back."

"I'm still here," she corrected. "And I'm still waiting for your answer, Rosen. What are you doing?"

"Dying. Dramatically. On-stage. This is Mass General. That's why I stayed away, then walked in unannounced. The world watches. People want to know. They ask, 'What is happening here?'"

She answered his rhetorical question after a long pause. "The Markarov Siamese twins were separated yesterday. Both girls are still in intensive care but doing better than expected. Pediatric cardiology did the first in utero fetal heart transplant this morning, and Bulkowski's knee will keep him off the Bruins' line-up for the season. That's what's happening here; that's what people want to know about. And you?"

"I want them to know about me. No, not about me. It's not about me at all. It's about them and about why I am dying. Death. My death, a warning, a call to arms."

She reached out and traced small circles on his forehead. "A friend who works on the ward told me you were here. She lent me her uniform and helped me get in. It was not too hard. There was no swarm of reporters and only one extra guard in the hall."

Rosen inhaled sharply. "They'll come. They have to. The truth needs to get out. This will be too big to ignore." His voice shook and his eyes moistened.

"My Rosen, always the same. So smart and so naïve."

"Are you really here, Millie, or is this some dying vision?"

"I'm here. I'll stay for a bit, while I can. I'm sure you're right," she reassured him, "they will know. Somehow they will know." She stood beside him, holding his hand, looking at him with love. He noticed.

"I did love you, Millie."

"I know."

"I was not good that way, you know, not then anyway," Tears pooled in his eyes. He reached to brush at them but was too weak to raise his arm more than a few inches. She tugged a tissue from the box by the bed and dabbed at his tears, then leaned over and kissed his forehead through her mask.

Then she was gone.

~ ~ ~

Dr. Goldin turned from the computer cart where he was updating the patient's chart and shook his head. "You know, I've been at Mass General for twenty-one years now, and I have never seen anything like this. A man staggers in here on Thursday and on Saturday he is dying. I still have no idea what we are fighting or how to fight it. The patient's organs are failing. We can't find a pathogen, not a plausible one. The ones we do manage to culture are clearly opportunistic infections. It's as if his body were at civil war, insurgents fighting rebel factions who are battling separatists—it's biological chaos, utter chaos. I asked for a consult and now they tell me a team of experts from the CDC arrives tomorrow, along with a specialist on tropical diseases from down in North Carolina, which makes no sense to me. I'm skeptical. And in any case, it doesn't look like they will be arriving in time."

"The patient, Doctor. He's trying to say something." The nurse's eyes were filmed with fatigue, and her voice was hoarse after a long shift.

"Okay, see if you can suction out his mouth."

Rosen looked up at the lights swimming, weaving a figure eight above his head. There was something he knew he was supposed to do, something he needed to say, but in his thoughts it kept bobbing and weaving, dancing like the lights before his eyes, beyond his reach, just out of his grasp. It was a rut in the road of life. A word. It started with a word. If only he could remember the word, the last word, the word that he was supposed to say to start, the word he needed to say to be able to finish. He could hear it in the distance, faint. Listen, he told himself. Listen. That's it. Listen. *Sh'ma*.

"*Sh'ma*," he said, a rasping, barely audible whisper squeezed from between his cracked lips, "... *yisrael* ..." The word faded into a hiss as his last breath escaped and his lips and tongue continued in silence until the lights stopped dancing before eyes that no longer saw.

There was a long pause while the doctor watched the man's lips flutter stubbornly one last time.

"Amen," he said.

"What did you say, Doctor?"

"I said," he hesitated, thinking, remembering something from his own distant past, a childhood of forgotten faith and reassuring ritual. "I said, 'I attest.'" The nurse gave him an odd look. "I attest," he repeated, thinking quickly. "I attest that the patient died at," he glanced at the wall clock, "11:07am, Saturday, 20 September." He reached for the pen in his pocket and stared at it. "It's Shabbat. I forget."

She gave him another odd look.

"Shabbat, Nurse Wilson, the Sabbath, a day of rest, no work. But it's a mitzvah, a commandment, to save a life—or to tend to the dead. Even on Shabbat." He finished writing the record and returned the pen to his pocket.

Millie had read the story at the library in the online edition of *The Boston Globe*. She didn't have cable, and the local paper hadn't even covered the news. "Hospital sounds all-clear," declared the headline. "Rare jungle fever not a threat, experts announce. Essex man, only victim, dies." For the drama it alluded to, the story was surprisingly succinct.

A spokesperson for Massachusetts General Hospital told reporters at a news conference today that the hospital, in consultation with experts from the Centers for Disease Control in Atlanta and medical doctors in the African country of Busanyu, had determined that there was no risk to Boston-area residents or anyone else in the Commonwealth from the fever to which an Essex man had succumbed over the weekend. "Idiopathic hemorrhagic fever, type 2, is a serious but rare tropical disease that is not highly contagious," said Linda Furtganger in a statement read to the reporters. "In accordance with established protocol, the patient was at all times kept quarantined in complete isolation in our secure unit."

The patient, earlier identified as Dr. David Rosen, a research biologist employed by the North Shore firm of Biontolics Research, LLC, apparently acquired the infection through improper handling of tissue cultures sent for analysis by the firm from doctors in Mbutsu City, capital of Busanyu in West Africa. Doctors there had enlisted the help of the Ipswich high-tech firm after President for Life, Edgar Jabari Mbutsu, succumbed to the fever last month.

Symptoms of the disease include high fever, violent tremors, and vomiting of blood and tissue as internal organs are destroyed by the virulent pathogen. After the onset of acute symptoms, death usually follows within 48

hours. There is no known treatment. Doctors at Mass
General reassured reporters at the briefing that all possible
measures had been taken to keep the patient comfortable.
He died quietly on Saturday morning. The body was
immediately placed in a special biohazard containment
coffin before being transferred to a facility in North
Carolina for further study.

It was bullshit, all bullshit. Rosen, who would not even scoop carrot peelings from the kitchen drain, would never have handled tissue samples of any kind, least of all in his work in mathematical biology. Surely the reporters would have checked his background and learned that he was just a computer geek, that 'biologist' had been a flag of convenience under which he sailed the seas of science. The North Shore Lab was not even the kind of facility that would have been called on to help diagnose Mbutsu. And, of course, it was not idiopathic hemorrhagic fever that had killed either of them. They had, she knew, died in a biological civil war as secessionist cell strains fought a losing battle against each other.

What infuriated Millie most unreasonably was that the reporters had not even gotten Rosen's name right. Still, she knew better than to contact the paper. She had been careful so far, and there was no point in taking an unnecessary risk just to score a personal point.

The school year had started weeks earlier, but she was not teaching. She was living in Falmouth Foreside under her maiden name, although she had kept the apartment in Cambridge and continued to pay the rent and the cable company. She had done all her research on public computers at the library, where she also made copies on a coin-operated machine. Since moving back to Maine, she had never even used her cellphone.

Millie chewed on her lower lip as she slipped one more speckled copy into the last of the thirty-two Express Mail envelopes. She knew they had underestimated her. Everyone underestimated Millicent, the scrawny little woman who taught middle school and banded birds on weekends.

She glanced over at the refrigerator where magnets in the shape of shore birds held printouts of the newspaper story, a quotation from Steve Jobs, and the action plan that she had drafted after talking with

Steven King. Red tick marks decorated all but the final item on her list.

She had considered using UPS Next Business Day delivery, but in the end worried that a corporation, even a big one like FedEx or UPS, might too easily be breached. If Mass General and the CDC could be compromised and *The Boston Globe* hoodwinked, who could she trust? She had settled on the U.S. Postal Service. She reasoned that it might be an inefficient and uninventive bureaucracy, but, at least, it was not corrupt and might not be corruptible.

Numbers were the enemy of conspiracies and the friend of whistle-blowers. Millie figured that the further she spread the word, the less likely it was that the word would be lost or silenced. They can't be everywhere, she told herself. The thick packets she had assembled contained most of the story and much of the documentation, at least what she could still dig up on the Web and could recover from the hard drive she had swapped out from Rosen's laptop before it had been stolen.

She was particularly proud of that maneuver, which meant that no one could find anything incriminating on his computer, regardless of what forensic methods they employed. There was nothing there to be found and never had been; it was a clean, factory-fresh drive with an unaltered OEM copy of Windows. One could not fault the level of technical support she had received from the computer company. Once she convinced them that the hard drive really was dead, the replacement had arrived the next day by overnight courier, and she had slipped away with the original. She liked to believe that Rosen had lived at least a little bit longer because of what she had done. She also hoped that the story in *The Globe* had been accurate, at least on one count, that Rosen had died peacefully, without pain.

In addition to Maine's two senators and the Governors of Maine and Massachusetts, there were packets addressed by name to people at *The New York Times*, *The Times of London*, and a dozen other newspapers, including one to a former student who had become a journalist at *The Sacramento Bee*. Millie was not sure whether the one addressed to WikiLeaks would ever be delivered, but she felt it was worth a try. Each packet also contained the full list of all the recipients. Her reasoning was that this way the disappearance of any one would let the others know that the story was real and needed to be gotten out as fast as possible.

The organization, as Rosen had referred to it, would come after her, she assumed, but it would be too late. By then, too many people would know too much. Even if they killed her, the damage would already be done. The scientist in her hoped to live to see how the story played out, what the world would ultimately do with the knowledge—the knowledge of good and evil as well as of life and death. The realist in her assumed that she would not likely live that long. Rosen's far-flung children might; protected by the anonymity of their own medically-assisted conceptions, they might live to see the dénouement. She hoped they would inherit his brains, then thought better of it and wished only that they would get his hair.

She walked over to the refrigerator to tick off the last item on her checklist. In the process, she knocked loose one of her magnets, and a sheet of paper fluttered to the floor, the note from Rosen that he had mailed to her old address in Cambridge before leaving for Quebec. She picked it up and reread the quotation before sticking it up again.

> No one wants to die. Even people who want to go to heaven don't want to die to get there. And, yet, death is the destination we all share. No one has ever escaped it. And that is as it should be, because Death is very likely the single best invention of Life. It is Life's change agent. It clears out the old to make way for the new.
> — Steve Jobs, Stanford Commencement, 12 June 2005

Millie grabbed her car keys from the pegboard by the door and left.

~ ~ ~

At the Post Office, Hazel Shaeffer greeted Millie warmly when she entered. Hazel had been a clerk in the small office for what seemed forever and had even remembered Millie when she had come in the week before to pick up the Express Mail envelopes and the multi-part address forms. Hazel was one of the reasons that Millie liked being in a small town again, a community where people knew each other and looked out for each other.

"Looks like some serious mailing you're into there, Millie. That'll cost a pretty penny. Sure you wouldn't prefer to send them just Priority Mail? Only takes a few days, you know. Usually. Most places."

"No, thanks, Hazel. I want them to go out overnight rate. There's a lot of work in those. I want to be sure they get there right away."

Hazel started weighing and stamping each piece. "The Governor? Do you have friends in high places, Millicent Geller?"

Millie laughed but said nothing. When Hazel finally finished with all the packages and had processed Millie's credit card for payment, Millie asked, "Now you're sure those will go out today and be delivered tomorrow?"

"Not the overseas ones. Can't promise when those will make it once they are out of the capable hands of the U.S. Postal Service. But the rest, don't worry about them. I'll take care of them myself."

Millie sighed and smiled. "Thanks," she said, as she gathered her purse. "It's important."

"I'm sure it is," Hazel responded. She watched as Millie left, crossed the street, and got into her car. Hazel was thinking about the man with the German accent who had started talking with her at the coffee shop the day before. She was also thinking about what retirement would be like on a decidedly modest USPS pension. And she was thinking about the little Geller girl, remembering how she used to stand on tiptoes to see over the counter and shyly ask if she could have a lollipop.

Hazel gathered the packets, balanced them in her arms, and pressed her chin on top to keep them from slipping. She headed for the back and walked over to the canvas sorting bags hanging in their frames. She paused for a moment in front of two of them off to one side, one labeled "Express Mail" in neat block print, the other with a hand-lettered sheet that read "Postmaster – Special Handling Only." She hesitated for a moment but knew that if she stood there for more than a few seconds, someone was bound to ask her if anything was wrong.

She had no idea why these particular packets were so important or why they might be worth so much to some foreigner, but she did know that she was an Assistant Postmaster in the United States Postal Service. Some things you do because that's just what is done, she thought. That's how it's done here in Maine.

She lifted her chin, letting the pile cascade noisily into the Express Mail bin, then turned resolutely on her heel and returned to the counter where another customer was waiting.

~ ~ ~

~ ~ ~

THE
MILLICENT
FACTOR

The thick envelope, with its official Express Mail label and its metered postage askew in the corner, thudded onto the desk. "There." Gustav Holzinger was not one to waste words when actions spoke loudest. He straightened his back and neutered the expression on his weathered Teutonic face. Behind his unblinking gray eyes and text-message brevity hid the taut discipline required by his ex-officio role as head of external security for the global empire that was Biontolics Holdings.

The office was a brooding patchwork of dark wood and bright spots from recessed downlights. The small corner suite overlooking Boston's financial district was not part of Biontolics itself. The sign in the reception area said it headquartered the Berkowitz Biomedical Foundation, but that was merely the current flag of convenience for one particular vessel in the flotilla of foundations and front companies that propelled the Biontolics operation and carried out its true mission: providing a very select clientele with unique medical services.

Across the bare expanse of the zebrawood desk, Bertrand Francoise Lyon, newly renamed and freshly reinstalled as head of Biontolics, did not even blink. His botox-steady face fronting a Kalashnikov mind was the edge he used to manage the messy dealings of his long and complicated life. In many ways, he and his security chief were siblings and looked like it, the half-century difference in age notwithstanding. He took his time before sliding his tablet computer to one side, then looked up. "What is this, Gus?"

"Frau Geller. She sent these to the press, politicians."

Lyon tensed almost imperceptibly. "And?"

"And I . . . intercepted them."

Lyon spun the envelope around and read the label. "Sanger at the *New York Times*. He's good, and he can be rather dogged in pursuit of a story, especially one with geopolitical implications. How?"

"When the woman at the local post office wouldn't cooperate, I went plan B. Those Postal truck drivers are seriously underpaid. This one rather appreciated the cash bonus I offered. He pulled into a rest stop on his way to the regional sorting facility and looked away from the unsecured truck while he took a piss."

"The woman at the post office?"

"A loose end at the moment, but not for long."

"Just this one packet?"

"No, that and thirty others. I thought you might want this for reference purposes. The rest are scattered ashes."

Lyon, who in an earlier life had fully earned his nickname as The General, stood and officiously extended his hand to Holzinger. "Good work," he said, with a quick grasp and release. "Once again. I do think it might be time to consider a suitable expression of the organization's appreciation. Something with greater . . . longevity, shall we say." His hand went to the back of his head, as if marking the thought in his brain for future reference. It rested there for a moment. As Atchison Douglas Dougherty, he had favored military-style haircuts, an affect-tation adopted in the Viet Nam War era as a reactionary commentary on the hippie look then coming into fashion among so many of his academic colleagues; as the freshly minted French-Canadian Bertrand Lyon, he was still getting used to the shaggier locks that better matched his always untamed eyebrows.

It was training, not temperament, that made Holzinger, the former German security consultant, nearly as unreadable as Lyon. "I'll leave that to you, sir . . . and the organization." He spoke as if reading lines from an email. "I just do my job."

"Yes, you do, and with quiet efficiency. What of Frau Geller, our erstwhile school teacher? Are we to expect more trouble?"

"I think not. I believe she can be . . . persuaded."

Lyon nodded and sat back down, a silent dismissal. Holzinger acknowledged with a nod of his own, took two steps back, pivoted smartly, and left the office, closing the door behind him with only a barely audible click.

Lyon was thoughtfully tapping the unopened envelope as his business partner, the dapper Dr. Charles Ferguson, reentered the office from the suite's private bathroom. Ferguson, despite plastic surgery and sartorial makeovers, still resembled Llewellyn Andras Cass, the Welsh wunderkind who had helped launch their enterprise over a half century earlier. Years of life abroad and many hours of voice coaching had long ago softened his accent into an indecipherable phonetic stew, but he had originally learned English by listening to the BBC as a lad, and some words still stood out. "News?" he asked, with the first letter of the word palatalized like a Spanish enya.

"No, the lack thereof, which is all the better."

"Was that Gus I heard? What's in the envelope?"

"It was Gus, and the envelope is filled with a void, the news that is not news and never will be."

"You still speak like a professor, one leading a seminar in creative non-fiction." He craned his neck to read the label on the envelope. "The biologist's wife, I assume, trying to blow the whistle."

"Indeed, but the whistle was muffled and went unheard, thanks to our ever efficient German friend. Millicent Geller thought she was being clever, but she was no match for a professional."

Ferguson forced a grim smile and did not pursue the matter further. "Business as usual, then, I suppose. I'm off for Moscow tomorrow, but I'll make a stop in Zurich on the way back. There's a supply-chain snag at Revic, a problem with some of the precursor chemicals. In Russia, I'm being briefed at the Nichevo labs regarding their innovative work on accelerating genome sequencing."

Lyon scribbled a note to himself, tore the top sheet from the pad, folded and creased it precisely, and slipped it into his shirt pocket. "How long do you think the Russians will keep looking the other way?"

"As long as we keep paying them not to turn around."

"Perhaps, but I hear Putin wants to join The Club. His FSB has sources in Africa and our sources say, in turn, that the Russians have already guessed much of the real story behind Mbutsu's rather lengthy reign over Busanyu."

"So? The FSB is rife with rebranded KGB from the Soviet era, now older and less reliable. If Putin wants to join, he will have to apply and pay the entrance fee just like everyone else." Among themselves, their complex organization had become known as The Club. Ferguson's scattered patients were its metaphorical members, but the tens of millions required upfront to join were no metaphor. The annual fee was also very real, and the consequences for falling behind in payments were permanent.

Lyon reached for his tablet computer again. "Perhaps. But Putin? Do we want one such as Vladimir Putin becoming a one-man dynasty and pulling strings in the Russian Federation for the rest of the twenty-first century?"

Ferguson shrugged. "Let's face it, we've accepted far worse. Putin may be a conniving kleptocrat, but even at his worst he can hardly match the reign of terror our dearly departed Dr. Edgar Jabari Mbutsu managed in Africa."

Lyon sighed with impatience. "The issue is about neither ethics nor methods, but that Putin is a bully on a bigger scale. The Russian Federation is not some small West African backwater. Given enough time, Putin would take over us and half of Europe. He has already begun his post-Cold War version of a slow march westward. No, I think it is in our own self-interest to turn down his application. I would hate to lose the lab in Russia, though. An entire city with only a number and a dot on a map is advantageous in our line of work. I'm not sure where we could go to continue that sort of research and development in such splendid isolation, especially not combined with such easy access to cheap and abundant scientific talent."

"Fret not, my dear Bertrand. I am already on top of the matter. There is no shortage of alternative sites. We could take Xander Quarry up on his standing offer to move out to his ranch. The weather is certainly better in northern California than outside Moscow. And if isolation is still a priority, there's always PanAfrica Pharmacometrics. Vanderwalter has already suggested we use his estate outside Cape Town. In any case, nothing has happened yet. While I'm in Moscow, I'll put out some feelers regarding Putin's fantasies. I'll see you in London at the end of the week, then?"

"Yes, London, the new flat. You'll like it—so much like the old one, just with better security. We would not want another incident, would we, like that matter with the deranged Dutchman? I hate being shot at even more than I hate having to shoot intruders. Besides, I'm just starting to get used to being Bertrand Lyon. What a nuisance it would be to have to go through this makeover mess again so soon. My jaw still bothers me from the orthognathic surgery." His fingers traced a line along his once square jaw line and absent-mindedly scratched at his new moustache above lips that had been subtly plumped with silicone.

Chapter 2

The news story from New England had upset him when he stumbled on it among his regular news feeds that morning, but Clinton was now on stage and the show was about to start. He knew that once he actually got into it, the rhythm of his role as a teacher would take over and the knot in his chest would ease. He looked up from the notes on his laptop and scanned the seventeen faces waiting for him to begin the seminar.

"Good morning. I'm Clinton Rodrigues and this is JOUR 129, Long-form Journalism, or, as I prefer to call it, 'Writing to be Read.' Let me begin with a few basics. First, no electronics in my class, so close your laptops, pocket your smartphones, and stow your earbuds. And yes, that means you, Roger Belknap; I'm onto your tactics of texting under the table. We're here to talk with each other and learn from each other, not to swap messages with faraway associates or to surf the World Wide Web.

"Second, I draw your attention to recent reports coming out of the Big Apple about students at Columbia, who have been demanding so-called 'trigger warnings' from their professors regarding any potentially discomfiting material. Here at Sacramento State, our journalism classes are only for grownups—at least mine are—so this is the one and only trigger warning you will get from me. I fully intend to make you uncomfortable. If I don't, and you don't get to thinking about your discomfort, I will have failed in my duty as a teacher." He attempted a menacing look, but his warm eyes and gentle Hispanic features made it hard to pull it off. A few students suppressed snickers.

"We will be reading and discussing some of the best contemporary examples of long-form journalism, and this stuff is full of violence, rape, drugs, sleazy sex, poisoned food, and dirty politics. And, perhaps ugliest of all, human stupidity in all its manifold manifestations. All this material is required reading, no exceptions. If you want to be a journalist, squeamish sensitivity needs to be left at the door. We will also be writing. Lots. Every week. And we will be reading our works aloud to each other and critiquing them in class." There were the expected groans and open-mouthed silent protests from the students.

~ ~ ~

The rest of the ninety minutes passed quickly enough and ended on a sharp cadence when Clinton introduced the first writing assignment. "If you want to write to be read, you have to grab readers, get their attention, and then drag them into the story. Long-form journalism is not like simple news reporting, where the first paragraph, the 'nut graph,' tells the gist of the story in condensed form. It's actually more like writing a book, which is part of why so many of such extended narratives end up being republished in book form. Note well, this is one of the few ways journalists might have a shot at the big bucks— unless you have the looks and charisma to become a network anchor.

"So, from the outset, you need to make your audience want to keep reading. That starts with the headline or title and the first sentence and the first paragraph. I am not talking about 'burying the lede' or teasers that withhold information; I am talking about compelling, engaging writing.

"We've heard some examples of that today, so you know what I'm talking about. Therefore, for next week, I want you to start the in-depth story of your life." Rolling eyes and groans spread around the room. "I said start, as if it were the beginning of an investigative series. I want you to devise a title for your series, a subtitle for the first article, and then write the first three paragraphs. That's all. See, not so bad." He swept the room with a searchlight grin.

"And let me give you some hints about what not to do. If your first graph starts 'I was born on blah blah in East Blah-blah-blah' you will earn an automatic fail. Does anybody here know the term *in medias res*? No? It's Latin, and it's one of the best pieces of advice for storytelling. It means 'in the middle of things.' So, one way to get readers into your story is to plunge them right into the maelstrom in the middle of it. Don't start at the beginning; you can save that for later when your readers are already hooked.

"And that, my friends, is why I did not begin this first class with a long set of dreary definitions or a protracted recounting of the origins and history of long-form journalism. Boring! I've saved that stuff for next week—now that I've got you hooked."

From the back of the room a male voice called out, "That's what you think, professor." A ripple of laughter intermingled with the shuffle of backpacks and the start of conversations as the students prepared to leave.

Clinton mimed throwing something toward the back of the room. "Always ready to bust my chops, Roger. You'll get yours when we start tearing into your writing. In fact, I think next week you can go first with reading your opening lines." Roger feigned taking a blow to the stomach.

One of the students, a young African-American woman who had arrived late but taken a front row seat, waited until most of the students had left before coming up to Clinton. She wore jeans with scuffed knees and a black tee-shirt featuring an indie band Clinton recognized by name but had never heard.

"So, tell me professor, how would the series on your own life begin?"

"Not fair. I want you to be original and find your own voice as a writer. Besides, I've done this exercise many times already."

"You said this was a seminar, that we were in this, like, together. So, what would you write? Off the top of your head, like, starting in the middle of things, as you said."

"Okay. How's this? 'After teaching the same seminar year after year, I was not expecting to be thrown off guard with the first class. A student, who was new to me, was standing with one hand on her hip and the other on the strap of her sling pack, glibly challenging me to walk the walk as a journalist.' Or something like that. It could use some editing; maybe it's a tad over the top."

"You cheated! You just took what was happening and . . ."

"Hey, it's my life story, and I'm starting in the middle of things. Don't you want to hear more? Who are these people, and where are they going? Would you be protesting if you weren't already hooked?"

Her eyes narrowed in concentration, but she turned and walked away without saying anything more. At the door, she paused and spoke without turning around. "Okay, you win, professor. I'll see you at the next class."

~ ~ ~

As part of the contract faculty, the underpaid migrant workers of modern academia, Clinton did not have an office of his own. The bullpen of four desks he shared with other part-timers was not even located with the rest of his department. He unlocked the door of the office and almost stepped on the fat envelope on the floor. It was addressed to him; the return address was the *Sacramento Bee*. What would his former employer be sending him? He settled in at his desk in the far corner and opened the envelope. Inside was another envelope, this one an Express Mail packet. Clinton noted the return address and started to feel sick.

Chapter 3

From the heat of the Central Valley to the autumn chill of New England was a journey of more than mere miles for Clinton. He had agonized over walking away from his students. He had stared at his computer screen, hand shaking above the mouse, until finally he had forced his own hand by confirming non-refundable roundtrip airfare to Boston. Even discounted, the tickets would take him time to pay off. Then he had agonized over how to ask Professor Grist for help with his classes.

Now he sat in his rental car with the heater cranked up as he stalled by rereading the local story. It had been front-page news in the *Portland Press Herald* when it happened, but now the follow-up story was tucked away inside, next to a report about gravestones overturned by vandals in a nearby cemetery.

Police Recover DNA Evidence from Trailer Fire

Sheriff Douglass McAlhenny confirmed that usable traces of DNA may have been recovered from the body found in a rented trailer home after the recent explosion and fire that took the life of one resident and destroyed five mobile homes at Gibson's Seaview Mobile Home Park. The trailer in which the fire started was reduced to ashes by the intensity of the blaze, but investigators said part of a fingertip from the body had not been completely consumed. Tissue has been sent to the State Police Crime Lab in Augusta to confirm the identity of the victim by matching it against a stored blood sample from Massachusetts. Based on the rental agreement for the burned unit, the victim was earlier reported by police to be Millicent Geller, a retired teacher and former resident of Essex, Massachusetts. A firefighter, who had been on the scene, said the body was little more than a pile of ash. "I don't think I ever saw one this bad," he told this reporter. The Fire Marshal and police are still studying the cause of the fire, which is regarded as of suspicious origin. A spokesperson for the Fire Marshal's Office, citing evidence of "accelerants," promised a "continued investigation." One neighbor described the presumed victim as "some kind of scientist, I think, a nice little lady but she kept mostly to herself." Residents of the small trailer park east of town reported an explosion and fireball from Unit 14, located at a back corner of the facility. A cellphone call to 911 was logged at 6:12 am last Wednesday, and the first of three firefighting companies was on the scene within minutes. The short-lived fire was so intense that firefighters could not initially approach and instead concentrated on saving other units and preventing the fire from spreading into adjacent woodland.

Clinton tucked the newspaper under his arm and struggled to slow his racing heart as he left the car and approached the large mobile home just to the right of the trailer park entrance. He attempted to put the best calm and unthreatening expression on his swarthy face. The screen door rattled against its frame when he knocked, but there was no response. He forced himself to breathe less raggedly and tried again.

A woman's tilted face, pale and puffy, slid into view at the edge of the screen. Her gaze circled over his face with the half-buried apprehension he remembered from growing up in the WASP-y small towns of New England. The demographics of the Northeast might have changed over the years, but the social bedrock remained—ever suspicious of strangers, especially those whose ancestors had not been pale early arrivals from France or England. The woman worked her lips as she waited. Then: "Yeah?"

"Ah ... I was wondering if ... if I could see where the fire was."

The woman, big but still a few dozen pounds short of obese, squeezed through the narrow doorway of the house trailer and stepped wearily out onto the concrete blocks that served as the front stoop. "You a reporter?" She glanced down at the Nikon on the strap around his neck.

He almost said yes but then caught himself. "No, I'm just ... I was a friend of the woman who was burned."

"She weren't burned, she was cremated. You ever seen what's in those little urns what come from the funeral home? Well, I heard there weren't much more'n that: just ashes, little pieces of bone 'n' such not.

Police said they couldn't even rely on dental records. You sure you ain't no reporter. Tha's some camera you got there—not a tourist-type camera. No."

"It's a hobby." He looked past the woman's bare shoulder, with its tattooed vine of green and blue winding halfway up her neck. He peered into the gloom inside the mobile home, and inspiration popped out of the shadows. "Some people do macramé; I take pictures."

"Macramé, huh. My daughter-in-law is a nut case over that, always givin' me some dang doodad all tied up like some sailor who don't know his knots and don't know when to stop tying. Got the stuff hanging ever' which way in there. I ask her whether she could tie me somethin' useful, like maybe a macramé hammock, and she jus' look at me and say, 'Amy Jane.' She keep on shaking her head and saying, 'Amy Jane.' I says, 'Tha's my name, don't wear it out.' and she laughs that big horsey laugh of hers. And . . .

"Even if I shows you the spot, you can't see much, you know, 'count of the police tape. I keep askin' them when they's gonna take that dang yellow tape down and let me clean up that section, but they jus' say it's a ongoin' investigation."

Clinton nodded sympathetically. "I understand. It must be a royal-ass pain. First you get a fire, and then you can't clean up the mess and move on."

"Tha's it. Dang right. C'mere. I'll show you where it's at. Jus' don't touch nothin' or nothin', okay?"

"I sure won't. Don't want to cause any hassles with the police. You from around here? Did you know the woman?"

"Do I sound the hell like I'm from around here? No way. You don't have a very good ear for these things, do you? These people here, they's all, like, 'Ah yup. Ah don't think you can get thay-a from he-ah.' Know what I mean?"

Clinton nodded again and fell into step behind her as she led the way down the dirt road into the heart of the trailer park.

Without turning to face him, she kept talking over her shoulder. "You knew Millie Geller, did you? I was never too sure about her. Mostly kept to herself, walked to the lib'ary lots, said she was a teacher, biology. Retired, I guess. She was a bird watcher, too. One of those always with them big field glasses, you know. What did you say you do?"

"I teach, at the University."

"University of Maine?"

"No, Sacramento State."

"I've heard of that. One o' them California types, huh? Long way away. If she was a friend, you should've come earlier." She stopped suddenly, wheezing as she caught her breath. "Well, here you are, such as it is. Fire took out all these." She swept a fat arm in a half circle. "Obvious where it started, but the others is damaged beyond repair. These here were all rental units. Most o' those over there are owner-occupied, as we say. They jus' lease the pad." She finally turned to face him. "You sure I can trust you? Ain't gonna touch nothin', right?"

"Right. I'll just get some pictures and be on my way."

"Well, I guess . . ."

"Don't worry, it'll take maybe five minutes. I can find my way back out okay."

"What you say your name was?"

"Rodrigues, Clint Rodrigues."

"Clint? Well . . ." She shrugged her tattooed shoulders and ambled past him without having offered her name.

Clinton took a series of wide-angle shots from around the taped-off perimeter, then zoomed his lens all the way out to 300 millimeters to get close ups of everything in the interior. He was no forensics expert, just an ex-reporter, but his journalist's instincts were kicking in. The residue of the fire looked all wrong to him.

Most of the structure was burned out, leaving a part of the kitchen area half standing, now shored up by two-by-fours placed by the police to prevent a further collapse that might destroy evidence. At the other end, where there would have been a bed, it was burned all the way through down to bare concrete, now discolored and heavily spalled by the intense heat. Somebody had worked hard to make sure no evidence remained. They may have almost succeeded if the article in the newspaper was right. It seemed unlikely that any DNA could have survived such a fire, but Clinton figured that if they could recover DNA from long-buried Neanderthals, maybe some tiny bit of the body could yield something useful.

Clinton pushed his stomach against the plastic tape and took two steps forward, stretching the barrier by a couple of feet. Leaning inward, he raised his camera overhead to point it down at the area now outlined with little yellow evidence markers. He snapped off a rapid-fire sequence as he panned the camera in spirals above the area. Redundancy was the key. With enough shots, he could stitch together a very detailed satellite view of the entire crime scene. He knew somebody back home who might be able to make sense of it. The slick-slick-slick of the camera's continuous-shot mode slowed, telling him the buffer on his D7200 was filled. He had enough anyway. He lifted his finger from the shutter release.

In the sudden quiet, he noticed the sound of trucks and cars whizzing by on the Interstate just the other side of the rise. A gusty wind huffed and sighed through the scrub woodland that bordered the trailer park.

Clinton made one last circuit around the cordoned-off remains of the trailer. On the far side, at the very edge of the well scuffed dirt, where singed trees recorded what might have become a forest fire, were two faint parallel lines in the ground. The short lines, shallow grooves just over a foot apart, led into the wet leaves and matted pine needles of the underbrush. Something, something with small wheels or runners, had been dragged into the site or out of it.

Chapter 4

The overnight package ("Guaranteed next-day delivery by 3 pm!") had reached Clinton nearly two weeks after it had been posted from Falmouth, Maine. It had been duly logged in at the mailroom of the *Sacramento Bee* the day after it was sent, but, because it had been marked to the personal attention of Clinton Rodrigues, who was no longer on staff, the mailroom clerk had followed procedure and set it aside. Several days passed before she got around to tracking down his current address to forward it by regular mail in a plain manila envelope. At the University, the envelope sat in the mailroom for a few more days before being dropped off with the departmental secretary, who slipped it under the door of Clinton's shared office late on a Friday afternoon.

~ ~ ~

After pleas and hasty arrangements with Bonnie Grist to temporarily cover his classes, Sacramento was now a continent away, and Clinton's stalled second career as a college professor was fast fading from his mind. He scanned the contents of the envelope fanned out on the small desk in his motel room. The subtle tremor in his left cheek started again, a motor-message from the damaged nerve in his jaw now clenched in concentration. It was not the first time he had puzzled over the package with such determination. Given the list of prominent and powerful recipients stapled to the back of the brief cover letter, by the time he had opened the packet on that fateful Tuesday, headlines around the world should have been screaming with the news. But there was nothing. It seemed impossible that the news-hungry staffs of both CNN and Fox could have been silenced or simultaneously taken a pass on such a story. Either the packet was a cruel joke meant just for him, or he would have to conclude that, of the thirty-two packages listed in the appendix, his was the only one to reach its destination. The rest must have gone missing.

The story was not quite a story. Millie Geller was a biologist, not a journalist, and there were different standards of evidence and different notions of proof in science and journalism. In aggregate, the documents from Millie Geller were only an outline supported by tantalizing teasers, a drama so preposterous that Clinton's first impulse was to think his former teacher had become a card-carrying member of the conspiracy wingnuts of America.

A number of the dramatis personae listed in her summary were already dead. Geller's husband, Dr. Rosen David, had died in an isolation unit at Boston's Massachusetts General Hospital, the victim of a mysterious hemorrhagic fever like the one that had earlier struck Edgar Jabari Mbutsu, the brutal dictator of the West African nation of Busanyu. A *Boston Globe* piece linked the two deaths, claiming that Dr. David had contracted the deadly disease after mishandling biological samples sent from Busanyu for testing by the Massachusetts lab where he worked. Atchison Dougherty, head of Biontolics Holdings, parent company of the lab, had been shot in his London flat by an intruder, leaving the firm now in the hands of a French-Canadian named Bertrand Lyon. The intruder, a Dutchman named Dekker, was also dead. Bernice Quarry, wife of billionaire octogenarian Alexander Quarry, was gone. So many dead. And now Millicent Geller.

He could still picture her in her classroom, a box of tissues always within reach, the wiry little biology teacher who seemed to be allergic to nearly everything. She had been one of Clinton's favorite teachers of all time, a bright light in a dark tunnel of his life.

After his father had returned to the Azores a step-and-a-half ahead of the law, his mother lost their house in Gloucester. Sarah Toledano was too proud to go begging to her parents, who owned apartment buildings in Manhattan but had disowned her when she married a gentile. So she moved with her son into a cheap apartment in Amesbury, where she got work as a waitress and used the liberal Massachusetts school-choice system to get her bright but over-anxious offspring into the better schools of Newburyport across the river.

It had been the right move, although Clinton hated the Nock Middle School at the outset. Isolated for being from the wrong town, bullied for his too-dark, acne-pocked complexion, and teased over his name, he had retreated into a cocoon of academics. There he fell under the spell of his science teacher, who set the stage for a career in journalism by teaching him how to notice things and how to write about what he noticed. She had been a diminutive dynamo who ignited sparks in her students. And now she was gone.

He wondered why was he here, now, back East, playing at a profession for which he had a passion but was ill-suited. He could face a classroom of young adults and be at ease talking about journalism in the abstract, but to knock on doors that he had never opened before or to approach strangers for interviews sent him into tailspins of anxiety. He was good enough as a writer and sufficiently adept at online and library research that it took a while before his editor at the *Sacramento Bee* had worked out that his avoidance of direct quotations was not a matter of literary style. He was not interviewing, not talking face-to-face with people. When Clinton headed over to the State House or to the mayor's office, he would hang back, hovering at the edge before slinking away to nurse a tall latte until it seemed like the right time to reappear in the newsroom.

To him, a classroom was controllable and predictable; people on the street were not. Clinton told himself that he was not agoraphobic, yet his life had become ever more channeled into those well-traveled lanes that minimized one-on-one encounters. It had reached the point where even placing phone calls could paralyze him.

Yet, here he was, on the road, pursuing a story again, all because a former teacher had sent him a package. "This is nuts to the nth, where do I start?" He was gathering string, as reporters called it, starting with the smallest lead and fishing for the next. He looked down at the packet. "The post office, dimwit, just like you would tell your students. Go back to the beginning, to a known source or location."

He had already deviated from the ethics of journalism by not identifying himself at the trailer park. It was not like he was working for a newspaper, he rationalized, more like playing detective on a personal mission. Besides, he figured he would get nowhere at the post office asking questions as a reporter, so he fished around for some motel stationary in the desk drawer, triple-folded several sheets, and stuffed them into the one remaining business-size envelope with the motel logo and return address. He addressed the fat envelope to himself in Sacramento, grabbed his keys, and left the room before he had time to panic and change his mind.

~ ~ ~

The Falmouth Shopping Center on Route 1 had seen busier days. The parking lot was more than half empty, and there was no line of waiting customers in the small post office, which upped the ante for Clinton. He would not be able to resort to his favored tactic of hanging back to listen in hopes of catching the name of the bear of a clerk behind the counter. Around the man's neck hung a lanyard with his USPS identification attached, but the badge was tucked into the ink-stained pocket of his shirt. That probably violated protocol, but otherwise the badge would have been always spilling off the slope of his barrel chest toward one armpit or the other.

Clinton filled his lungs and exhaled. "Hi, there. I wonder if you could help me."

"Depends." The man tilted his head down to peer over his old-fashioned half glasses. "Wha' do ya need?"

"I need to send a letter to California and want to get it there as fast as possible. You know, like FedEx overnight."

"There's a FedEx office two miles south of here. This is a post office."

"Yeah, I know, but, like, how much would it cost to mail it, like, airmail special delivery?"

"What you want is Priority Mail Express. What's the zip code?"

"Like where it's going?"

"Yeah."

"Ah, 95819."

"Let's see it."

Clinton pulled the envelope from his back pocket and handed it over.

"Here. Put it in one of those flat-rate mailers over there and fill out that form. Cheaper that way."

Clinton completed the multipart form, slipped his envelope inside the stiff mailer, and returned to the counter. "I don't suppose you get a lot of rush packages to California from here."

The man scowled over the top of his glasses. "You might be surprised. Few weeks back we must've had maybe three dozen go out in one day. Not all to the Coast, mind you, but, like, lots of places."

"Were you here at the time? Do you remember who mailed them?"

"Naw, 'tweren't me. I'm just filling in as Assistant Postmaster for Hazel Shaeffer."

"Uh, she was the one here at the time?"

"Yup."

"Could I talk with her?"

"Don't think so."

Clinton was wondering how many questions it would take to get anything from the man. "Why not?"

"On account she got herself killed."

"Killed?"

"Yeah. Poor Hazel, she was headed home after work and skidded off the road into a tree. She was nearing retirement, too." He studied the screen of his terminal. "That'll be $19.99."

"Ouch, maybe I'll just send it first class."

"Your choice. Need stamps?"

"No, I have stamps. Thanks." He shook the envelope out of the flat-rate mailer and returned it to his hip pocket. "Er, when was the accident, when did the woman die?"

"Two, two-and-a-half weeks ago. I say it was no accident. I've known Hazel for decades, and she drove like a little old lady, if ya don't mind me saying. Speeding? They said she was speeding, took the curve too fast. Doesn't add up."

~ ~ ~

Clinton sat in his rental Ford in the parking lot and tried to calm himself. He was not succeeding. He was thinking that the woman who was at the post office when Millicent mailed his packet was killed shortly after. The other thing he had gotten from his visit was indirect confirmation that his had not been the only packet mailed. Something had happened to the others, but his had slipped through.

Back in his motel room, Clinton sat on the bed and tried to think about his next move. He was at a loss for ideas. When in doubt, write it out, he thought, just like he would tell students. He fired up his laptop and started writing a post for his class blog.

American education is in crisis, and the crisis deepens every time a good teacher is lost, whether to retirement, to burnout, to a higher paying job in industry, or to the nothingness beyond. The world lost one of its great teachers recently. Millicent Geller taught general science to generations of awkward and uncertain middle-school students in Newburyport, Massachusetts, but she did more than that: she inspired them to delight in discovery, to take pleasure in exploration, and to pursue the better parts of their unique potentials.

She did that for me, opening doors that would take me across the continent and into new worlds. If the world were just, teaching would be one of the highest paid professions, and great teachers would live out their lives in comfort, surrounded by friends and family and former students, rather than dying alone in trailer parks. That Millicent Geller seemed to be allergic to almost everything never stopped her from being a field biologist who took her charges along on the ride. On field trips, her backpack was stuffed with guidebooks, pocket magnifiers, and extra packets of tissues. She delivered her magic between sneezes, and posed her questions punctuated by sniffles. And we loved her. I loved her. And she will be missed.

Ferguson gunned his nimble red-trimmed black Porsche out of the last curve and into the long straightaway heading directly toward the isolated Russian facility. There the road dead-ended at a town without a name, a gated community rescued from communism's fall. Ferguson and his friends called it *Nichevo*, Russian for nothing. There was only one way in and one way out of the Soviet-era "secret city." It had been a bargain when they bought the whole thing outright from the cash-starved Russian government during the chaos of *perestroika*. The labs, once used to design death, had been repurposed to study life. The organization had had its pick of some of the best scientists from across the new Russian Federation, and the assembled team had been churning out a stream of brilliant studies that would never be published—could never be published. The fetal stem-cell research alone was worth the many millions The Club had invested. In the current climate, it was research that could not easily be replicated anywhere else.

Stands of bare birches, like mottled white flag poles planted in mounds of early snow, flew past. Ferguson was in his prime, a perpetual forty-something with middle-age looming but kept ever at bay, a man who always stretched the rules just so. It was strictly against agreed policy for any of The Core, the four principals who steered the Biontolics ship, to drive themselves, but Ferguson kept the Porsche garaged at his Moscow apartment in defiance of policy. He supposed Bertrand knew. There was no point in even trying to keep secrets from Bertrand, whose eyes were everywhere and fingers reached into everything, but The General had bigger concerns than doctored expense reports and fudged travel logs from his partner.

Speeding down the deserted two-lane road in defiance of rules was both exhilarating and mesmerizing. For just a moment, the image of a lab technician at the compound flashed before him: Sveta, smart, sexy Sveta, with hips and breasts to match her oversized ambitions. Then he blinked. Sveta was dead. The General had decided her ambitions were too great and her loyalty too limited. Within The Core, it was better never to get involved, never to develop relationships that lasted. The life of the road could be lonely, but flying first class was some compensation. His old-style Hollywood good looks complemented by no-limit credit cards meant there was never a shortage of passing companionship.

"What the ... !?" Ferguson sprang into action as he deftly downshifted and slowed. In the distance was something in the road just ahead of the entry gate. As he approached, the dark shape resolved into the angled profile of a camouflaged armored personnel carrier. The BTR-80, with its duck-boat front and blunt rear, was angled across the road, the barrel of its 30 millimeter cannon pointed straight down the long approach. Two *Kozlik* jeep-style vehicles flanked the road. As Ferguson eased toward the roadblock, lounging soldiers straightened up and readied their weapons. A soldier manning the carrier-mounted machine gun pivoted to face the approaching Porsche.

Over a megaphone, Ferguson was ordered in Russian to stop. He was already stopped. A soldier with a Kalashnikov approached. "You cannot be here. It is forbidden. Turn around."

"What is going on?" Ferguson asked in Russian. "I want to speak to someone in charge. This facility belongs to my company, Slavic Estate Enterprises." He started to open the door to step out of the car, but the soldier used his knee to push the door closed again. "Look, I have a right to be here. Get your commanding officer."

The lieutenant ambling toward the car looked too young to be an officer, but a braided scar on his face suggested he had seen combat. "The town is closed," he said in heavily accented English. "It is being ... returned. You had better go back the way you came before I am forced to ... detain you."

"This is the first I have heard of any closure. It's my company, and these are our laboratories."

"I wouldn't know. I have my orders not to allow anyone into the town after the evacuation."

"Evacuation? When?"

"Yesterday, the day before—it was ordered, some emergency."

"Ordered? By whom?"

"Just ordered. We follow orders here. It is best. You should, too. Turn your car around and go back."

There was no point in arguing. The man was just a junior officer. But Ferguson would not be following orders exactly. He would not be heading back to the Moscow apartment, neither would he be going to Sheremetyevo International to catch his flight for Zurich.

He saluted the lieutenant, smartly turned the Porsche around, and drove until well around the first curve before pulling over to check his cellphone. It still had one bar from the tower that served Nichevo. He scrolled through his contacts until he found the entry for Oleg Zabrovski. "Hello, Oleg? Yes, Ferguson here. File for Hamburg but fuel for London. I'll be there within the hour."

He hesitated before dialing his Moscow office, then the extension that was a direct link to London. He realized, though, that Bertrand would need as much advanced notice as possible. "Hello, Prudence. Dr. Ferguson here. Yes, yes, I would assume Bertrand is not yet in the office, but I need you to track him down and get a message to him: 'The President took Nothing.' Got that? Yes, just those words exactly. I'll see him at the flat tonight."

He activated the app to wipe the call log and messages from his phone before slipping it back into his pocket. The tires squealed and gravel flew as the Porsche shot off the shoulder and rocketed down the empty road.

Chapter 6

The post-modern terminal at Ostafyevo Airport, with its gridded glass façade and arched roof, resembled a cross between a boxy commercial office building and a gussied-up maintenance hangar. Ostafyevo, a converted military base south of Moscow now operated by Gazprom, catered to business travelers with private jets and private agendas. Zabrovski Aviation, another Biontolics front, operated a small fleet of Gulfstreams that served as a source of revenue from Russian oligarchs and an escape route for emergencies.

Ferguson left his Porsche with the keys in it for later delivery elsewhere by a driver. As soon as he entered the terminal, an aide in the teal-trimmed black uniform of Zabrovski Aviation signaled him to follow. He was led quickly through a side door, down a long corridor, and out onto the tarmac where a G650 with a stylish blue-green Z brush-stroked on its tail was waiting. Ferguson mounted the stairs, shook hands with Oleg Zabrovski and his co-pilot, and surveyed the empty cabin before seating himself in the leather-upholstered swivel seat nearest the cockpit. A flight attendant with pixie-cut hair dyed an improbable maroon, came up from the galley with a tray. "Orange juice or champagne, Dr. Ferguson?" She was almost as tall as Ferguson but still short enough to wear heels and not graze her head on the ceiling.

He shook his head. "Drambuie, neat, thanks." He watched the sway of her hips as she returned to the pocket galley at the back. Maybe in London, he thought, before her return flight.

There seemed to be nothing special about her, but that in itself was an appeal: nothing to hook his interest, to draw him into wanting more or to stretch things out. He was thinking how odd it was that, given enough time, variety and change and newness could themselves become boring. And he most definitely had enough time, years that he no longer kept track of, years that had begun to blur into sameness despite an endless string of adventures and problems and crises that should have kept his attention. Others might envy his globe-trotting lifestyle, call it exciting and count him lucky for his very long life and unblemished health. He, however, was beginning, at times, to wonder about the path he had taken. Was it worth it? What would most people give for the extra years?

The plane started taxiing away from its hardstand almost as soon as the attendant finished raising the folding stairway and closing the door. Within minutes, they were cleared for takeoff and airborne. When they reached their cruising altitude of 40,000 feet, Oleg came back to chat with his passenger. He was carrying a brown box with a handle and a handset atop that resembled an old-fashioned car phone.

"The big boss told me to always carry this whenever I flew with you. I assume it's a secure satellite phone of some sort, but in my job, I don't ask a lot of questions."

"Wise practice. And thank you for the prompt departure on short notice."

"It's what we do. Air traffic control is already asking us some questions. Hamburg and London are almost but not quite on the same flight track. We'll be fine once we're out of Russian airspace and take a slightly more northern route over the Baltic. I'd sit tight with the phone until we're clear in about ten minutes. We've asked Malvina to join us on the flight deck, and I'll close the door behind me for your privacy. Okay?"

"Excellent. Thank you again. And thank Malvina for me. How long until we arrive in London?"

Oleg checked his watch, a flashy oversized Omega chronograph that did not look like a knockoff. "Less than three hours to London City Airport. Closer in is worth the higher fees. There will be a car waiting for you."

"Perfect."

Ferguson waited fifteen minutes before trying the encrypted phone. "Hello. It's Chas. I'm flying over Latvia at the moment, headed for London. Did you get my message?"

"I did. What the hell does it mean? What's going on? What is with Putin?"

"They have evacuated Nichevo—some kind of an emergency as pretext. It's now cordoned off by the Russian army, or three vehicles of it, I should say. It doesn't take much for a town with only one road in or out. I presume the orders came down from the top, regardless of whatever the official word might be. Putin obviously thinks he can bully or blackmail his way into The Club. Typical. Knowing this government's history, I decided it would be prudent to get out immediately. In any case, we're stuffed. We've lost the entire lab, decades of work. It's gone, in the hands of Putin."

"It's a setback, that's all. All the data and findings are already duplicated on our own servers. We can start quietly getting some of our star players out of Russia, and we can be up and running in South Africa within a month or two. Revic in Zurich and PanAfrica in Cape Town will keep up the flow of pharmaceuticals and cell strains, and you and your flying doctors will keep up the preventive health services."

Ferguson grinned. "Quarry Ranch has a bigger swimming pool than Vanderwalter's estate. Besides, California is a lot more stable and easier to reach than South Africa."

"Precisely. Remoteness and a certain amount of social chaos are good screens. Much of the research we did at Nichevo could not have been done in a more stable, more exposed locale. Imagine trying to do the fetal stem cell work in California. Now it's time to move on. This is a hiccup—a costly one, I'll admit—but just a bump in the road. We have already acquired some of the needed lab equipment at PanAfrica. We're only talking about an extra few million or so."

"What about Nichevo? The Russians now have everything: all the specialized equipment and all the paperwork. What will they make of it and get from it?"

"You still think too much like a country doctor, Chas. The Russians will get nothing. I'll see to that. They really have no idea who we are or what we are capable of. As soon as I'm off this call, I'll look into it. That's why they call me The General."

Static poured from the handset; the call had been ended.

~ ~ ~

Heavy traffic slowed the ride in from London City Airport, and Ferguson took the opportunity to get to know Malvina better. They both knew what the agenda was when he offered her a lift into the city. With the exodus from Russia behind him and Bertrand already alerted, Ferguson felt no urgency. A quick lunch was followed by a long stopover at his place before he had the limo drop Malvina at her hotel. Buoyed by a pleasant dénouement, Ferguson decided to dismiss the driver and walk the two kilometers to Bertrand's flat: the entire top floor at one of London's toniest addresses.

Ferguson deplored the ostentation that Bertrand relished. It drew attention to Biontolics and could jeopardize the entire operation. With a few notable exceptions, members of The Club led comfortable lives, quietly building wealth over the long haul and calling the shots from offstage, out of the limelight. Edgar Jabari Mbutsu had been one of the exceptions, but he had been a necessary early compromise because it was his billions that had bankrolled the launch of The Club. Even the formerly flamboyant Xander Quarry, another of the founding underwriters, had settled down since becoming a father and losing his wife. The drug-fueled orgies for which Quarry Ranch had once been notorious were now history.

At the private elevator for Bertrand's flat, the uniformed guard nodded and used his keycard to summon the car. "Welcome back to London, Dr. Ferguson."

"Thank you, Tony." He stepped into the lift, smiled back as the doors slid shut, and waited for the stomach-lurching ride to the penthouse suite. Bertrand was waiting for him in the ivory-walled canyon that was the sitting room. A curved seven-foot wall screen mounted to one side was carrying a news feed in Russian. Lyon tapped a remote and muted the sound. "I was wondering when you would finally show. Did you catch the news on the way in?"

"I did not. I napped through the traffic, then I caught some lunch and stopped off at my place . . . for a shower." On the screen, spotlights played over streets filled with rubble and dotted with smoky fires. "Where is this?"

Lyon smiled. "Nichevo."

"What? What happened?"

"Terrorists. Maybe Chechen rebels. Who knows? Lots of speculation and little specifics so far. Whoever they were, they had surface-to-surface missiles, which means they were well-funded—or well-connected. When they attacked the town at dusk, all hell broke loose. It went up, just like that. People heard the explosion clear over in Moscow, and the fireball could be seen twenty kilometers away. The media think the town housed some kind of munitions store or weapons research facility."

"But . . ."

"Of course, no one knows for sure. Maybe the former occupants of the facilities had rigged it against just such a contingency."

"You mean . . . ?"

"I mean that our Russian bad boy now knows who he is dealing with, and by letting the news out so promptly, he is effectively informing us that he knows. Look, one of us has to think like a general, anticipate, plan ahead. Your head is always buried inside your lab results, titrating treatments, monitoring patients."

"That's what's needed. The science is still shaky. It all has to be watched and tweaked or we lose someone, and then there's another mysterious death to cover up with doctored documents and a benefactor to be replaced. There are only two of us tending more than a dozen members. I also manage all of the medical infrastructure and oversee most of the research and development. I don't have time for war games."

"War games." Bertrand laughed his incongruously high-pitched snigger. "You do worry, Chas, but about the wrong things. Revenue sources are everywhere. With over two thousand billionaires in the world, nearly all of whom would probably pledge the bulk of their net worth for our services, there is no shortage of candidates for membership."

Ferguson stared, open-mouthed, at the devastation on the wall screen. "I hope the town really had been emptied."

"Or not. Either way, the evidence is gone. Of course, Putin has, no doubt, already figured out who was behind the rebels, but he will be powerless to do anything about it directly. Some rebel faction will be blamed because he cannot expose us and risk completely closing off any future prospects. One might say the livestock have already fled the barn, and now the entire farmstead has been razed. His ex-KGB heavies might try to extract information or take revenge on some of our former employees, but most of them knew next to nothing about the real mission, and some of them are already on their way to Cape Town."

Ferguson backed away from Lyon. "You really don't care about these people."

"They're just people. Ordinary people die all the time. It happens. For all but a handful of the very unordinary, it happens sooner than they would want."

"Maybe death always arrives sooner than we want, even for the ones lucky enough to be members of The Club. We still don't know how long treatment can be sustained or how long it will continue to be effective."

"As long as we want. It's biological stasis."

Ferguson shook his head sadly. "You don't read my reports anymore, do you. The real problem is not in the genetics but in the epigenetics: how the genome responds to the unique conditions each individual faces, how genes are turned off or on by circumstances. At the start, we had a method, a treatment plan that could be followed like a formula. Now we've learned that there is no plan but, at best, a template tailored to each person and constantly updated. For the oldest of our members, we are already having to up the treatment frequency just to stay even. The induced mosaicism and multiplicity of cell lines is an ever increasing challenge to manage. Even a short delay in scheduled treatment can trigger a runaway condition, a cascade of cell death."

"Enough, Chas. You are not explaining this to some grad student or new hire. I do read your reports as well as every goddamned paper our legions of research scientists crank out. I prefer to put my faith in science, and I don't mean medical science, which is really more craft and hand waving than science. We'll figure it out. I don't know about you, good doctor, but I don't intend to ever hang up my stethoscope.

"We have spawned a singularity, old friend, a discontinuity in human history. We have mastered human life, given permanence to a temporary trajectory, conquered death. Nothing is the same, all bets are off, and we will witness the outcome of the game—and the next and the next."

Bertrand reached for the remote and turned up the sound. The announcer was calling the frantic scene Armageddon in the Russian countryside.

Chapter 7

At the faux-country building housing the Falmouth Police Station, Clinton leaned on the counter like a cub reporter, reaching for all the nonchalance he could muster and trying to keep his hand steady. "So, what can you tell me about the fire over at the Seaview?"

"At the what? What fire you talking about?" The lieutenant working the desk, a beanpole with big hands, looked up from the form he was laboriously filling out on a Panasonic Toughbook, pecking away at the keys with a well-chewed Bic pen as if he had never quite completed the transition from paper forms. His pen hung suspended over the keyboard, as though he were expecting the interruption to be brief.

"The trailer that burned last week."

"Oh, you mean over at Gibson's. What can I tell you? Nothing." He looked back down and tapped away at what Clinton guessed must be a cursor key.

"I'm a reporter, working on a story." He flashed an outdated identification card.

"I don't care if you are Ernest Hemingway writing about the Spanish civil war. What I can tell you is nothing. It's an open case, possible arson."

"Okay, so that's good. Arson. You must have some good people working on it, then."

The officer gave him a dyspeptic look.

"I mean, you'll probably know pretty soon, one way or another. I can come back tomorrow."

"Tomorrow won't do you no good. The HTA expert from Seattle doesn't arrive until Tuesday. And the State Fire Marshal is handling it."

"So, you're calling in an HTA expert. Makes sense." Clinton scribbled "HTA?" in his notebook before flipping it closed.

The officer was warming to the conversation. "Yeah, I guess they had a series of these big building fires out there back twenty years or so. Took time to figure them out."

"Big buildings? But this was a little house trailer."

The officer scratched at his forehead as if uncertain whether to continue. "Well, it's about the accelerants, high temperature, you know."

"Oh, yeah." We're doing okay, Clinton thought, just keep him talking. "Do they know what the accelerant was yet?"

"No, that's why they're bringing in this West Coast hotshot."

"So, tell me, what do you think it is?"

"What do I think? I'm a detective, but I think maybe Hal Nordquist is right. He's a welder, uses something called DuWeld, burns like hell on a stick. He says it sounded maybe like that to him: welding chemicals."

"And you,

"Me, I think she had chemicals stored in the trailer. She was some kind of science type. When the fire started, the chemicals went up and took her, too. That's what I think."

"That's a great theory. Can I get your name?"

"It's Lieutenant Sweden, Delmar Sweden."

Clinton flipped open his notebook again. "And how do you spell your name?"

"Sweden, like the country. But you can't quote me. I'm not the department spokesman; Rita Kleimer is. Spokesperson, I should say."

"And your first name, how do you spell that?"

"Delmar, just like it sounds."

"Oh, right." Clinton drew a squiggle and closed his notebook.

~ ~ ~

Northbound traffic on Interstate 95 was approaching gridlock, but southbound was not too bad once Clinton got away from the Portland area. He wasn't sure why he had checked out of his motel early and headed south. His flight home wasn't until Monday, and he had considered heading up to Bar Harbor for a break over the weekend.

The rental car's compass heading began to make sense soon after reaching Massachusetts. He crossed the Merrimack River under the baby-blue twin arches of the new Whittier Bridge and spotted the sign for Newburyport. Without thinking, he began slowing for the exit. It had been so many years that he was driving more on instinct than memory. He took the left off the ramp, then hung a right onto Low Street.

He was thinking about the crime scene and the odd residue of the fire when, near the other end of Low, he noticed girls practicing soccer drills on the athletic field while scrawny, sweaty boys in assorted tee shirts puffed around the outside track. He suddenly realized he had driven right past the Nock Middle School. He turned in at the skating rink, circled, and headed back toward the school. After slipping into the last open visitor parking space, he sat quietly in the car for a minute, thinking that it was a grim impulsive pilgrimage to a school he had hated for a teacher who was no longer there.

A new security system stopped him from simply walking into the building. He had to show identification and explain his reason for visiting before he could be buzzed in. "I'm a former student and . . . I was in the area. Just wanted to stop in."

By the time he reached the office, he had decided that he might as well explain the real reason to the woman working there. The scarecrow in a print dress and gray cardigan looked at him expectantly. "Yes?"

"I was a student here eons ago. I just learned that my favorite teacher died recently, and I felt like visiting the old place, maybe dropping in on her classroom."

"Oh, you must be talking about Mrs. Geller. It was so sad. And she was really quite young. She didn't come back for the start of the term this fall, you know. I think it was a family matter. She had just lost her husband, and, well . . . and then this. How terrible. You know, there's a tribute page started for her by former students. You'll find a link to it on the school website. Do you want me to write down the web address for you?"

"No, I can Google it. Could I just stop by her old classroom? I mean, it's not school hours."

"Mr. Collingwood, head of the department, has taken over her classes."

"Could I drop in on him anyway?"

"You have to sign in and wear one of these visitor badges. I can walk you down to the room after I finish with this form. Or I could page him and have him come to the office."

"No, that's all right. He wouldn't know me, and I'm sure he's busy. I can find the room on my own."

"I'm sorry, but visitors have to be escorted, you know."

"I keep forgetting how much schools have changed."

"Well, we can't be too careful, now can we. I mean, those school shootings and all. And we certainly can't have some pedophile just waltzing in here and roaming the halls, now, can we?"

"No, and we certainly wouldn't let kids ride school buses without wearing seatbelts, right?"

"What do you mean? School buses don't have seatbelts."

"Ah, right. Anyway, I am happy to be escorted safely to Mr. Collingwood's classroom." Do temper your sarcasm, he told himself.

"Yes, well, it will only be a minute before I'm through here."

~ ~ ~

The visit to the classroom and chat with Mr. Collingwood were both disappointing. The room looked nothing like Clinton remembered, and Arnold Collingwood was given to droning on in response to the simplest question or the most casual comment. Clinton finally extricated himself with the excuse that he had another appointment. He stopped in at the school office to return his badge and sign out. So much for requiring an escort, he thought. Clearly, it depended on who was interpreting the rules. "Is there a place in town where I could get a burger or something. I mean, not McDonald's."

"Try the old Fowle's on State Street. Name's changed but the old sign is still there. I hear they have, like, a dozen kinds of fancy burgers now."

"Thanks, I'll give it a try."

~ ~ ~

After decades of decline, the historic seaport of Newburyport had undergone a renaissance starting in the 1970s that had transformed its downtown into a brick-sidewalk tourist mecca of galleries, funky shops, and diverse eateries. Following a stroll along the boardwalk from the municipal parking lot, Clinton settled in at the retro 17 State Street Café and began working his way through a near-perfect half-pound hamburger smothered with jalapeño barbecue sauce. Between dripping bites and quick dabs with his napkin, he was trying to figure out what to do next.

The part of him that panicked when knocking on doors or approaching strangers just wanted to fly back home and return to his quiet life in Sacramento as adjunct faculty in the Department of Communication Studies, Journalism, and Film. The part of him that loved puzzles and mysteries wanted to get to the bottom of Millie Geller's crazy story and tragic death. She had believed in him when he was just a scared middle-school misfit; she had inspired him to reach for something; and she had remembered him. He owed her at least a best try.

Somehow the very real danger that he might be getting into did not frighten him. He knew his social anxiety was completely irrational and that he should not give in to it, yet it had grown to nearly rule his life. Now here he was launching an investigation into a mysterious group that seemed quite capable of murder, and he was calmly thinking through his strategy. People are strange, he thought, and you, Clinton Jorge Rodrigues, are one of the strangest.

He wondered how much danger he was actually in? His name was on the list attached to Millie's cover letter, but as far as he could tell, none of the other packets had reached their recipients. Had they been intercepted? Lost? Destroyed? He would have to conclude, at least for the moment, that no one knew that he had received his copy.

If anyone knew, he would probably already have met the same fate as Millie and the woman at the post office. If he drew attention to himself, though, if he started poking in the wrong places or talking to the wrong people, it might not take long for someone to figure out that he had a copy of the documents. He would have to hold his cards close to the chest and play his hand with poker-faced calculation.

He opened his laptop but quickly discovered there was no Wi-Fi in the café. He paid his bill with a twenty tucked under his untouched water glass and left for the Starbucks a few doors down. The place was full, and the line for ordering was doubled back the length of the counter, past an odd assortment of mermaid paintings and carvings by some local artist, almost to the door onto State Street. When he finally reached the register, he ordered a grande latte, then squeezed into a spot at the end of the bar where he could stand while waiting for his drink. On impulse, he reopened his laptop and searched for the tribute page for Millicent Geller. He was surprised that it topped the search results and even more surprised to find hundreds of messages posted. She had touched a lot of people.

He was about to add a note of his own when he remembered about the game he was now playing. He would need to reduce his visibility, maybe go incognito. He scanned the guestbook and made note of a couple of local people who might be worth following up on. He didn't know Betsy Whitman, but her post mentioned she was now working at the nearby Crane Estate in Ipswich. He had already heard of one of Newburyport's best known and most successful graduates, venture capitalist Felix Templeman, who was now busy reinvesting his first millions at Boston's Enventia Capital.

Clinton switched over to his web-mail page. There was email from the chair of his department. Clinton realized he would have to decide soon whether he was going to teach this semester. Bonnie Grist was covering his classes for another week, but that was all they had negotiated before he left. There was also email from a student.

> *When are you coming back, professor? I read your blog about the*
> *biology teacher. She must have been good. Like you. Hurry back, that*
> *other prof is just not as good as you. I miss you.*
> *--Julia Sousa*

Clinton was picturing Julia Sousa, the pretty black girl who always arrived late and always sat in the front row. Was she trying to butter him up for a better grade? She had done fairly well on the first writing assignment and had aced the first quiz. The tone of the email seemed rather personal, but then, students these days tended toward instant familiarity, even with teachers.

After the barista slid him his coffee, Clinton stood sipping while staring at the screen and thinking about Millie's story. Was Atchison Dougherty, the former CEO of Biontolics Holdings, really nearly a hundred years old when he was killed by an intruder? Was the late President-for-Life of Busanyu even older? It was hard finding pictures of Dougherty, but there was no shortage of shots of the African dictator, whose battle-battered face was hard to judge. Neither of them looked anywhere near as old as Millie's materials claimed. Was the kind of life extension that medical quackery and fringe science were always touting as just around the corner already a reality?

Clinton made two quick decisions. He was going to stop being Clinton Rodrigues for the time being, and he was going to pay a visit to the Biontolics lab.

Chapter 8

Bright sun and a warming fall day had already inspired Clinton to drive with the windows down as he turned left out of the driveway of the Country Garden Inn in Rowley. Growing up in the area, Clinton had thought of the tiny town as essentially a geographic placeholder between Newburyport to the north and Ipswich, the next well-known colonial seaport to the south. Rowley had no real town center, and its one nominal claim to fame seemed to hinge on a weekly flea market of some renown along with the stretch of antique dealers that dotted the secondary road leading to Ipswich.

The About Us page on the company website for the North Shore Laboratories of Biontolics Research, LLC, placed it in Ipswich, near the end of Argilla Road, the street leading to duly-famed Crane Beach. Clinton knew of the beach and the adjacent Crane Estate by reputation, but he had never been there. Living up in Amesbury, his mother had always headed to the closer and cheaper Salisbury Beach for relief from midsummer heatwaves.

Trees speckled with the first colors of autumn crowded Argilla Road, and the pavement was slick with dew-wet leaves. Clinton knew he had missed the turnoff when he reached the entrance to the beach at the end of the road. He circled around outside the gatehouse and headed back toward the center of town, driving slowly and searching for a sign. He would have missed the unmarked driveway a second time had there not been a blue minivan just pulling out, a discreet Biontolics logo painted on its sliding door. Clinton waited until the van was out of sight before turning into the curving driveway. The low sea-blue sign that confirmed he was in the right place was halfway up the long approach, where it would have been invisible from the road. If you didn't know where you were going, you didn't belong here, it seemed to proclaim. It was another reminder to Clinton that he was back in New England, where signage had a reputation as often being confirmatory at best, mostly useful only if you already knew the way, and confusing to all others.

Clinton parked in a visitor space out front and walked up the broad front steps onto the porch of what had once been a large private residence. The façade was vintage New England, a gentleman's farmhouse fronting on a sprawling complex of converted old lap-sided buildings and newer board-and-batten construction, all painted in drab grays and muted greens to blend in with the surroundings. Except for the sign at the entrance and the two large parking lots, it could still be taken as a bucolic estate with its gabled main house, a barn, and a guesthouse linked by covered passageways.

"I saw an ad," he told the guard at the desk just inside the front entrance. "It said that you were hiring, looking for a statistical programmer. I know R and have worked with Matlab. Can I talk with someone?" It was blurted out, the rehearsed lines he had settled on after scouring for references to Biontolics on the Web. He stood there, suddenly feeling awkward, telling himself there was no point reciting his résumé to a guard.

"Yeah, sign in here, put the number of this badge next to your name, add the time of arrival, and initial. I'll buzz Dr. Kenilworth."

Clinton wrote "Neal Blake" in neat block letters on the bottom line of the register, scribbled initials and a wavy line in the signature box, and copied the three digits from the badge at the end. "What time do you have?"

The guard looked at his computer screen. "It says 8:33. Clock over there looks like 8:37. Take your pick. You can take a seat over there."

Clinton split the difference to fill in his arrival time, then sat down. He feigned interest in the copies of *Nature* and *Science* neatly arrayed on the coffee table in the reception area. For the next twenty minutes, he pretended to read as his anxiety kept rising.

The man who approached looked like a middle-aged Harvard humanities professor in shirtsleeves and bowtie. "Hi, I'm Rich Kenilworth. Sorry, but I was just settling into my morning routine, which involves responding to a deluge of overnight dispatches from overseas before it gets too late there. Bill here says you're a statistical programmer. Did you see our little ad in *New Scientist* or what?"

"I ... yeah, I saw the ad and happened to be in the area for an interview with New England Biolabs. It seemed a shame not to check you out."

"Ah. So, they're also looking. Interesting. You know, we are nowhere near as big and not as well known, but we're doing interesting work in genomics and epigenetics. Of course, it all ultimately comes down to numbers, which is where our statistical programming team comes in. The stats team works hand-in-glove with our subject-matter experts from the get-go: experimental design, data processing and quality control, right through to data analysis and visualization. Did you file your résumé through our website?"

"No, but I will. As I said, this was a last minute decision to drop in. I mean, the job over at New England Biolabs is basically mine already, but I really wanted to check them out in person before committing. That's why I'm in the area. It's a big move from . . . UCLA."

"That's where you're working now?"

"Yeah, until recently. I've been doing R programming and teaching it to undergrads for five years." The only truth behind the claim was that he knew what the R language was, having once mistakenly signed up for an elective in statistics that was taught using the popular open-source programming language. He hoped he would not be called on to demonstrate any expertise. "I realized awhile back that this—the programming and statistics—is where my heart really is. And now it seems time for a jump, time for a West Coast native to check out New England. This sure isn't Los Angeles. I don't think I have ever seen so much green. Know what I mean?"

"Yeah, I imagine, what with the drought and all, Southern California must be pretty much all brown. Well, as long as you're here, let me show you around and see if I can convince you to consider Biontolics. We can worry about HR and the paperwork later. Just follow me."

"So what do you do here?"

"I'm head of the Statistical Programming Team. As I was saying before, we are trying to take some of the number-crunching heavy lifting off from the shoulders of our scientists and researchers, give them more time for the think work. This is a relatively new way of doing business for us, and we are still finding our way. It requires a particular kind of person, with a deep knowledge of statistics, experimental design, and fluency in statistical programming, especially in R, which is our go-to-ground language for most applications, but at the same time you need an ability to collaborate closely with research scientists, who are another species altogether.

You gotta have your head wrapped around R code at the same time you're talking turkey with geneticists and biochemists and neuroscientists. You know what I mean?"

"Yeah, but I meant what does this lab really do? The stuff on the Web about Biontolics was not all that informative."

"Well, we're about basic research at the leading leading leading edge in human biology: genetics, epigenetics, genomics, cell energy economy, apoptosis mechanisms, gerontology, you name it. We're funded some by government grants but mostly by a few private sources, like the Berkowitz Biomedical Foundation. We pitch our ideas to them, they write a check. It's a lot more efficient than the whole drawn out drama with government grants and peer-review panels and funding cycles and stuff like that. But that's not my bailiwick. As I said, I'm a numbers nut, but I trained as a biochemist. Everyone here is a trained scientist in some area, some in more than one, even if they are crunching numbers or pounding out programs. What's your PhD in?"

"Ah, doctoral work ... seems like a lifetime ago." Clinton was thinking fast. He needed something plausible but with little risk of being caught out on. "I started out—would you believe it?—in sociology, ended up doing a dissertation on the sociology of science, which got me interested in what real scientists do. It was a little too late to take a U-turn, but I found I had a real knack for stats and cutting code, started doing little things with Systat and MatLab as favors for other profs." He was grinning at his own BS. "You know how it goes. The rest is history. Not sure I could even tell you much about that other life."

"I understand. I'm not sure I could even make much out of the molecular structure of chiral cytokines anymore—my dissertation subject. Anyway, here we are in our Neuroscience Section. They're doing basic science but focused on the aging brain." The elongated room with a wall of windows along one side was occupied by half a dozen people in front of computer screens, most of them wearing headphones or earbuds. "Not much to see, unless you read their papers. The functional MRI and positron tomography pictures are stunning, but the actual imaging is farmed out or done at our Research Triangle Park facility, our headquarters down in North Carolina. Anyway, I hope you don't mind if I don't do introductions. I hate to interrupt when people are deep into it, you know."

Clinton followed Kenilworth down the aisle between the desks. Just past the open door into a conference room, someone called out. "Clint! Hey, Clint."

Clinton stiffened and tried not to show any reaction, but he could feel the spasm starting in his cheek. He kept walking and turned around only when he felt a gentle tap on his shoulder. "What?"

The woman, about his age, with sun-hued skin a shade darker than his, was dressed in jeans and a magenta silk blouse. A matching reddish smudge marked her forehead above black eyebrows and near-black eyes. She looked perplexed.

"Clint, don't you remember? Sahana, Sahana Patel. From high school."

Kenilworth was now watching both of them with narrowed eyes.

"I ... I'm sorry," Clinton said, before Kenilworth could jump in with questions. "I think you have me mixed up with somebody else." He held out his hand. "But I'm glad to meet you, Sahana Patel. I'm Neal Blake. I'm applying for a job here. I take it you're a neuroscientist."

"I am. But OMG! You look so much like him, like this Portuguese guy I knew in high school. You sure you're not Portuguese, maybe with a long lost twin brother?"

"I'm sure not either of those. English on my father's side, some Cherokee way back on my mother's." It was the sort of quick thinking that had earned him a reputation as a master bullshit artist. "But I would definitely remember you if we went to high school together. I don't think we had many future scientists where I went to school in Oakland." His focus kept shifting between her dark eyes and the red dot on her forehead. He did remember her, and now he found himself hoping the mark did not mean she was married.

Her head pivoted slowly to one side as she kept her eyes on him. "It's uncanny. You look so much like this guy. A bit older, of course, but, like, still the same. Anyway, I'm sorry for interrupting. Good luck with the job app. Maybe I'll see you again."

"I hope."

As they left the room, Clinton could feel the aftereffects of the rush of adrenaline. It had been a close call. He had no intention of following through on any job application, but he now knew he had a potential inside contact at Biontolics, and he would follow up with Sahana. He was already thinking ahead to how he might do that.

He meticulously managed the rest of the interaction with Dr. Kenilworth to make it increasingly clear that Biontolics and Neal Blake were not a good fit. At the same time, he knew he had to make the mismatch seem natural and mutual without raising suspicions. He wrapped things up with a halfhearted promise to forward his résumé, a promise that they both knew would not be kept. As he left the main building, he was thinking that maybe he was not so bad as an investigative journalist as he had once thought. Or at least he was not too bad as an actor doing somewhat risky improv.

Chapter 9

Tracking down Sahana proved to be easier than expected. If she had been a Paula Smith or a Joan Brown, there would have been several hundred thousand hits on Google, but Clinton was able to locate the right Sahana Patel in only a few minutes of digging. She lived in Ipswich, and her name showed up among top finishers in local short-distance races, such as, the Thanksgiving Day "Run for the Pies" and the annual "Chase the Gorilla Down Argilla" sponsored by the Ipswich Y. A search for her name and first digits of the local telephone exchanges turned up two PDF documents that included her phone number. Clinton called.

"Sahana? Sahana Patel?""

"Yes?"

"You may not remember me, but this is Clinton Rodrigues. We went to Newburyport High together."

"Ohmagod, this is just too weird. You won't believe this, but I saw this guy today who looked like you. I mean, just like you."

"That's funny. I met someone today with the same name as you. How unlikely is that?"

"Wait a minute. Is this some kind of a prank? Are you trying to pull something?"

"No prank, but I am trying to pull something. I'm a journalist now, and I'm working on a story but couldn't take a chance on playing it straight under my own name at your laboratory. I had to play it cool when we met today."

"You have to tell me. I mean, you absolutely have to tell me. What is this about?"

"I'll tell you, but not over the phone. Can we meet somewhere that's nowhere? A quiet bar? Or maybe a really loud bar, out of town but not too far? Or better yet, I'll buy you dinner."

"This is sounding better and better. Do you like seafood?"

"My favorite."

"Then there are a lot of possibilities nearby. Of course, we might be spotted by people I know. How about heading down to Gloucester. Do you know Gloucester?"

"I know it. I was born there."

"Well, there's a place called Latitude 43."

"I don't remember it—it's been a few years since I was back—but I'll find it. Eight o'clock work for you?"

"Sure, I'll meet you there."

~ ~ ~

Latitude 43 turned out to be a classy bar-restaurant, all glass and exposed wooden beams, next to a craft brewery on Gloucester's renovated waterfront, itself a quirky blend of working fishing harbor and upscale tourist target. The online ratings of the venue and the food had been promising. After a little pleading and negotiation over the phone, Clinton was able to get an 8:30 reservation for an inside table overlooking the harbor. He was gambling that they might be able to be seated early, so he didn't text Sahana about the change in time. When she arrived, they ordered two glasses of sauvignon blanc and appetizers at the bar. While they waited for their table, Sahana broke the ice.

"I remember you—from AP calc—this mysterious brainiac who always hung back." She winked. "You had this knowing half smile most of the time, like you already knew all this stuff and found everyone else's struggles marginally amusing."

"That? Just cover for my paralyzing shyness. And I remember you from AP calc, too: this brainy girl with the exotic looks who was always in the center of a circle of friends, talking nonstop."

"Was not." Their wine arrived, they raised their glasses in a toast, and she took a sip. "Mmm, nice. Mind if I ask you something, something personal I always wanted to ask?"

"No, I don't mind. Go ahead."

"Your name. I remember you getting teased over it. Was your mother a Hillary fan or something?"

"No. Clinton is actually a pretty popular boys name in Portugal— at least it was then. It was my father's choice. He made all the decisions when I was young. Then he disappeared, and my mother made all the decisions. That's how I ended up going to school in Newburyport. So now it's my turn. Personal question."

"Okay, fair is fair."

"The little dot on your forehead, which was magenta this morning and now has turned bright blue, like some kind of magical mood mark. What exactly is that all about?"

"You mean my *bindi*? It's decoration, a Hindu tradition. It actually has religious significance for some people—chakra stuff—but I just like the look. And I changed it to blue to match my blouse."

"So it doesn't mean you're married or something?"

"No, not that, definitely not that. And you? You're not married?"

"No, definitely not."

After their shrimp and scallop ceviche arrived, she sprang the big question on him. "So, now that we cleared up names and marital status, what is this really about? I mean, you pretending you don't know me, claiming to be somebody else. What is this story you say you're working on, and what does it have to do with the lab?"

"Wow, a lot of questions. You know, I probably shouldn't be having this conversation with you, but my instincts tell me to trust you. I hope my instincts are right."

"Ooo, you make this sound all cloak-and-dagger-y."

"It is. I'm investigating the death of someone, someone you knew, I think." She waited for him to continue. "You remember Mrs. Geller, the middle school science teacher? Did you have her?"

"Yes, I remember Mrs. Geller. Who can forget? I heard about what happened to her from Betsy Whitman. It was terrible. I was going to post a note on her tribute page."

"Well, I have good reason to believe what happened to her was not an accident. The police are looking into it, of course, but I'm doing some investigating on my own. Did you, by any chance, know her husband, Dr. Rosen David? He worked at Biontolics."

"He was her husband? I didn't know that. I didn't actually know him personally, except for what a friend told me. I mean, everyone knew about him after that story came out about his dying of Ebola or something. We all knew the story was bullshit. The hospital and reporters got it garbled up somehow. He couldn't possibly have been handling tissue samples. He didn't do that kind of work. No one up here does. The clinical stuff is all done down in North Carolina. Up here, we're mostly computer nerds with fancy titles."

"Can I ask what you are working on?"

"Well, you know all our work is very hush-hush."

"You mean, like military stuff?"

"No, not that kind of confidential, but the company is absolutely paranoid about tipping its hand. Maybe, like, half the requests to publish are turned down by corporate. We joke about them as the 'science censors.' I swear, it seems they only let the crap be submitted to journals; the really good papers mostly get filed away."

"What kind of papers? Any of your stuff?"

"Ah, I don't know. We're not supposed to talk about our work."

"Well, just talk about what you can, then. Anything." It was a reporter's ploy, an end run around the confidentiality excuse.

She stared at her food for several seconds. "You won't name names, will you? If you do the story, I mean."

"Look, I'm a journalist. We protect our sources. Or you can talk off the record, if you want." At that point, he figured he had her.

She leaned her head close to his and lowered her voice. "Well, I had this one paper. I was doing work on cognitive decline in normal aging, not field work or clinical studies, but theoretical work on the functioning of memory consolidation and retrieval and changes over time in the aging brain. I devised this systems model, very detailed, then collaborated with a guy down at Research Triangle—that's the other East Coast unit of Biontolics. It checked out. I mean, this was breakthrough work, maybe Nobel material eventually. Squelch. Then Rustum—that's my co-author at Research Triangle—says the funding source wanted some added runs in the clinic from another population using a convenience sample. That means people not really picked at random but who just happen to be available. Well, he does it, and all of them are outliers, off-scale for their recorded ages. It completely breaks the model."

"That must have hurt."

"No, don't you see? This is science. Whatever you find is good. So what if the model was wrong? Models can be fixed. Besides, the results on these five subjects were so far out of line that this was another must-publish result. Once again, no go. So, two-and-a-half years of work with no new papers.

"But—and get this—Biontolics doesn't care. Rustum and I got hefty bonuses and commendations for 'outstanding contributions to neuroscience.' What the fig was that all about? You tell me."

"I see. So you think your work is being suppressed?"

"No, I wouldn't say that, exactly." She paused to take another sip of her wine. "Oh, I don't know."

"Okay, we'll leave it at that. Back to Millicent Geller. You didn't know Dr. David personally and didn't know he was married to Mrs. Geller. What about this friend you mentioned? What was his name?"

"*Her* name. Jeannine Carston, one of my best friends here—actually got me my job at Biontolics. She was having an affair with him."

Clinton tried not to look too interested. "You don't happen to know how I might get in touch with her, do you? I'd like to get her story."

"That would be a little hard, unless you believe in communication with spirits."

"She's dead?"

"Yeah, cancer. She died in his arms, so they say. After she was diagnosed, they both dropped out for a while. Eventually he reappeared, promoted to a new position at the lab, but he was never the same. It must have hit him very hard. From what Jeannine told me, they were really in love. I really didn't know he was married. Of course, not long afterwards, he too was dead." She set her fork down and scowled in concentration. "That's three people, closely connected, all dead within a few short months. Wow! Is that why you started your investigation?"

"I started out because of Millicent Geller. She was one of the best teachers I ever knew, because she changed the course of my life and I owe her something. Now I may have more reasons." He held her gaze for several seconds before she suddenly found her drink interesting and looked down. "I need you to take me seriously. I don't think it would be safe to talk with anyone about this or even to mention that you know me."

"I am taking you seriously. I'm expecting the same from you." She stared out across the dining area toward the windows with the lights of the harbor beyond. "I just thought of something. Jeannine had two sisters living in the area. I don't remember their married names—the family was Catholic, so they probably didn't keep their maiden names—but you might be able to track them down."

"I already have an idea how to do that."

"I bet you do. You might have been a pretty good scientist if you had stuck with biology."

"I might have been a pretty good journalist if I had stuck with journalism."

"What do you mean? I thought you said you were a journalist."

"Well, I teach journalism. You know what they say: those who can do, those who can't . . ."

"I don't buy that for a minute. The best teachers teach from what they know and what they do." She suddenly looked up. "Ah, here comes our bouillabaisse. I think they are finally going to seat us."

~ ~ ~

Dinner lasted longer than either of them expected, and a stretched-out stroll along the harbor boardwalk extended the evening even further. On the way back to Sahana's car, Clinton made a detour into the still-open Walgreen's on Main Street and bought a prepaid phone with cash. He turned off location tracking, deleted several junkware apps, and disabled text and call logging, then entered his cell number into the contact list before handing it to her. "This is what they call a burner phone. It's only for messages between us and only in an emergency. After one use, we dump it or replace the SIM card." She took it and slipped into the pocket of her jacket.

"One more thing," he said. "Do you know about public-key encryption? Do you know what PGP is?"

"I have a *pretty good* idea."

"Ha ha, right: Pretty Good Privacy. Well, set yourself up to exchange PGP email so we can be in touch without eavesdroppers. And don't ever use your computer or the phones at work to contact me, okay?"

"Wow, you really are looking out for me."

And for me, he thought, as he gave her a quick hug.

~ ~ ~

It was past midnight when Clinton got back to his motel. He immediately slipped his laptop computer from the backpack on the bed and booted it up. "Well, Jeannine Carston, whoever you are or whatever part you played in this story, I think it is time to see what we can learn from Google."

Clinton was in his element when online: digging, dodging and weaving from link to link, uncovering unexpected resources through sophisticated searches, and doggedly chasing down information. It did not take him long before he had unearthed citations to scientific papers linking a Jeannine Carston to Dr. Rosen David. An obituary in a newspaper archive provided further details, giving the cause of death as cancer and saying that Jeannine Carston was "survived by her loving husband, Dr. Rosen David of Essex." So, they might have been married. Were Rosen and Millicent divorced, was he a bigamist, or had it just been an affair? The obit also named the two married sisters, Elise Carston McDermott and Angela Carston Farini, along with the names of three nieces and a nephew. He had done his journalistic duty: he had his multiple sources of confirmation linking the three deaths.

Jeannine Carston had worked with Rosen David at Biontolics and been involved with him, yet Clinton didn't remember seeing the name in the packet from Millie Geller. He got the envelope from his suitcase and slipped out the documents. On the cover letter was a smudge near the bottom that he had not noticed before, a smear where something in pencil had been erased. He held it at an angle, trying to make out the faint traces of what had once been written there in firm block letters. With the light just right and his eyes squinted, it was just visible, one word: Carston—Carston with a question mark.

Millie Geller had made an annotation on his copy of the letter, then changed her mind. Or was it intended to be discovered, a tantalizing teaser or, in this case, a clear confirmation.

The deaths were linked. How? Biontolics, obviously. How else? What else did he know? The dictator in Africa who died the same way as Dr. David. Perhaps he could learn something in the Republic of Busanyu. It would be a logical step for a reporter. Not as logical as getting some interviews with the top dogs at Biontolics, but that route looked like it was probably strewn with landmines. Staying in the area much longer also had begun to feel risky. Ipswich was a small town, and it would be all too easy for determined parties to track him most anywhere around Boston's North Shore. The whole quest was beginning to seem quixotic, but maybe he needed to put some distance between himself and New England.

Before turning in for the night, he picked up email. There was another note from the girl in his journalism class.

Your sub is so boring. She drones on like a UAV flying over Iraq.

(Nice simile, huh?) I want you back. She gives the weirdest assignments and she doesn't even stick to the syllabus. I don't think she likes me. Please come back soon. –Julia

Chapter 10

Bertrand Lyon rechecked the transaction summary, then tapped the Enter key to complete the electronic transfer paying off the renegade commander for the attack on Nichevo. He was ahead of schedule, but he liked tying up loose ends as quickly as possible. It was one of the reasons he had come to trust and rely so much on Gus Holzinger. Gus finished the assigned job, whatever it might be, quickly, quietly, and without leaving tracks.

Bertrand retrieved the Express Mail package from his briefcase for one last check for tracks that might need erasing before it was digitized and destroyed. He scanned once more through the double-sided attachment to the cover letter that listed, in alphabetical order and conveniently numbered, all the recipients and their addresses. They were a mix of well-known journalists and news editors with others he had never heard of. He stared at the last entry on the flip side: Giles Underwood at the *Sydney Morning Herald*, number 32 in the list. Something bothered him.

He fished his smartphone out of his pocket and tapped a contact icon. "Gus. Lyon here. Sorry to bother you at this hour, but I wondered if you remember how many mail packets you intercepted. And remind me: what exactly happened to them?"

"I saved one for you and shredded and then incinerated the other thirty."

"So, thirty-one, you say. And you're sure of that?"

"Sure as I can be. I was rather surprised by the size of the stack that I slipped from the bag in the truck. I counted them on the spot and again when I disposed of all but that one. Why?"

"We have a problem. The packet itself lists thirty-two recipients."

"Shit."

"You should have cross-checked against the list. You missed one. Presumably it was delivered."

"I didn't ... I ..." He stopped protesting. "Yes, you're right, sir, I should have examined the contents and cross-checked."

"And you destroyed the others, so we have no idea which one is missing."

"I thought it was prudent."

"Prudent. Right." Bertrand considered his words. "Well, we have our work cut out for us, Gus. We can cross Sanger off the list because his packet is in front of me right now, but we have thirty others to eliminate—and one to sniff out, someone who did receive the material but hasn't acted on it, at least as far as we know. This could bring down the whole operation. Get on it, Gus. Now!"

"Yes, sir. That's not going to be easy. We can't just go up and ask everyone on the list. What do you propose?"

Lyon took the phone from his ear and looked at it in disbelief. "I don't propose anything." His voice had taken on a hard edge. "Figuring out how to do this is what we pay you for."

"Yes, sir. Send me an image of the list, and I'll start on it right away."

"And Gus, I don't need to remind you that we do not want to tip our hand to anyone—not those who didn't get their copy and certainly not the one who did."

"No, sir. You don't need to remind me."

~ ~ ~

Holzinger's mind raced through possibilities. There had to be a way to find out which packet had been delivered. The US Postal Service was hardly at the center of his area of expertise, but there would have to be some sort of audit trail at the post office where the packets had been posted. He looked at his watch. Another drive up to Maine would be the tedious but easy part; getting access to records would be far harder. And a third unfortunate accident in the same area, should it become necessary, would magnify the attention that was already being focused on just one small town.

It was time to slow down in order to speed up, get some background on how the packets were sent. Express Mail. He remembered the labels. He could go to the local post office and ask. Or he could just go online.

A few minutes later, he was calling back to the Sellian Atlantic offices in London. "Sir. Holzinger here again. There should be a number on the label of that packet. Would you please read it to me?"

"What good will that do? We already know what happened to this one."

"I have an idea, sir. That number might help."

"All right then. Ready?" He read off the letters and digits of the number.

Holzinger had guessed that the Express Labels at any given post office would be numbered sequentially, or at least be issued in blocks. He clicked through to the USPS tracking page and stated entering numbers, varying the last two digits, but every number he entered was rejected. He tediously checked all numbers within 100 to either side of the one he'd been given. No luck. Maybe the numbers printed on the labels were not used for tracking. He checked his watch. The post office would be closed; he would have to find another way.

Clinton, who had told no one about returning to Sacramento State or about his immediate plans, hiked across the river on the elegant Guy West footbridge and slipped onto campus without announcement. He was sorting through the file drawer of his desk, when he heard a voice from the doorway, high and melodious, with the laid-back rhythm of California's Central Valley.

"Hey, professor. Welcome back. How long you staying this time?" It was Julia Sousa. When he swiveled his chair to face her, she flashed him a megawatt smile that dominated her round, milk-chocolate face.

"Not staying long. Just until I can arrange my next trip. I'm afraid you'll have to grit it out with Dr. Grist this semester. If you're really so sold on the superiority of my teaching style, maybe you can take my journalism ethics class next semester. If I'm back by then."

"When do you leave for Africa?"

Clinton's mouth hung open in astonishment. "What? What makes you think I would be going to Africa?"

"You make me think. Simple: trip, arrangements. Sounds like big-time prep, maybe visa application, might not be back by next semester. You were out east, posted about a teacher who died recently, dateline was Falmouth, had to be this Millicent Geller, wife of Rosen David, worked with Jeannine Carston at Biontolics, she died, then he died of the same tropical shiz as that African dude, both tied to Biontolics. Four weird deaths within months, all tied to the same company. You already were out there, now you're back here. Simple deduction. Next stop: Mbutsu City, Busanyu, West Africa."

"Holy shit. You put all that together just now?"

"No, I did my Google research while you was away."

"Were. While you *were* away."

"Yeah, you were. When you said you were leaving again, I guessed. If not Africa, one of the other places Biontolics operates. I got lucky." She crossed her arms across her chest, displaying a tattoo on her left forearm: "YOLO" encircled by barbed wire: You Only Live Once.

Clinton was shaking his head. "That's not luck, that's professional-caliber investigative work. I wish you were already through with the program and working for me."

"Your lucky day. Your wish is granted. I'm through with the program."

"What are you talking about. You have at least another year of coursework plus an internship."

"No way. I quit today. A whole fricking term of Dr. Bonnie Grist grinding away like some millstone—you like my plays on words?—that's not in my plans."

"But you didn't know until just now that I wasn't teaching any more this semester."

"That's when I quit."

"Just like that?"

"Just like that. How long do I have to get my visa and that shiz?"

"Hold on there." He held up both hands in protest. "What are you talking about? You're not going with me to Busanyu. No way."

"Click." Her index finger tapped an imaginary touchscreen in the air. "Confirmation. Destination: Busanyu. Thanks, professor. I better start packin'."

"Now you're talking crazy." For no reason that Clinton could figure, the girl started humming the chorus of "Beware the Dog" by The Griswalds. "No, I said no. I am not taking a student with me to Africa. Absolutely no. Look, I don't have time for this. I have a lot of things to do over the next three days."

"Click. Departure date confirmed. See how good I am at getting people to tell me details? You need me."

"Why? Why do I need you?"

"Portuguese."

"What about Portuguese?"

"You, you're Portuguese?"

"Well, yes, I am part Portuguese, on my father's side, and Moroccan Jew on my mother's side. But what has that got to do with—"

"O senhor fala Portugues?"

"No, I don't speak Portuguese, but I do know a few phrases. Like that one. And I remember how to curse in Portuguese, thanks to my father, who had a talent for it. That and chemistry, the kitchen variety. *Merde!* That's pretty much the extent of my Portuguese shit."

"Exactly. I'm fluent. Both my parents are from Cabo Verde. I was born here, but at home we spoke nothing but Portuguese. You'll need a translator."

"But I'm not going to Cabo Verde or Angola or Mozambique. I'm going to Busanyu." He zipped his backpack closed and stood.

"Without doing your homework, Professor?" She wagged her index finger like a metronome, then straightened and stood with her hands to her side as if reciting. "Owing to its historic roots, the two official languages of the Republic of Busanyu are Lusanyu, the dialect of the dominant tribal group, and Portuguese. Do you speak Lusanyu?"

"No, I—"

"Didn't think so. Neither do I, but I can sing the national anthem in Lusanyu. It's on YouTube." She sang out in a dramatic soprano voice. *"Basanya kyahm ngala, ga'atni o mkam a'ana."*

Clinton waited patiently until she finished the first verse. He clapped. "Very impressive, but you are still not going with me. It would be against the rules for me to take a student with me on a trip, certainly not on an international trip."

"Exactly. But I'm not your student, not even a student anymore."

Clinton dropped his backpack into the chair in exasperation. "Look, you're underage, you—"

"Am not. I'm twenty-three. I know, I look young for my age. It's the Cabo Verde genes, I think."

Clinton turned back to shuffling through files and tried to ignore her.

"Okay, then," she said, turning to leave. "I'll meet you in Mbutsu City. Try the Hotel Palácio Real. It's cheaper than the name suggests, and the bar is a favored hangout for journalists."

"How the hell would you know something like that?"

"By doing my homework. See, you need me."

"NO!"

"Then I'll meet you there. I'll be staying at the Palácio Real. Later, professor." She pivoted and started strolling away.

"No, wait. You realize, the country is on a State Department caution list. I can't have you flying to West Africa alone."

"That's chill. Then I can ride with you to the airport." She returned to his desk.

"Wait. How are you going to get the right tickets? How can you afford this? How—"

"I'll get the right tickets because we'll both be on the only connecting flight that leaves in three days. Like, there's only a couple of flights a week unless you do something weird like fly through Japan or something. And I can afford this because I have a travel grant built into my stipend from the Strathmere-Lewin Foundation."

"Strathmere-Lewin? Never heard of it. Wait a minute. I thought you quit."

"I did. Or will. I'll do the paperwork at the end of the semester. Right now, I have to go see the bursar to get the travel funds for a study trip abroad. You will be listed as my sponsor, of course, but you don't have to tag along. I can forge your signature."

Clinton didn't know which part of her whole improbable story to confront first. "You . . . you are . . ."

"Awesome. Yes, I know it. So are you." She hugged him and danced away. "Later, professor," she said, without looking back.

He was still sorting papers into his backpack when she returned a few minutes later.

"I just wanted to thank you, professor." She hugged him once more. "We're going to make such a team in Africa. I am so there." She skipped out of the room again.

Clinton put his hands over his eyes and bowed his head. "What am I in for? This is nuts to the nth."

Chapter 12

Clinton picked up his email one last time before leaving his apartment. There was an encrypted message from Sahana. He drummed his fingers on the table as he waited for the plaintext to appear.

> *I've been doing a little digging on my own, covering my tracks so as not to set off alarm bells. I've found evidence that the archives at the lab have been sanitized. There are occasional citations of internal working papers that ought to be in the system but seem to have been deleted. Almost everything by our friend Dr. David is "unavailable." I'm now using my own system and Internet resources to keep poking around. In my experience, if you dig long enough, you find that somebody somewhere has an unauthorized PDF copy saved on some server. I'll keep you posted. And thanks again for dinner.*
> *–Warmly, Sahana*

Clinton tapped out a quick reply.

> *Be careful. I'm traveling and may be out of touch for a while, so don't panic if there is a delay in responding to emails. Check out the attachment and let me know what you think of it, but don't discuss it or show it to anyone. –Yours, Clint*

He attached an encrypted digital copy of the two unpublished papers that had been included in the packet from Millicent Geller.

~ ~ ~

When he arrived to pick up Julia at her mother's place, she insisted on introductions all around at the curb. "Hey all, this here is my professor who I'm working for."

"Whom," he corrected in an aside, "for whom I'm working."

"Right. I'm working for him. This is my mother, Anabella Sousa. And that's my kid brothers, Denzil and Daniel. They're twins, but you wouldn't know it. And standing in the doorway is my stepfather,

António, but he won't talk to you. Or me."

Clinton waved in the man's direction. "So, your parents are all right with this trip?"

Julia gave him a surreptitious scowl just as her mother took a step toward them and reached to take Clinton's hands. "It is so wonderful you to do this. And I am so surprise that the University pay to study abroad for students. America! Amazing! You take care of daughter. And all students on trip."

It was Clinton's turn to frown at Julia. "Pay? Study abroad? All students?"

Before anyone could say anything else, Julia started hugging her mother, with air kisses to the left and right. "We really need to leave. It's a long drive to the airport. I'll send email through Denzil or Daniel. Okay?"

"Okay. *Adeus*. Go with God."

~ ~ ~

Clinton concentrated on his driving through the heavy traffic getting out of town, which spared him from making conversation until they were speeding down the I80 freeway. "Uh, your mother's English is pretty good. I thought you spoke only Portuguese at home."

Julia pulled out her earbuds. "What did you say?"

"I said your mother speaks English better than I would have expected, considering you spoke nothing but Portuguese at home."

"Well, yes. But mother is smart, and she has learned a lot. I also tutor her. She . . . ah . . . practiced before you arrived."

"She practiced, huh? And you? Did you practice?"

"What do you mean?"

"Nothing. Look, we have a long drive and a couple of even longer flights ahead of us. On the way to the airport, why don't you tell me a little about yourself so I have a better idea who it is who manipulated me into this trip."

"Who me? Manipulated? You asked for my help. That's the only reason I'm doing this. I figure you'll owe me big time and give me good grades in the class."

"You're not in my class anymore. Don't you remember? You quit school."

"Oh, yeah. Right. But I'll probably have other classes with you, so, like, it's an insurance policy, sort of, for when I'm back in school."

"Back? Isn't it time you came clean and told me what this is really about? I checked. You're not enrolled as a regular student at the university, and you're not on any stipend or scholarship that the administration knows about. You are taking one class—mine—and you are behind on the tuition payment for that class. What gives?"

"Must be some kinda records screw-up. You know how the California universities are at messing up records and stuff."

"Cut the crap. You are trying to bullshit a BS champion. What is your story? You tell it to me straight, or you don't get on that plane."

"Then you'll be the one who gets stuck for my plane ticket."

"How do you figure that? You bought the ticket."

"On your credit card."

"What the fuck? You're a thief, some kind of hustler. How did you manage that?"

"I boosted your wallet when you were getting ready to leave. Took down your Visa card number and the little code on the back. That's all they need through the website. Slipped it back to you when I returned."

"You little ... how the hell am I going to pay for two tickets to Mbutsu City via London. I should pull over at the next rest area and have you arrested."

"No you shouldn't. You really do need me. My Portuguese is actually pretty good; I didn't lie about that."

"What else didn't you lie about?"

"That you're a great teacher, that I'm really learning lots from you, and that I really want to someday be a journalist like you."

"Oh, no. You may want to be a journalist, but you really don't want to be a journalist like me. You—"

"Yes, I do."

"No, I don't think you understand. I ... oh, never mind."

"No, tell me." She reached over and placed her hand on his forearm. "I really want to know."

He glanced down at her hand. It felt warm against his bare arm. "It's just that ... well ... the work can be a little scary at times."

"Well, yeah, which is what makes it exciting. Hell, you packed up for darkest Africa on a whim. Flying half way around the world to chase down some bad guys: that sounds pretty brave to me."

"It may sound like it, but, believe me, it's a lot harder tapping a state senator on the shoulder and asking him questions."

"Yeah, I suppose. Never tried that, but I did lift a radio from a state trooper once."

"No shit! How in . . . ?"

"Roadblock, he's running a field sobriety check, I stumble into him. He says, 'You flunked, young lady.' I insist on a breathalyzer, and it comes out clean. He walks back to his car perplexed. Got into trouble, I would guess, when he showed up at the end of the shift without his radio. I tossed it in a dumpster on my way back to my boyfriend's place. It was his car, and he would've been royal pissed to have to get it out of impound."

"I don't get it. You have a nice home, a family, you're studying journalism. What's with being a scofflaw or a pickpocket."

"Scofflaw? Now there's a real vocab word. But I don't live there, you know, at my mother's place. I just stopped by in time for you to pick me up. I've been living on my own since I was sixteen—hustling, boosting, whatever pays for groceries—ever since they kicked me out."

Clinton changed lanes to pass a slow truck train. "What happened? I mean, why did you get kicked out?"

"My stepfather was trying to hit on me, but when my mother caught him, he said I was coming on to him. She believed him. Hey, I don't blame her. He was the one paying for groceries; I was the one eating them. Simple economics."

"And why are you coming with me to Africa?"

"Why not? I'm between gigs. Besides, I was about to get kicked out of school for not paying my fees, but I wanted to keep learning from you. You're a good teacher. And I like you. The way I figure it, just give us some time on the road, and maybe you'll like me, too. Anyway, now we're stuck with each other." She loosened her seatbelt enough to slide down and stretch out. "I'm gonna catch some dreamtime. You drive careful."

"Carefully. I'll drive carefully."

"Right, like I said." She closed her eyes.

He looked over at her, so lovely in repose, and shook his head. "Danger in denim," he whispered to himself.

Chapter 13

Holzinger's hands hovered above the white-lit letters of his laptop keyboard. He was running out of trick ponies to call into the ring. His own hacking skills, once first rate, had not kept up with the rush of advances in cyber-security and the malicious tools that exploit their vulnerabilities. In recent times, he had become too much a jack-of-all-trades, too much a hands-on enforcer. Not long ago, he could have hacked into any number of facilities on his own, as he once did with the arXive servers at Cornell University to make an unpublished paper vanish. That was then, this was now, and the US Postal Service was proving beyond his flagging skills.

His hands, still poised an inch above the keys, were beginning to cramp with tension from the struggle with an inner self that had long ago been paved over. It was a self that wanted to form his hands into fists and pound the laptop in helpless fury, a self that had erupted in rage when he was offered no explanation of why his security clearance for a promotion in Germany's BND had not been approved. It was the self that turned red in the face when a target recovered from the poison Holzinger had carefully painted on the inside of a coffee mug. It was the self that Gustav Holzinger had vowed to defeat, to keep sedated in a straightjacket in a well-guarded mental prison at the back of his brain. Training, discipline, perpetual practice: these had enabled him to maintain his calm and controlled exterior for all the years he had worked with Sellian Atlantic and Biontolics and Pan-Africa Pharmacometrics.

The responses from his extended network of hackers in China and Russia were not placating that dark inner self. They all had different ways of expressing it, but the answers were, at the heart, the same. It would take too long and cost him too much to hack into either the USPS databases or, alternatively, the systems of more than two dozen separate organizations to which the packets had been sent. Money itself was not the issue—it never was with Biontolics—but too much money chasing one job could attract unwanted attention. In any case, just putting such a job out for bid could be a bad idea because it had too high a risk of exposure.

Holzinger looked up from his tense hands to focus on a spot in space just above his laptop screen and a half meter beyond. He watched as his smoky visualization of his breath jetted out and then was drawn back in, an unseen but not unreal cloud, pure thought, pure vapor. He followed his thoughts and his feelings without judgement, without response, letting his mind stray from the breath that ebbed and flowed, allowing its return to that living vapor that sustained him, letting go of everything wanted or needed. With this meditative practice, the tension gradually drained from his fingers, which floated upward as if buoyant. Somewhere, beneath the waves of nothingness that spread over his being, a desperate and angry inner voice muted, grew silent, and once more slept inside his head.

"More than one way," he said in the whisper of a slow exhale. "What do I know? What are my assets?"

He imagined his problem floating above and beyond the laptop screen in the void wiped clean by his breath. He pictured a glowing list of names on the left and a bright single name on the right. He visualized a line slowly materializing in the space between, jumping around erratically like the artificial lightning from an electrostatic generator, finally establishing a bright connection from the name on the right to one of those on the left. That was it. He did not need hacking skills that he no longer had; he only needed to do some clever online research. Thirty-two names against one. What were the matchups?

He shifted his focus back to his laptop screen and let his fingers tap away at the keyboard. He first established a secure connection through the Sellian Atlantic VPN tunnel, then launched a browser inside a software sandbox that would isolate it from the rest of his system and make everything he did disappear when he shut it down. The queries were straightforward, variations on "Frieda Abinger" AND "Millicent Geller" or "Johnathan Beltram" AND "Millicent Geller"; "Washington Post" AND "Millicent Geller" or "Times-Picayune" AND "Millicent Geller." He created a simple text file, then wrote a script to crawl through the file, posting all the combinations against both Millicent and Millie Geller. He launched the script. In a few minutes, he had the consolidated results from Google, Bing, and Yahoo.

Among scattered pairings that were easily dismissed as spurious, one stood out: Clinton Rodrigues at the *Sacramento Bee*, tied to Millicent Geller by a blog post. He popped it up in a new window and skimmed through the blog lauding the late teacher. He was about to close the window when he noticed the dateline: Falmouth, Maine. "Son-of-a-bitch!" He had been right there. What the hell was a reporter from California doing in a suburb of Portland, Maine, if not responding to a packet sent to him from there?

Holzinger checked his watch. Three hours earlier on the West Coast. It was worth a try. He Googled to get to the contact page of the newspaper website, then dialed the main number. He got a voice menu and selected the option for a dial-by-name directory. Entering the first letters of the first name got him a voice mail for someone in the finance department. He decided to try for a live operator by holding down the zero-key. After a seemingly unending series of rings, an operator finally answered.

"I'm looking for Clinton Rodrigues. Can you connect me?"

"Just a moment." He was put on hold. "I'm sorry, there is no one by that name in our directory. What department are you looking for?"

"News?"

"I'll connect you."

The news room was no help except to say that Rodrigues didn't work there and they could not help locate him. The secretary who answered the phone suggested he try searching on the internet. Holzinger was already launching a new search as the woman on the other end droned on about what he might do. He disconnected.

And there it was, on the first page of results for "Clinton Rodrigues"—a half dozen publications, a blog, and an entry in the faculty listing for the Department of Communication Studies, Journalism, and Film at California State University Sacramento. He dialed the number in the entry but got shuttled to a voice-mail message. "Hi, you've reached the robo-domo for Clinton Rodrigues, lecturer in Communication Studies, Journalism, and Film. If you are a student, please use your SacLink account to contact me. Anyone else, send me email. Don't bother to leave a voice message; it will only get swallowed by digital demons."

"All right, Mr. Rodrigues. Now that we know who you are, I think it is time we make your acquaintance in person."

Chapter 14

On their tickets it had looked so straightforward: SFO to LHR to MBI. The reality was two brutal days of flying. Clinton had never been good at sleeping on airplanes. He spent much of the ten-hour-plus overnight flight from San Francisco to London's Heathrow reviewing the pages from the packet that he had photographed and stored in an encrypted file on his laptop. He wearily plowed through a second reading of the two unpublished scientific papers that he had passed on to Sahana. Most of the first, "Cancer expression, cell longevity, and mosaicism in *Rattus norvegicus*," made little sense to him, but the accompanying material suggested it was behind the anti-aging strategy that scientists at Biontolics had devised. Of the four authors listed on the typed cover page, he recognized only Atchison Dougherty, former head of Biontolics. The other paper, by Dr. David Rosen, "Role of selected oncogenes in regulation of telomere activity in genetic chimeras: a multi-factor meta-analysis," made even less sense to him in detail, but the overall conclusion was clear enough.

Julia, with the resilience of youth augmented by a couple of little white pills, had slept through the whole flight and awakened, refreshed, in time for breakfast before landing. As she fairly bounced through the day of enforced tourism in London, Clinton shuffled along like one of the living dead until their return to the airport. Finally overcome by exhaustion, Clinton slept on the overnight flight to Mbutsu International.

~ ~ ~

"Hey, my sleepy professor, wake up. We're in Busanyu. Can you believe it? We have to get off before this plane takes off for Cape Town."

Clinton opened his eyes to see a smiling, wide-eyed face hovering inches from his. He managed a sleepy smile in return and struggled to orient himself. "What?"

"We're in freakin' Africa, professor. Awesome. Grab your stuff and let's get to work."

~ 283 ~

Perched on the shaved-off top of the once-majestic Mount Durban, the airport, small but surprisingly modern, overlooked Mbutsu City and the valley beyond. Passengers were efficiently escorted across the tarmac toward the multi-colored glass face of a graceful terminal. The building, an architectural monument to the excesses of the previous regime, seemed to float amidst jets of water spraying into early morning air that smelled of a recent rainstorm. Black-draped portraits of the late Dr. Edgar Jabari Mbutsu greeted new arrivals as they entered the building. The country, still in official mourning, was under the guidance of a caretaker government trying to fill a power void until the elections promised for early in the next year.

Edgar Mbutsu had been a brutal despot, but his violent and heavy-handed regime of more than four decades had brought prosperity to the country—at least to those in his favor—and had helped stabilize the region. The latter had made Busanyu's President-for-Life the darling of the West even as its leaders condemned his undemocratic regime. His sudden but not entirely unanticipated death had made many in Busanyu uneasy about the future. The rebel group, *O Exército de Unidade Nacional*, the self-styled Army of National Unity, had taken advantage of the unease and the power vacuum to up its game and stage increasingly bold incursions into the nation's heartland from the remote regions where it exercised its own brand of repression.

Despite the abundant presence of soldiers patrolling the airport armed with AK-47s, the customs and immigration clearance was perfunctory. Almost before they knew it, Clinton and Julia were standing outside in the still morning air looking for a taxi into town.

Clinton turned toward a queue near a covered kiosk painted in the ubiquitous national colors of blue and orange, but Julia tugged at his arm. "The taxis, when they get around to showing up, will charge you big time. That's for ignorant tourists or business travelers who can afford to throw money away. See that guy over on the other side of the parking lot, the one with the red jacket? We tell him where we are going and get there much cheaper and faster."

"How do you know that?"

"Got it from the PlanetStudentwise travel site."

"You sure it's okay? Is it legit?"

"No, it's not legit, but it'll be okay. Those guys are the ones taking the chances. They park here at the airport and stay out of sight until the flag—as they call the guy in the jacket—signals them by texting their cell phones. Then they pop up from under a blanket in the back seat of some old Peugeot, and, ba-bing, you have your own private driver, half-price."

"Don't the airport police or whatever know about this?"

"Of course, and the driver will slip some cash to the guy at the gate, who will then spread it around. Don't you know anything? Haven't you ever been to Africa?"

Clinton thought about lying, but just shook his head. "And you?"

"Once before, when I was little. Back to Cabo Verde to meet my grandparents. I was maybe six. I remember the way my grandmother smelled of sour sweat and wood smoke and the way this sand beach we visited seemed to stretch forever. Not much else. Anyway, let's talk to the man in red and get to our hotel."

~ ~ ~

The newly paved road from the airport zigzagged down the mountainside, past tin shacks and tiny terraced vegetable gardens interspersed with elegant mountain-side retreats protected by high concrete walls. The driver kept up a running commentary in a mix of Portuguese, English, and a language that seemed constructed of gutturals, grunts, and tongue clicks. Clinton thought it might be Lusanyu, but Julia said it was another dialect. "You can tell," she whispered, "by the nose that he's not a Basanya. Didn't you check out the photos on Flikr?"

Commuter traffic into the city slowed them to a walking pace once they were off the mountain. Sprawling suburban slums slowly gave way to blocks of businesses in buildings that kept getting higher as they approached the city center. There, office buildings sheathed in bronze-tinted glass towered over squat pocket malls with open stalls in their parking lots. Black Mercedes limos with darkened windows competed for the right-of-way against bicycles piled high with goods and produce. The cacophony of horns and curses and shouted conversations pummeled them from every direction.

The Hotel Palácio Real was a four-story yellow-brick building on a quiet cul-de-sac a few blocks from the central business district. It displayed three stars on a painted plaque beside the entrance, but Clinton had his doubts. Maybe Busanyu had its own rating system.

The lobby was dark and austere. A gray-haired housekeeper marched a whining upright vacuum cleaner back and forth over worn carpeting. At the unmanned front desk, Clinton tapped the nickel-plated bell and waited. The housekeeper turned off her noisy cleaner and said something to them in heavily accented Portuguese as she walked around and took up her spot behind the desk.

"She says her brother is at the market, but she can help us," Julia said. "It's a family that runs this place. Don't worry, I'll take care of this." She turned to the woman and started talking in Portuguese. The maid-turned-clerk responded in a sing-song variant punctuated by smiles and pulses of laughter. The registration process dragged out for many minutes as Julia and the woman talked amiably. "She was telling me about her boys, Alejandro and Filipe. Oh, she needs our passports. She will photocopy the identification page and return them to us later. It's the law here. She also needs your credit card for the deposit. It's also the law. She promises the deposit will be credited once the bill is settled."

Clinton fished out his passport and Visa card from his travel wallet and handed them to Julia, who delivered them with her own passport. The woman took an imprint of the card on an ancient hand machine that jammed twice before finally passing over both card and slip. She then studied each of their passport photos and glanced up at their faces. She laughed and said something in Portuguese before turning to fetch two keys from a cubbyhole behind the desk. Julia took them and handed one to Clinton. *"Obrigada, muito obrigada,"* she said to the woman.

Clinton nodded and said, "Yes, thank you."

"Your wife speaks very good Portuguese," the woman said, switching to English as she turned toward Clinton. "I hope you both enjoy your visit to Busanyu. It is a poor country, but is beautiful."

"She's not m—"

He was cut off by Julia's elbow in his ribs. "Let's go check out our room," she said to him, as she shouldered her backpack and started dragging her duffle bag toward the stairs.

The room on the third floor was clean but spartan in its furnishings, with two narrow beds pushed together on one side and an open armoire against the opposite wall. Straight ahead, French doors opened onto a balcony deep enough only for standing.

Clinton slid his luggage into the space beside the nearest bed. "So what happened to the two rooms I reserved?"

"I changed the reservation. This way we get a 'deluxe room with balcony' for less than the two rooms."

"And we just got married, did we?"

"Well, just for our cover purposes. And to save money."

"Cover? You do realize we are journalists, not spies. Or at least I'm a journalist. But I am grateful that you are looking out for my financial wellbeing, especially after you had me pay for your airfare."

"Chill. I'll pay you back."

"What century will that be?"

"This one, right after we win the Pulitzer." She noticed him studying the beds. "Hey, don't worry. There are two beds. We can pull them apart. I get the one closest to the window."

"Fine, as long as you keep to yours, and I'll keep to mine."

"Duh. What else?"

Clinton sat down on the bed and leaned back against the headboard. "I suppose we better start to work. We only have four days and three nights to decipher the connection between Biontolics and Busanyu and figure out what that has to do with Millicent's death. But first, I need to pick up email, which might not be easy in Mbutsu City. We have to figure out where we can get Wi-Fi service."

"There's an Internet café two blocks away." She slipped a map from the outer pocket of her backpack and unfolded it. "See? I already marked it. PlanetStudentwise again."

~ ~ ~

The Internet café was no Starbucks. Rows of young people, mostly male, sat at simple wooden tables outfitted with old-style small-screen glass monitors and grimy keyboards. Julia asked if there was Internet *"sem fios"*—without wires—and the tall man at the table nearest the door shook his head, but he reached under the table and pulled out a coiled cable with Ethernet connectors at either end. He gestured toward the back of the room where barstools were lined up in front of a deep shelf running along the wall. A power strip was taped to the wall alongside a network router with flickering green lights. It took a few seconds for Clinton to realize why all the stools were empty. Since it required owning a computer, it was probably beyond the reach of most of the other patrons.

Clinton plugged in, connected the network cable, and booted up his laptop while Julia tried to talk the man at the front into providing another cable. She returned with a pout on her face. "He says no more cables. Besides, only the far left port on the router is working. We'll have to take turns."

When at last he worked his way past a string of connection problems, Clinton found an encrypted email waiting for him.

> *Not sure if I should keep emailing you. The head of the lab has been finding excuses to drop into our section, and the section lead has been watching all of us like a lioness over her cubs. I've been trying to be careful and clever, but espionage is not in my job description. I think they may have smart monitors on "selected papers" that raise a flag whenever these "land mines" are accessed or even referenced. Where are you? I tried to call you at the university and got your stupid voicemail. I copied your telephone number from the burner phone (didn't think this qualified as an emergency) but kept getting an "out-of-service-or-out-of-area" message when I called. Are you okay? Should I be worried? Well, I am worried. Find a way to get in touch with me. Oh, there was nothing in the system about either the Dougherty file or Rosen David's paper. Very suspicious. Should have known. –Warmly, Sahana*

Clinton swore under his breath and quickly tapped out a reply.

> *I'm all right, just out of reach for a while. Better not do anything connected with me or this story at work. Nothing. Sit tight, and don't worry. –Clint*

"My turn," Julia said. "You can chat with your girlfriend some other time."

"I wasn't chatting, and she's not my girlfriend. She's ... she's an old acquaintance. We went to high school together."

"Sure you did, now scooch over and let me log on."

"I've got several more emails. Just hold on." He opened the next one. "All right. This is the one that counts. We have a 9:30 interview tomorrow morning with the Deputy Minister of Tourism."

"I didn't know Busanyu had any tourism."

289 ~ The Millicent Factor

"It doesn't, really, but that doesn't stop them from having a full cabinet post. Another opportunity to spread the wealth from blood diamonds, yellowcake, small arms, and everything else that gets skimmed as it enters or leaves the country."

"So why are we talking with Tourism?"

"Because we have to start someplace, get a foot in the door. So, here's the deal. We are doing a feature story on the state of Portuguese-speaking Africa, working our way from Angola, Busanyu, and Cabo Verde to Guinea-Bissau, Mozambique, and São Tomé and Príncipe. Who in the government would feel the most need to spin such a story their way? Who is a small enough player that he would care? That's why tourism is our entry point. As we discussed in class: find a door, then go through it."

"What do we do between now and our interview?"

"We do some poking around, man-on-the-street, study the lay of the land and get some background that we can use going into the interview tomorrow. What I am hoping is that after meeting with the deputy minister, we'll draw the interest of someone more important than our Mr. Rúben Magellan. So, watch what I do, take notes, and learn from the master."

"I will, after the master gives me the damn network cable."

Chapter 15

Gus Holzinger did not act precipitously, but he also did not hesitate to move quickly when needed. Before booking a flight to California, he had called the main number of the Department of Communications Studies to verify that Rodrigues was still with the university, obtained the location of his office, and attempted to get his home address. When that request was denied, he went online to track down where Rodrigues lived, then turned to the university site to verify that the man had a class scheduled for the term. The seminar was being taught Tuesdays and Thursdays in a Mendocino Hall classroom. That would probably be the best starting point to intercept and follow Rodrigues. There was even a convenient picture of Rodrigues on the man's LinkedIn profile.

The Core were having a late meeting at the clinic outside London when Holzinger made his Skype call. He was put on speakerphone. "Gus, this is Ferguson here. Can you hear me all right?"

"Yes, just fine, sir."

"Good. Sorry I missed you in Boston. Bertrand, Xander, and Ysabel are also here with me. Bring us up-to-date on the situation."

"Dr. Lyon, Mr. Quarry, Dr. Mandelova, you must know already that one set of the documents was actually delivered. I tracked it down to one Clinton Jorge Rodrigues, presumed to have been a reporter at the *Sacramento Bee*. He is now on the adjunct faculty at Sacramento State University. I am about to leave for California. I have a plan, subject to revision as needed, to deal with the problem. It will be resolved within twenty-four hours."

"Ysabel here. What about the other problem?"

Holzinger, caught off guard and unsure how to respond, probed. "What about it? What is your specific concern?"

"The woman at the North Shore lab, the one who has been making inquiries on Norwegian rats and other sensitive matters. Have you followed up on that?"

"That's next on my list." He was already scrolling through his recent messages. There it was, a text message from Bertrand that he had somehow overlooked: "Check on possible mole at NSL." He was slipping; he had seen it but not understood the urgency. "I'll take care of her, too."

"Wouldn't it make more sense, since you are already on the East Coast, to deal with her first."

"I considered that," he lied to buy time. "I believe Rodrigues is the priority, since he has the material and is almost certainly the instigator. We need to stop him before this spreads further. Besides, she's inside where we can keep tabs on her; he's not."

"Good enough. Under the circumstances." It was a typical response from Ysabel Mandelova, who never expressed unqualified approval or outright disapproval. Of The Core, she had always been the most difficult for Holzinger to read and to work with.

"This is Bertrand speaking. We'll up internal surveillance at the North Shore lab. You deal with Rodrigues and check in before moving in at North Shore."

"Of course."

"Hey, Gus, this is Xander Quarry speaking. While you're out on the Left Coast, stop in at the Ranch for a dip and a recharge. You're always welcome, whether I'm there or not. Tell Nadia I sent you. I'll be back at the end of the week, but I imagine you'll have moved on by then."

"Thank you, Mr. Quarry, I'll consider it if I have time."

"You know what you have to do, Gus." It was Bertrand Lyon's unmistakable voice again, the voice of command. Whatever the official definitions might say, there was never any question who led The Core.

"Yes, sir." The call was terminated from the other end. Holzinger lifted his palms from the wrist rest of his keyboard, where two sweaty imprints now glistened.

Chapter 16

The West African morning, still cool from the rains, had been spent exploring the city, a city of deep contrasts, where lighter-skinned descendants of the colonial Portuguese jostled natives with blue-black faces and where a checkerboard of buildings advertising wealth abutted crumbling proof of permanent poverty. White faces were rare and mostly seen entering or leaving the tall buildings of the central business district. In the *Jardim dos Exploradores*, the city's botanical gardens, Clinton and Julia encountered their first genuine tourists: pasty-faced elderly Brits and bored German youth ambling through the maze of plants from around the tropical world.

The former responded eagerly to their questions with complaints about the tour company that had disappointed them with second rate accommodations and a charter flight that had left two days late from London's Gatwick airport. The German young people, part of a joint Portugal-Germany initiative to raise awareness of Sub-Saharan Africa, found Clint's name and his stumbling German riotously funny. "A day here and a day there," said a slim blond girl with a boyfriend's arm permanently dangling around her neck, "it raises the awareness so much. You can learn more on Wikipedia. But, this is also free. And we get away from classes."

By the afternoon, Clinton and Julia had swapped places. She was the journalist taking the lead with spontaneous interviews, and he was the photographer tagging along to document everything. Clinton was surprised to find his anxiety abated as long as Julia was fronting for them, and her easy bravado escalated with every encounter.

Striding in the lead late in the day, she suddenly pivoted and pushed through the revolving door of a glass-and-stainless fronted office building. Quickly scanning a short building directory posted on a stand in the lobby, she approached the sleepy, bleached-hair receptionist with the announcement that they had an appointment at Berman and Gillmere, Limited. "Can you tell me what floor they are on?"

"Third floor." The woman reached for a telephone handset. "And who is your appointment with?"

Clinton swallowed his impulse to correct her grammar and waited to hear what Julia would say.

"We are meeting with Mr. Gillmere," she said.

"I'll have to call ahead."

"Oh, please don't. We're late for this meeting already, and you know how those types can be. Calling will only make us look bad, worse than already." She held her hands prayerfully in front of her.

The receptionist pursed her lips and hesitated, then broke into a smile. "Okay. Go ahead. Lifts are on your right."

In the elevator, Clinton admitted he was impressed with Julia's quick thinking. "But what are you going to do when we get there?"

"Watch. And learn from the master." She winked.

The elevator doors slid open to a reception area paneled in Bubinga wood with the blue-and-orange Busanyu flag draped behind an expansive desk. A grim-faced young man in a short-sleeved white shirt and patriotic blue-and-orange tie stared and waited as they approached.

With her warmest smile radiating, Julia started in Portuguese. "We are from the Sacramento Bee, and we are doing a story on companies doing business in Mbutsu City. We understand that Mr. Gillmere would help us with this story."

"Sacramento Bee? What is that?"

"The newspaper. We're reporters."

"You have identification?"

"Of course. Rodrigues!" She gave Clinton an impatient flick of her chin and switched to English. "The man wants to see some identification." Playing his part as lackey, Clinton dutifully extracted his expired press pass and a business card from his wallet. He fanned and turned them to face the receptionist, then promptly put them away again. The man looked dissatisfied but said nothing.

Julia filled the gap. "Would you please let Mr. Gillmere know we are here. He should be expecting us. My editor said it was all arranged."

The man, clearly operating well outside his comfort zone, reached reluctantly for the desk phone. "Your names again?" He held out his hand expecting them to supply business cards.

"Julia Sousa. And Clinton Rodrigues."

The man smiled briefly at their Portuguese names before tapping out an extension on the telephone keypad. "Yes, I have Senhorita Sousa and Senhor Rodrigues here from the newspaper, the Sacramento, uh . . ."

"Bee, the Sacramento Bee."

"From the Sacramento Bee. They said it was already arranged with you." He listened for several seconds. "Yes, of course." He replaced the handset. "Mr. Gillmere asked that you have a seat and make yourself comfortable. He'll be with you in a few minutes."

They took seats on the padded black-leather chairs lined up on one side of the room. Julia inclined her head toward Clinton's and spoke in a low voice. "See, that's how it's done."

"You're good at thinking on your feet, but we're not out of here yet."

Clive Gillmere, a red-cheeked dumpling in suspenders with fly-away hair that might have crowned a mad scientist, emerged from the far door a few minutes later. "Welcome to Busanyu. I am not sure what this is about, but please come along to my chambers." His British accent was as crisp as the conditioned air in the suite.

A short corridor led them to an airy office with an entire wall of windows overlooking the terraced plantings of the Garden of the Explorers. The rest of the office was paneled in pale boxwood. "Imported from good old Mother England," Gillmere said, when he noticed Julia admiring the surroundings. "A bright reminder that not everything is dark in Africa. Now, what is this all about?"

Julia continued to take the lead. "We're working on a feature series about Portuguese-speaking Africa for the business section of our paper. My editor was supposed to have okayed this with you and your firm."

"And are you from Portuguese Africa yourself?"

"My parents emigrated from Cabo Verde; I was born in the US. And you?"

"Manchester by way of Cambridge. But I've been here twenty odd years. Closer to twenty-five, but definitely odd. So, what is it you want to know about Berman and Gillmere, Limited?"

"We would rather hear it from you, in your own words. Tell us about your business. What brought you to Busanyu? What is it like working here in Mbutsu City? How do you think the business climate might change with the elections next year?"

"What brought me to Busanyu was the pound sterling. The money was the draw for Otto Berman and me, certainly not the culture or climate. Rising into the moneyed ranks was far swifter here. Better sweating through hazy tropical nights than clawing up some London law-firm ladder. My wife—ex-wife, I should say—was from Angola, originally. It was easy to switch sides when Busanyu gained independence and Mbutsu started rewarding his closest and most loyal supporters. He needed import-export help, and Otto Berman and I were ready to supply it. That's what we do, handle the paperwork side of moving goods internationally. It's more exacting than exciting, but it covers expenses and buys much more here than it would in London."

"I would say so, judging from your offices."

"Oh, you should see the laddies down the street. We are small and spare by comparison."

"Laddies down the street?"

"Mbutsu's own crew of expert exporters and . . ." His voice trailed out and his lips pursed as he considered whether to continue.

"Please, go on."

"This is Busanyu. It is a country peopled by fact-fakers and nimble-fingered skimmers. Import-export here is a business based on playing with labels and taking liberties with bills-of-lading. At least, though, we do not all make our millions on outright fraud."

"Now that is interesting. Could you elaborate?"

"No. I thought you wanted to know about our business. People who talk out of turn around here do not stay in business for long. The country is classified as a democracy, but that mostly means we can vote to keep our dictators in office. Mbutsu was elected President-for-Life by a landslide, as will his hand-picked successor, that toady Raul Gomes. People will vote for him because he appears to be benign, and because nobody dares vote against *O Partido da Revolução*. The Revolutionary Party is everywhere." He paused. "Even here. And, of course, they are also a force within certain interests back in Britain."

"Can you say more?'

"Oh, I could say a lot more, but that does not mean that I will. As I said before . . ."

"These interests, more financial than political, I assume. And British?"

"Is the Queen English? It's no accident that regular air service from London was among the first on the scene after UN recognition. I can tell you that an awful lot of money flows from here to London."

"And how is it that you know this?"

"You forget how small this slice of a continent is. Little happens in Mbutsu City that is not known to nearly everyone. You did not hear it from me, but nearly anyone can tell you how much is lost to graft and corruption in the government. Gomes, our former Minister of the Interior, may not prove to be as brutal as his predecessor, but he is no more trustworthy. Those bloody bastards in the Ministry of Industry and Trade get their percent of every deal handled by this office, and we are nothing special. Not that I would complain. We all get our nibble of the pie, all except the poor bastards on the street and in the countryside who get the crumbs left on the plate."

Julia pretended to be checking her notes before continuing. "We're meeting tomorrow with the Deputy Minister of Tourism. What should we ask him about?"

"His salary. And how, on his salary, he can afford a second home and second family in South Africa. No, I jest. And I said nothing, remember that."

"Of course, off the record, all of it, not for attribution."

"Good, we understand each other. I wish you luck tomorrow —and after." He stood and came out from behind his desk. "You are a lovely and clever young woman." He took her hand in both of his. "You just might get what you are after, whatever that may be. Rúben Magellan is a fool for pretty young women and an easy mark for anyone with intelligence, something he has no abundance of."

He turned to Clinton and held out his hand. "And you, good sir, do keep watch over the young lady."

~ ~ ~

It was the cocktail hour, but the hotel bar at the bottom of the stairs off the lobby was nearly empty. A middle-aged German couple had barricaded themselves in one corner behind schooners of warm beer and a rampart of guidebooks and maps. A man in shirtsleeves and wrinkled khakis sat half-on, half-off a barstool; a leather-trimmed canvas courier pack was stowed at his feet. All three patrons and the bartender eyed Clinton and Julia as they entered.

The man slid off the barstool and walked toward them holding a near-empty martini glass in his left hand while extending his right. "Olá! You must be the American journalists that Suzana mentioned. I am Hidalgo. I work for the Valley Free Press, which is an absurdist name for our sorry excuse of a newspaper. 'Why?' you ask, as you are journalists yourself and naturally curious about the curiosities of life. 'Because.' I answer, 'our office is on the road halfway up Mount Durbin and in Busanyu the press is decidedly not free.' But the press part of our name is valid. And you?"

"Sacramento Bee. I'm Julia Sousa. This is my photographer, Clinton Rodrigues."

Hidalgo shook hands with each of them and gestured toward the bar. "Come, please join me. I'll buy you a drink. Sacramento, you say. Central Valley. You are a long way from home."

"You know California?" she said.

"Oh, yes. I have visited there. I have cousins who live in Oakland. I would like to live in Oakland, too, but it is hard to get away. And hard to get in. Under Mbutsu, curse his memory, some sought asylum and were admitted to the US, but not many. Most who were in actual danger were simply eliminated by Mbutsu. Who was left to flee? Not me. They ignore me because I am nothing, and the Valley Free Press is published in English. Who reads English in Busanyu? A few tourists and no one else who is not already part of the Mbutsu machine, that is who."

Julia climbed onto a stool, leaving one between her and Hidalgo. "But there is now a caretaker government and elections coming after the first of the year. Don't you expect things to change?"

"Yes, I expect things will change. There will be new faces to fear, new pockets to fill, and new rules to memorize—and circumvent. What will not change is that the few will live well off the backs of the many. But that is hardly unique to Busanyu; it is the way of things nearly everywhere, and your much lauded land of opportunity is no longer an exception. But please pardon any offense."

Julia shrugged. 'No pardon is necessary for the simple truth. The US is now a nation of haves and have nots, with no road forward other than toward more of the same."

"Ah, I see you are a cynic. How does one so young and so beautiful succumb to such a disease of the soul? That malady is understandable in the old and disillusioned, like your jaded photographer here, but you and I, we have no excuse for catching the contagion of lost hope."

"I for one haven't lost hope," she responded, "but neither have I lost my eyesight. What's happening back home is plain enough to see. But tell me, what is happening here?"

Clinton, content to hang back, smiled his approval of her tactics.

Hidalgo leaned across the intervening seat and arched his eyebrows. "What is happening here is that we have somehow suddenly been blessed by an influx of reporters, including a clever young journalist who no doubt writes as well as she speaks and who brightens our dark city with her lovely face."

"Oh. My. God." Julia spread her hands in mock surprise. "Do all Busanyu males slather it on so thick? Or is it just lonely journalists."

"I am a journalist, true, but I am no longer lonely since you arrived. What would you like? I promised you a drink."

"Caipirinha."

"And you, sir?"

"Cerveja."

"The beer will be warm, you know. One of the few British influences, warm beer, an unfortunate legacy at that."

"Then I'll have what you're having."

"I'm having the vapors above a vanished dry martini, shaken not stirred."

"Then make it two James Bond martinis. Are you a spy in reporter's clothing?"

"No, just a lifelong Ian Fleming fanatic. Marmdu,"—he raised his empty glass toward the bartender—"two more of these, please."

"Are you staying here at the hotel?" Clinton asked him.

"Hell no. On the earnings of a reporter in Busanyu? No, I came here when I heard that there were foreign journalists in town. They always stay here and hang out in the bar because all the online crap says this is where journalists hang out. I don't know how that particular urban myth ever started, but it is self-fulfilling and self-sustaining. I suspect Suzana and her husband first planted the story to bring more business travelers to the hotel. A clever invention."

"Like the plaque out front with three stars?"

"No, that's legitimate, like the wall at the entry hall of your CIA. It means three people have been killed here. No, no, just a jest. Many more than three have been killed here. The stars are the official rating by our own Ministry of Tourism. One star if you have a bar, two if you have private toilets, three if you pay the substantial fee for the 'special review' by the Tourism Board."

"Four and five stars I suppose cost extra."

"No, they are reserved for hotels run by members of the royal family, that is, the brothers and sisters and cousins and children of our late President's many wives. Well, not so much his children, who are mostly still quite young, since he had rather a preference for young women, some of them very young themselves, some of them not quite women."

"I see."

"It is even said that one of the young women who he picked for special attention tried to kill him, but nothing came of it. He lived, and she disappeared. There were reprisals against her relatives, yes, but these were justified by the regime as attacks on rebel strongholds, strongholds that had always been remarkably well disguised as peaceful villages, if you understand what I am telling you."

Clinton smiled grimly. "Mbutsu was the Energizer Bunny of despots, wasn't he? He seemed able to survive every attack and to outwit every enemy, even old age."

Hidalgo finished his drink and signaled for another. "Yes, and in the end our survivor succumbs to some mysterious disease, despite being under the personal care of an entire company of physicians and specialists from England. One wonders."

Clinton set his drink down. "Tell me more about these doctors from England."

"What can I tell you? Nothing is known, but everyone knew. The Presidential Palace had its own fully-equipped hospital, and doctors would fly in regularly to give Mbutsu some kind of special treatments. I once interviewed an old man named Fallu who said he had been taken to that private clinic to be used as some kind of guinea pig for the treatments Mbutsu was getting, but some English doctor talked Mbutsu out of the idea. The man was let go, perhaps because no one knew he understood English. Shortly after I interviewed him, he was found dead outside his village, supposedly the victim of a random attack by rebel forces. Supposedly."

"Can anyone confirm any of this? Do you have evidence?"

"You need to understand about this country. We do not have confirmation or corroboration. There are no witnesses, no evidence, not even facts. Ours is a country of rumors and supposition, of stories unproven but universally known. The bankers in the central business district could tell you the exact number of millions that flow every day from here into numbered accounts and private investment arrangements. They could tell you, but they won't. Hell, the bartender here could tell you about secret deals and undocumented transactions. This is how the country works. And it does work. Why would anyone want to replace a proven regime, a stable system that works, with the uncertainty of genuine democracy and transparency. Who would favor a government that might distribute wealth away from those who have it, those who sustain the current system on behalf of wealthy patrons here and elsewhere?"

"But . . ." Clinton left the word hanging in the air.

"But. Yes, but what about principles, justice, equity, fairness, freedom? Empty words, like my martini glass again." He ran his finger around the rim, filling the bar with a sweet ringing. The bartender started making another martini as he talked with Hidalgo in Lusanyu. Hidalgo leaned toward Julia. "He says you should ask the Minister tomorrow about his garden."

"He's been listening? He understands English?"

"He's a bartender. Listening is his profession. He understands everything and everyone and betrays no one. I have been trying to tell you, this is the way Busanyu works. Everyone listens, everyone knows; no one speaks, no one does anything about what they hear. Even the rebels, the self-styled Army of National Unity, are also part of the system. They have no chance of victory, and they cannot be defeated. They need the government as the source of the plunder that sustains them and to seed the discontent that supplies recruits to their cause. The government needs the rebels to divert attention away from real problems and as a scapegoat on which to blame those problems. Everyone knows this is how it works, but no one ever says so."

"Except you, you are telling us."

"But who am I? I am no one. And who are you? In a few days you will be gone, with nothing but stories and suppositions in your notebooks, the ravings of a drunken reporter in a shitty little bar."

"Are we in danger?"

"What danger could you be in? If anything happened to you, American visitors, then there could be real problems. But if you return home, knowing everything but with nothing you can tell, you are harmless. Besides, who cares what happens in this tiny African country that no one can even place on a map? You have enough problems back home." He chug-a-lugged his last martini and slid off his stool, swaying as he bent over to retrieve his courier pack. "Do ask the Minister about his garden. That should be amusing."

Chapter 17

It was mid-morning in California, and Holzinger was pacing the empty corridor outside a classroom in Mendocino Hall, waiting for his target to emerge. The door opened and a gaggle of chattering students burst out and spread in all directions like water from an open hydrant. He watched attentively while trying to act uninterested. No one who came out matched the mental snapshot he had of Clinton Rodrigues. He decided to risk a quick glance inside the room.

At the front stood a Kathy Bates look-alike with close-cropped gray hair and large eyeglasses, two blue-outlined perfect circles covering half her face. She glanced up at him with a questioning look magnified by her glasses. "Yes?"

"I was looking for Professor Rodrigues."

"Well, he's not a professor, and I am not him."

"Do you know where I might find him?"

"No, do you? No one knows, except he is not here teaching his class. I am." Annoyance flashed in her eyes. "And I am none too happy to be doing his job for him. I should right now be writing, working on a textbook, the final draft, that is, and that's what I should be doing. I have better things to do with my time than to be holding the hands of third-year students who think they already know something. It was unprofessional and irresponsible of Rodrigues to pull out at the very last minute."

Not expecting the rant or the disappointing news, Holzinger took a moment to gather his thoughts. "And do you know what he is doing if he is not teaching?"

"I don't even know where he is, much less what he might be doing there. Of course, there are rumors, but journalists don't traffic in rumors."

"But these rumors—what do they say? It really is rather important that we find him."

"And who, exactly, is this 'we' who must find him?"

"Jackson, Polan, and Lieberman. We're attorneys." It was one of

Holzinger's favored instant covers because it carried a certain implied threat and lent an aura of legitimacy and power.

"Is he in legal trouble of some kind?"

"No, not trouble, but our client is eager to locate him. I'm not at liberty to discuss details, but the stakes are rather high. Anything that you could tell me that might be of help would be most appreciated. What sort of rumors are making the rounds?"

"Well, this is an interesting story. A student from this class said he thought that Rodrigues had taken off with one of the other students."

"Another student?" He leaned in to encourage the talkative professor to keep talking.

"Well, I don't know, but there is a student, female, who has also stopped showing up for class, an African-American girl, rather attractive, I would say, who kept asking after him when I started teaching his class. It could be just a coincidence. I didn't know Mr. Rodrigues that well, but he always seemed to be very responsible in his teaching—at least until dropping his course load—and much liked by his students. Of course, one can be too well liked. It's not our job to be liked by students but to teach them what they will need to know to become journalists."

"Of course. Did any of these rumors hint at where Mr. Rodrigues might be headed?"

"Well, the girl was from Africa—Angola or something like that."

Holzinger was suddenly more interested. "The student who dropped out. You know her name?"

"Yes," she looked down at a class list. "But I couldn't just tell you."

Holzinger followed her eyes. One inverted name drew his attention; it looked like Sousa. "Of course, I understand. Student privacy. Still, thanks for your time." And thanks for pointing the way to Portuguese Africa, he said to himself. He was beginning to get a clearer picture of just how messy the scenario he was facing might be.

~ ~ ~

AfrikAire was yet another of the Biontolics companies. It had been started specifically to service the newly recognized Republic of Busanyu and to serve as a captive conduit to Mbutsu City and on to Cape Town, where the vital facilities of PanAfrica Pharmacometrics were located. Like most of the Biontolics operations, AfrikAire was no mere front; it had exclusive rights to the routes, ran a robust operation, and traded with other parts of the financial hydra that was The Club, helping to channel earnings back to the coffers of the parent company.

Except for Bertrand Lyon, even the four in The Core did not know the exact extent of the many companies and organizations they controlled. Gus was not privy to the financial details, but his job required him to know which companies were theirs and which were not and who to contact and who to leave alone.

He checked his watch, retrieved the number for the Atlanta reservations service center that handled the AfrikAire account, and wracked his brain for the name of the woman who worked at the extension he was calling. He was never sure of it. That was the mnemonic.

"Shirley, it's Gus Holzinger here. I need you to check into passengers on recent flights to Busanyu."

"How are you, Gus? We never see you around here anymore."

"I've been busy. Traveling. Can you do a search for me? See if a Julia Sousa or a Clinton Rodrigues has recently flown into MBI."

"Sure thing. Do you have an authorization code?"

"Give me a break, Shirley. If you want to put me on hold while you call corporate, that's just fine with me, but you'd only be making more work for yourself."

"Okay, okay. Your caller ID is right, and I'd know your voice anywhere, but you gotta promise you'll find a way to swing through Atlanta on your way somewhere. I know a great little Jamaican place here."

The great little Jamaican place was actually Shirley's apartment, which had been an occasional stopover when Gus was working his way up in the organization. Now, though, he had no use for the Shirleys of the world and no interest in overnight delays. "Sure thing. I'll let you know. Can you do that search?"

"Already did. They traveled together, LHR to MBI, arriving Thursday. They have a return booking next week. They should be there right now. Do you want me to link over to the hotel system and see if I can find where they are staying? It might take a few minutes to get through the layers."

"Yes, do it. Send me a text message when you find them. And I'll catch you at that Jamaican place sometime soon." He disconnected before she could press him for a more specific commitment.

He checked his watch again, did the math, and decided to call London. He got the administrative assistant at Sellian Atlantic who told him that Lyon and Ferguson were having dinner at "the Table." Holzinger knew exactly where she meant. It was a touristy beef-and-ale place called Nights of the Round Table where private dining was available and no one who really was anybody in London would ever be seen. Holzinger called Lyon's cell phone, but there was no answer; he got an answer on the second ring when he called Ferguson's cell.

"Holzinger here. I found Rodrigues. He's in Mbutsu City with one of his students."

"Bloody hell. Well, at least he's isolated. Do what you need to do."

"What about the mole at the North Shore lab?"

Ferguson hesitated. "I . . . Look, it's practically on your way. Make a stopover in Boston en route to London and Busanyu. In the meantime, we can be sure our pair are tied up until your arrival in Mbutsu City. I'll see to it. You better get moving. Take care of that woman."

"I'm on my way. I'll catch the red-eye to Boston."

Chapter 18

Clinton opened his eyes, suddenly aware that he did not know where he was. It was not his apartment in California, not the motel in Massachusetts. The night sounds of a city drifted in on muggy breezes stirred by a slow-turning ceiling fan that buzzed with each rotation. He stared up at the turning blades, barely discernable in the darkness. Mbutsu City. It was a sound in his head more than words or letters.

He lifted his left arm and strained to make out the faint glow of the hands and the cardinal points on his watch. The hands were an italic L: a few minutes after three, so predictable. Whenever he crossed too many time zones, in either direction, he would awaken the first night right around three, suddenly alert to some internal alarm that did not actually keep time but merely reliably complained that something was off kilter.

He stared at the ceiling, letting his eyes adjust until he could make out the swirls and swipes in the sand-finish plaster. He started thinking ahead, as he often did when awake in the middle of the night. In the morning, they would be making their first open move into Busanyu officialdom. A meeting with a second-tier appointee was only the beginning. If they could parlay it into connections closer to the real seats of power, perhaps they could learn something. If need be, they could extend their stay.

But. There was always that word in Clinton's head. But what if they were going about it backwards, what if the real sources they needed were not the faces at the front, but the ones at the back, the ones in the crowd or the backrooms? Perhaps they needed an unconnected but knowing informant. Hidalgo had said that was how Busanyu worked. What if they were wasting their time with the Deputy Minister for Tourism?

Clinton tried to smooth over the anxiety that was rapidly rising, taking over his breathing, squeezing his throat. He rolled restlessly onto his side, and there she was, not even an arm's length away, eyes closed, her face turned toward him, sweetened in sleep into an innocence that was such a contrast to the tough, streetwise exterior of her daytime self. In the heat, she had shrugged the thin sheet down off her shoulder almost to her breasts.

As he studied her face in the dim light and watched the steady rise and fall of the sheet, his thoughts danced around the obvious. She was smart, pretty, inventive, and her affection seemed genuine. And she is your student, he reminded himself, and you her teacher. It would be a tough few days, but just that: a few days, only that. He could resist.

He closed his eyes, rolled onto his back, and lay there, willing himself to sleep.

Julia tentatively opened her eyes, watching as his breathing slowed and grew more even. She studied his profile until he was asleep and sleep finally came again to her.

~ ~ ~

There was a message at the front desk when Clinton dropped off their keys in the morning. Their meeting with Rúben Magellan had been moved from the downtown office of the Tourists' Bureau to the ministry's main office on the grounds of the Presidential Palace. When they asked the young man at the desk how to get to the Palace, he raised his eyebrows and whistled. "Taxi. But it is many miles out, very expensive."

"Are there buses?"

"Buses? Why would there be buses to the Presidential Palace?"

"How expensive?"

"Maybe fifty American dollars. It might be cheaper if you have euros."

"We have Busanyu *cruzeiros*. How much would that be?"

"Oh, a taxi would not accept *cruzeiros* from you. They would want hard currency. But . . ."

"Yes?"

"My brother has a car. I think he would take you for maybe thirty dollars. Do you want me to call him?"

Clinton shook his head in amusement. "Everybody here is a hustler. How long before he could be here?"

"Not five minutes. He is parked in a lot just near here."

"Will there be enough time to get us to the Presidential Palace for a 9:30 meeting with the Deputy Minister of Tourism?"

"Oh, I am sure Filipe can do that. Yes."

"Alright, then, call your brother."

~ ~ ~

The ride out of town to the Presidential compound was harrowing. First, there was the traffic getting out of the city, then there was the road without traffic, a deserted stretch of paved but narrow highway that snaked alongside meandering streams and made sudden hairpin turns for no apparent reason. Filipe attacked these switchbacks like a Formula One driver gunning for position.

They finally approached the gray fortress-like walls and gate of the compound at twenty past the hour. Guards on either side of the open gate stepped out of their booths and watched warily as Filipe sped toward them. Clinton cringed and involuntarily slunk down in his seat. At the last second, Filipe slammed on his brakes and skidded to a stop. The guard to the left lowered his rifle and grinned. Apparently this was not the first time Filipe had hurriedly delivered visitors to the Presidential Palace.

Filipe and the guard laughed as they chatted in a mix of Portuguese and Lusanyu. "My brother-in-law," Filipe said, as they were waved through the gate. "He is married to my youngest sister. I do not envy him. She is a princess born into a poor family, and her fantasies for him are as rich as the palace here." He drove them through the gate and down a wide avenue between stately eucalypt trees. Ahead, framed by the rows of trees, was a white marble building with broad steps mounted by massive marble columns. They pulled beside closely spaced concrete bollards that prevented vehicles from getting closer than fifty feet. "It is a security measure. You will have to walk from here. I am sorry."

"And we owe you how much? Thirty American dollars?"

"Oh, my little brother, he always does this. He knows it is forty dollars, but he always tells people less. I do not know what I am to do with him. I am sorry."

Clinton stood with his wallet in his hand, not moving, not sure whether to argue or surrender to the scam. "I am also sorry. We changed most of our money into *cruzeiros*, and I only have thirty American dollars left. Ah, but I can give you *cruzeiros*. At the official one-for-one exchange rate, that would be forty *cruzeiros*. Whichever you prefer is fine with me. *Quarenta cruzeiros ou trinta dólares?*"

"I will take the thirty dollars and get the rest from my stupid little brother." He reached for the bills that Clinton held out to him. "Call the hotel when you want to come back. Maybe my little brother can come and pick you up on his Vespa."

~ ~ ~

The rush to arrive on time had been for nothing. Deputy Minister of Tourism Rúben Magellan was still in a meeting with the Acting President. It was nearly an hour before they were ushered into an empty office decorated with antique maps and paintings of fifteenth- and sixteenth-century sailing vessels. A gentle breeze drifted through tall open windows.

Magellan arrived to find them studying one of the paintings. "It's an oil, not a print, but it's only a copy. The map over there, however, is authentic sixteenth century."

"Are you related to the original, to Fernão de Magalhães, the explorer?" Julia asked. Clinton stood and started snapping pictures.

"Naturally, not directly—his two sons died young—but to the family, I think. My father anglicized the name to Magellan after studying at Oxford." He pretended to be oblivious to Clinton clicking away. "Now, what is this interview about. Suddenly, out of a cloudless sky, a fax arrives saying you are on your way and doing a story on us. Most amusing."

"Well, to be honest, it's only a small part of a bigger feature series about the countries of Portuguese Africa."

"Why all of a sudden?"

"Mbutsu. When he died, it put your country on the map with the media. The American public started thinking about this young country and its future. We wanted to do something to counter the Fox News sensationalism over Mbutsu, and, in the process, introduce our readers to some of the diversity of the former Portuguese colonies."

"We were never a colony. We were born a democratic republic."

"Yes, of course. Well, then, let's begin there, with the early days. Were there tourists right after independence from your neighbors? Fill us in on some of the history."

"That you can get from the national website. Or Wikipedia. Let me start instead with the last few years, since I was appointed by the late President-for-Life Dr. Edgar Jabari Mbutsu o Busanya."

Once started, there was no stopping Magellan, who droned on about numbers of endemic bird species and hectares of national parks and thousands of passenger arrivals at the airport as well as plans for expanded tourist attractions in the country's only real city.

Julia took advantage of a brief pause in his narration to jump in. "Speaking of tourist attractions, what exactly is the story of your garden?"

The man's face reddened noticeably. "Who told you to ask that? I want to know who."

"No one. I think it came from an Internet search. What is the story. Apparently, it is quite an interesting one."

"The *jardins botânicos* were under-budgeted, the contractors dishonest, the market in exotic plants volatile, and the accountants incompetent. That is the story. I personally benefited in no way except for the satisfaction of seeing the city gain a valuable and successful attraction for visitors. If anyone tells you otherwise, they are traitors. Or jealous of my . . . our success."

"I see. But of course. Charges of fraud and corruption fly like bats at dusk around here. None of it is to be taken too seriously."

"Oh, it is to be taken most seriously. I could tell you many things to be taken seriously. My garden pales by comparison to what I know has been paid into accounts administered by Revic Investments and other firms in Switzerland. I . . ."

"No, don't stop."

"I forgot myself. But you are interested in tourism, business not politics."

"Financial stability or impropriety is certainly of interest to visitors. In any case, we are broadly exploring the state of business in the countries of Portuguese-speaking Africa. Busanyu is the youngest sibling in this diverse family. It will interest our readers to compare and contrast. Cabo Verde, for instance, is widely regarded as one of the most democratic countries in Africa, Busanyu as one of the most—"

The Minister held up a hand in warning. "I would be careful. We have rather strict slander laws here, and you are in the Presidential Palace."

"We are, and we are your guests. As journalists, we do sometimes forget our manners in the course of trying to do our jobs. So, why don't you lead the way and tell us as much as you can about tourism here and your role in the business."

He opened his mouth to speak, but was interrupted by the ringing of the telephone on his desk, a brass and ivory model made to resemble an antique. *"Baya,"* he answered in Lusanyu. There followed a rapid exchange during which he kept glancing at the two of them. Just as he was hanging up, two armed men in camoflage uniforms entered.

"I am afraid you will have to go with these . . . gentleman."

Clinton started clicking away, documenting the scene. "What is this about?" he asked between shots. "We're journalists. You have no right—"

One of the two soldiers crossed the room in two strides and took hold of Clinton's Nikon. *"Fotos são proibidas.* No pictures. Forbidden."

"But, we're journalists." Julia came to his defense just as the other soldier took her arm, turned her toward the door and pushed against her back with the side of his rifle. "Where are you taking us? You have no right." Her voice was demanding, but it cracked with the last words.

Clinton was fighting to retain his camera, but the soldier heaved and spun, breaking the strap and leaving a friction burn on the side of Clinton's neck. They were pushed out of the room and were met by more soldiers, who escourted them to an office several doors down. They were shoved roughly through the door, which was slammed behind them and then locked.

Chapter 19

Julia kicked at the door after it closed. "What the hell is this all about? At least now I understand why they don't get that many tourists. These people have a warped sense of hospitality."

"Ha ha. Easy for you to joke. You didn't just lose several thousand dollars worth of camera and lens. And remember their reputation here. People they don't like tend to disappear. We are in a deep cesspool, swirling in shit." Clinton slumped down in an upholsterd chair.

Julia paced impatiently. "Not for long."

"But we're locked in."

"Der. Does this look like some kind of dungeon to you? We're in a frikken office wing. Like, they're improvising; they must be winging it on short notice. Hey, turn around. Check out the windows behind you. They're wide open, and it's only six or eight feet to the ground. Let's go while they're busy extracting their thumbs from their asses and trying to figure out what to do about us."

Before Clinton could argue, Julia climbed onto the broad window ledge, swung her legs out, and lowered herself from the window. He looked out in time to see her dusting herself off. She looked up and beckoned him to follow suit.

As soon as he was beside her, she led the way around the corner of the building, down an alley, and into the shadow of the private hospital positioned back from the main gate and to its left. They stood there for several minutes, waiting to see if there was any sign their absence had been discovered. There were no sounds of running feet, no shouts, no alarms. "We don't know how long we have," she said. "They might come back to the room in two minutes or leave us to cool our heels for hours. Let's get out of here."

"How?"

"Same way as we arrived. Just don't panic, don't run. Whatever happens, act normal. It's just like walking away from a department store that you just relieved of some merchandise."

She stepped out of the shadow and started walking casually but briskly down the avenue leading to the main gate, keeping to the edge in the broken shadows of the eucalypts. Clinton caught up and got in step with her. "What are we going to do?"

"You are going to shut up unless it's to use one of the nine words of Portuguese you know. Let me do the talking."

They reached the front gate and Julia walked up to the guard who had spoken with their driver on the way in. She greeted him warmly in Portuguese, and he responded with a smile. "And tell your brother-in-law to get his sorry butt in gear," she said. "He was supposed to be here to pick us up after the interview."

"Ah, that is just like Filipe. He thinks he is such a businessman, but he is always screwing up. I will call him." He pulled a cellphone out of his fatigues and punched in a number. "Filipe, you desert donkey, your riders are here at the gate, waiting for you. They are finished and want to return to the city. Where are you?"

He covered the phone with his hand. "He is in Rio Frio. It is in the hills. He says he can be here in fifteen minutes, but he lies. It will be twenty." He took his hand off the phone and put it to his ear again. There was a rapid exchange in Lusanyu before the soldier returned the phone to his pocket.

"Thank you so much." Julia held out a fistful of *cruzeiros* for him.

"Oh, no, that is not necessary. I am glad to help a visitor. And my brother-in-law is a stupid donkey." He took the money despite the protests.

Julia and Clinton sat down on the sloping grass a few feet from the guardhouse. Twenty minutes passed with no sign of Filipe. Suddenly there was a commotion inside the gate and loud cries: "*Fechar o portão! Fechar o portão!*"

Clinton turned to Julia. "What are they shouting?"

"Close the gate. I think they have discovered we are no longer where they left us."

The two guards looked at each other and shrugged. They had been given an order, a simple, direct order. Reentering the guardhouse, one of them flipped a switch, and the armor-plated gate rolled ponderously closed. It banged shut just as Filipe's dusty Peugot came into view. He skidded to a stop as he had done earlier and waited for his passengers to climb in.

"Okay," Clinton said, "let's go."

"First, I have to say hello to my cousin, then we have to agree on the price."

"Your cousin is busy, and the price is forty *cruzeiros*."

"One hundred."

"Fifty."

"Eighty, no less."

"For that, we'll wait and call a taxi."

"Sixty, then. But that hardly covers the petrol and oil."

"Okay, sixty. Let's go."

Filipe threw the car in reverse, spun the wheel, and braked in time not to slam backwards into the closed gate. His spinning tires left rubber on the pavement as he raced forward again.

"Filipe, is there any other way back to the city?"

"No, only the Presidential Highway."

"No back roads or turnoffs?"

"Only the road to Rio Frio, but it is just a tiny village in the hills. There is nothing there."

"Isn't that where you just came from? There must be something there."

"Well, there is my pretty Ovita, but . . . Do not say anything of this to my brother. Alejandro has a mouth that never closes. He will tell my wife."

"Don't worry, we will not tell him. And you will not tell anyone you took us first to Rio Frio." Clinton reached around and dropped an extra stack of *cruzeiros* onto the passenger seat.

Filipe smiled at them in the rearview mirror. "Unlike Alejandro, I know when to close my mouth. We will take the turnoff just around the next curve and spend the afternoon visiting the village and exploring the trail along the river."

"Most excellent. And when you make the turn for the village, try not to leave any skid marks."

"Ah, but yes, I do understand. I do."

They made the turn toward Rio Frio without squealing tires. As the Peugot climbed the steep unpaved road toward the village, they could just hear the sound of distant sirens fading as a caravan of vehicles from the Presidential compound rushed toward the city.

~ ~ ~

Clinton counseled against returning to the hotel, but Julia insisted. All their clothes and Clinton's laptop were there, and she was convinced that if they waited long enough, they could get back in without being spotted.

Filipe finally drove them back into town well after dark. "This way, we can see lights on the road if they have any patrols out," he said.

Julia had Filipe swing by the hotel and run in to retreive their room key from behind the front desk, then drop them off a block away. She led Clinton around to the back of the hotel, where she used the room key to open the after-hours entrance. The hallway on the third floor was deserted. She slowly turned the key in the lock and opened the door a crack. When there was no sound, she opened it the rest of the way. The beds were made, the armoire was open and empty, and their things were gone.

Chapter 20

Clinton, standing just outside the door to their room, lowered his voice to a whisper. "What are we going to do?"

"Not stay here, that's for sure." She left the room without closing the door, grabbed his hand, and pulled him back toward the rear stairway. At the sound of hurried footsteps coming up the stairs, she spun around. "Quick, out the front." She led the way down into the darkened lobby and toward the front door. They froze at the sound of steps behind them.

"Wait, it is me, Alejandro, Filipe's brother. Filipe called me while you were visiting Rio Frio. Your things are in the storage room, the door behind the front desk. It is not locked, and I will be asleep when your things are taken. I will not know what happened to them or who took them. *Entenda, Senhora?*"

"Yes, I understand. Thank you."

"Here." He slipped a piece of paper into her hand. "It is Hidalgo's telephone. He said to call him if you need help. I think you should call."

"Yes, I will. *Muito obrigada.*" She hugged him and kissed both his cheeks.

They were startled by a flash of blue light through the front windows. "Quick, before they get here," he said, "take your things and go that way. At the end of the corridor is the door for the help to take the *lixo* to the back, to the rubbish bin. I will delay them."

As they fetched their bags from the storage room, Alejandro positioned himself in a drunken sprawl across a sofa in the lobby. When the pounding at the entrance began, he stood and staggered slowly to the door.

~ ~ ~

Three blocks from the hotel, Clinton stopped to catch his breath. He flattened himself against a building, set his suitcase down, and slid the strap of Julia's duffel off his aching shoulder. "Whew. We'd better call Hidalgo, although I can't imagine why he would help us. I got the impression he was a failed reporter, resigned to the regime and to shuffling his disillusioned way through the rest of life. Of course, he seemed enthusiastic about hitting on you."

"Well, maybe your impressions were wrong. I saw him as a pragmatist with deep but disguised ideals. And he wasn't hitting on me. It was just a game we were playing."

"Well, let's call him. Maybe he can settle our disagreement. I think the only reason he would help us is to see you again."

Hidalgo answered on the first ring but asked for Julia to be put on the phone. Clinton raised his eyebrows and squinted in a smug look as he handed the phone over to Julia. "He wants to talk with you."

"Obviously, because he is more comfortable speaking Portuguese. That is why he wants to speak with me." She talked with Hidalgo in rapid Portuguese punctuated by quiet laughs. She disconnected and handed the phone back to Clinton. "He said we should be waiting in the alley behind a tobacconist several blocks away. I think I can find it, but we must hurry there."

When they reached the specified rendezvous, Hidalgo was already waiting. He threw their luggage in the front passenger seat of his car and hurried them into the back. "We must move quickly without attracting attention. And tell me what you did to bring the army and the police down on you. No, don't tell me. What I don't know I can't betray under torture." He smirked at them over the seat back. "Now, duck down and try to think small until we get to my cousin's place."

Clionton laughed. "It's always cousins: a cousin's car or a cousin's apartment. Is everyone a cousin here?"

"Yes, mostly. Family is what people turn to when they can't trust institutions. I learned that at the University of Porto, but it's true."

The cousin turned out to be an old woman, Safima, who spoke neither Portuguese nor English and had an unused room at the back of her cottage where they could hide out for a few days. "Until you leave to return to America. She will bring you food, and I will bring you news."

"Will they stop us from leaving at the airport?"

"They might, and they might not. It depends on what offense they think you are guilty of. But the caretaker government is indecisive, and they might be more than a bit wary of angering the Americans, who supply nearly half of their arms, either directly or through Israel. Unless you are spies or have committed treason—in that case, you could be shot on sight—otherwise, I think it will be in their best interest to let you go and be done with it."

Julia put her arms around Hidalgo's neck and kissed him. "Thank you, so much. Return with news soon."

"I will. Oh, I will."

Chapter 21

Dr. Silvio DiGiorno had the best publication record in the Neuroscience Section at the Ipswich labs, which, to Sahana, meant he churned out a steady stream of mediocre papers, none of them good enough to warrant sequester by the "science censors." She surmised that he had been elevated to Section Lead precisely because he had learned to play the game reliably according to its hidden rules, which meant he required no special attention from the management above him. It also meant that his own output was largely superfluous, hence the time he spent on administrative duties was no real loss to the organization.

He was as incompetent as a manager as he was as a researcher, but his limited ability seemed to match some need of the organization to keep a certain number of unproductive people on payroll. This at first had bothered Sahana, who had been raised by her Indian immigrant parents to excel at everything and never to settle for her own second best. DiGiorno, on the other hand, seemed to settle for second or third place in everything. As it became clear that his muddle-through methods were no barrier to her and no real drain on the section, she accepted the state of things. She herself did not aspire to move into management; it was the intellectual thrill of the science that drove her.

Of late, DiGiorno had been spending more time actually in the section than in his second-floor office. It was as if he had become a sudden convert after reading some popular book on the philosophy of management-by-walking-around. His version of the approach was to begin each day with a ritual stroll through the section, pausing at each workstation to peer over the shoulder of a researcher, studying intently what was on the screen, and nodding for several minutes until the researcher became sufficiently uncomfortable to take out her earbuds or turn around and ask if there was anything he wanted.

"No," he would say, "nothing special, just interested in what my people are doing." It was always "my people." He would give a flick of his long fingers in the general direction of the screen and continue. "Tell me about this. What exactly are you working on?"

This morning was different. DiGiorno strode in with purpose, accompanied by a taller man with an expressionless face and gray eyes that constantly darted and scanned his surroundings. The two of them walked down the corridor between workstations directly toward Sahana, stopping at her desk. Her heart sped up as she tried to concentrate on the paper she was reading on-screen.

"No, next one," DiGiorno said. He turned to Sahana. "Where is Nina Bracken today?"

"I don't know. She didn't say anything to me. Maybe she's tied up in traffic. She lives in New Hampshire, you know."

"Well, when she comes in, tell her I'm looking for her. She should see me in my office right away." He flicked his fingers. "Carry on."

"Yes, of course. And I'll tell Nina you are looking for her."

Nina Bracken, the youngest member of the section, showed up only a few minutes later wearing a too-tight tee-shirt and a short skirt over leggings with the sparkle of metallic thread. "There was a bad accident at the Whittier Bridge," she said. "95 was backed up for miles."

"Anyone hurt?"

"Well, there were ambulances, so I guess so. I don't like to think about that stuff. It was such a drag being stuck in traffic so close. I probably should have taken Route 1, but by the time I got stuck it was too late. I thought—"

"Silvio is looking for you, wants you to see him in his office as soon as you come in."

"Well, he won't see me until I get my coffee. He'll just have to chill for a bit."

Nina took her time filling her mug and adding soy milk from her private stash in the refrigerator. She smiled back at Sahana and then started up the back stairs with her coffee. She returned an hour later with a grim look on her face.

"What was that about, Nina?"

"That's what I'm wondering. They asked me a lot of questions about stuff I have nothing to do with, papers I never heard of, research that's not in my specialty. They seem to think I've been doing stuff on the side or extracurricular work using lab facilities."

Sahana turned toward the scientific abstract displayed on her screen, hiding her expression. "Were you?"

"No way. I told them that. I don't have time for everything that is already on my plate. Why would I take on anything else?"

"You told them that?"

"Yeah."

"And they believed you?" Sahana was hoping for reassurance.

"I guess so. Although they said they would be watching me closely, whatever that means."

"Are you . . . well . . . worried?"

"Shit no. I can walk into half a dozen places on the North Shore and have a job within fifteen minutes. I know I'm good, and if they don't recognize that, screw them."

"That's the attitude, girl." Sahana swiveled around to give her a high five.

~ ~ ~

Gus Holzinger suggested that Silvio DiGiorno should find somewhere else to work for a while and to close the door on his way out of the office. Gus used Silvio's computer to access the secure link to London. He slipped his Bluetooth headset out of his belt pack, paired it with the computer while he waited for the connection, then asked to be put through to Bertrand Lyon."

"Sir, it's Holzinger here."

"What's up, Gus?"

"I interviewed the girl."

"And?"

"Not sure, but she seemed genuinely perplexed by the questions. We know that the queries came from her workstation—the IP addresses matched—but she might not be our mole. If somebody else used her computer or fudged the IP address, it could be anyone."

"Or she could be lying."

"Yes, well we'll be tailing her, and we're now tracking all traffic in the entire section. We'll find whoever it is."

~ ~ ~

Sahana waited until she was back in her apartment before using the burner phone. She finally got Clinton to answer after many rings.

"I'm sorry it took so long to answer. What's up?"

"They may be onto me. A guy showed up today with my boss. They interrogated one of the researchers, apparently about the archive searches I did from her workstation. I knew she had the habit of not logging out when she quit for the day, so before the connection timed out, I would launch a program on her system to keep it logged in until everybody else was gone."

"Clever. But if you haven't already stopped doing that, stop now. They'll catch you. I told you not to do anything at work."

"Yeah, but you told me that after I had already done it."

"Hey, it's bridge water."

"What?"

"Water under the bridge, whatever. Look, it's the middle of the night here. Despite the adrenaline you started coursing through my veins, I'm not fully awake."

"Where are you?"

"Somewhere else. Better you don't know."

"Who is that talking in the background?"

"Uh, another reporter, my . . . my interpreter."

"A female reporter, from the sound of it."

"Well, yeah, we're working together on this story."

"And sharing a room." It sounded catty and insecure at the same time.

"No, it's . . . we're in a . . . a conference room, working late, planning our strategy for interviews tomorrow." He covered the phone with his free hand. "Cut it out, Julia. Just wait until I'm off the phone."

Over the phone came a tinny voice. "Are you still there, Clint?"

"Yeah, I'm here. Look, pick up a clean SIM card tomorrow. Pay cash. And destroy this one. Call me once and hang up right away so I have the new number in my phone. Sit tight at work, and don't worry. You'll be all right."

Chapter 22

Holzinger was becoming weary of living at 35,000 feet sharing a long, narrow room with hundreds of strangers, but he needed to conference in person with his employers, and he needed to pass through London on his way to Busanyu. After the stopover in Boston, he caught an overnight flight to Heathrow. He always found that flight to be too long to stay awake and too short to sleep. He popped a couple of uppers on arrival at Heathrow, rented a car, and drove out to the clinic, where he amused himself with Sudoku puzzles until Lyon and Ferguson arrived.

"Good morning, gentlemen." He stood and shook hands with each of them. "I will not take much of your time today, but I thought we should agree on what to do with the two we are holding in Mbutsu City."

Bertrand took the lead as usual. "We are not holding anyone in Mbutsu City. While you were winging across the Atlantic, we learned that they escaped from custody."

"How the hell did that happened."

"It doesn't matter how; it happened. The alert is out for them. It would not be easy for them to slip out of the country unnoticed, particularly without help, which it does not seem they had, at least according to the local police."

"But they are there, still?" Holzinger said. "All we have to do is ferret them out. I can leave on the next flight."

"Let us not act too precipitously. So far, you seem to manage to be always in the wrong city or on the wrong continent when it comes to dealing with Mr. Rodrigues and his friend."

"But, I . . . Yes, of course, but now we know where they are, and they are, effectively, trapped. Busanyu is a small country."

"And mostly jungle, peppered with tiny villages connected only by footpaths and rutted tracks. They could be anywhere."

"They could be, but they are not. I am certain of that, sir. I—"

Fergusson interrupted. "Wouldn't it be far simpler if we let them come to us."

Holzinger pondered this for a moment. "What exactly do you have in mind?"

"They have return tickets, with the return booking in two days: San Francisco via London. They are amateurs. It would be far easier just to let them come to us. We can intercept them at Heathrow instead of chasing after them through a million square kilometers of back country."

"That's if they do use the return. What if they don't."

"Then you can chase them on horseback or by Land Rover if you wish, but we have little or nothing to lose by waiting."

"Little is not nothing, sir. What if they approach the news media, as the Geller woman tried."

"Tried. That is the operative verb. Forewarned is forearmed. We now have our own people planted at every media outlet on her list. No, if they try to go to the press, they will get nowhere, and we will get them. Besides, there is no press as such in Busanyu. It is all controlled by the government or too small to be of consequence."

"Really, sir, I should—"

"Two days, Gus." Lyon was back calling the shots. "That's all. You know, I think you are becoming a little impulsive and impatient with the years."

Holzinger nodded and let the blinds fall over his expression. "Perhaps. I'll go ahead and book my flight to Mbutsu City and be ready should that be needed."

~ ~ ~

Holzinger was finishing a bowl of soup in his hotel room when the text message came in.

Our intrepid reporters, ready to call it quits and head home, telephoned AfrikAire for required 24hr advance reconfirmation of return flight K0-12, MBI to LHR, leaving tomorrow at 21:00 GMT+1, arriving LHR 05:25 GMT. Be there.

Clinton had dozed off again. There was little else to do in the hot, dark confines of the fly-filled room, their temporary prison that might soon be bartered for a more permanent one. The sound of muffled laughter came from the high-fenced garden behind the house, a plot that was too small and too shaded to grow more than a handful of scraggly tomato plants with yellowed leaves and shrunken fruit.

Clinton pushed through the rear door that would not close completely and into midday sun that made his eyes water. Hidalgo and Julia were squeezed onto the single stone bench shaded by overhanging branches from a tree on the other side of the fence, talking quietly, as much with their hands as with their words, gesturing and touching, crinkling their eyes with the pleasure of the secret language building between them.

Clinton nervously cleared his throat. "What news, Hidalgo?"

"The soldiers seem to have given up. The official newspaper, *A Gazeta*, says only that two people were reported to have been on the grounds of the Presidential Palace without permission."

"And you still think it will be all right for us to leave tomorrow."

"I think the dogs have been officially called off for whatever reasons. As you requested, your return flight has been reconfirmed, and there has been no sudden manhunt, no massed militia in the streets. All is quiet."

Clinton half closed his eyes in an expression of deep skepticism. "Do you know any of the old American westerns, the classics? No? The soldiers in the fort always say when all is quiet that it's too quiet out there. What do you think is going on?"

"Perhaps they want you to come out in the open, to try to make a run for it. Perhaps they no longer care. Whoever 'they' are."

"Did you find out anything more about the doctors, the ones who took care of Mbutsu?"

"Only that they stopped coming after his death, and yet the money still flows out to the same accounts. So, perhaps you were wrong that the money was for medicine."

"Perhaps."

Julia stood and stretched. "I think it is time for a siesta myself. I'm going in, out of the sun. If you talk, talk quietly. Okay?" She bent and kissed Hidalgo on his sweaty forehead. To Clinton she gave a wink.

When the door had creaked nearly closed, Clinton walked over to Hidalgo. "Is there a back way out of here?"

"Over the wall, if you can manage. A footpath runs behind the houses and to a spring-fed stream that once supplied water to the residents but no longer can be trusted to be safe. Can you manage?"

"I can manage. Let's go for a walk."

Once they were away from the back garden, Clinton inched up close behind as Hidalgo led the way along the narrow path. "I don't even know your last name," he said.

"Laredo. Spinoza e Laredo. I should have properly introduced myself."

"Spinoza? Really? Are you also . . ."

"Yes, I am also. I am both a heretic and a Jew, like Benedito de Espinosa. And, in case you were wondering, there are no Jews in Busanyu—none that I know of—but no shortage of heretics. And you?"

"Both, you could say. My mother was Jewish, from a wealthy Mizrachi family, Moroccans originally, but when they disowned her, she disowned them and the entire tribe in turn. I was raised chameleon."

"Chameleon? I do not know that religion."

"I meant that she raised me to blend in, to disappear into whatever religious crowd I might find myself in. It proved to be useful training for doing journalism."

"I would imagine. I was raised *Catolica*, but like most Portuguese men, I outgrew it not long after my confirmation. My sisters, on the other hand, still live it, the religion, as do most Portuguese women. I only learned of my Jewish ancestry at university in England, where my classmates told me that a Jew is a Jew is a Jew, and a Jew by any other name would still smell. This I was told, repeatedly. And so, in response, I now call myself a Jew, although I have no real knowledge of what it means. It is a declaration that, though I may live here, I do not belong."

"Then you are. Then we are both Jews. As long as we are talking personally, can I ask whether you are married?"

"Ha. I know what this one is about and why you are asking. Yes, I am married, and no, I am not chasing your Julia. It is just a game, a most fun game that we Portuguese play. She and I both understand that."

"Are you sure?"

"I am sure. All she talks about is you. It is what gets us both to laughing so much. She has become my new little sister, the smartest and most interesting of the lot."

Clinton fought to keep from smiling too broadly. "Well, if we are to get Julia safely out of here, we had better do some planning. I don't like the idea of going to the airport right out in the open. Is there any other way down from the mountain in the event we need to change plans at the last minute?"

"Yes, there is a disused construction road from the other side, dating back to the mining that stripped the top of the mountain. It might still be passable in an off-road vehicle."

"Tell me, Hidalgo, what do you really think are the chances that we can board that plane and get away?"

"Those may be two different things."

"What do you mean?"

"They might not be letting you get away. They might be reeling you in."

"And then what?"

"What happens to fish that get reeled in? Still, you should get on the plane."

"Why?"

"Because you are not fish; you are smarter. And I will help you."

"Why?"

"It is your favorite word: why. Do not forget the other words that every reporter learns are the keys to a story: who, what, where, when, and how. But why do I help you? Because,"—he put his hand on Clinton's shoulder and squeezed—"we are both members of the same tribe."

"Jews?"

"No, heretics. Now, let us figure out the what and how of your story. Then we will return before your Julia misses us."

~ ~ ~

Clinton and Julia had showed up at the airport at the last possible minute and were inching forward at the very back of the check-in line at the gate. Julia was clearly perplexed and trying not to show it. "Why are they letting us do this? Why would they let us get away?"

"Maybe they are not letting us get away. Maybe they are reeling us in like fish?"

"Then why are we getting onboard."

"Because we're not fish. We're smarter. Hidalgo said that."

They reached the front of the line and handed their boarding passes to the ground staff at the gate. While the woman examined their passports yet again, the man checked them off on the passenger list on a laptop computer, then they were ushered outside, the last to board the shuttle bus that would take them out to the aircraft.

At the door to the plane, they showed their boarding pass stubs to the purser, who ticked off their names on her copy of the passenger manifest. The aisles were crowded with people stowing bags and negotiating seat changes. It took them a few minutes to reach their seats in row twelve.

~ ~ ~

From his spot against the windows on the observation deck of the terminal building, Hidalgo watched as the shuttle carrying the last load of passengers arrived at the bottom of the steps. He saw Julia and Clinton climbing the mobile stairs. At the top, Clinton paused and looked around nervously before entering the cabin. Hidalgo waited patiently until the cabin door was closed, the steps were rolled back, and the catering truck servicing the plane backed away to return to the building. Through the layers of glass he could hear the engines revving up as the plane inched forward and turned to roll toward the end of the runway. Hidalgo could sense the others watching the same scene. He shifted his gaze to focus on the reflection in the tinted window. A man in a business suit was just putting his cellphone away as the plane started its takeoff run. He was immediately escorted out by a uniformed guard.

As the plane gained speed, lifted from the runway, and began its steep climb to avoid the next peak in the chain of mountains, Hidalgo pressed his face to the glass and spoke quietly. "Godspeed on your journey, my friends."

Chapter 24

Heathrow Airport's Terminal 5 was especially busy, and, owing to a security alert, extra patrols and security personnel were everywhere. Holzinger edged toward the front of the milling crowd at the meeting point outside International Arrivals. An overnight connection meant his quarry would have to retrieve their luggage and clear customs and immigration in London. Gus was dressed in black slacks and a white shirt with epaulets and a shoulder patch that identified him as a member of airport security. A Glock 17 was holstered at his hip. He preferred a Kimber Custom or a Beretta, but the Glock, a favorite of United Kingdom law enforcement, was part of the disguise.

The rest of his people were stationed throughout the terminal, ready for any contingency. He watched as passengers on an Iberia flight from South Africa emerged through the swinging doors from the secure area, then the first arriving passengers gradually slowed to a trickle. At last, the AfrikAire crew came through the doors.

Holzinger stepped forward. "Excuse me, can you tell me if everyone is off the AfrikAire flight K0-12 from Cape Town and Mbutsu City?"

"Everyone is off. We're the last of the flight crew. There's only ground personnel aboard now."

"Are you certain?"

"Yes, of course. I'm the Captain."

Holzinger walked away. He pulled a compact radio from his pocket and pressed the Page All button. "Everybody, heads up. They slipped past us somehow. Fan out, cover the exits. We can't let them get away."

~ ~ ~

As they stood waiting beside the fat sculptured trunk of a baobab tree, Clinton turned toward Filipe. "You know, we almost didn't make it. Our little princess-of-all-she-surveys is so used to being in charge of everything." Julia bared her teeth at him and imitated a low growl before smiling sweetly.

"So, there I am," Clinton continued, "sitting on the aisle, row twelve, watching, checking my watch and eyeing the front of the cabin where the ground crew were finishing up. I wait until the maintenance guy steps out and the flight attendants close and secure the forward cabin door. The purser ducks into the cockpit with the flight crew as the other flight attendant starts down the aisle taking the passenger tally, clicking away at a little hand-held counter. I wait until she is past us before unbuckling my seatbelt. I tell Julia, 'We're both heading for the toilets. Now.' and she says, 'Not yet. Wait a minute.' Well, I don't want to wait a minute or even another second, so—"

"He says 'Move it!' and then practically drags me to the front where one of the catering guys closes the cockpit door in order to open the forward lavatory door, kind of blocking off the flight deck."

"Right. So, I push Julia ahead and reach behind me to open the door of the coat closet just aft of the galley, which blocks the view from the rear. A woman in a FoodForward Catering uniform nods to us."

"And he practically throws me toward this, like, platform extended from the food service truck. Two guys grab us and pull us inside— somebody's cousins, I guess."

"Yeah, and right behind us, the last two ground crew nimbly stepped across the widening gap as the catering truck backed away from the plane with the platform already starting to lower. The truck swayed as it swung wide to clear the wing of the plane—"

"I thought we were going over."

"—and it speeds across the tarmac toward the terminal. We reach the terminal building, the catering truck backs up to the loading dock, and we get hustled out of it and into the back of the Range Rover that heads us down the back way off the mountain." He took a little bow. "Just call me Harry Houdini. We checked in, got on the plane, were counted aboard, and yet, when the plane lands in London, we have vanished in midflight. Hidalgo and his friends are absolutely brilliant. And their brilliance bought us an extra nine hours before the discrepancy could be discovered and maybe a few hours more before they figure out we weren't actually on the flight."

"What I wonder, Mr. Houdini," Julia said, "is what about our luggage? It was checked. It left for London."

"Not the contents, just the cases. Our stuff is in the bags in the back of the car. And now we pull another disappearing act. Right, Filipe?"

"Right. We are just waiting for the signal. The border here is very—what do you say?—porous."

Clinton nodded to confirm the word. "And we are going to just walk across, get escorted to a remote airstrip, then leave from a different city by a different route on a different airline. It may not be perfect, but it will certainly buy us more time."

Julia looked puzzled. "I still don't see how we are going to afford this. I thought you were close to broke."

"While you were getting to know Hidalgo, I was busy hustling with of some of Hidalgo's scruffier friends. I maxed out my credit cards—well, nearly—for down payments on three expensive cars from three shady dealers, then fenced them on the black market, pretending I had stolen them. Then I fenced the credit cards."

"You cheated the cheats."

"Pretty much."

"You know, you're not as dumb as you look." She crinkled her nose at him.

"Neither are you, but you're not the only one who can pull off a stunt. Anyway, I . . . look, there's a light flashing over there."

"Yes, that's the signal: three short, then two. Quickly, grab your bags and hike over to that spot on the rise. Your border escort is waiting."

They embraced and said goodbye to Filipe and Alejandro, before shouldering the simple military-style canvas bags. "And tell Hidalgo *muito obrigado* from both of us," Clinton said, "especially thanks for helping us get away."

"Wait," Alejandro said. "He told me to give this envelope to you, but you are not to open it until you are someplace safe."

"What is it?"

"I think it is a reporter's notebook."

Chapter 25

Bertrand Lyon, his usual self-control fleeing like crows before a hound, paced as he ticked off events. "They cleared passport control, that was verified by our contact in the Border Protection Service in Busanyu. They got on the plane. AfrikAire confirmed it from the gate records and the passenger manifest. The passenger count tallied with the manifest. They were on that plane at Mbutsu International, and they were not when it arrived at London Heathrow. The plane was searched after they were reported missing on arrival.

"Unless they parachuted out somewhere over Morocco with no one noticing an open cabin door, there are only two possibilities: they never left Busanyu or they somehow managed to disappear at Heathrow in the midst of a security alert—with you and your men watching."

Holzinger nodded. "I'm already booked to Mbutsu City, sir. I think they must still be there someplace."

"Then tell me how in God's name they could have gotten on the plane and gotten off again."

"I don't know, yet, sir, but simple logic says it's far more likely for them to be able pull the wool over the eyes of security down there than at Heathrow. Think about it."

"I am thinking about it. And I'm also thinking about whether we need another major restructuring of our entire security operations. From the top down."

"Yes, sir. Let me find and take care of them first. Then, if you want my resignation, I will tender it."

"I don't want anyone's goddamn resignation. I want those two found and taken care of. Have I made myself clear?"

"Yes, sir, perfectly clear."

As he left the building, Holzinger took a grim mental inventory of his future prospects. Failure was not an option. No one ever resigned from Biontolics, not anyone at his level at any rate. That is not to say no one ever left the organization, but leaving was rather permanent and absolute. That precedent had been set from the earliest of days when Bertrand Lyon was still Atchison Dougherty and had quietly offed the young woman who was the first person to dare step outside the clearly drawn limits. Holzinger had no illusions that any exception would be made in recognition of his long service and unquestioned loyalty. If anyone knew there was no escape, no hiding from The Club, it was he.

~ ~ ~

The light across the Busanyu border must have been farther away than it had seemed. Either that, or they had misjudged the direction. It flashed once more—three quick flashes, then two—as they crossed a gravel-strewn dry creek bed. "Over there," Clinton whispered, "to the left."

"No, I thought it came from over there, to the right a bit."

"Just keep walking. They won't wait for us forever."

They crested the rise but there was no one in sight. A rocky trail led along the ridge, then down into the shadows below. Clinton started following it. Suddenly there was the sound of pebbles kicked aside and a muffled cry from behind him. He spun around and faced a man with a machete held high. Two other men were holding Julia, one with his hand over her mouth. She writhed trying to free herself. A man put a revolver to her head and said something to her in a low whisper. She nodded several times and the hand was taken from her mouth.

Clinton was too worried to say anything. Suddenly they were surrounded by half a dozen men in camouflage fatigues armed with machetes and Kalashnikovs. A man with a bandolier over his shoulder came up to Clinton and smiled. "Americans. I am General Cabral. You have money?"

"We have your money, what you were promised: three hundred dollars."

"Six hundred. It will cost you six."

"The deal was three. That's all we have."

"Six. Six or we bury you here. First we have some fun with the girl. Even in the dark, I can see she is pretty. And she has spirit. I like that—more fun. Perhaps she will fight to the end." There was quiet laughter around the circle.

"Six it is. We pay when we reach the landing strip."

"Ah, American, so you do have more than three hundred dollars. Rich American, yes? Perhaps we just take the money, all of it, and leave you here to walk back where you came from. First, some fun, of course. The girl, is she fun?"

"I wouldn't know about that. She's my daughter, and you better not touch her."

"I better not touch her? Very funny." This time the laughter was deeper. "And so, the father has spirit, too. Well, I am a father, also, and my daughter is only a little younger, so we will take you to the airstrip where the plane waits. See, we are men of honor, but we are also in need of better arms, so the price for safe escort is six hundred. Now, pick up your things and stay close. The trail is hard to follow in the dark."

~ ~ ~

They walked nearly through the night. The sky was already beginning to lighten when they reached the grass airstrip where a single engine Cessna 206, a favorite among African bush pilots, was waiting. Two of the escorts walked ahead out to the plane, where they banged on the cockpit to awaken the pilot. The other four sat at the edge of the field talking and sharing rations.

Julia looked at Clinton. "What do you think?"

"I think we may be screwed," he said, keeping his voice barely audible. "I don't trust these guys to let us go. Why should they? Kill us and everything we have is theirs. Maybe they are working a deal to split with the pilot. What do you think we should do?"

"Throw money at the problem, like any good American." She looked to see if he understood. "And follow my lead."

He gave a tiny nod just as the two rebels who had been talking with the pilot sauntered back. "He says wait," the General announced as they approached. "He warms up the plane."

"While he's getting the plane ready,"—Clinton gestured—"you can put our bags aboard." The two men looked at each other, uncertain. "Just put the bags in the plane," he said. It was a voice with authority. The leader, asserting his own position, snapped his fingers to one of the men and pointed to the two bags, then to the plane. The man shrugged and started dragging the bags toward the open rear cargo door of the Cessna.

"Now, where is our money?" the General said, grabbing Clinton's collar.

"I have it." Clinton glanced toward the plane, as the bags were thrown aboard and the pilot signaled a thumbs up. "Julia, you go get in the plane and make sure the pilot is ready while I pay our most honorable guide here." She started walking toward the Cessna as the pilot gunned the engine and turned the plane away from them to face into the wind.

"General, let me pay you personally." Clinton half winked.

The leader took a few steps closer to the plane and away from the other men. Clinton withdrew a wad of twenties and started peeling off bills like a bank clerk counting cash for a customer. "Twenty, forty, sixty, ..." As he counted, he rocked from foot to foot, slowly side-stepping around so the leader was turned away from the plane. He kept watching as Julia climbed aboard through the open cargo bay. The pitch of the engine picked up again. "... five hundred eighty, and six hundred." He thrust the stack of bills out as the breeze picked up, letting go of it just short of the man's hand. The gust took the bills and spread them in a flutter.

As the men dashed about trying to grab the bills, Clinton ducked and made a dash for the plane, yelling, "Go! Go! Go!" The plane turned slightly, presenting its tail to them as it started to accelerate. Clinton pushed for all he was worth and lunged for the open cargo door. He caught the lip of it and tried to roll himself in, but the plane was picking up speed. Suddenly, he felt a tug on his pants belt and was propelled in. He rolled over as he tucked his legs inside and looked up into Julia's grinning face. The pop of gunfire from behind them could be heard above the roar of the single engine as the Cessna bounced down the field, took off, and climbed steeply to avoid the trees.

"That's some wedgy you just delivered, girl."

"You deserved it, slowpoke."

"Are we good with the pilot?"

"Yes, but I had to promise him five hundred more. Are you all right?"

Clinton was squirming, trying to push his pants back down. He grimaced. "Oh god. I think I banged something getting in." He put his hand to his side. "Oh, that really hurts."

"You're bleeding."

He pulled up his blood-soaked shirt and looked down. "Yeah, looks like it. A chunk is ..." His eyes rolled and he fell back against their bags.

Chapter 26

Holzinger wasted no time after his early morning arrival in Mbutsu City. He took a cab directly from the airport to the Presidential Place, paid the driver in US dollars, and told the guard at the gatehouse that he wanted to see the Acting President—immediately. When he was informed that it was impossible, he handed his Biontolics business card to the guard. In a tone that bordered on a growl, he suggested that, if the man valued his neck, he should get in touch with his superior officer without delay.

Within minutes, a limousine arrived, flying miniature flags of the Republic of Busanyu and escorted by Jeeps fore and aft bristling with armed soldiers. The motorcade carried him all of a half kilometer to the front of the Presidential Palace. There he was met by a slightly disheveled and clearly sleepy Chief of Staff, who escorted him up the Palace steps and into an anteroom the size of a small ballroom.

"I regret that the President is not available at this moment, but he assures me he will be with you as soon as he can manage. In the meantime, he has asked that I see to your breakfast." He snapped his fingers and a small platoon of waiters with carts entered through double doors at the side.

Holzinger held up his hand with a commanding gesture. "No, please. I'll just wait for the Acting President to arrive." He audibly underscored the word *acting*.

"Are you sure? Not even a coffee? Okay, as you prefer. I will see to the President and be back in a moment."

The moment was nearly forty minutes long, which Holzinger judged as about twenty minutes longer than the time it actually took to awaken, dress, and ready Raul Gomes for the world. The discrepancy he chalked up to a mandatory cooling off period intended by Gomes to send a message to his visitor, the gist of which was that Raul Gomes was not Edgar Mbutsu, but he was still a man to be reckoned with. Holzinger considered all such games of social or political one-upmanship to be silly, but that did not stop him from playing them with his own mordant style.

When Acting President Gomes arrived, Holzinger was not in the anteroom. The French doors to the terrace were open, and Holzinger could be seen outside inspecting the potted palms and climbing passion fruit vines, apparently oblivious to the President's arrival.

"Touché, Mr. Holzinger, well played. Now, would you care to come back in and tell me what this unexpected visit is about? Surely not an agricultural inspection."

"No, not agricultural. You know perfectly well why I am here. We asked you to retain two Americans, and you let them get away. That is not the sort of thing that makes us happy. I am here to make sure no effort is spared in retrieving these errant Americans and that no similar incompetence occurs in the process."

"Now, just one minute. I remind you that you are a guest in our country and that I am head of state."

"And I will simply remind you that we know the numbers and balances of all your off-shore accounts. As the majority of these are managed by Revic Financial, it would be most unfortunate if you suddenly found your balances in these accounts reduced to zero."

The President's bulging eyes widened enough to show nearly full circles of white, but he said nothing.

"Now that we understand each other, I expect you to direct your generals and the head of your police to cooperate fully and to put their entire forces at my disposal. I intend to find those two if we have to shake every tree in the entire rain forest and overturn every rock on the savannah."

Chapter 27

Julia huddled against Clinton as she looked out over the sun-dotted seascape stirred into a stippled surface by a stiffening breeze. "Why are we here?"

"Because," Clinton said, keeping his voice low, "Madeira is where my father said to meet." The two of them were standing on a white and black stone-tiled sidewalk in front of the small airport terminal on the Island of Madeira. "And please don't squeeze so hard. My side is still sore as hell."

"Just be glad the bullet only grazed you. Of course, you had to go and pass out as if mortally wounded."

"Hey, can I help it if the sight of my own blood makes me faint. Hell, the mere thought of it . . ."

"Now don't you go trying to get more sympathy from me. And again, why are we meeting here?"

"As my father told me, security at the airport here is very lax. You may have noticed that we walked from the plane, picked up our bags, and walked out without so much as anyone looking askance. Officially, we are not here." They had arrived by a tortuous route that had taken them first to Luanda, from there to the Canary Islands, and finally on a turboprop flight to Madeira. Rising crosswinds had almost prevented their plane from landing on Madeira's famously challenging runway that perched partially on concrete stilts marching out over the sea. The pilot had managed a steep drop and sudden flattening on the second approach, garnering sustained applause from the relieved passengers.

"I thought your father was from the Azores," she said. "Didn't he go back there when he ditched you and your mother?"

"He did, but apparently he was not welcome for long, so he's moved around a lot over the years. He sends a postcard to my mother every year or two with nothing on it but a new phone number, which she has never called. Not that she uses the telephone anymore. It was a long shot, but I tried the number I had copied from the last card he sent, and it worked."

"Your mother doesn't use the phone? What's that about? I don't think you've ever said much about your mother."

"What's there to say? She's in a nursing home south of Sacramento. I moved her out there after she developed early onset Alzheimer's. I visit her several times a year, but she usually doesn't know who I am. Anyway, we're here to see my father."

"Are you sure about this? I mean, the man is wanted in ... how many countries?"

"I only know about two: the US and Spain."

"Isn't that enough? What exactly is he wanted for?"

"Drugs. He's a chemist, brews designer drugs, constructs new molecules just beyond the reach of current law. Under his pseudonym, Chemo Sabé, he actually has quite a reputation for concocting safe legal highs."

"Not all of his creations must have been just beyond the law or he wouldn't be wanted in at least two countries."

"Well, he started modestly in the States with a synthetic cannabinoid analog, but his synthesis was a little rough and yielded a mix that was contaminated. Some of the residue species were actually already on the Feds' list. He was self-taught, learning by doing. And then, of course, there are the sorts of people he has to deal with—not always your most upstanding citizens. I don't know the details of the Spanish misadventure."

"You sound pretty casual about a father who abandoned you and your mother."

"It's bridge water."

"You know, you're the only person I ever heard use that expression that way."

"It's a reference to a prison in Massachusetts: Bridgewater State. I picked it up from my father when I was too young to know what it was about. My mother once told me he had picked it up from a buddy who had done time there but would never talk about it. He'd just say it was bridge water, obviously meaning water under the bridge."

A short man in a plaid hunting cap approached them from the end of the walkway. "You want a taxi into town?" He gestured back toward a lemon-yellow cab with sky-blue trim parked in a lot at the end of the terminal building.

"No, thanks," Clinton said. "We're meeting somebody."

"And you would recognize this somebody if you saw him?"

Clinton was a little taken aback by the question. "It's been many, many years, but I think so."

"So, many years have passed," the man said, "It's all bridge water."

"Dad?"

"Angelo Rodrigues, in the flesh, Clinton. Get in the taxi before they come over and cite me for an unlawful passenger pickup." He reached for Julia's duffel. "I'll get that for you." He stepped up his pace to reach the cab ahead of them and open the trunk. "Oh, you two will be staying with me while you're here. It'll be a little cozy, just one extra bedroom, but I assume you two are . . . well . . ."

Clinton cleared his throat. "I can sleep in the living room."

Angelo looked from Julia to Clinton and back, shrugged, and said, "Whatever." With a hand placed loosely in front of his mouth, he turned to Clinton and spoke in a half-whisper. "You're not gay, are you?"

"Would it make a difference?"

"Not really."

"Then I'm not."

"You mean you would have told your old man that you were queer if I had said it mattered?"

"Probably."

"Now I see what kind of boy my Sarah raised."

The twenty-minute trip into town was a rush of tunnels and bridges and interspersed vistas over the sea, with Angelo constantly turning in his seat to explain what they were seeing. "That was more bananas we just passed, small bananas, not the super-sweet monsters you find in stores in the States. These *quintas*, little plantations, are all over the place. There's plantings of bananas and other produce even in the heart of the city. There's one right next to my apartment building, another behind the Modelo—that's the supermarket where I get my food and stuff." He turned back and slammed on his brakes to keep from rear-ending the car ahead that was slowing at the entrance to another tunnel.

"The whole island is gopher-holed with these things. People say there's more concrete in the roads and tunnels of Madeira than there is rock in the whole damn volcanic island. It's political currency. The politicians buy votes with promises of a new road and tunnel to someplace."

In fifteen minutes, they were emerging from a tunnel and looking out over Funchal, a city of stucco houses with terra cotta tile roofs all stacked up the steep hillsides. Within minutes, they were through yet another tunnel and into the Western districts. "That was Funchal. I'll show you around the waterfront and the Old City later after we get you settled in."

Angelo's building—"I own it, outright, thirty apartments"—was on a narrow street that looked too steep to drive. Angelo gunned the engine and shot up the road, just missing a scrawny feral dog stretched out by a boarded up building.

"Funchal's like that: classy next to crappy." He slowed and pressed a button on his key fob. A sheet-steel entry gate slid slowly aside, followed by an overhead door opening to an underground garage. "Perks of owning the place: indoor parking spot and an apartment with the best views. What's the point of having a place in Funchal if you don't have a view of the harbor, right? Wait until you step out onto *a minha veranda*, uh, I mean my balcony. I talk more in Portuguese than English these days. After I started the cab company, I made myself the relief driver—mostly because it meant I could chat with British tourists. A lot of Brits come to Madeira. Also Germans and Russians, but I don't speak German. Or Russian."

Inside, they took an elevator to the fifth floor, where Angelo escorted them into an airy apartment with windows on two sides facing the sea and the city. After he showed Julia to the spare bedroom, he asked Clinton if he really wanted to sleep on the sofa in the living room. Clinton nodded emphatically.

Julia returned from stashing her things in the bedroom. "I thought you said you had only the one extra room. What are those other doors to?"

"This is my home office."

Clinton sighed. "What he means is that he has to have someplace to cook."

Julia raised her eyebrows and pointed through a doorway. "I thought that was the kitchen."

Angelo smirked. "Not that kind of cooking."

"Right. Should have known," she said." So, like, I'll be sleeping next to a meth lab?"

"Oh, I don't do that kind of shit," Angelo said. "In fact, my newer work involves GMO yeast. You know, even high school kids can now do genetic engineering. I don't do much with anything that could explode. Not much, anyway."

"Not much? That's reassuring, Dad."

"I'm not trying to reassure you. I'm just giving my son and his . . . friend a place to stay. Hey, let me show you the view." He reached for the handle of a sliding door.

Julia started back down the hall. "You two go ahead. I'm going to freshen up."

Standing on the wrap-around balcony looking back over the tiled roofs of central Funchal, Angelo lit a cigarette and turned to Clinton. "So, why did you suddenly contact me? I don't imagine it's about recreational drugs."

"No, it isn't. We need paper, and I figured you would know somebody you could refer us to."

His father studied Clinton's face and took several slow breaths. "Yeah, I know somebody, more than one somebody. I assume you need the best, something that can get you through airports and the CBP."

"Yeah, the best. We need to get back home without people knowing."

"These days, that can really cost. You know it's all electronic now, embedded chips, biometrics, RFID, and stuff. The blanks have to be stolen, real thing. Lots of people to pay." He was shaking his head slowly.

"How much?"

Angelo held up his thumb and index finger in a circle. "For you, nothing. It's on me. And I won't even ask what this is about. You're my son, and I was no father to you. This is the least I can do." He closed one eye and scratched at an eyebrow. "Of course, I might have to sell one of my yachts."

It took Clinton a second to react. Then he laughed and reached out to slap his father on the back. Angelo grabbed Clinton's arm and in a split second had his wrist in a lock and twisted behind his back. "Sorry," he said, releasing his grip. "I don't let anyone touch my back. Just a thing. You two must be hungry. Let me fix dinner for you. I'm a pretty good cook, and I do mean the food kind."

~ ~ ~

Dinner was spicy chicken with black-beans, a dish that Angelo called *frango piri-piri*, accompanied by mashed white sweet potatoes with slivers of red onion. Julia raved about the chicken. "This is fabulous. I haven't had piri-piri from Africa in years. The Asian and Mexican chiles are just not the same."

"I know what you mean. I love that touch of smoky-sweet that real piri-piri has. You should take a few jars of it back with you. Here in Madeira you can pick it up at any supermarket."

After dinner, the three of them sat out on the balcony sipping a fifteen-year old tawny Madeira. Angelo broke the silence. "You don't have to, but if you want to tell me what this is about, it might be useful in picking who we go to for your new papers. No sense approaching the mafia if that's who's after you."

Clinton held up his glass and studied the amber liquid lit by the late sun. "Not the mafia. Actually, we're not exactly sure who is after us. We assume it's some part of this corporate medusa." He gave his father a quick summary of what they knew and a run-through of their adventures in Africa.

"Wow, cool! You know, you could join my business—both of you. You guys are pretty resourceful. Let me tell you, life here is pretty damn good, and being rich makes it even better. I don't have to drive a cab, you know, but it makes for better appearances. Gives me a way to pay taxes and be a good citizen above suspicion."

Clinton looked at Julia before turning back to his father. "I don't think so, but thanks anyway. This is a problem we have to deal with. But there is something else besides getting the passports that you could do for us. I know you are not a biochemist by training—"

"But I am, just not with the degree. I can design and cook circles around the best psychopharmacologists in the world. So what do you want?"

"I want you to take a look at a couple of old papers I have stashed on my laptop, and tell me what you think of them."

Chapter 28

Clinton looked on as his father closed the second file. "So, what do you make of them?" he asked.

"I'm not going to pretend I understood every word—especially the second paper, the meta-analysis of all that research—but here's what I think. These people found a way to essentially stop aging at the cellular level by tricking oncogenes into replenishing the protective telomeres at the end of the DNA strands. At least that's part of the trick. It involves mosaicism, where a person's cells become a mix of multiple genetic lines creating a chimeric individual with more genetic resources for warding off pathogens and biological degradation. This happens naturally to a small degree whenever a woman has a baby. Fetal cells enter her system, are incorporated into her tissues, and improve her biological fitness."

"But this isn't about pregnant women, I mean . . ."

"No, this new treatment revolves around creating a more robust organism through an elaborately orchestrated balancing act between competing cell lines on the one hand and triggering cancer on the other. It depends, in part, on what is called hormesis, that longevity and stress tolerance can be enhanced by calibrated cellular challenges—kinda what doesn't kill the cell can make it stronger. Something like that. The summary of the second paper, the more recent one, suggests this could actually be put into practice with human subjects—or already has been."

"Thanks, Dad. That's pretty much what I thought. If we are right, the people who are after us have actually been doing this—secretly—and they're willing to do almost anything to keep it to themselves and to prevent anyone else from finding out. They even killed my old biology teacher for trying to expose them. She's the one who tipped me off and passed on these papers—papers she had retrieved from her husband's laptop."

"Wow, I'm beginning to see what you're up against."

The next week was a mix of spy games and idyllic excursions. After a day of hiking along the gentle footpath of one of the island's myriad *levadas*, the narrow water canals that zigzagged the mountains, they returned to the apartment to work on small changes in their appearances in anticipation of getting fresh passport photos. "Nothing makes more difference than a change in facial hair," Angelo told them.

"Maybe I should grow a mustache?" Julia teased.

"No, but he should. He should ditch the half-shaved look for smooth cheeks and a hairy upper lip. And you, you should maybe shorten and straighten your hair. We're not talking about plastic surgery here, I hope, just enough so you are not too easily spotted in a crowd. Like maybe a pixie cut for you, little lady."

They did as Angelo suggested, then got new photos made at a little second-floor, second-rate studio near the *Lojas da Cidade* in the city. As they waited for their new documents to arrive, Julia started using evenings to study the notebook from Hidalgo. "There's a lot of good stuff in here, including interviews with people who once worked at the private hospital in the Presidential compound. It's pretty clear on the connection between Biontolics and Edgar Mbutsu. And there's a member of the presidential staff who verifies that large, regular payments were made to a South African company. According to a correspondent of Hidalgo's, that company is owned by Biontolics. And you know what else?"

Clinton looked up from his laptop. "No, what?"

"Our Hidalgo was a poet. Interspersed among his interview notes are a number of poems, most in Portuguese but a few in English."

"Any good?"

"Judge for yourself. This one is called 'Dark Forest, Bright Tutor.'" She started to read aloud.

> Dark forest, bright tutor, show me a path,
>   the secret math
>   of counting stones and steps unknown
>   until the turning point is reached.
> With leafy fingers point me down the road,
>   the rock-hard trail
>   where once I failed to learn what others failed to teach.

Teach me to listen with uncovered heart
  to the silenced part within the noise:
  the whisper of the rising sun,
  the soundless ticking of impending death,
  the echoes unending of my own doubt.
Let me learn to see by darkened beams
  to find hidden routes out,
  the unspoken dreams in shadowed uncertainty.
Spread above me your canopy of indifferent caring,
  that I may be sheltered
  as I stand staring into emptiness,
  from darkness still learning,
  always learning,
  still.

~ ~ ~

Most days were spent touring the island with Angelo in one of his cabs.

"Don't you ever have to work?" Clinton asked him one mid-morning, as they headed for the western tip of the island.

"No. Never have to, not anymore. But I love what I do. I design happiness for people who can't get it from friends or lovers or work."

"What a noble and bullshit reframe. You're a drug pusher."

"I don't push, and I don't get people hooked. I know how to dial down the addictive liability of my compounds."

"Are you a user yourself?" Julia asked.

"Nope. I always test them on myself, but I get my kicks out of molecular biology and biochemistry and tweaking the shape of a new molecule that neither nature nor man has ever seen before. I'm working on one right now that induces a deep calm without drowsiness. It's like being completely mellow and excitedly alive at the same time. So, maybe I am an addict; I'm addicted to playing god, making things possible that never were before. I—"

"Watch out for that truck!"

Angelo turned back to face the road and an oncoming delivery truck. He hugged the jagged cliff face on the right as the truck edged toward the unguarded drop-off on the ocean side of the road. It sped on as if the near miss were all routine. "Well, that was a little close,"

Angelo announced over his shoulder. There was a sharp crack as a protruding rock took off the passenger-side mirror. "Shit!" He leaned over and back to assess the damage as they approached the next hairpin turn.

"Better keep your eyes on the road, Dad."

"Look, son. I have a hundred thousand kilometers on this piece of shit, and I've replaced more mirrors than you could count. Cost of doing business, that's all. You don't have to worry about me. I'm fine." He braked suddenly for an unmarked turnoff, then accelerated up another steep road.

~ ~ ~

It was a rare stormy fall day with afternoon rain coming down in sheets when Angelo trudged up the hill from the waterfront with a hand-couriered package tucked under his rain jacket. "Okay, so here you are." He handed each of them a passport and driver's license. Clinton looked down at his. "Sean Collin Metzger? I see you shaved a year off my life."

"Yeah, and I added a couple to hers. Makes it look better with you traveling together, not so much like you were robbing the cradle or anything."

A look of horror spread over Julia's face as she opened her passport. "You made me Shandrise Barrows? You gave me one of those trendy made-up first names. Sounds oh so very 'black'. I hate it."

"Hate it, love it, who gives a shit? You look the part. Anyway, in the envelope is the rest of the paperwork, birth certificates, the works. This is almost as good as witness protection. These guys charge an arm and a leg, but they do good work, the best. The courier brought it in from New York just yesterday. You can go through airports, whatever. Hell, you can even buy a house with these. What you won't be able to do is buy a cup of coffee, so you'll need a little walking-around money." He handed each of them a fat business envelope. "There's $9,000 each. That's so you stay under the $10,000 reporting limit when you reenter the country."

"This is too much. We can't take this from you, Dad."

Julia punched his arm. "What do you mean we can't take this. Your father is trying to be generous, and you are being an ungrateful son."

"She's right, son. And there's more. This is a key to a safe deposit box, Progress Cooperative Bank of Sausalito. There's enough there for a down payment on a house. Well, not in San Francisco, but . . .”

“I don’t know what to say.”

“Well, son, at least I know what to say. Thank you. Thank you, Clinton, for giving me a chance to do some small thing to make up for skipping out on you.”

“Why didn’t you ever help while I was growing up? Do you have any idea how hard Mom worked just to keep it together and get me through school?”

“Yes, I do know—and I tried. Your mother would never accept a penny from me. It was drug money, tainted, she said. But that doesn’t mean I didn’t keep trying and waiting. Weren’t you relieved when you learned that she somehow magically had long-term care coverage?”

“You?”

“I’m just grateful for the chances to try and set things right.”

Clinton threw his arms around his father. Angelo winced. “I’m sorry,” Clinton said. “I forgot.”

“It’s all right. It’s . . . Here, I’ll show you.” He lifted his shirt up to his armpits. His left side and much of his back was angry scar tissue and what looked almost like exposed muscle.

“What happened?”

“Necrotizing fasciitis, flesh-eating bacteria. These bastards cut me bad, swabbed me with the superbug, and left me to die a slow death. I knew what to do, though, so I got myself to London for treatment with piperacillin/tazobactam combination therapy and debridement, but, well . . . Anyway, I lived. And now I’ve lived to see my son again. I wish I could go back to the States, but . . .”

“Why couldn’t you pull the same thing as we’re doing, start with a new identity?”

“Because the people who did your papers are the people who would never let me. We have a détente, a division of responsibilities and distribution of the spoils. They need me on the design and production side, and I need them on the sales and marketing side: a perfect symbiosis.”

“And they helped you help us.”

“Right. Put enough zeroes after the first digit and miracles can happen—like living to a couple hundred years.” He winked. “Look, I have some errands to run. You two figure out your itinerary from here, then we’ll get you off the island.”

He slapped on his hunting cap, grabbed his keys and wallet, and left.

Julia studied the passport with her new look and new name. "How many zeroes do you think it took to give us new lives?"

"I don't know. Four, maybe? Maybe more."

"We owe him a lot."

"True. And I am in the funny position of going from thinking I had the worst father on the planet to . . . now, I don't know. Maybe I owe him my life, yours, too. Becoming Sean Metzger will be hard enough; being Angelo's son is even tougher to wrap my head around."

"You have it easy. I have to be Shandrise Barrows."

"What's your middle name?"

"Jana. What kind of a mother would name her daughter Shandrise Jana?"

"Well, you could go by your middle name and be Jana to your friends. And we should get used to calling each other by our new names. What do you say, Jana?"

"What's your middle name?"

"Collin. I'll do the same. S. Collin Metzger. And C. Jana Barrows. Hi, Jana."

"Pleased to meet you, Collin."

Chapter 29

The connection was not very good. The voice on the phone was distorted and drowning in waves of static. Bertrand Lyon almost shouted into the handset. "What? What the fuck did you say, Holzinger?"

"I said we tracked them to a second-rate hotel in Mbutsu City, but they had already skipped out without paying—right after they escaped from the Presidential compound. We enlisted the help of the local military to apply a little persuasion to the family that runs the hotel. It seems that the late President trained his army interrogators better at administering pain than obtaining information. They learned very little before the two sons were 'taken ill'—the exact euphemism used. All we know is that our targets disappeared over the border. We . . . lost them again."

"You lost them again, Holzinger, not 'we'. You. Lost. Them. Again."

"Yes, sir."

"Don't bother to call or text me again until you have taken care of the matter." He hung up before there could be a response. He looked up to see Ferguson watching from the doorway. "What?"

"I heard you yelling. I think you need to get out to the clinic for a psych eval. Hell, we should run the whole battery on you. I think you may be at the edge of the cliff."

"I'm not at the edge of anything. I'm just goddamn fed up with dealing with idiots like Holzinger."

"Since when did your German golden boy become an idiot? I thought you were about ready to canonize him for entry into The Club."

"I was, but I was mistaken about him. And maybe you."

Ferguson recoiled visibly. "That sort of talk can be an early sign of cellular cascade. If it starts with the brain—"

"Fuck you, Charles or Andras or whoever you are now. I'll check myself in tomorrow for the full battery of tests just to prove you wrong."

"I hope you do. I do want to be wrong about this. We've never been able to pull anybody back once the cascade gets past stage one. And it's not a pretty way to go, with all your cell lines attacking each other." He turned to the sound of someone approaching. It was Prudence Tanner, latest in the very long line of Bertrand's personal assistants. She would have been vaguely attractive were it not for the look of constipation that continually camped on her face.

"Gentlemen, I am sorry to interrupt, but there is a man down at reception who is quite adamant that I hand deliver his calling card." She stepped into the office. "He says he has something to tell you and that you would know him."

"He gave his name?"

"He declined, but gave me his card to pass on to you, Dr. Lyon. He said you would understand." She handed him a small envelope such as might contain a gift tag. Inside was an embossed plain white business card printed in black ink with a classic typeface: Toto Brancaccio, Palermo, Import/Export Consultant. There was no address or telephone number.

Bertrand held the card out toward Fergusson, who took it. "Well?" he said with impatience as his partner studied the card. "Should we . . . ? I mean we do know who this is even if we don't know the man by name."

"Quite. And that's why we make it a policy never to deal with them."

"Would it do any harm to hear him out? We don't know what he wants to tell us."

Prudence cleared her throat. "He mentioned that he understood you were looking for some people."

"In that case, show him in, and then leave us undisturbed."

'Of course, Dr. Lyon," she said, then left.

Fergusson was clearly bothered by developments. "We do not deal with the mafia. Once we start, there will be no stopping them."

"You're being an alarmist, Chas. We are not dealing with the mafia; we are talking with one man, a businessman from Sicily. Here he is now."

Prudence ushered in a stout man wearing a charcoal gray Savile Row suit tailored to make him seem slimmer. She paused before closing the door behind her and glanced toward Bertrand with a carefully modulated look of disapproval.

Bertrand stood and offered his hand. "Mr. Brancaccio, I'm Bertrand Lyon, CEO of Biontolics Holdings, and this is our Chief Medical Officer, Dr. Charles Fergusson. Please take a seat and tell us about the nature of your visit."

"I'm here as an exporter. I have overseas information to sell."

"Yes? What information?"

"Are you buying?"

Bertrand steepled his hands, fingertips to fingertips, in front of him on the desk. "That depends on the cost and the content."

"I know about a couple of journalists. The price is entry into your country club."

"Out of the question." Bertrand stood, rounded the corner of the desk, and walked to the door. "I'll have my assistant show you out."

"You're making a big mistake. I have connections. I could be very useful to you."

"Connections? We're not in the market. We have an abundance of connections, and you can keep your information."

"Wait, okay. Fifty big ones, then."

"We're not in the market for overpriced imports, either. Ah, here's Prudence now." He smiled in the direction of the doorway. "Prudence, please see Mr. Brancaccio out."

The man stood, clearly agitated. "No, wait. Really, I know where they are. Twenty big ones and I'll tell you."

Bertrand raised his hand partway, palm in the direction of his assistant. "Perhaps Mr. Brancaccio will be staying for the moment. If we need you, Prudence, I'll buzz."

"Of course, Dr. Lyon." She slipped out again and closed the door.

"So, Mr. Brancaccio, first tell us how you know."

"A package was couriered to them."

"Where? Where was the package delivered?"

"Oh, no. Money first."

"I'll see that you are cut a check for twenty thousand as soon as you tell us what you know. So, what was in the package?"

"That, I don't know, but it was for this Rodrigues chap."

"From your firm, you're saying."

"Well, sort of, in New York. But look, that's it. You got all the freebie tasting you're gonna get. Twenty, and no check. Hard currency only."

"Regrettably, we don't keep that much petty cash on hand, Mr. Brancaccio. I'm afraid ten thousand is the best we can do on short notice. Take it or leave it."

"Show me the color of your money first."

"Well, we are talking about British pounds, so the color varies with the denomination."

"I meant, show me the . . . Wait a minute, you're joking, right?"

"Right. So just tell us where they are, and I'll have my assistant arrange for the money to be waiting at the guard desk in the lobby for collection on your way out of the building. It'll only take ten minutes or so."

The man licked his lips in concentration. "Okay. But if you fuck with me you will know who you fucked with."

"Of course, Mr. Toto Brancaccio. Now, where are they?"

"Madeira, the island, you know, in, ah, Funkle." He mispronounced the name of the city. "You know, the capital."

"Right, okay. Please wait here with Dr. Fergusson while I arrange for the payment." He smiled broadly at Charles as he left the room.

~ ~ ~

Ferguson watched with amusement as the Sicilian was finally ushered out of Bertrand's office. "You played our Italian visitor rather well."

"I knew the moment he walked into the room in his brand new suit that he was no mafia don, probably just a courier himself. And he bargained like a foot soldier, first overplaying his hand and then letting himself be talked down to a price tag that won't even give him bragging rights. Even before he told us where Rodrigues is, he told me plenty, including that the Sicilian mafia knows what business we're in and they somehow knew we were looking for the journalists."

"Obviously, there are leaks in the pipelines. My guess would be either in Busanyu or Russia."

"You see the Russians more often than I do. Do you think the Russian mafia would deal with the Sicilians?"

"Somebody somewhere did. It only takes one overly ambitious or overly talkative person. Perhaps we should arrange an accident for our Sicilian businessman. He strikes me as the type who would tell all for just a beer or two."

"It's already arranged, but not here. Back in New York."

"Holzinger?"

"No, he's about to be on his way to Madeira in a G6, courtesy of the Acting President of Busanyu, who is temporarily rather in our debt after failing to get either the people or the information we needed. Even if he wins the upcoming elections, I don't see Senhor Gomes getting into The Club like his predecessor. Added to his ineptitude, we would have to factor in that he is not nearly as corrupt or brutal as Edgar was, which translates into a much lower net worth."

"Does it always come back to that? Wealth?"

"As you were lecturing me not so long ago, Chas, operations are becoming ever more expensive, and it is harder and harder to keep the lid on things. By my projection, we will need at least another decade, maybe two, before we have cornered enough wealth to really be in charge. Then we can step out into the sunlight because there will be no one and nothing to stop us."

"You really think in terms of world domination?"

"No, not really. For me, power is merely a means to an end, and the end is living at least a few hundred years."

"Well then, my French-Canadian colleague, you had better keep your appointment at the clinic."

Part Six ~ Return
Chapter 30

Clinton's cheek finally stopped twitching after he and Julia exited Terminal E at Boston's Logan airport. He took a deep breath of air heavy with exhaust from the idling taxis, limos, and buses. "Well, it worked. We made it through US Customs and Border Protection."

"I was more worried about dropping off the package from your father at the stopover in the Azores."

"I guess it comes with the tickets. If you fly SATA, you stop in Ponta Delgada. Hey, at least it gave us a chance to see a bit of the island and sample some of the local cheeses."

"Do you know what was in the package?"

"I assume it was chemical, but I didn't ask." He looked down the line of cars waiting to pick up passengers. A state trooper was walking up along the queue, telling drivers of cars that had overstayed their welcome to move on. "I should have thought more about what we would do when we got here. I can't use my old credit cards without risking tipping off our pursuers that we're back. We have a bundle of cash, but it won't last long if we're staying in hotels, renting cars, and taking taxis all the time."

"What about the safe deposit box in Sausalito?"

"Oh, yeah. I forgot about that. Problem is I have work to do here: research and people to see. I want to find out what happened with Dr. David's laptop that Millie Geller had. Did it get destroyed in the fire? Was it stashed someplace before? Or what?"

"I could fly back to California to collect the contents of the box while you stay here and keep digging. If you trust me, that is."

"That's a good idea, and I do trust you. But before you fly off again, let's take care of a few things. We need to figure out a place to park ourselves. For now, let's get a taxi and head up to one of the cheaper motels, preferably near a shopping center. We need to set up fresh email accounts, get new burner phones, buy a couple of pre-paid debit cards, get new clothes. And I need a camera. I'm going to miss my Nikon, but I suppose I can make do with one of those new compact superzooms that go for a few hundred—not very professional, though."

"My poor, poor professor, having to make do with a slick new camera." She put on a pout and patted him. "Let's get in line for a cab."

~ ~ ~

Returning from his daily shopping trip at Modelo, Angelo hip-checked the apartment door closed behind him and looped his keychain over the deadbolt latch so he wouldn't forget it on his way out again. He flipped on the lights, walked into the kitchen, and set the bag of groceries down on the counter. When he turned back to hang up his jacket and cap, there was a man with a drawn handgun standing in the entryway.

"Hello. You must be Rodrigues," he said. "I understand you took delivery of a package not so long ago."

"And who are you?"

"You could call me a talent scout. I'm looking for a couple of creative young people. One of them happens to have the same last name as you, so I am guessing from the look of you that he's related somehow, maybe your son. And he's traveling with a young girl, African-American, very pretty, I'm told. Does this jog your memory?"

"Nope. I do have a son, but I haven't seen him since I left Boston more than twenty years ago. Didn't know he had a girlfriend. Good for him."

"What was in the package?"

"Package? Oh, you must mean the DHL shipment from New York. Wait here. I'll get it for you, but I don't think—"

"No, thank you. Just tell me where it is. I'll get it."

"Sure, suit yourself. It's on the bench, second door on the left down the hall, box about so big marked DHL."

"I do hope you don't mind if I make sure you don't go anyplace while I check it out." He spun Angelo around, grabbed his left wrist, and handcuffed it to the handle of the refrigerator, all in a single unbroken movement. "I'll be right back." He paused in the doorway and looked back. "Do understand, I'm just doing a job. Your son and you got in the way. Nothing personal." There was the weariness of a veteran in his voice, and his shoulders slumped as he left.

He returned with a sealed carton and set it on the kitchen counter along with his 9 millimeter Beretta. "You haven't opened it yet?"

"Didn't need it yet. Already know what's in it."

"Which is?"

"Laboratory glassware, ultra-high-temperature."

"Sure, right." Holzinger slipped a paring knife from the wooden block on the counter, slit the sealing tape, and pried open the carton flaps. The box was filled with green packing peanuts. He pushed some aside, spilling them onto the counter and floor and exposing an inner liner of heat-sealed plastic. He cut through the heavy film revealing the top of a large glass flask. He freed it from the liner, and lifted it from the box to hold it by the neck at eyelevel. "Smooth, almost slippery." He placed his other hand beneath to keep from dropping it.

"Must be residue of the manufacturing process," Angelo said. "Maybe a film from the final oil quenching."

"Looks rather ordinary to me."

"Looks can be deceiving; take a closer look."

Holzinger stared at the empty flask as if studying some work of art. "What? What the fuck . . . ? How in hell do they do that? The colors, swirling . . ."

Holzinger slumped slowly to the floor and rested with his back to the under-sink cabinet. "How did you . . . ? What did you do to me?" His head lolled slowly from side to side.

"I'm a chemist. It's a small molecule, a sulfone that easily penetrates the skin, quickly enters the bloodstream, and passes the blood-brain barrier. The visual hallucinations should be rather entrancing. I wouldn't know myself, as this particular compound is rather toxic. By now you should have absorbed a lethal dose. Nothing personal."

Holzinger dropped the heavy flask, which shattered on impact with the tile floor.

Angelo clucked his tongue. "Now, look at the mess you've made. I should make you clean it up, but I don't think you're quite up for much in the way of housework right now."

Holzinger's eyes widened, and his mouth started opening and closing as if he were a fish gulping water. He struggled to reach up for the handgun on the counter behind him, but only succeeded in knocking the box and the gun to the floor. His chin dropped to his chest and his arms started to spasm. When he stopped moving, Angelo kicked the man's legs to one side. He used his free right hand to roll the body over and retrieve the handcuff key.

He stood over the body as he rubbed his left shoulder that had been wrenched behind him. "You should have checked the date on the DHL package, you dumbass. And you should learn what the terms 'customer loyalty' and 'customer service' mean. My New York people warned me you might be coming by. Now, for some more chemical magic—a little smelly and not as colorful, but very effective. Let me go fill the tub for your bath." He stepped carefully around the shards of glass and started toward his supply closet.

He felt the sharp pain in his back at the same instant he heard the sound. The second shot went wild, and the bullet ricocheted off the metal door of the circuit breaker box in the entryway before lodging in the wall next to the doorframe. There was no third shot. Angelo realized what had happened and cursed himself for not kicking the gun away and not making sure the man was dead. He tried to stand but found that his legs didn't work. He dragged himself over to the straight-back chair in the entryway and pulled himself partially erect. At his waist, his shirt was already dark and soaking, and he wondered how long he had before he bled out from the wound in his back. There was not much he could do himself, and by the time an ambulance arrived, it would likely be too late. It was coming down to what he might do with his last minutes.

Chapter 31

Julia gave Clinton a big hug before going through security for her early morning flight to San Francisco. He watched as she put her new backpack on the conveyor into the x-ray machine, then held her arms above her head in the scanner. On the other side, she looked back to see him still standing there. She blew him a kiss. Poor girl, he thought, as he walked slowly out of the terminal to wait for the shuttle back to their hotel.

In the room again, he booted up his laptop and scanned his notes. He reminded himself that, even as S. Collin Metzger, he would have to be careful. He did not know how extensive or efficient the Biontolics espionage network might be. Too many contacts or inquiries by him might set off alarm bells, and his new cover would be blown.

He started by working with what was available. Luckily, before losing his camera, he had swapped out the SD card with the photos of the burned out mobile home and had uploaded the pictures to his laptop. He spent several hours studying them at full magnification and eventually spotted what he was convinced were the melted and charred remains of a cellphone, but nothing that looked like it might have once been a laptop. What could have happened to it? Was it now a carefully labeled bag of charred wreckage in some evidence locker? Had Millicent earlier given it to someone for safekeeping or stashed it somewhere?

He started by making notes about what he knew and what he could guess about. Three people had died in succession. When people die, they usually leave wills bequeathing their estates to other people. Jeannine Carston died first. Might she have left everything to Rosen David? Or maybe her sisters or nieces and nephews? With Rosen's death, his estate would have passed to his wife, Millicent Geller.

He decided it was time to start acting like a reporter again. Through online records, he was able to track down Carston's younger sister, Elise Carston McDermott, at an address in Manchester-by-the-Sea. Clinton had never been to Manchester, but he remembered hearing of it as a child, a place his mother had described as full of rich people, "most of whom are full of themselves." He remembered the mix of envy and resentment in his mother's voice, but it wasn't until many years later that he learned there was a personal story behind it, a well-to-do boyfriend who had unceremoniously dumped her not long before she had met Clinton's father.

Clinton could feel the twitch in his cheek start as he slipped the strap of the new Canon PowerShot around his neck and put the keys to his rental car in his pocket. He knew there was no alternative; it would require talking in person to get what he needed from the sister. He would have to knock on the door of a stranger.

~ ~ ~

The door to the house on the way to Singing Beach in Manchester was dark walnut, deeply carved, massive, and flanked by leaded-glass sidelights with an art nouveau floral theme. Clinton climbed the wide pink marble steps and rang the doorbell. A young woman in a white-ruffled maid's uniform opened the door and asked him in Spanish-inflected English if she could help him.

"Is Mrs. McDermott home? I'm looking for Elise Carston McDermott."

"And who should I say is calling?"

"My name is . . . Collin Metzger." He handed her a business card he had printed at Staples the day before. "Tell her that I knew her sister Jeannine. I would like to talk with her for a few minutes, if she wouldn't mind."

"I'll see. Please wait here." She closed the door on him. It reopened after several minutes. "Mrs. McDermott asked me to show you in. Please follow me; she's out on the back patio."

He was led through a cathedral-ceilinged living room, past a stone fireplace with a hearth almost tall enough to stand in, and out onto a patio facing a teardrop-shaped swimming pool. At a glass-top table under an umbrella of blue sailcloth, a woman in velveteen sweats and matching plum hoodie sat with a drink in one hand and his card in the other.

"You'll forgive me if I don't stand, I hope." She set down her drink and held out her hand toward Clinton. "Have we met?"

"I don't believe so." Clinton took her hand lightly for a moment; it was cold from holding the drink. "I'm Collin Metzger."

"Elise McDermott." She brushed back her hood to expose diamond stud earrings and long hair dyed in a subtle ombré of brown ochre and spun gold. "You knew Jeannine?"

"Yes, and I do apologize for barging in this way and doubly so for bringing up your sister. I am sorry for your loss."

"Of course you are." She closed her eyes wearily. "Would you like a drink? I know it's really too late in the season for mint juleps, but I so dearly love them." The ice in her glass rattled as she took a sip. "Jimena!" The maid appeared quickly. "Please get Mister ..."—she raised his card and squinted at it—"Metzger a drink. What are you having?" She raised her glass toward him.

"Nothing, thanks. Or just water, please. I don't drink before noon."

"Oh, come now. How are you going to be ready for the afternoon cocktails without a morning warmup?"

"I guess I'll just have to face that challenge when I get there."

"All right, then, a mineral water for Mr. Metzger, Jimena. Ice or no ice?"

"No ice, thank you," he said.

The maid returned with a glassful of ice and a small bottle of San Pellegrino on a tray. Elise stood and swayed. "Damn it, Jimena, he said no ice."

The woman backed away with the tray. "I am so sorry, madam. I'll not be a moment, sir."

"No, that's all right," he said. "Ice is fine." He reached for the glass and the bottle, leaving the woman holding an empty tray and looking unsure about what to do next.

"You may go, Jimena." Elise gave her a stern look, then shrugged as she turned back to her guest. "These Latina types. My husband picks them. Because they work for less, he says. He's a lawyer, but he doesn't bother about checking their documents. He says the younger ones learn faster, but, I'm the one who has to train them, and ..." She trailed off and stared into her glass. "My husband likes ..."

Clinton waited, but she didn't complete the thought. "If this is not a good time, Mrs. McDermott, I could come back."

"One time is as good—or bad—as another. The house is empty, the kids are in school, and my dear husband is, mercifully, in Hong Kong or some other God-forsaken place for the week. What is it that you wanted."

"I'm a journalist, working on a story about small-cell carcinoma. I understand that is what your sister died from."

"I thought you said you knew her."

"Uh, yes, I did. I worked for a while at the lab in Ipswich."

Elise stood again and steadied herself on the table, setting the umbrella to swaying. "I ought to ask you to leave. You're all bastards. It was the chemicals that killed her, that's what I think.

"And that doctor she fell in love with. You know, Jeannine left everything to him, including her share in our lakeside place up in Maine. Can you imagine that? The family compound, and she leaves it to this Hebe. How did she think that was going to work? I mean, sharing the house and cabin with one of . . . them? We were fighting that in court, but then the bugger goes and dies, too. What a mess."

"I can see how it must have all been a shock. So, was that it? I mean in her estate."

"Just her share of the place on the lake and her own land in northern Maine—wilderness, really. A modest retirement account, some personal things, a wine collection, stuff—you know. But I thought you were interested in this cancer thing."

"I am. It seems there have been an unexpected number of deaths recently from this very rare form of lung cancer. Your sister appears to have been part of a pattern. I wondered if you might have some information that would help me figure it out: papers, correspondence, medical records, anything."

"You think it might be, like, chemicals from your lab?"

"Not my lab, and I wouldn't know. I only worked there for a few months . . . as a technical writer."

"I see. Well, I don't think I have anything about Jeannine that might help, but I can give you the name of her doctor: the one who treated her, not the one she, well, fooled around with."

"That would be great. Just one more question: Is there any chance you might have a copy of her will?"

~ ~ ~

Clinton now had two places to look for the missing laptop. Both were longshots, but longshots were all he had. He called Julia to let her know he was heading back up to Maine to do some poking around, starting with the Carston summer compound. "The death certificate I got from public records shows that Carston drowned at the lake. But a contributing cause was that she was weakened by lung cancer, a rare form called oat-cell carcinoma on the certificate but otherwise known as small-cell carcinoma."

"Does that mean anything?" she asked.

"I don't know yet. Before I head north tomorrow, I'm going to check in with Carston's doctor, Bradley Jervis, at a clinic in Peabody"

"Be careful, Clint."

"Collin. After all this time, Jana, I would think you could re-member my name."

She laughed. "Right. Oh, say, I met your mother. I drove down to the nursing home. I hope you don't mind."

"Why did you do that?" There was annoyance in his question.

"Because I wanted to know her, too, not just you and your father. You're right, she's not all there, not hardly at all. She kept on talking about Angelo—my Angelo, she called him—about how he had called and they talked on the phone."

"See what I mean? And the sad irony is that she's still fairly young and healthy, at least her body. She could have decades left of advancing dementia until there's nothing left but a body, just a shell stubbornly holding onto life."

"I'm sorry."

"It's okay. Did you get over to Sausalito?"

"Not yet. Tomorrow, probably. Oh, guess what. I'm meeting with friends tonight, some of your students from the seminar. Isn't that way cool?"

"No, that is not way cool. You were never in my class. You have to remember who you are now: Jana Barrows. We just cannot take chances at this point."

"Hey, chill. I think you're worrying too much, but I'll play it cool. If you want, I can tell them I can't make it."

"It's not about what I want, it's about staying alive. I'd rather you play it smart than play it cool. Remember, we're investigative reporters working on a big story. Blow your cover, and the whole thing blows up in our faces. Anyway, I'll talk with you again later. Well, tomorrow. I'm seeing somebody tonight."

"Seeing somebody. As in . . . ?"

"As in a contact inside Biontolics, that's all. Anyway, bye for now."

"Yeah, later. I . . . whatever." She paused before disconnecting.

~ ~ ~

Since Clinton's motel was not far from Route 128, the beltway ringing Boston, Sahana suggested they head over to Woburn to eat at a South Indian restaurant. "It's the real deal," she had told him, "literally like my mother's cooking. I'll pick you up at your hotel. I insist."

Later, as she pulled out of the parking lot at the down-market all-suite hotel where he was staying, she chided Clinton about his taste in accommodations. "Not sure whether this is a step up or down from your last motel."

"Well, the Wi-Fi's faster and there's more room, but we're still kinda living on the cheap for now."

"We?"

"Well, my student intern has to sleep someplace. Don't worry. She has the bedroom, and I have the sofa-bed in the sitting area."

"I'm not worried, and I'm certainly not prying into your personal life."

"Maybe you should. I think the poor girl has a crush on me."

"Men always think that, especially male professors." She slowed at the top of the on-ramp and slipped into southbound traffic that was still fairly heavy. "I remember this prof I had for Neurochemistry of Memory and Learning. I was a senior, and by that time I was really hooked on neuroscience. I kept pushing for extra readings and answers to tough questions, and he acted as if I were coming on to him. I finally had to tell him straight out that I was only interested in the subject matter, nothing more. He said, like, 'I understand,' but it became clear before long that he thought this was just another ploy in some game."

"What happened?"

"He finally took the hint when I left a copy of the student guide on his desk open to the page on sexual harassment with the number of the reporting hotline highlighted in yellow. The ultimate pisser is that he stopped answering questions and gave me a C on my term paper, which brought my grade down to a B. I appealed, of course, but he only raised the mark to a B-, which still left me with just a B+ in his class, so my straight A streak was broken. It was only the second B I ever got in twenty plus years of school."

"How very, very sad."

"Hey, don't mock me. This is serious. I deserved an A for that paper. It was a complete meta-analysis of dozens of studies on neurotransmitters in the hippocampus. In fact, I expanded and polished it up a bit over the summer before I started grad school, and it was accepted for publication in PLoS Biology. I sent my professor a link but never heard back from him, the jerk."

"I guess it's different at different times."

"Yeah, like different for guys."

"Maybe. I can't say I've ever had a female professor come on to me, but I've had crushes on teachers, women, that is."

"So have I. Actually both—men and women—but that's adolescent stuff. Well, or post-adolescent. I had this one course, Feminist Theory and Scientific Progress, with a lesbian lecturer I thought was gorgeous. She had a mind that could wrap around layers of inference and implications, and I loved the fact that she never wore a bra. Let's just say she had a way of inspiring the curious experimental side of more than one of the women in her seminar. "

"I think I understand. I really had the hots for one of my teachers in middle school. She was . . . oh, wait a minute, now I remember. You said you had Mrs. Geller, too."

"I did. I can see how you might go for her. She was cute and bouncy and non-threatening."

"Do you always put that kind of spin on things?"

"What kind of spin do you mean?"

"I mean like, gender politics, male-dominance sort of stuff."

"Hey, it's all gender politics if you're an aggressive, over-achieving female trying to make it in any field dominated by men, which is most of the really interesting ones. That's a big part of why I'm quitting Biontolics. The atmosphere there is heavy with rancid testosterone, and it oozes down from the top. I met The General once, the previous CEO. He was exactly the kind of domineering dick that unenlightened research assistants or grad students fall for if they haven't been clued into what goes wrong when he tires of them and moves on to the next younger one in line. Then it's dump city, girl."

"There's a new CEO, right?"

"Yeah, and frankly, from what I've gotten from his memos and seen on his all-hands pep-talk videos, he was cast from the same mold as his predecessor. I wouldn't trust him closer than ten meters."

"Is that why you're leaving Biontolics?"

"Hold on, this is our exit." She down-shifted as she took the off-ramp. "In a sense, yes, that's part of it, but I'm not so much leaving Biontolics as moving on to something better. I'm joining a startup in the Bay Area. I'll be out in your end of the country. Isn't that cool? It's a woman-headed software house that's building some innovative new brain-training and cognitive enhancement apps."

"Is that stuff real? I mean, from what I've read, it's fairly solid pseudoscience."

"Most of it is, but this is different. That's why they're hiring me. Anyway, here we are; this is the place. Doesn't look like much from the outside, but get ready for some of the best Indian food you'll ever taste, that is until I invite you home to meet the family and you get to try my mother's cooking for real."

~ ~ ~

They were back in the parking lot of his motel, still talking after a long dinner, when Clinton suddenly interrupted her. "Sorry, but I just flashed on something you said earlier. How soon do you actually leave Biontolics? Or are you already gone?"

"No, I'm still there, finishing out the month. Why?"

"I wonder if you could get something for me, but only if you can do it without putting yourself at risk."

"What do you want?"

"I was wondering if there was any way you could get me copies of a couple of those videos: one from the current CEO and one from the previous guy, the one you called The General."

"I don't think so. There really is no way of getting digital copies out of the building, no open ports or USB slots or ... I certainly couldn't email them to you. No, I don't see how. Why?"

"I've just got a funny hunch. You said they were both cast from the same mold. That got me thinking. Oh, well."

"If I think of anything, I'll let you know. Okay?"

"Okay, but no heroics."

"Is this more macho posturing or are you simply being unnecessarily protective of me?"

"I just—"

"Shut up. I'm teasing." She leaned over as far as her seatbelt would allow and gave him a conciliatory look.

"I had a great time this evening," he said. "Thanks for a wonderful dinner." He hesitated, then gave her a quick kiss and started to reach for the door.

She took his hand and pulled him back for a longer kiss. "I wish it wasn't a week night. But it is, and I really have to go."

"Yeah, me, too. Both. All of it."

Chapter 32

It took persuading to get Jeannine Carston's doctor, Bradley Jervis, to agree to meet in his Peabody office, a suite in one of the string of medical facilities arrayed behind the North Shore Mall. Jervis insisted on waiting until the end of the day. When Clinton arrived, the doctor told his nurse that he would be using Examining Room B. "I know it's unscheduled, but Mr. Metzger is only in town this afternoon and needs to be seen right away."

In the room, Jervis closed the door, turned on the water in the sink, and sat down on his stool. "Now, tell me what this is really about."

"Jeannine Carston. Her sister told me you were her doctor. She died of a form of cancer she shouldn't have had. What's the real story?"

"I'm sorry, I can't help you. Medical records and patient information are confidential. Without a release or a court order, I'm afraid there is nothing I can tell you."

"Then let me tell you some things. I assume you know that Carston's lover, Dr. Rosen David, died not long after. Did you know that Dr. David's wife, Millicent Geller, also died recently?"

"You're talking about the teacher, from the Middle School up in Newburyport? I don't see—"

"The death was suspicious, a fire that shouldn't have happened. I was investigating it, and now people are trying to kill me. Informed sources cast doubt on the reported cause of death for Dr. David, supposedly the same rare tropical disease that killed that African dictator, Edgar Jabari Mbutsu. Except, I just returned from Busanyu, and that story doesn't hold water. What's clear is that some people are very determined not to have the real story come out, determined enough to eliminate anyone who threatens to expose them. I believe you know something about this, Dr. Jervis."

"If I did, why would I tell you . . . or anybody else?"

"Because it keeps getting worse. Your proximity to Carston puts you on the radar. Sooner or later the beam will swing around and shine on you. These people are relentless, and they have enormous resources."

"Then let somebody else put themselves in the radar beam. I know nothing about these mysterious and malevolent people you refer to, and there is nothing I can tell you about any of my patients without releases or court orders. Besides, even that would get you nothing. Do I make myself clear?"

"Perfectly."

Dr. Jervis escorted Clinton out, then slumped into a chair in the waiting room with his head in his hands.

~ ~ ~

Clinton left the office convinced that Jervis knew something important but would say nothing about it. It was time to try different channels. He headed back toward the Interstate but immediately whipped across traffic into a strip mall where a Starbucks beckoned him to refuel before hitting the highway. He ordered a latte and fired up his laptop while waiting for the barista to work her way through the queued orders. On impulse, he tried a new Google search, combining oat-cell carcinoma with Biontolics. Below a stack of misleading hits, the results page included references to two papers out of Biontolics Southland in North Carolina. A switch to Google Scholar netted him abstracts that reported development of a strain of exceptionally virulent oat-cell carcinoma that was actually communicable.

It was possible, then, that Jeannine Carston had been deliberately infected with lung cancer. Could that have been what had killed Rosen David and Edgar Mbutsu, too? It didn't make sense. Hidalgo's notebook had included interviews with staff from the Presidential Palace that claimed Mbutsu had died when the so-called rejuvenating treatments failed or were stopped.

Okay, Clinton told himself, time to head north. He looked at his watch. It would be after dark by the time he reached the lake. Good, he thought. He closed his laptop, retrieved his latte, and left.

~ ~ ~

The Carston family compound proved to be a small lake-front property with a two-story cedar-shingle house and a small outbuilding that looked as if it had long ago been a large storage shed. Both buildings were boarded up for the winter, and signs warned that they were protected by a central alarm system. Clinton wondered how long it would take for anyone to respond to an alarm. It was a mile of deeply rutted dirt road back to the turnoff, then nearly ten miles of country roads to the nearest town. How long would he need? He switched his flashlight to low and kept it pointed downward as he scouted out the property. At the back of the house he found the electric meter missing. The electricity had been disconnected. What were the odds that the alarm system had no power?

He decided to chance it. He retrieved the tire iron from the trunk of the car and slowly pried one of the plywood panels off the back porch. He used a pocket knife to slit the screen enough to crawl through. The door from the porch was locked, but one kick sent it swinging open.

Inside smelled dusty and dank. Sheets were draped over most of the furniture. It did not look promising as a place to stash a laptop, but he went through the house anyway, opening drawers and cupboards, looking under beds and along shelves. He was about to leave when he noticed a small door under the stairs to the second floor. It was secured with a padlock, but the hasp was easy to pry off. Inside were stashed a stereo, a small-screen television, and a DVD player. No laptop. He closed the door and pushed the screws of the hasp back into their holes. "Good as new," he said.

He left the way he had entered, doing his best to make it look like the place had not been broken into. He worked the same procedure on the outbuilding, which consisted of a single room with two sets of bunk beds. He felt bad about the breaking-and-entering but forgave himself. Nothing was missing, and the repairs would be trivial. He put the tire iron back with the spare before closing the trunk. He was about to start the car when he saw a light out over the water and heard a motorboat approaching. He hadn't thought of that. The lake was only a mile across.

Hide? Run for it on foot? No, tear-ass back up the dirt road, he concluded. He started the car but left the lights off. In turning around, he backed into a tree, then struck a boulder with his right front bumper before aligning with the road out. In the pale light of a waning moon, it was almost impossible to see the road ahead except as an absence of dark shapes. He twice struck rocks or tree roots before he reached the paved two-lane road again. He headed north, tromped on the accelerator, and turned on the headlights after rounding the first curve. Behind him he heard sirens, first approaching and then fading.

Carston's wilderness parcel was even less likely than the family compound, but the satellite view on Google had shown what looked to be two small buildings of some kind nestled in the woods. He had come this far; he might as well keep going.

Chapter 33

When Fergusson arrived at the office, Bertrand Lyon was pacing, wearing a figure-eight path into the carpeting. "What is it this time, Bertrand?"

"Well, it's bad enough getting test results that say I have to go back in for an early treatment,"—he waved a stapled sheath of A4 paper— "but now Holzinger seems to have dropped off the edge of the earth. Nothing from him in over two days."

"Gus Holzinger has been known to go incommunicado before. He'll phone home when he's ready. But what's this about the tests?"

"Borderline."

"Let me take a look at the results." He reached for the papers.

"And you think you'll see something I didn't? I invented this whole thing, remember."

"We invented it. Technically, it was Janella Kai who ought to be credited, since it was her discovery of the anomalies with the mosaic lab rats that was the basis of everything that came after."

"Janella was nothing but a pretty young lab assistant with a nose for trouble, nothing more. It's a dead issue."

"Appropriate choice of words."

"Fuck you, Charles. I protected our interests. From the very beginning, I protected our interests."

"My, we are touchy. When do you go back for the unscheduled treatment?"

"I'll admit myself tonight after I clear up this Holzinger business."

"Just send somebody else to go in after him."

"The problem is I only know what city he's in, not his exact whereabouts."

"Surely, there is somebody else on our security team who has the talent to track him down."

"There is, but I'm hesitant to send her in."

"Now I get it. Who is it? The Chinese girl, the one I told you to leave alone?"

"She broke it off anyway, once she learned she couldn't sleep her way into The Club. Of course, she didn't actually know what all the membership perks were, just that the members were all fit and fabulously wealthy."

"So, you don't trust her?"

"No, that's not it. Zhu Huang is trustworthy, I suppose, as most all true mercenaries are—so long as they're well paid. I just hate to send a girl on a man's mission."

"And right there, Bertrand, is the nub of the problem, why you can't keep administrative assistants for more than a year. You should hire a competent male secretary, preferably gay." While the open-mouthed Bertrand was pondering a retort, Fergusson left.

~ ~ ~

Before she landed in Madeira, Zhu Huang had checked the online editions of local newspapers, relying on Google Translate to give her the gist of stories that interested her. She had also already cultivated a contact among the *Bombeiros Municipais do Funchal,* the local firefighters. He was Han Chinese by descent but had been born on the island. Like Zhu, he preferred a physical to a cerebral life, which had been a profound disappointment to his parents, both professors at the University of Madeira. She guessed that Bohei had taken much teasing over his name when he was growing up in Funchal. She caught up with him after he finished his shift at the station on the steep thoroughfare of Avenido Calouste Gulbenkian.

"Yes," he told her, "there was only one body recovered from the burned building, an intruder, the police believe." He spoke to her in Mandarin, but so heavily accented that Zhu had difficulty under-standing him. She asked if he spoke English, but he hung his head in shame and told her no.

"And the others all escaped unharmed?" she asked.

"No, four victims were hospitalized: burns and smoke in the lungs, one of them also had a gunshot wound. He was the one who sounded the fire alarm about the time of the explosion. They found him in the stairwell outside the apartment where the explosion set off the fire. He had dragged himself there."

"Was the body identified?"

"No, nor did anyone claim it. The matter is still under investi-gation. A pistol found in the wreckage near the body was not registered and could not be traced because it had been altered."

"This pistol, do you recall anything about it? What kind? What caliber?"

"I don't know. I am sorry Zhu Huang. I think it had an Italian sort of name."

"Beretta?"

"Yes," his face lit up. "That's what the papers said."

"What about the explosion? Has anything been figured out about that?"

"It seems some chemicals in the apartment were ignited when the gun was fired. That is the theory, but it is still being investigated."

"And these victims? Where are they now?"

"They were taken to the main hospital, at Cruz de Carvalho. I would not know if they are all still there, but I think the man who was shot might be."

"His name, would you happen to remember his name?"

"Yes, he was Portuguese. It was Rodrigues, but I do not recall his Christian name."

"Thank you, Bohei Wong." She bowed. "You have helped a great deal in this. Do not speak of this meeting. I trust you understand it is a matter of national security and very sensitive."

"I am honored to be of service to you, Zhu Huang." He bowed in return and respectfully did not ask her which nation's security was at stake. "I hope your long trip here has not proved to be a disappointment to you."

~ ~ ~

At the hospital, Zhu inquired at the reception desk whether anyone spoke English. "I speak a little," the woman said.

"Good, I am here to find out about a patient named Angelo Rodrigues."

"I am sorry, but we can answer questions about patients only to people in the family."

"We are investigating the fire." She showed the woman an Interpol identification that she used with people who would not know what the real thing looked like or what it meant. "I need to talk with Mr. Rodrigues."

"Oh, but that would not be possible."

"Why not?"

"Because he is not here. He was discharged yesterday, in the company of some of your colleagues."

"Colleagues?"

"Yes, from Interpol."

Chapter 34

It was bitter cold, nearly dark, and after almost two days of trudging the wilds of northern Maine, Clinton had found nothing. He turned away from the frozen lake to skirt a fallen tree. As he trudged uphill, there was a brief flare of white, then yellow, through the trees. He stopped and held his breath, but now there was nothing. He took a step back, and there it was again, in a narrow gap between tree trunks: a light. He walked slowly forward on the unmarked trail up from the water, gradually turning his head to keep his eyes fixed on the same spot some distance away. Finally, through another somewhat wider break between trees, he saw it once more: two lights, flickering, seeming to float in space about chest high. Candles.

The snap of a twig underfoot was followed almost instantly by the double-slap of a pump-action 12-gauge shotgun being cocked. Clinton froze, his foot in the air as if he were about to step into a bear trap.

"If you want to keep your balls," a voice said, "you better turn tail and head right back down the path. This is posted property, and you are trespassing."

Clinton tried to place the direction of the voice, but the trees and uneven snow cover played tricks with the sound. He glanced from side to side without turning his head, but darkness was advancing over the forest like a fog rolling in, and Clinton could see no one.

"I'm looking for someone," he called out, still frozen in place.

"Well, no one by that name is here. Better look somewhere," — there was an audible intake of breath and a sharp sneeze— "somewhere else." A triplet of sneezes followed.

Something was oddly, impossibly familiar about the staccato sneezes. "Who's there?" he said. "Do I know you?" There was no reply. "I'm,"—he hesitated for a moment before using his real name—"It's Clinton Rodrigues."

"Are you alone?"

"Yes. I mean no. Someone is waiting for me in my car, back on the fire road."

"Rather fond of that name: someone. How do I know whether to believe you or not."

"I received a package. One of thirty-two identical packages mailed at the same time. Who else would know that?"

"Anyone who intercepted any of them would."

"Okay, fair enough. Mine had a scribbled note, written and then erased."

"Clinton? Is it really you?"

"For real. Would you shoot a former student?" He turned toward the sound of boots breaking the crust on the snow to his left. A small woman, with short-cropped corn-silk hair peeking beneath her knitted ski hat, smiled at him. She was dressed in jeans, Bean boots, and a blue fleece under an open red-plaid outer shirt. Clinton grinned back at her. "My, Mrs. Geller, don't you look the part of the Maine woodsman."

"You'd think it were the dead of winter the way you're dressed, Clinton. That California sunshine must have softened you some. You look like the Michelin man in all that puffy down outerwear. Come on up to the cabin and get some of those layers off before you start sweating and catch cold." She tugged at his arm and steered him to the left. "And try to stay on the trail instead of trudging cross-country like you've been doing. Tramples down the underbrush and leaves tracks that are too easy to follow. Step over that creek and come up this way. And watch your step. Getting too dark."

She marched on ahead of him, deftly sidestepping deadfalls and skirting large rocks as if she were using night-vision goggles. They reached the cabin and Clinton could see that the light he had spotted came from two candles on a table near a small window.

She noticed him looking. "Friday night, Shabbat. I never miss lighting the Sabbath candles, although I don't always bake challah. You're in luck tonight; I had two eggs and decided to use them and some of the flour. Only one loaf, though."

"You need more? Isn't one loaf enough?"

"Jewish tradition, two loaves, proof of plenty. Plus, then you don't bake again during Saturday." She reached around the rough-hewn door jamb and tugged at a hidden pull cord that lifted the latch. "Hurry on in. Don't let the heat out."

It was surprisingly warm in the cabin, a twelve-by-sixteen slope-roofed structure that looked like it had started as a lean-to hiking shelter before being closed in and weatherized. A green painted spindle-leg table and two matching chairs stood by the only window. Split logs burned in a field-stone fireplace on the opposite wall where a ladder led to a sleeping loft under the sharply angled peak of the roof. Along the wall to the left of the door was a shelf that held stacked jars of food, books, a pair of binoculars, and a microscope under a dust cover.

"I see you haven't lost the bug for biology," he said.

"I'm researching changes in insect pest populations with changing climate. Another five years and I should have enough data to publish. I'll pass it on covertly to someone who still has a name and a career. So, do you really have someone waiting in a car?"

"No. That was just a bluff."

"Good. It gets pretty damn cold up here at night. You'll have to wait until morning to hike back out. I have a spare sleeping bag. It's a little drafty on the floor, but you can curl up close to the fireplace. Well, not too close. Fire screen has a tear in it I haven't gotten around to fixing." She twisted one of the chairs out from the table. "Here, sit. First take off some of those layers or you're going to be sweating like a pig that just ran the Boston Marathon." She paused and looked at him expectantly. "What? Don't you remember anything from eighth-grade science? We covered this. Pigs don't sweat to cool off; they wallow in mud."

"Right, I don't remember much about eighth-grade science, but I do remember my amazing teacher."

"Whom you and your friends called Sneezy behind her back."

"At least you weren't called Grumpy like the shrunken Mr. Duff."

"He wasn't all that grumpy, maybe a little dyspeptic."

"Great choice of words, but that makes me think you actually have read some of my writing, because that's exactly how I referred to him in one of my essays: the dyspeptic Mr. D."

"Of course, I was plagiarizing you, testing you. I read everything you wrote. Why do you think I put you on my special mailing list."

"You know, don't you, that your packages didn't get delivered — except for mine—and they think you're dead."

She punched the air. "Yes! It worked."

"Well, I can see that you're not dead, but they identified the body.

They actually got a DNA and partial fingerprint match from . . ."

She was holding up her left hand. The tip of her fourth finger was missing.

"Oh, wow, you did that? You really, like cut off . . . ? How could . . . ?"

"I'm a biologist. Had to do something that no one would imagine I would have done. No big deal. Didn't even hurt all that much until the next day."

"This is some story. You have to tell me everything. How in hell did you pull this whole thing off?"

"I'll tell you, but first hang up your things on the pegs by the door and sit down while I make tea. This is a celebration."

~ ~ ~

Clinton wrapped his hands around the mug with the broken handle and sipped. "The tea is really good. Is it Lapsang souchong? I think I detect just a hint of smokiness in the blend." He winked and nodded toward the fire.

"Okay, so I mostly use the fireplace for my cooking. I do have a propane camp stove, but packing in spare cylinders is a nuisance and then there's the problem of disposal. And please excuse the mug. I've had exactly one visitor since my untimely death, and that's you. I'm not used to entertaining and intend to keep it that way. Understood?"

"Understood. But please tell me how you did it. I get that you left behind the tip of your finger but . . . I mean, there was a whole body burned, a superhot fire, like . . ."

"Well, I got a little warning, and I had done my prep in advance. A clerk at the post office said there had been a stranger chatting with Hazel Shaeffer, so I guessed they would be coming after me next. There was aluminum powder and oxidizing compound—homemade thermite—under the body, with more on top to melt into it to destroy it from the inside also."

"But the body . . ."

"I robbed a grave and covered the fact by knocking over gravestones. It was an old cemetery, pretty much abandoned. I knew it would be awhile before the vandalism was noted and figured no one would connect the two events. The body was going to end up cremated down to ashes anyway, so they wouldn't know it was old remains."

"The fingertip?"

"It was stuck in the mouth of a beer bottle packed in dry ice, which protected it and sublimed with the heat. No evidence to find. Same with the aluminum oxide from the thermite, which just wafted away with the smoke. Besides, like most mobile homes, mine was aluminum, so traces of metal or aluminum oxide wouldn't be an issue. Same for the bullets. My assassin stepped just inside the trailer, fired two shots to the head from a .22 caliber handgun with a suppressor. As he left, he smelled gas—methyl mercaptan, part of my plan—and got inspired. He loaded a tracer shell, got clear, and fired into the trailer. I triggered my little primer remotely, and the rest is history."

"It was just some random body in the bed—right?—under a blanket, I assume. How do you know exactly what happened? "

"Because I had an infrared Wi-Fi webcam that I was recording remotely. Another insurance policy."

"And you got out just before this guy arrived, towing your roll-aboard luggage."

She gave him an open-mouthed smile. "Oh, you are good."

"Well, I noted the tracks but didn't figure it all out until just now. So, you are dead. Everyone, including your enemies, is convinced you died in that fire."

"Exactly, and that's the only way I get to stay alive—by being dead. Now it's my turn. How did you track me down?"

"I was following the trail from your husband—late husband, sorry—and from the material in your packet figured you had his laptop, must have stashed it someplace. He inherited this parcel from, well, you know . . ."

"Jeannine, his lover. You don't have to tiptoe around things with me. I actually left him before those two connected."

"I see."

"Probably not, but that's not important. So you thought a little like I did, trying to figure someplace that was not really directly associated with me. So, here I am."

"But, living out here, alone—that must be hard."

"I do miss teaching, but otherwise it's not so bad. I'm a real biologist again, doing real science. That part I love. And I don't need much more. So, sit, relax, tell me about your life while I serve us a lovely Shabbat meal. It's been cooking all day: rabbit stew with *Daucus carota*. If you remember our unit on edible wild plants that's Queen

Anne's Lace: wild carrots. I hope you don't keep kosher, though. It's just so hard to find a kosher butcher in these parts, and rabbit wouldn't qualify anyway."

Clinton laughed. "No, I don't keep kosher. I'm not even Jewish. Well, I'm half Jewish."

"Hey, half-Jewish is Jewish in my book. I never really practiced except for Shabbat. Everyone should have a day of no work, a time to just be alive in the world and appreciate it. The Jews invented the weekend, you know—isn't that something?—the punctuation in the grammar of daily life. Greatest invention in human history." She walked over to the shelf, picked up a plate covered with a polka-dot hand towel, and lifted it to her face. "Smell that?" She passed the plate under his nose. "Fresh bread. Life is good. I even have wine. Rosen was always a connoisseur of good wine. When he passed, his cellar went to me. It's now down in the cellar—the root cellar." She tapped a foot on the floor. "At the rate I drink, it should be enough for years."

~ ~ ~

The simple dinner and a bottle of an Argentine Malbec kept them talking for hours. At length, she reached across the table and took his hand. "What are you going to do next?"

"Publish the story, expose them."

"I tried that route. They are not going to let the story get published. Did you ever see that old Robert Redford movie, *Three Days of the Condor*? At the end, his character and this CIA guy, Higgins, are standing on the street outside the New York Times Building. One of the last lines, by Higgins, is something like 'How do you know they'll print it?' I can now see how this poison vine has it's tendrils into everything, everywhere. If you try to publish, they'll get you. They got Rosen, and they got me. Millicent Geller is dead. Now I'm just the crazy nameless bird-and-bug lady of the Maine backwoods."

"I'll find a way."

"I hope you do." She stood up still holding his hand. As he rose, she put her arms around his waist, and they stood, embracing, for long seconds. She rested her head on his chest. "I guess there are other things I miss bedsides teaching."

He looked down as she tipped up her face, lit by the light of the waning fire and the guttering candles, to give him a warm, almost embarrassed smile. "I'm sorry," she said. "Not much human contact."

He bent to kiss her. When they stopped, she caught her breath. "I don't think this is a good idea. No. You're very sweet, but—"

He put his finger on her lips and shook his head. "I had such a crush on you. Did you know that? I hated that there were these stupid rules and that I was just a kid to you."

"It happens, adolescent hormones, crushes on teachers. Kids outgrow it."

"Not all of them."

She kept shaking her head with short pulses of laughter. "You . . . but I'm feeling so, so old. I'm old enough to be your—"

His finger was on her lips again. "No, be still."

"Not my way, being still. Let's sit back down and talk."

In the morning, she insisted on hiking with him back to his car. She scoffed when she saw the fresh dents and scratches. "My, you sure are driving one beat up automobile."

"Wasn't that way a couple days ago, but it's a long story. I'm going to have to figure out what to tell the rental agency. Right now, I should get on the road."

"Remember: no one must know. You cannot tell anyone."

"I know. I know."

She stepped up and put her arms around him. "Thank you," she said, as she held him. "Thank you for spending Shabbat with me and for . . . for being understanding."

"Thank you, for sharing a very special evening. You know something funny? I'm still learning from you; you're still my teacher. I'll be going back home with some new insights."

"You're just saying that to make an old teacher-lady smile."

"Well, I do like that smile. I used to live for that bright spot in the dark days of my middle-school angst."

"And you had to mess up the moment by reminding me of your long-ago school days." She beamed up at him.

He kissed her forehead gently. "I'll be back, I promise."

"Don't make promises like that. I might not be here." She turned abruptly and started back up the trail from the fire road.

Chapter 35

Clinton tried to concentrate on driving, but his mind kept going back to the night with Millie. That was how he now thought of her: no longer as Millicent, certainly not as Mrs. Geller. It took nearly an hour of slow going on back roads before Clinton was in range of a cell tower. Minutes later, his phone tapped out a drum solo announcing the arrival of a delayed text from Sahana. He slowed and glanced at the short message: "Home sick. Call on burner. News 4 u."

There had been no traffic, but habitual caution kept Clinton driving until he found a wide spot in the road where it would be safer to pull over to call Sahana. "Hi, what's up?"

"I was working on your request."

"I hope you were careful."

"Der. Since I couldn't actually download the files, I tried shooting a video of my monitor with my smartphone, but it was terrible, so I started thinking about what you might be interested in. Among the videos I watched were some full-face close-ups of Atchison Dougherty and some of Bertrand Lyon. I freeze-framed on the faces and started comparing them. At first they looked quite different to me—different hair, face shape, mouth—then I noticed the eyes. Lyon has slightly darker eyes, but—get this—when I zoomed in on their left eyes, they both showed exactly the same irregularity in the iris: dark inclusions at 3 o'clock and 11 o'clock. I really think it's the same guy, maybe with contacts, a little plastic surgery, hair dye, that stuff. All in all, it makes him look younger by ten years or more."

"Great work!"

"That's not all. At home I did some online research into the background of our new CEO. Everything in his official bio checked out. I was a little suspicious, because every fact was linked to a page that confirmed the claim, almost like they wanted you to click through their prepared links rather than do independent research. So, I decided to verify his birth date on my own. Sure enough, I found his Canadian birth certificate through a genealogy site.

"But, get this, I thought some of the old news stories about him linked from his bio read like they had been written by public relations people. So, I got inspired and looked for them on the Internet Archives, the Wayback Machine. They're not all there. In other words, some were created recently with doctored dates, even in the metadata."

"Wow, that's huge."

"Yes, Bertrand Lyon, the supposed head of Biontolics, is a fiction. It's really Atchison Dougherty. And whoever he is, he has the resources and expertise to plant false documents in government databases and create a fake online presence. And why this charade? Because Atchison Dougherty should have been dead long ago. He would be a centenarian by now. Do either of the men you've seen in pictures or videos look like frail, hundred-year-olds? No."

"Hmmm." Clinton let it sink in. "There is another possibility. Dougherty might have been secretly replaced by someone else, someone much younger, who now styles himself as Bertrand Lyon."

"Doesn't wash with what you told me. No, these people have bioengineered what Ponce de Leon sought in Florida. They've stopped aging, and they are determined that nothing and no one will stop them."

"Then lay low, chill out, and finish your month at the lab without drawing any attention to yourself. I'll catch up with you in California after your move."

"Do I have to wait that long?" There was a sudden change in the tone of her voice to something between teasing and petulance. "I mean, you owe me now, not only for my sleuthing. It's also your turn to buy dinner."

"I don't know. Things have gotten a little complicated."

"Your so-called research assistant? No, wait, you called her—what?—your student intern."

"Not her. Not that sort of thing. I mean it's this story I'm working on."

"And I'm not working on it, too?"

"No, you're not. You need to get on with your new job and leave this to the pros."

"Ouch."

"I didn't mean it that way. Look, it's better if you forget this whole conversation and the stuff you uncovered."

"Okay, but we have to at least have a going-away dinner before I head west."

"I don't think that would be such a good idea. I'm trying to keep a low profile, not be seen too much in public."

"Then how about dinner at my place? I'm not quite as good a cook as my mother, but she thinks I'm not bad."

"I don't know . . ."

"Friday, my place, seven o'clock. It's a date, no argument."

"Well . . ."

"Great! See you then." She disconnected just as Clinton's phone started winking that its battery was low.

~ ~ ~

He was back in the motel room, stretched out on the couch recovering from the long drive, when the call came in. "I have some news." Julia's voice on the phone was brimming with suppressed excitement.

"Me, too, absolutely amazing news. But you go first. Mine may have to wait until you get back here."

"But I thought you were coming out here, to our home turf."

"Precisely why we shouldn't be hanging out around there. Sacramento is the first place they would look for us."

"But we're no longer us. We're Jana and Collin."

"It's temporary cover to let us get back to the States, not like actual witness protection, despite what my father said. And to really stay gone, we would have to leave behind all the places and people we know. Hanging around the same haunts with the same friends is one sure way to be found. But we can hash all that out later. What's your big news?"

A sharp sigh was just audible over the phone. "Okay. I went to the bank. It's a good thing I brought my backpack with me. I almost couldn't close the zipper."

"What all was in the safety deposit box?"

"Money, that's all. Nothing but dollars: over a hundred thousand in twenties and fifties. I don't think I ever expected to see so much cash in one pile in my life. We're rich."

"Well, I wouldn't call a hundred K rich, but it certainly would do as the down payment on a house. Wow. Not bad.'

"Now, what about your news."

Clinton resisted the impulse to blurt out anything about his discovery in the north woods. "Bertrand Lyon is really Atchison Dougherty. The same guy is still the head of Biontolics. He is actually over a hundred and doesn't look a day over fifty."

"How do we know this?"

"My contact at Biontolics analyzed some photos." There was a long silence over the phone. "Pretty neat, huh?" he said. "She was able to show the eyes are the same."

"Right, pretty neat, I guess. Look, I gotta go." There was another extended pause. "What should I do with the money? Open a bank account?"

"No! Absolutely not!"

"You don't have to yell at me."

"Sorry. Look, we can't deposit it. Large cash deposits are reported. We'd have to be able to explain where we got it. The feds would assume it was drug money."

"Well, that's what I'd assume, too."

"Yes, of course, which is why we will just have to hold onto it and only use a little at a time. We can split it up when I get out there."

"So, at least you still trust me."

"What's that supposed to mean?"

"Oh, whatever . . . just forget it. I'll figure out some place to stash it. You just go and have fun with your . . . your inside contact. Cheers." She disconnected.

Chapter 36

"Sir, this is Zhu Huang. I located Holzinger. He's dead. I located Rodrigues. He's gone." The voice on the phone barely hinted at the frustration Zhu was experiencing.

"That's not good, really not good." Lyon ran a hand through his hair. "What's our next move? Rodrigues and his girlfriend are high value targets."

"It was a different Rodrigues. This one was in the building with Holzinger. He was shot. Left the hospital in a wheelchair. I checked the airport. No recent wheelchair passengers on commercial flights, no medivac flights. He's here or he left by boat."

"You said it wasn't the right Rodrigues."

"Oh, it was the right Rodrigues, just not the one you were looking for. Someone, some organization with real resources, got to him first. They posed as Interpol and took him away under armed guard."

"Was he wanted by the government, some government?"

"Yes, but I doubt that was who took him. Others have an interest in him and his work. He owned the apartment building where Holzinger died. Burned. There was a drug lab."

"So . . . organized crime."

"Probably. I suggest we let him run. I have another angle. With your permission, I want to head for the Ipswich lab. The security breaches there were never resolved. I have a hunch."

"Okay, Zhu. Bring this business to the right conclusion and you can have Holzinger's old job."

"One job at a time, sir."

"Okay. And Zhu . . ."

"Yes?"

"Be careful."

~ ~ ~

For the rest of the week, Clinton's world was bounded by the motel and by his own circadian rhythm set adrift by time-zone transitions and tension. He took his once-a-day meals just as room service was closing down for the night and would awaken from a few hours' sleep when the maid knocked on the door in the morning. Five days of frenzied research and writing was fueled by coffee, cola, and barbecue chicken pizza.

Taking his cue from Sahana, he started systematically checking information about the heads of Biontolics by comparing current web pages against earlier versions and data recorded in the Internet Archives. In some cases, he was able to find multiple revisions of the same biographical tidbits that arranged themselves in a neat timeline of successive doctoring. He made dozens of quick phone calls to libraries, schools, newspapers, and professional associations to triangulate his findings and get quick quotes for use in an article. As the anomalies piled up, he began typing up his notes in the first draft of a five-part exposé: "Archivist Talia Brucher confirmed by telephone that records showed Llewellyn Andras Cass, M.D., had been Board Certified in Oncology in 1986, but a hardcopy of the *Directory of Medical Specialists in Massachusetts* dated 1980 listed L. Andras Cass as having been Board Certified in 1972. When asked about the conflicting information, Brucher said she would 'look into it'."

After a week of erratic hours, Clinton almost forgot his promise to Sahana to come for dinner on Friday. At the last minute, he realized he had no clean clothes. With the clock ticking, he sprinted to the shopping center up the road and bought a French-blue dress shirt and a pair of khakis at TJ Maxx. On the way back, he stopped at a package store and impulsively purchased an expensive bottle of a German auslese Riesling that he thought might do as an aperitif.

He was nearly an hour late when he pressed the buzzer outside Sahana's apartment. She greeted him at the door dressed in a red-print sari with gold-thread trim. "Please come in."

"I'm so sorry I'm late. I was trying to find the right way to wrap up an article and just lost track of time."

"It's not a problem. South Indians have their own sense of time, one that's not slaved to either the clock or the sun. Welcome to my place."

The apartment was spacious, furnished in a sophisticated blend of contemporary furniture with traditional Indian wall hangings and bric-a-brac that suggested Sahana had an artistic side to complement her scientific talent. Dinner started with an appetizer of small pancakes served with an assortment of chutneys and sauces. "These are *dosa*. Perhaps you remember them from that restaurant, only I'm using them as appetizers. They're not hard to make, but for the authentic version, like these, the batter has to be fermented."

Dinner stretched over a leisurely several hours of talk about trivia and transcendence, with Sahana serving a succession of Indian delicacies between disagreements over the risks and rewards of weak ethics in science and the state of investigative journalism in America. After a full week of pizza and Pringles, Clinton's taste buds were savoring the onslaught of spices. "How did you manage all this? You must've cooked for days."

"Not quite, but I did take today off. I've accrued a gazillion sick days and weeks of vacation time. Besides, things have gotten weird at work. They've hired a new woman in the Neuroscience Section, supposedly my replacement. She's Chinese, speaks English with a British accent, but if she has a doctorate in neuropsychology from Oxford, as she claimed, I'll eat my sheepskin from Stanford. She does a good job of faking it, but it doesn't all hang together. She's always hovering around me and Nina Bracken. Asks lots of questions, not all of which make sense from a scientist."

"Maybe she's not a scientist. This could be more snooping to follow up on your earlier brush with exposure."

"But I haven't done any more of that stuff at work. Besides, I'll be out of there soon enough. Look, can we not talk about that sort of stuff tonight?"

"Sure."

"Thanks." She reached over and refilled his wine glass. "And are you ready for desert?"

"Desert? I'm not sure I have room for—"

"It's non-fattening, I promise. Wait here." She slipped back into the kitchen with the last of their dishes. When she emerged a minute later, she was unwrapping her sari, just exposing a glistening mat of jet-black pubic hair. Clinton held his breath as she let the sari fall to the floor. She narrowed her eyes as she approached. "I think it's time we expand your understanding of the culture of India, starting with the meaning of the much misunderstood word *tantra*."

Chapter 37

Bright morning sunlight reflected off the water and rippled on the ceiling. Clinton stared at the light show above him and realized he had only slept a couple of hours. Beside him, Sahana lay, one brown leg bent atop a pillow and the other half wrapped in the silk sheet. The night had been a slow swirling blur that had seemed to stretch on like a wormhole through the dark.

Clinton attempted to slip from under the sheet and out of bed without disturbing her, but she stirred just as he stood and began searching for his clothes.

"They're in the living room," she said. "But don't go yet. It's Saturday morning; there's no hurry."

He gave her a cockeyed smile. "Not for you, maybe. You don't have to worry about pleasing your boss anymore. I, on the other hand, have work to do."

"And who is this boss who expects you to work weekends?"

"Immediate supervisor or top boss?"

"What?"

"Well, the former is a real taskmaster and the latter is the ultimate in guilt-trip manipulators."

"Who are you talking about?"

"Whom. Well, me, in the first instance: I'm a really tough taskmaster. And ultimately, it's all my mother's fault. She used six thousand years of Jewish perfection of the art of guilt tripping to inculcate me with a work ethic that never slacks off. I can hear her in my head even as I excuse myself to use your shower before I duck out of here."

"Well, we're going to have to do something about that overinflated work ethic, mister. I'm a hard worker, too, but I don't bring it home with me. If we're going to make this relationship work, there will have to be some rules."

Clinton stopped in his tracks at the words "this relationship." "I . . ." He reached for a response, then gave up searching for words. "I think I better take a shower and be going," he said, without turning around. "I really have a lot on my plate right now. Maybe some other time." He walked into the bathroom and closed the door behind him.

When he emerged, the bed was made, and his clothes were neatly laid out on the side closest to him.

~ ~ ~

Back at the motel, Clinton turned the room key and pushed the door open. It banged against the taut security chain. "What the ...?" He heard soft footsteps approaching, then the door slammed shut in his face. The chain rattled, and Julia opened the door halfway.

"Oh, it's you," she said.

"I thought you were in California. I ..."

"I was. I decided you were right. We should be staying clear of the home turf for a while. I took the red-eye from San Fran to Boston. I wanted to surprise you. Guess I did. Did you have a nice night?"

"I ..."

"That good, huh? She made quite an impression on you, I take it. Left you speechless."

"I don't know what to say."

"Not a good sign for a journalist in pursuit of a Pulitzer. You need to have some sound bites ready for awkward moments like this."

"I just wasn't expecting you."

"That much we've established. Anyway, I get the picture. After all, who am I to you? I'm just some kid who hitchhiked a ride on your breakthrough story, a college student with a dream who thinks ..." She was fighting off tears. Clinton put his arms around her, and she hugged him for a moment before pushing him away. "Don't you goddamn patronize me."

"I wasn't, I was trying to—"

"And don't be sweet either. That's even worse. It just makes it all the harder for me to get over you." She turned away from him and growled into empty space. "Shut up, stupid little girl."

"You're not stupid, and you're no little girl. Sit down and talk for a minute."

"I don't want to talk. I feel betrayed: stupid and betrayed. I want to get on the next plane back to San Francisco. But I won't. I'll be a professional and finish this work with you. It's a job; we've a job to do. That's all." She was suddenly aware that he was still just behind her.

When she pivoted into him, he embraced her again, this time resisting her half-hearted efforts to pull away.

"If you won't talk, I will," he said. "It's . . . it's more than a job, more than mentoring. We, you and I, . . . It's a total mismatch, completely impossible, maybe wrong, but I want to find out. Do you understand? You terrify me, but I don't want you to leave. I don't want you to go back to California—not without me."

"What are you saying?" She looked up at him, and he kissed her tears before giving her a slow but very chaste kiss.

"I'm saying I don't want to rush into anything that we might regret, but I'm willing to follow you."

"Why? Why now? Why this sudden, like, change of heart? What about your sexy scientist?"

"It's not what you think. Hell, it's not what she thinks. I wish I could explain, but I don't really understand it myself. In any case, it's over. For now, let's just say I've been learning a few things. In time, I'm sure we'll talk more, but for now let's leave it there. Okay?"

"Okay." She hugged him harder and put her head against his shoulder. "Maybe we both will have second thoughts later, but right now, right now I could stay like this forever."

"Forever will have to wait. We have work to do. Let me bring you up-to-date."

Part Seven ~ Merge
Chapter 38

Zhu Huang sat in the empty offices in Ipswich as she finally finished going through the recent activity logs for all the workstations in the Neuroscience Section. The only discordant note was from Nina Braken. Late the previous Friday, Braken had spent a long time watching two all-hands videoconferences: one with Bertrand Lyon and one with his predecessor. The oddest thing was that, according to the badge-reader data, Nina Braken had left the building at noon and not returned that day. On the other hand, Sahana Patel had exited shortly after the videos were viewed and Nina Braken's account had been logged out. Zhu switched to the human resources system to retrieve Patel's home address. There was a note on the file scheduling an exit interview the following week. She was leaving Biontolics.

Zhu considered paying a home visit over the weekend or sitting in on the exit interview. Time was not on her side, but if she moved too quickly or aggressively, it could frighten her target. She thought for a moment, then updated the HR record to move the exit interview up to Monday.

~ ~ ~

Clinton and Julia spent the rest of the weekend holed up with take-out food, motel coffee, and their research and writing. Julia kept arguing that Clinton's approach was doomed, that he was writing an article that could never be published.

"I have to write it. I have to get the whole story down. There must be somebody I can send it to who will act on it. Once I finish, I can send it off to everybody on my contact list. Maybe Millie's mistake was using snail-mail to deliver paper copies; I could send it all by email."

"Look, those people were able to infiltrate the US Postal Service. What says they haven't penetrated Yahoo or Google or whoever provides your email? Hell, maybe they have access to everything the NSA vacuums up."

"That's Star Wars thinking; this is the real world. They can't be everywhere and track everything." Even as he said it so emphatically, he was thinking of what happened with Millie. "In any case, we need to move fast, finish the story with all the documentation, and figure out how to get it out there. We don't need all your negative attitude."

"My negative attitude? Who flew the red-eye from SFO to get back here to help you while you were banging that Indian super-scientist."

"Oh, we're back on that, are we? I thought I made it clear: it's going nowhere."

"You didn't make anything clear." Each word was louder than the last. "And you're still keeping me at a distance."

"Distance? What do you want: a fuck? I told you—"

"No, I don't want a fuck. From you, I don't want anything. It was a mistake coming back. You're right. It's all wrong. I don't know what got into my head that you were something special. You . . ."

He was standing by the door, his hand on the knob, shaking. "What is it with us? The same thing happened last night: a big blow-up after midnight, one or both of us reduced to tears, you stomping off to the bedroom while I go fetal on the couch."

"Isn't it pretty obvious?"

"No, not to me."

"Is it men who are so clueless or, like, just older people like you?"

He smiled and wiped at his eyes. "I've got a double handicap. Are you going to enlighten this clueless older male or not?"

She stood across the room, clearly uncertain whether to be the first to say it.

"Okay," he said, "I'll go first. I think I'm falling in love with you. No, wait, I don't think it; I am. No, that's not quite it either. Rewrite: I'm not falling; I've already fallen. There, I said it. And that's what scares me, because we are skating on the edge of the void here, and the thought of anything happening to you is unbearable."

She stared back at him, not moving, tears welling up and spilling over her cheeks. "I love you, Clinton, and I want you. And the thought of anything happening to you is unbearable. But, we're in this together. Look, if you're not ready for more, could we just sleep together tonight. I mean just sleep, just hold each other, because I've always been this tough street kid and now you're in my life and I'm so scared." Her shoulders shook as she broke into sobs.

"Me, too. Yes. We're both tired. Let's go to bed."

It was after ten in the morning when they were awakened by the ring of Clinton's burner phone. Half-asleep, Clinton padded out of the bedroom to find his backpack and fish around for the phone. "Hello?"

"It's me. They moved my exit interview up to this morning. The Chinese woman was there with lots of questions, not about neuro-science either. She asked if I knew a Clinton Rodrigues. I told her I didn't recognize the name. She asked me again at the end of the interview when she stood and blocked the doorway as I was about to leave."

"Where are you now?"

"At work, sitting on a bench out behind the main building."

"Hang up, go back to work, and play it straight for the rest of the day. Is there anyone you can stay with for a while? I mean besides me."

"Betsy Whitman, maybe. She's an old friend, works down the road from here."

"Okay. Figure out how to do it without drawing too much atten-tion, but get to her. Lay low until I contact you."

"But . . ."

"Good luck." He thumbed the phone off.

"What was that all about?" Julia called from the bedroom.

"A wakeup call. We gotta move." He entered the bedroom. Julia was sitting up against the headboard, naked. He stared at her, mouth open, stunned.

"What?" she said.

"My god, you are beautiful."

"You're not so bad yourself."

He looked down and realized he was naked. "Did we . . ."

"No, too tired, but it was damn delicious waking up with your leg over mine. It's not too late to do something about our poor performance last night." She made a point of looking down at his growing erection.

"Not now, we gotta move, and I do mean move. Get dressed, pack up all your stuff. I'm going to get rid of the car and report it stolen, then we're going to get a new one. When I get back, we'll check out. Be ready to go." He hurriedly dressed and left with the car keys.

When he returned more than an hour later, Julia was sitting on the couch, typing on her laptop. "You ready?" he said. "We have to go over to the rental place and file a report."

"What did you do with the car?"

"Drove it to another mall, one of the big ones off 128, left it in a deserted back corner of a lot where I crashed it up against a lamppost. Teenage joy riders, obviously. Also explains the dents and scratches. Then I hiked back. What have you been doing?"

"Worrying about you, taking care of some loose ends out West, worrying about you. Oh, did I mention worrying about you?"

He gave her a hand up from the couch. "Me too. Let's check out of here and get a cab to the rental place. We'll keep the replacement car for a couple of days, then switch to another company—try to throw the dogs off the scent."

"What about the police?"

"We'll go all, 'oh, we were so upset we didn't think of that' and tell the rental people we'll take care of it, like, right away."

"You know, we could get in trouble for this."

"Tell me something I don't know. Hey, we're running for our lives until we get this story out. Even then, I don't know."

She gave him a long, deep kiss. "When we check in at the new place, the first thing we do is hit the bedroom. Understood? I don't want to, like, you know, well . . . without first, you know . . ."

"You are something else, but . . . let's get there first."

~ ~ ~

It was Julia's idea to drive back to the same area after getting the new car. They took a room in a second-rate strip motel on the other side of the divided highway. "See, this way we can keep an eye out for police or caravans of black limos or whatever across the way. That way we'll have some warning."

"That is, if we spend our time watching out the front window." He pulled the curtain back enough to peek out.

"Later. Now we're going to spend our time checking out the mattress in this dump." She took his hand and pulled him toward the bed.

Chapter 39

Despite an uncharacteristic sense of panic that periodically swept over her like a rogue wave, Sahana managed to play-act through the rest of the day. When she left early, she pulled out of the Biontolics driveway, headed for town, and then turned toward her apartment, checking behind her frequently. At her building, she parked in the front lot, went up to her apartment, and hurriedly changed into jeans and a sweater-jacket. She tied her hair back in a tight bun and used a cleansing pad to remove the bindi from her forehead. To finish the transformation, she put on a head scarf and a pair of blue-reflective sunglasses. Checking herself in the mirror by the door, she judged the look to be cliché but effective.

In the parking garage beneath the building, she hopped into her silver Mazda Miata, pressed the door opener on her keychain, and gunned the low convertible through under the still rising overhead door. Reaching the town center, she shot past Argilla Road and took the long way around via route 133. As she turned off the highway, her anxiety rose—she would still have to drive past the lab. At the last moment, she realized she better call to confirm that Betsy was still working at the Crane Estate.

"Wow, Sahana, this is unexpected. Here we work not five minutes apart, and we hardly ever see each other. What's happening?"

"Oh, you know, the usual stuff. I thought we could catch up over dinner, which is why I called. It was a long shot but . . ."

"You mean tonight?"

"Yeah. Is that possible?"

"I don't know, it's pretty short notice. My partner and I usually eat takeout on Mondays: Chinese."

"Well, I love Chinese. I know it's pretty presumptuous of me to suggest it, but you don't suppose I could invite myself to join you. I mean, if . . ."

"You're right, it's pretty damn presumptuous. But, hey, what are friends for, right? Let me call Chris and see if that's okay. I'll call you right back."

Five minutes later, as Sahana was approaching the turnoff for Castle Hill, her phone rang. She answered on hands-free.

"It's me, Betsy. Chris says sure. Do you know our address in Essex?"

"No, but look, I'm right here, you know, just down the road. Why don't I pull in there, and then I could follow you."

"Well, okay, I suppose. Just come up to the main building and ask Elliot at the entrance to point you to my office."

Sahana negotiated the long winding driveway up the hill and pulled into the gravel parking lot nearest the hilltop building. The imposing brick mansion had once been the summer residence of the wealthy Crane family from Chicago. Now the estate and the adjacent beach were administered by the Massachusetts Trustees of Reservations, and Betsy worked for them as an event planner for the property, managing private parties, Christmas craft fairs, and open-air summer concerts.

Betsy was waiting in the hallway with a warm, dimpled smile. "It's been a while, but you haven't changed a bit, Sahana."

"Neither have you. You're looking great."

"Right, still prematurely gray. Did I ever tell you how much I hated that my mother wouldn't let me dye it. I was so embarrassed, but by the time I was in college, I was used to it this way and never did get around to coloring it. But, lucky me, Chris loves my hair. You'll love her, too: big, warm, sweet. She gives my life direction; she's my true north. Oh, where are my manners? Would you like a tour of the place before we head out? Or have you been here before? From the balcony up on the rooftop, the view down the *grande allée* toward the water is just breathtaking."

"No, that's okay. I got the grand tour right after you started working here and invited all your old friends from high school to one of those summer concerts."

"Oh, right. I forgot. The whole gang was here." Beneath her permed gray hair, her round, baby-smooth face broke into an incongruously lopsided grin. "Well, then, shall we go?"

"Can I ask another favor?"

"One's not enough, huh? Well, shoot."

"Could I leave my car here and ride with you?"

Betsy was suddenly serious. "This is not about some random impulse to reconnect with an old friend from high school, is it? You're in some kind of a pickle, right?"

"Yeah, some kind."

"Okay, girl. You don't have to tell me more, at least not now. The look on your face says it all. Big mama Chris and little mama Betsy will take care of you. We got plenty of room. You can stay with us tonight, and I'll bring you back for your car when I drive back tomorrow. Let me grab a temporary parking sticker so you don't get towed overnight."

"Thanks, I don't know what to say."

"Then don't say anything. Instead, you can pay for the moo shu chicken and spring rolls tonight." Her laugh was big and loud.

～ ～ ～

Allowing for the time difference, Zhu decided to leave a voice mail for her boss even though their history made her hesitant to depart from protocol. "I've talked with our scientist-spy from the Ipswich lab. She played innocent, but was unconvincing. I'm all but certain Rodrigues is here in the area, and this woman is going to lead me to him. I'm on it and will finish the job within the next few days. I'll let you know when I have news."

Zhu sat in her car down the road from the apartment building where there was a clear view of the parking lot. Sahana's car was where she had left it, and she had not re-emerged. There was only the one road off the point and back toward town, so Zhu could relocate every so often to avoid suspicion and be ready to tail the woman whenever she left.

Sahana's cellphone was being monitored by the little box on Zhu's dashboard. The blue box was a sophisticated device that pretended to be a cell tower and could be programmed for a variety of tasks. At the moment, it was set to connect only with a specific nearby phone that was programmed into it. Zhu had read the identification off the cellphone while Sahana had left for the ladies' room at work. Now, the device listened for calls in the approaching endgame.

It was nearly ten o'clock when Zhu was suddenly blinded by a spotlight in her eyes followed shortly by sharp raps on her window. She fingered the button to lower it and looked up into a woman's face, the face of an Ipswich police officer, her blond hair neatly tucked under her cap. "Is there a problem, constable?" Zhu said.

"A resident in the neighborhood reported that a car she didn't recognize had been stopped here for several hours." The officer bent low to survey the interior of the car. "Is there a reason you're still sitting here?"

'Not particularly, officer. I was fatigued, pulled over, and fell asleep. I'm sorry. I didn't realize this was a restricted zone."

"Can I see your license and registration, please."

Zhu fumbled around in her jacket "Here. It's a British permit. The hire car agent said it was acceptable here. I don't know about the registration, since this is a hire car. Do you want to see the contract?"

"Yes, I need to see the rental agreement. And your passport please."

Zhu pretended to be flustered and confused as she first rifled through the door pocket, then opened the glove compartment. "Ah, here's the contract." She handed it through the window. "Oh, and here's my passport."

"Please remain in your car and keep your hands in full view. I'll be back." The officer left for her patrol car with the documents. It was nearly ten minutes before she returned. "I need you to step out of your car, please."

"Why? Is something wrong?"

"I need you to step out of the car." The officer took several steps back and moved her hand toward the holster at her hip.

Zhu assessed the situation and considered whether to draw her own firearm, to make a run for it, or to cooperate. She opened the door slowly, and got out of the car.

"Have you had anything to drink tonight?"

"Yes. I have a bottle of Evian in the car."

"Evian?"

"Mineral water."

"Oh. I'm going to ask you to do several things. Please follow my finger with your eyes without moving your head. Okay, now I need you to walk heel-to-toe in a straight line for nine steps away from me, then turn on one foot and return the same way. Is that clear?"

"Yes, officer." Zhu imagined herself as once again a young girl on the balance beam. She marched away, spun smartly, and returned.

"Now, I want you to stand on your left foot, raise your right foot six inches off the ground, and hold that position while you count aloud slowly to thirty."

"How many centimeters is that?"

"What?"

"Inches. We don't use them anymore. What is it, now, like fifteen centimeters?"

"The height of a Coke can, ma'am. I don't know it in centimeters."

"There. How's that?" She stood statue-still as she began to count. "I can raise it higher if you would like."

"No, that won't be necessary. Here are your license, contract, and passport. You can return to your car, but you can't remain stopped here. Please move on to your destination."

"Of course. Thank you, officer. Have a pleasant evening."

Zhu did not wait for the patrol car to depart to start her car. She was angry at herself for not thinking in terms of small-town New England rather than big city Europe. She drove to the end of the road and made a three-point turn. She gave a polite salute to the policewoman as she passed, being careful to keep her speed down until she was well away. Once back through the center of town, she turned onto Argilla Road and sped toward the Lab. She figured it was better to drop the tail than risk another interruption by local police. She could pick up the track in the morning when the subject arrived at work. In the meantime, she could catch a few hours of sleep stretched out on the couch in the reception area at the Lab.

~ ~ ~

The arrival of the day-shift guard awakened Zhu. After using the toilet, she returned to her car where she connected a cable from the blue box into her laptop and reviewed the overnight logs that were uploaded. Nothing.

Always methodical, Zhu used the downtime to review files and check that all her equipment was in order. She was just returning her Beretta to her cross-draw holster when the LED on the blue box winked at her and her laptop screen brightened. She looked around and checked her rearview mirror. No one had entered the rear parking lot. She started the car and drove around to the small visitors' parking area at the front. It was still deserted.

She got out to walk around the building on the outside chance somebody had approached on foot. Through the trees, she heard the sound of a small sports car being worked through the gears as it raced past on Argilla Road. Zhu trotted to her car, spun her tires on the gravel as she reversed, then sped down the twisting driveway. A Miata was disappearing around the far curve as Zhu fishtailed out onto the road. As she accelerated down the road, the blue box blinked again, indicating that it had reacquired the signal from the cell phone.

Zhu slowed to keep from overtaking the car. The box on her dash flashed yellow, indicating an attempt to place a call. The box itself scanned for the nearest legitimate tower and passed on the request, keeping itself in the middle of the link, decrypting and recording the call in real time. Zhu punched up the volume on her laptop speakers as the caller waited for an answer.

The voice on the phone was tinny through the small speakers on the computer. "Yes, hello?"

"Mom, it's me. I'm sorry for calling so early."

"I was awake. Your father is snoring beside me. You should be sorry that you never call your parents, not that you call so early." The voice on the line had the distinctly voiced consonants of the Indian sub-continent.

"I'm sorry, Mom. Much is happening. Did you hear? I got a new job. With a high-tech startup in San Francisco."

"And where would I hear that you got a new job, if not from you? Who could tell me that? Would the airlines call me and tell me? 'Oh, Mrs. Patel, your daughter is flying to California for her new job.' No, I don't think so."

"Mom, it hasn't been that long since we last talked. I asked you for that recipe just, like, last week."

"You asked me by email; you asked for a recipe. That is not calling and talking."

"Look, I'm sorry, Mom. I'll try to call you more often."

"From San Francisco you'll call?"

"Well, that's what I'm calling about. When do you and Dad head south?"

"The same time as always. Your father and I never leave before Thanksgiving. We've been leaving for Florida for the winter the week after Thanksgiving every year for the last seventeen. Why do you ask? Do you want to visit your poor mother and father?"

"Yes, I want to visit you, but that's not why I'm asking. If it's all right with you, I'd like to stay in the condo for a few weeks. Is that okay?"

"You're in Florida? I thought you were in California."

"Not yet, Mom. I'm taking a little break before starting the new job."

"In Florida? There's nothing but old people down there. You need to be meeting people your own age. You're not getting any younger . . . or prettier."

"Thanks loads, Mom. Look, just don't start."

"You know, you should have let us arrange a marriage for you while you were still, well, you know . . . of the best age. But, no, you had to be modern and get your degrees first. We should have had a son. Is our unmarried daughter who is moving away going to help us when we are old?"

"Thanks, Mom, for your support and approval. I remember the one match you tried to push me into. Even back then, I made more than that orthodontist you picked. What a . . ."

"He was a third cousin and everyone considered him to be a good match. He—"

"Mother, he was a little boy with little-boy fantasies about sex and marriage, an absolute weirdo. But, please, just for once can we not talk about the fact that I'm not married? I'll get married when I'm ready and when I find the right man."

"Are you seeing anybody?"

"Mom!"

"A mother can ask, can't she?"

"Yes, you certainly can, Mom, like pretty much every time we talk."

"Which is very seldom."

"Mom, just tell me if I can stay in the condo for a while."

"Of course, dear. Oh, your father is waking up. I'll have to tell him the terrible news. He'll be heartbroken."

"What are you talking about, Mom? I'm just borrowing your condo."

"No, I mean that you're leaving us to pursue some fantasy in—what is it called?—Silicon Valley."

"It's San Francisco, and it's not a fantasy, and tell Dad I love him."

"You can tell him yourself, since your call woke him up. Here he is."

The voice was grainy with sleep and two octaves lower. "*Namaste.* How is my favorite daughter? And what is this about terrible news?"

"Your favorite daughter is still your only daughter, and the news is not terrible. I'm moving to San Francisco to take a job with a startup doing brain-training apps."

"Oh, that's wonderful news. Brain training. That's good. Be sure you get some equity in your package. Are they giving you stock options?"

"Yes, they're giving me options, Dad. You taught me well."

"That's my girl. Send email as soon as you settle in."

"I will."

"Look, do you want to say goodbye to your mother? She's right here."

"No, you do it for me. Love you."

"Me, too. bye."

The light on Zhu's blue box winked out as she braked to keep from coming too close to the silver convertible. As she did, she saw the driver put a cellphone to her ear. The indicator on the blue box flashed yellow, then red. It was not a phone for which the box was programmed to intercept, but there was a way to override the programming and grab the signal anyway. Zhu reached toward the laptop on the passenger seat and tried to position the mouse pointer over the correct button. The car bounced as the right wheel left the road. Zhu looked up and spun the wheel to the left but not fast enough to avoid the tree. The car bucked and swung to the side, the airbag exploded in Zhu's face, and the engine died.

The Miata was already out of sight, making the turn off Argilla Road.

Chapter 40

Sahana was finishing her yoghurt and granola in the kitchen just as Betsy Whitman barged through the door from the garage carrying two suitcases. "I think I got everything you asked for from your apartment." She set the luggage down in front of Sahana. "Here are your keys back. The suitcases weren't quite big enough for everything, so there's still some loose stuff in the backseat of the car. You can borrow my old backpack to take up the slack. You should be good. Where did you say you were headed?"

"I didn't. It's better you don't know."

"We're talking serious paranoia here, you know. I wish you could tell me what this is about."

"I told you last night."

"Well, yes, you did. Three or four sentences worth about how you were helping some reporter with a big story. I get it that you're in some kind of danger but not why?"

"I'm trying to be smart—and to protect you and Chris. You were both so sweet to take me in like that."

"Hey, we needed somebody to pay for the Chinese takeout. You just happened to come along at the right time." She winked broadly. "And you're sure you want to leave that cute little car with us?"

"I'll get a rental when I land. You might as well enjoy it—small compensation for your help."

"Look, is there anything else I can do for you before I go back to work?"

"No, not really. I'll be gone by the time you get home tonight. Thanks again."

"Don't mention it. We enjoyed seeing you. Be careful, now. I hope you know what you're doing."

"I don't know what I'm doing, but I'll try to be careful."

~ ~ ~

Zhu watched as the wrecker pulled away with her rental car in tow. It had taken some fast talking to convince the police officer who arrived on the scene that it was not a simple single-car accident. She finally talked the policeman out of issuing a ticket by her story of swerving to avoid a dog crossing the road and her convincing picture of an adorable mutt scampering off. A traffic ticket would not have been a disaster but certainly would have complicated her task.

Fortunately, she had stashed her computer, the blue box, and her Beretta in her duffle before anyone showed up. A quick swap of identity would distance her from the messy situation long enough for her to finish the job here and get back to London. The next step was clear. Just before the crash, the box and her computer had gotten enough data to identify the phone being called from the Miata. Once her replacement car arrived, she would head back to the Lab and use the system to call the phone and locate it. Sahana Patel was not her ultimate target; Sahana could wait.

~ ~ ~

Clinton was annoyed. His burner phone was ringing, and he had told Sahana not to call it again. He picked it up and looked at it. He didn't recognize the number. Second time this morning, best to ignore it, let it go to voicemail, he thought. Then the ringing stopped. He was unsure about what to do, but if the phone was compromised, it would be better to dump it and start with a fresh one.

Julia was just returning with groceries when Clinton came back from the dumpster behind the motel. "What's up?" she said, as he held the door for her.

"Something odd with my burner phone. Just to be on the safe side, I destroyed the SIM card, wiped the phone, and dumped it out back. How are you doing? You were up late last night."

"Follow-up on some more leads, working California time, you know. How close are you to wrapping up your work?"

"Pretty close, first final draft, anyway. I'll have to stay away from it for a bit so I can go back to edit it with fresh eyes."

"Hey, what about me? I could review and edit it for you."

Clinton looked to one side and frowned. "That's odd. I hadn't thought of that. I guess I still think of you as the student, I as the teacher."

"Me as the teacher," she corrected. "Object, not subject."

"Ohmagod. You're starting to sound like me. Now you're correcting *my* grammar."

"Hey, I learned from the master." She smiled and kissed him. "Let's put away these groceries, brew some more coffee, and get to work."

~ ~ ~

The morning and early afternoon passed with Julia working away on the draft and Clinton trying to look over her shoulder. "Cut that out. I'm almost finished here," she said. "You can read through my edits when I'm done."

There was a knock on the door. Clinton gave Julia a questioning look. She shook her head, shrugged, and went back to her work. He sidled up to the door and peeked through the security viewer. A tall woman stood outside holding a tray covered with a napkin. "What is it?" he said through the door.

He could see her lips move, but he couldn't hear her answer. "What is it? What do you want? I can't hear you." Again, the woman seemed to be answering but he couldn't hear. He slid the security chain into its channel and opened the door the two inches the chain allowed. "Yes? What do you want?"

"Room service."

"We didn't order room service, you have the wrong room."

"This is room 122? You are Mr. Rodrigues?"

"But," he answered without thinking, "we didn't order—"

The chain was ripped from the wall as the door was kicked open and the woman entered with a drawn handgun. "Compliments of the manager, Mr. Rodrigues." She shoved the empty tray at him as she kicked the door closed behind her. Julia quickly tapped the Enter key on her laptop, closed it part way, and pushed it aside.

~ ~ ~

Traffic was chockablock at the airport. Sahana fished in her wallet for an extra twenty as the cabbie unloaded her luggage from the trunk. He took the money, eyed the bills, and said, "Do you need change?"

"No, that's for you. Thanks."

"Thank you, miss. You have a good flight."

As the taxi pulled away, she stood at the curb watching, wondering whether she was doing the right thing. Was she running away? If she was, what was she running away from? The Biontolics cabal? Clinton Rodrigues? Men in general? Life in general? She could hear her mother's voice in her head, exhorting her to be careful—and to find a husband. It was her father who always believed in her as a scientist, but it was her father who seldom had more than a paragraph of conversation with her before he would pass the phone to his wife.

What would be the purpose of hanging around except to put herself in more danger? And what was the point? Clinton had obviously made his choice. He clearly preferred his cute little student. It was the story of her life. Maybe her mother had been right. She should have gotten married, had a baby, then gone back to school.

"You okay, miss?"

Sahana looked up to find a state trooper standing in front of her in his calf-high boots and Smokey-the-Bear hat. "I . . ."

"Can I help?" It was a professional courtesy, but there was also a look of concern on his face, as if he actually wanted to be of help.

"No, not really. I'm just thinking about getting a cab."

"Taxis can't pick up at this level. You'll have to take the escalator down to arrivals. You'll see the line down there."

"Thanks, I'll do that." She picked up her suitcases and headed into the terminal. As she approached the down escalator, she was already shifting mental gears, strategizing her next move. What could she do? She was smart enough, but she was a scientist, not some kind of clandestine operative. She knew the barest outline of the story, but now that she had been exposed at Biontolics, there was nothing more she could do there. Clinton and his student were obviously way ahead of her. She had to admit, she had none of their drive to become a knight errant out to expose evil. What she wanted to do was survive, to get some armor against becoming herself a victim of Biontolics. She figured she would need something on them, something to hold over their heads against their coming after her.

She stood at the top of the escalator, looking out through the wall of glass at the skyline of downtown Boston, with the towers of the financial district reflecting beams of sunlight her way. She had an idea.

~ ~ ~

Zhu looked over the documents spread out on the bed in the motel room. "False identities. You were registered under fake names. That's why I had to describe you to the motel clerk. And,"—she held up their new passports—"these must be what was in the package delivered to you in Madeira. How clever of you and lucky for me. It should make it all the easier for you two to disappear without a trace. An investigation will show that you left the country for Busanyu but never returned. It will become apparent that something happened to you in Africa. How tragic. People can so easily get lost or vanish in these small, unstable African countries. Now we just have to make sure you disappear completely—and soon."

She had them empty their pockets. Both surrendered their smartphones. "You're going to have to hang out a little longer here while I work out some arrangements." She had them sit down on the two kitchen-style chairs and put their hands behind them. She used zip ties to fasten their wrists and ankles to the chairs, then taped their mouths. "I'll be back later. Don't get into trouble while I'm gone."

Chapter 41

Sahana waited in the reception area of Enventia Capital, rehearsing her story.

"Mr. Templeman will see you now." The slim receptionist bent over her like an anglepoise desk lamp. "Just follow me; I'll show you in."

Felix Templeman had never been particularly handsome, but now he had the good looks that money and a surplus of time could acquire. His dark, naturally wavy hair looked as if it had just been razor cut that morning, his orthodontist-perfect teeth gleamed in his smile, and his skin had the warm glow of a recent Caribbean vacation. He buttoned the jacket of his custom-tailored double-breasted suit as he rose and came around from behind a desk that could have served as a banquet table for eight. "What a surprise. I couldn't believe it when Tonia said who was here. You are looking good, Sahana."

"Thanks. I just came from the airport, so I'm a little more disheveled than usual."

"Well, the word disheveled would never have occurred to me. You look great to me."

"Thanks again." She glanced around the office. "And you seem to be doing rather well."

"I've been lucky. I keep picking the right numbers on the roulette wheel of new ventures, I guess. I understand you've done all right for yourself, too, with a PhD in neuroscience and a position at Biontolics. I'd love to get a piece of Biontolics or a company like it, but it's closely held, and they make it hard to see exactly what they are up to. I don't suppose you could enlighten me."

"Maybe I could. Maybe you could enlighten me."

"Now this is beginning to sound interesting, almost as if this were not some random visit."

"It's not. Just how good are your financial research skills, Felix? I mean, can you really get the real scoop on companies you might be interested in?"

"My skills? Well, they're not bad, but I have an amazing staff that does the real leg work. They put together the research and then I sniff the report. I have a nose for what makes sense and what doesn't."

"Have you ever taken a whiff of the Biontolics empire?"

"Well, as I said, they're a closely held corporation, and they do not seem to lack for capital. So, no, other than casual curiosity, I haven't spent a lot of time looking into them. Should I have?"

"Maybe. If a big privately held company like Biontolics were to suddenly find itself in deep trouble, what would be the consequences? Would there be ripple effects on other companies?"

"If the company is big enough and critical enough, a collapse or crisis could trigger tsunamis in the financial markets. Look what happened after Volkswagen got caught cheating on emissions. Think of what would happen if, say, the Koch brothers empire went south. Everything is connected to everything else in the global economy."

"Would it be worthwhile to a venture capital firm to know if some such company were, shall we say, at risk for being compromised?"

"Whoa, there. I do hope we're not talking about insider trading."

"Biontolics stock isn't traded, and this information doesn't need to come from inside. I'm talking about what your brilliant staff could do on their own."

"This is starting to sound really, really heavy. Are you sure you want to continue?"

"I don't know. I'm trying to figure that out right now. Other than the fact that we shared the platform at graduation from Newburyport High, we don't really know each other."

"And I always regretted that."

"Really?"

"Really. But my parents kept me on a tight leash during high school. I didn't get to date a shicksa until I got away to college. Of course, I did end up marrying a nice Jewish girl I met at Wharton. It pleased my parents and hers, but it was a mistake."

"So, you're . . . ?"

"Divorced. Happily so. No kids. And we had a prenup—at her insistence, by the way. She was so self-deluded, convinced she was going to be a billionaire. So here I am: not quite a billionaire but on the path." He spread his arms.

"I see. But look, as you quickly concluded, I'm here for a reason, and I'm still trying to figure out whether I can trust you."

"Fair enough. So let me earn your trust: first by showing you what I've been doing with Enventia and second by taking you to dinner. Then after dinner, if you don't trust me, I'll put you in a cab and wave goodbye. If you decide you do trust me, we can come back here to start some research wheels rolling before we go for a nightcap. How does that sound?"

"It sounds like you move pretty fast."

"I do. It's one of the secrets of my success. I don't dither or delay over decisions. If I find myself wavering or temporizing, then I know that whatever it is, it's a no-go. Consider yourself warned. By the end of dinner, I'll know whether I can trust you and whether I can let you trust me. So, permit me to start by telling you about our investments in solar, hydroponics, environmental remediation—a fancy term for cleaning up chemical disasters—and genomics." He tapped at an iPad on his desk and a wall-size display sprang into life with the opening slide of a PowerPoint deck.

~ ~ ~

The maître d' at the restaurant recognized Felix and greeted him by name. "A private table, Mr. Templeman? But of course. We're fully booked for the evening, but I am sure I can get Luigi to prepare a table for you in the wine cellar, and you can have the place to yourselves. The usual?"

"Yes, that would be splendid."

"Excellent, I'll alert the staff. They'll be delighted. If you care to have a seat in the bar, I'll get everything ready for you, *subito*."

Sahana smiled at Felix as they slipped into their seats in the small bar tucked into a corner. "Very impressive. I take it you're a regular here?"

"Now and then. But they know me. I helped finance Montero when he started Firenze Sempre. Now he owns three restaurants and three homes, a sort of domestic parity."

"And the usual? What is that?"

"Oh, you're in for a treat, a succession of small plates and perfect Italian wine pairings to enjoy while we get acquainted. Or reacquainted. What did you think of this afternoon's corporate tour."

"Very corporate. I always wonder about the reality behind slick slogans and polished PowerPoint."

"Yes, I noticed that. You are a skeptic and have a knack for asking the right questions, usually rather pointed ones."

"I hope I wasn't too aggressive. I know I can be off-putting at times."

"On the contrary, I rather liked that. I trust you found my answers direct enough."

"And then some, though I would like to hear more about—"

She was interrupted by the arrival of the maître d'. "Your table is ready, Mr. Templeman. Please follow me."

~ ~ ~

After spending the afternoon finalizing arrangements, Zhu Huang returned to the motel. When she unlocked the room and turned on the lights, she found her prisoners on the floor, still strapped to their toppled chairs. "Just in time, I see. What did you think you could do, squirm your way out of here? You want to leave, do you? Okay, that can be arranged. First we'll separate you from those chairs and cuff you again. Then let's go for a ride."

The small boat bobbed in the swells of a wind-driven incoming tide. Clinton knew from the sounds that they were at a pier in some harbor. They had been blindfolded during a car ride that had taken what seemed like hours, with two unexplained stops along the way. Given the time, they could be anywhere between Portland and Providence, but some instinct told Clinton that they were actually somewhere on the North Shore, Cape Ann, maybe even Gloucester. There was something familiar about the pattern of turns they had made near the end of the ride.

The edges of the zip-tie around his wrists were cutting into his skin. The smells of fish and diesel were heavy in the air. Suddenly, the incessant seagull cries were submerged in the rattling of the boat's engine being started. It coughed and sputtered before settling into a deep throated rumble. They moved slowly at first, but after some minutes, the pitch of the engine rose sharply and Clinton could feel the pounding as they sped over an increasing chop.

He lay on his side on the floor, leaving just enough room for Julia with her back to the wall and her knees doubled up. She had been still, but once the boat was up to speed, he could feel her moving against him. Suddenly, his blindfold was yanked off, and he blinked in the dim light of a cabin below deck. The tape over his mouth was suddenly and painfully ripped away. "What the . . ."

"Sshh. Keep it down, sport," she said.

"How did you get loose?" he whispered.

"Brains. A trick from the street, you twist and flex your wrists when the zip-tie is put on, gives you enough slack to later slip out. At least that's the idea." She held up her bloody left hand. "Sometimes you leave a little something behind."

"Are you all right?"

"Not yet, not until we get out of here, and not by the route our Chinese lady has planned. Turn over."

"What are you going to do?"

"Cut your zip-tie. Unless you want to do as I did and end up scraping off half your hand."

"How are you going to cut anything?"

"With the edge of this drawer handle I just acquired. Try to keep your wrists out of the way. This is going to take a while."

Many minutes and several bloody nicks later, Clinton was able to snap the last narrow strand of plastic and free his arms. "Wow, you are pretty clever."

"What have I been telling you?"

"What next, oh clever one?"

"There's two on board: China-girl and some guy. I heard them talking. It'll take one of them to handle the boat, so we only have to deal with them one at a time, starting with whoever comes down here."

"And how do we get *whomever* to come down here?"

"Just follow me." She tried the handle of the cabin door; it turned. "I had guessed she didn't lock it, probably didn't see the need, what with us tied up. Look, you get over there, in the shadows, just behind that ladder thingy coming down. I'll make a racket, and you find something to use to bean *whomever* climbs down."

Clinton looked around and spotted a fire extinguisher on the wall. He pulled it from its bracket and flattened himself up against the bulkhead beside the ladder.

Julia used the drawer handle to bang on some pipes running along the side, but the light clanking was drowned out by the throb of the engine and the slap of waves as the boat raced out to sea. She rummaged around in cabinets along the side until she found a set of tools. She grabbed a heavy pipe wrench and raised it to bang on the pipes again, but Clinton stopped her. "We don't want to break anything connected to anything important. This is our transportation back, too, you know."

She looked around, shrugged, and took a swing at the ceiling. She kept hammering away until she had smashed a hole in the wood overhead. There was no response. She picked a spot closer to the bow and started hammering out a pattern of thuds that Clinton recognized as a crude SOS.

As the hatch above was lifted, Clinton signaled her to stop. A man wearing a sailor's watch cap peered down through the opening.

Topside was almost as dark as below deck, but the man was silhou-etted against the retreating sky glow from on shore. As he waved a handgun back and forth as if it were a flashlight, Julia pulled back to-ward the bow as far as she could. He hesitated for a moment, then started to lower himself down the ladder. Just short of the bottom, he spotted Julia and brought his gun up. Clinton came out from behind and swung the bottom of the fire extinguisher against the man's side, causing him to drop the gun. He turned and caught Clinton's second swing in the side of his face. He pitched forward and sprawled on the deck.

Julia held out the wrench to Clinton. "Here, better than that thing." She knelt and picked up the gun, checked to make sure the safety was off, and waved Clinton up the ladder. She climbed up behind him, squatted beside the open hatch, and pointed toward the bow where the Chinese woman was at the helm. As Clinton started forward in a running crouch, the man's grizzled head emerged from the hatch. "Huang," he shouted, "look out!"

Julia swung her foot around, slamming his head against the side of the hatch. He tumbled down the ladder and thudded onto the deck below.

Clinton was nearly to the wheelhouse, when Zhu Huang turned and fired at him. As Clinton fell, Julia took aim. The pitch and roll of the boat threw her off, and the shot went wild, slamming into the controls beside Zhu. With one hand on the wheel, Zhu turned the other direction to fire at Julia. Julia dropped to the deck and flattened herself. With a two-handed grip on the pistol, she pressed her wrists against a fitting on the boat and fired, emptying the magazine in a steady pulse of paired shots. Zhu slumped, clinging to the wheel as she dropped to the deck, sending the boat into a wide arc.

"Get to the controls!" Julia yelled at Clinton.

Clinton swayed as he tried to stand. He staggered the rest of the way to the wheelhouse and pulled himself up the several steps. He shouldered the woman's body aside, grabbed the wheel, sussed out the controls, and pulled back on what he guessed was the throttle. The boat pitched forward, slowed, and chugged at a crawl through the water.

Julia climbed up beside him. "Is she dead? Did I get her?"

"Looks like it. Also looks like you killed a lot more than just our kidnapper." He swept his hand toward the control panel, which was decorated with broken glass and bullet holes. "We don't know where we are, and I don't think we're going to find out. I'm guessing this is the radio. Well, if it was the radio, it looks dead now."

"Do you think we can use a phone out here?"

"We're probably out of range from any cell tower. Besides, who has a phone?"

"I do." She smirked. "Maybe she does, too."

"You have a phone? But she took ours away."

"Not the little burner phone I had tucked in my underwear. She patted us down, but not very good."

"Not very *well*."

"Oh, for God's sake. Just can it, at least until we're back in civilization. Which is where?" She turned in a half circle.

"West. If we can figure out where west is. The compass seems to be among the victims of the slaughter."

"Der. Which way do you see the sky still faintly glowing after sunset? What we don't know is where we would reach shore if we sail toward the receding sun. It's already pretty dark, and even us California girls have heard about the rock-bound coast of New England."

"Well, what about that phone of yours?"

She flipped it open and looked down at it. "Nothing, no bars. We're too far out."

"See if our kung-fu kidnapper has a phone."

Julia finally found a phone in a pocket of the woman's vest. A bullet had smashed through one corner. Julia pressed buttons and tapped the screen. "It's dead, like literally dead."

"Okay," he said. "I've an idea. We head slowly back, roughly westward, until we do get a signal on your phone. Then we call the Coast Guard."

"And the number of the Coast Guard is . . . ?"

"9-1-1. At least that's a start."

Clinton slowly brought the bow of the boat around until it pointed toward the last faint glow on the horizon. "Okay, we're going to take it slow. You keep checking for a cell signal."

They were underway for only a few minutes when the engine slowed, coughed, and finally died. Clinton figured out which button was the starter, but the engine stubbornly refused to turn over. Without the generator, the main lights had cut out, and they were left with only emergency battery lighting.

"We're adrift, in the dark, in an area crisscrossed with shipping lanes, and . . ."

"Thanks for the cheery pep talk." She gave him a sour-face look. "For real, what are we going to do?"

"See if we can find flashlights or maybe battery powered lights below."

"Like, in the dark, we're supposed to find these?"

"Do your best, I'll keep trying to start the engine."

~ ~ ~

Julia emerged from below with a hand lantern she had found, and Clinton had figured out where the emergency flares were stowed in the wheelhouse. "We need to save these until another boat comes near. Keep listening."

As the last glow of dusk left the sky, they sat huddled together in the partial shelter of the wheelhouse as a cold wind picked up. Clinton studied the overcast sky, searching for a break through which he might spot some familiar constellation, but the cloud cover was solid.

"Look, Julia, you go below out of the wind, see if you can find something to keep warm. I'll keep watch up here."

"Don't pull that macho crap on me, mister. We're in this together. You can have first watch, one hour, but then we switch. Okay?"

"Okay."

"If . . . if we don't . . ."

"Just get below. We're going to be fine. None of that if-we-don't shit."

"Okay. Come get me in an hour."

~ ~ ~

Clinton let an hour go by as the wind continued to pick up. He was about to go below when Julia emerged from the hatch wearing a heavy man's jacket. He recognized it as the one worn by the assailant they had dispatched. As she came up beside Clinton, she pointed astern. "Are those lights? And look at the sky; it's noticeably lighter, like sky glow from a city."

"You're right. The wind must be coming from the east. It's blowing us toward shore."

"That's good."

"Or not. Remember what you said about the rocky coastline in New England."

"Well, then let's hope we can reach the Coast Guard before we reach the coast."

Ever so slowly, the lights along the horizon were becoming more distinct and separate as the breeze stiffened. Suddenly, Julia started bouncing. "I got a signal. It's one bar. Should I try it?"

"Go for it."

Julia started entering a number.

"What are you doing? That's more than three digits. 9-1-1. That's all you need. Who are you calling?"

"Just in case we don't make it, I've another call I need to do first. Be quiet; it's ringing." She listened. "Answer, damn it."

"Hullo?"

"This is Chandrise."

"You mean . . . ?"

"Yes, Roger, it's a go. Just do it."

"Right. Are you okay?"

"Just do it. Now." She disconnected and looked over at Clinton.

"What was that all about?"

"Insurance. Now, let's try the Coast Guard."

~ ~ ~

At first, the operator did not believe her, but eventually Julia convinced the man to patch her through to the Coast Guard.

"So where are you, ma'am? Please tell me your coordinates."

"I don't know. The navigation equipment is . . . well, dead."

'Do you have GPS on your phone?"

"Nope. It's a cheapie."

"Well, if you're calling us by a cellphone, you can't be too far off the coast, but there's a lot of coastline in New England. You really have no idea where you are?"

"Not a clue."

"Can you see anything around you?"

"Yeah, we can see lights on the horizon. Like, one of them seems to be blinking on and off very slowly."

"Okay, that's good. It could be a lighthouse or an airport beacon. What else can you see?"

"Well, a little to the left of the blinking light is a pretty bright blob of light."

"How far to the left? Like on a clock face."

"Well, we're still pointing roughly to where the sun set, I think, sort of west, so the blinking light is like eleven o'clock and the bright blob is maybe ten-thirty. Does that help?"

'It does, because we just heard from Verizon with the identity and location of the cell tower that you are linked through. Do you have running lights on?"

"Er, no. Clinton, can you turn on some lights?" Clinton tried a number of switches. "Oh, there. Now we have lights. At least while the batteries last."

"Okay, sit still. We have a rough idea where you are. We're sending a cutter to search for you."

~ ~ ~

They were on the Coast Guard cutter headed back to shore and into police custody when Clinton leaned over toward Julia and asked in a soft voice what her first phone call had been about.

"You'll find out soon enough if it worked. If not, we're dead."

Chapter 43

As Roger Belknap finished the final edits on his blog post, the smartphone on his desk vibrated. It was a text message with one word—"Yo!"—the last of the confirmations from his team. Operation Chandrise was cocked and ready. Thirteen students were now poised at their keyboards, waiting for his signal. It was a scattershot exercise in which near simultaneity was essential. His tweet would be their shot heard 'round the world, triggering the first wave. A second wave, powered by sock puppets, would follow in ten minutes, then hundreds more reinforcements at random intervals over the following hour. Each of the team would be recruiting others on the fly to multiply the effort. If one medium or channel didn't succeed, there were others. His favorite was a hilarious video from two film-school students: "The International Geriatric Beach Volleyball Tournament." Nothing like California girls in bikinis to spice up YouTube. It had a shot at going viral. He started laughing just thinking of it.

Roger was both anxious and relieved to have gotten the go ahead. He wasn't sure how much longer he could have kept everybody in check without a leak. He switched over to Twitter, pasted the preplanned text, and clicked to send it off. "Game on!" he said to his sleeping roommate.

~ ~ ~

Sahana and Felix were finishing dessert accompanied by a small glass of Brachetto when he put the question to her. "Are you ready to trust me with what this is really about?"

"Is that fair after all this wine?" She blinked hard.

"If you're the person I think you are, you already made the decision by the time the first appetizers arrived."

"Before."

"Me, too. In fact, before we left the office, I had already asked a crack team in my London office to start working overtime on Biontolics. I just got a text message that said they were already finding interesting things: interesting being a code word for details that couldn't be shared over open communications. I'm going to fly over tonight, want to tag along?"

"Slow down. You are exceeding the speed limit here."

"Business, I'm just moving at the speed of business."

She looked at her watch. "I had no idea it was this late. I didn't think there were any flights out at this hour."

"There aren't. I have my own jet. Well, it's actually a time-shared Gulfstream—makes more economic sense—but we can be ready to take off in an hour or so. What do you say? You told me you just came from the airport, and you had my receptionist stash your bags, so what's to stop you?"

"Nothing. Let's do it."

Chapter 44

Ferguson's helicopter wobbled in the urban crosswinds before settling down on the helipad atop the Sellian Atlantic Building in London. Despite the unseemly early hour, the plaza below was already crowded with the media and the curious. Overhead, a SkyNews chopper circled. Hustled into the building by his security team, Ferguson was greeted inside by a tall man, as gray as the polished granite of the building façade. "Morning, sir, I'm Kevin Wellbern, Acting Head of Security. I'll brief you on the way down."

"Are the others here?"

"Dr. Mandelova is already waiting in the ninth floor conference room; Mr. Quarry is on videoconference from America. I'm afraid Dr. Lyon is still in hospital."

"Not good. Make sure security is upped at the clinic."

"Already taken care of, sir. I've had the facilities cordoned off, barricades are in place, and we've created a pretense to close the lane at either end."

"Excellent. Now, what the hell is going on?"

"It's a social media blitz. The Information Technology team has been working with us, but we haven't identified the original sources yet. That can take a very long time. It appears that a number of near-simultaneous postings, largely from America, were responsible, starting sometime between midnight and one GMT. It had to have been an orchestrated attack by numerous agents through a wide variety of channels: YouTube and Vimeo videos, posts on Twitter and Tumblr as well as several smaller and more specialized networks, pictures via Instagram and photo sharing sites, and posts and comments on Reddit and elsewhere. The topics were trending within an hour and went viral before dawn here. Our MediaTrax system detected the trend on references to Biontolics shortly before things went viral, and the tech team triggered takedown orders, but the curves were running against us. By the time IT people alerted us, some posts had been retweeted sixty thousand times."

"What are they saying that spreads that fast."

"You'll see in the briefing, but one of the YouTube videos is built from newspaper file photos and other sources. It has face shots of Douglas Atchison Doherty slowly morphing over time, eventually becoming Bertrand Lyon. Underneath, claimed chronological age is displayed. It finishes with a question: How many centuries will this man live? Then it gives the Biontolics main telephone number and Dr. Lyon's company email address. The telephone lines were jammed within hours and our email servers had to be taken down. The main hashtags on Twitter have been #AgelessBiontolics and #FontOfYouth. The most retweets are for a message with an animated GIF. The animation shows side-by-side headshots of Dr. Doherty and Dr. Lyon with their birthdates. The animation zooms in on the left eyes, which are seen to be identical. The text below says: 'Just how old is the #AgelessBiontolics CEO? Has #Biontolics found #FontOfYouth?' There are others, including links to stories about that African dictator and hints of criminal activity."

"Is Twitter cooperating to stifle this?"

"They were until the live social media like SnapChat picked it up. Live broadcasts are much harder to take down because by the time we know about them, the sources are done. Then the American authorities stepped in. It seems that not long after the social media blitz started, an extensive exposé was posted on half a dozen somewhat obscure blogs. Unfortunately, by the time our people tried to remove the articles, they had already been re-blogged in hundreds of places. Huffington, Wired, Daily Dot, The Register here, and dozens of online publications are already doing their own stories with links to copies of the original blog on their own servers."

Ferguson stared ahead and didn't move as the doors of the lift opened. Prudence Tanner was waiting and handed him a thick folder before leading the way into the conference room. "Coffee and tea are on the credenza along with bangers, toast, whatever you like. I'll leave you to it." She turned to leave.

"Prudence, I think you should stay. I want somebody to take notes and handle things as they come up."

"Of course." She took a seat away from the conference table and opened an old-fashioned steno pad.

Ferguson nodded to Ysabel Mandelova and gave Xander Quarry's image on the videoconference screen a tip of an imaginary hat as he seated himself. "Okay, what do you two think."

Ysabel pursed her lips but said nothing; Xander arched his eyebrows. "If you have to ask," he said, "then you don't know what is happening . . . has happened. We're fucked. The party's over."

Ysabel turned toward the videoconference screen and let her sour face express her disapproval to the camera.

"What's that for, Ysabel? You don't like my saying it or the way I said it?"

"I think you're wrong. It will take some time and resources, but we'll get this under control again. We've squelched things before."

"You have your head up your fucking corn hole, Ysabel. This time it's everywhere. I don't think you understand how the digital world works. The whole goddamn world knows all about us. It's Pandora's fucking box. Once it's out there in cyberspace, it's out there forever."

"Let me guess, your daughter is away from the ranch."

"She is. Why?"

"Just noting your language is suddenly saltier. She doesn't tolerate you using the F-bomb."

Xander snorted out of the corner of his mouth. "I'll fuckin' F-bomb as much as I like. Those kids, those students here in sunny California, absolutely gazumped us. They screwed us six ways from Sunday, them and their goddamn teacher."

Ferguson leaned forward. "I thought we didn't know who did this. Our head of security—what the hell is his name, Prudence?"

"Wellbern, Kevin Wellbern."

"Right. Well, he said the original source . . . sources had not been identified."

Xander looked heavenward and shook his hands. "You're not fully awake, yet, Chas. They identified themselves. Hell, this Rodrigues chap has his byline right at the top of a 25,000-word article. There's another, shorter piece, from one Hidalgo Spinoza e Laredo in, of all fucking places, Busanyu. And the student network that handled the media campaign have claimed responsibility. This one kid, Roger Belknap, is already an Internet celeb, and it's still the middle of the night here.

"Un-be-fucking-lievable. A group of kids, undergrads from Sacramento State, journalism students, takes down one of the most powerful, secretive companies in history. They had an advance copy of the Rodrigues piece and did more footwork on their own. They put together this multimedia, multichannel campaign with graphics and videos and the works, then sprung it all at once all over the place. Some of it is pretty slick."

He laughed. "One of the videos to go viral is a fake ad for Biontolics. It starts with a wide shot of this wrinkled old crone partially silhouetted as she's walking naked along a beach. As the camera slowly dollies in, she gets younger and younger. The camera finishes with a head-and-shoulders shot, and she's this beautiful twenty-something. She turns toward the camera and whispers: 'Thank you, Biontolics.' Then there's a telephone number and an email address. Because of the nudity, YouTube took it down, but not before it got downloaded, duplicated, remixed, and spread all over the Internet. It didn't hurt that they picked some real hard-body goddess for the close-ups."

Ferguson swiveled in his chair. "Prudence, get Media Relations to set up a press conference for this afternoon. Between now and then, no one is authorized to speak to the media, and any questions are to be met with 'no comment.' Understood?"

Xander was laughing onscreen. "What the fuck are you going to say in a press conference?"

"I don't know. That's what we pay people for. In the meantime, we all just say 'no comment' and leave it at that."

Ysabel sighed. "You know, this could drag out for years, with parliamentary inquiries, congressional hearings, special prosecutors, God knows who or what. It's over. You think you're going to be able to keep up treatments for members of The Club with this going on? We're dead, quite literally."

Prudence touched the Bluetooth earpiece in her right ear. "Excuse me for interrupting, but there's word from the clinic. Dr. Lyon wants to speak with you. Shall I route the call through the conference phone?"

"Yes, do that." Over the speakerphone in the middle of the table came a buzz and a click and then the sound of medical monitors beeping in the background. Ferguson unmuted the mic on the speakerphone. "Hello, Bertrand. Are you there?"

"Mostly." The voice was weak and hoarse. "I just wanted to tell you that the singularity is real. It's just not the ..." A fit of coughing and spitting lasted several seconds, and the voices of conferring medical staff could be heard in the background. "It's not the one I expected. Should have. We all face it: the ultimate singularity. And you were right, it comes sooner than we expect or wish."

"Look, Bertrand, we'll pull you through this somehow. We have the best medical people on the planet."

"That may be, but I'm done here. I don't want to go out like Edgar or Rosen, dissolving into a stew of my own tissue and fluids. I'm grateful parliament finally passed the Compassionate Termination Act. I'm all set. All I have to do is have them start the drip. I just wanted to say my farewells and acknowledge my failures first. I don't know what I should have or could have done different, but I do know I went down the wrong road."

"Maybe not, Bertrand. Ysabel thinks we might still be able to stuff the djinn back in the bottle."

"Ysabel, dear Ysabel. She is a dour optimist with never a good word or idea but an eternal faith that things will somehow work out. They will not."

Ysabel opened her mouth to speak but Ferguson gave her a cautionary shake of the head as more coughing came over the speakerphone.

"It's time, Andras, old friend. Your turn will come soon enough. Llewellyn Andras Cass will follow Atchison Douglas Dougherty down the discontinuity. The staff here will brief you on the situation—two other members of The Club are already here, nearly as far down the slope as I—but I have neither the energy nor the time." There was a pause filled with several audible breaths. "Start the drip, please."

"Douglas!"

"The one true singularity, but it's private and personal, and we ..." The voice faded and trailed off.

"Douglas?" There was no answer. A steady chirp in the background turned into a long, steady tone, then silence as a monitor was turned off.

"This is Dr. Phradip, acting Head of Service here at the clinic. I have just pronounced Dr. Dougherty ... I mean Dr. Lyon, dead. We should schedule a consultation in person at your earliest. Please excuse me now, as we have other patients in need of attention."

Chapter 45

By the time Felix and Sahana landed at London City Airport, the Biontolics story was monopolizing the news. "Orange juice for you?" Felix asked, once they were settled into the waiting limo. He handed her a glass from the bar. "I hope you don't mind me channel surfing on the way into the city, but it's obvious the big surf is up and I want to catch the wave."

"I don't mind. I'm just as interested as you are. I guess the question of going public or not is academic now."

"We may have some flotsam to add to the waves. We'll meet with my London team after breakfast and strategize our next moves, but I don't think either of our lives are on the line over this any longer. Your reporter friend and his crew have blown things wide open. After this drubbing, I don't think Biontolics will have room to sneeze, much less pursue ex-employees."

"You're probably right."

"This is life, not statistics, sweetie; no probably about it." He thumb-typed another message on his iPhone.

"What are you up to?"

"Giving some marching orders to my private investment team, making sure we're ready to take advantage of some volatility in big pharma and life extension. Their stocks will take a hit, then slowly rebound. We'll buy at the bottom and then move out when enthusiasm is highest just before new government regs and reality set in. Hop aboard, Sahana. We're on track for an exciting ride."

"You think so?":

"Oh, I know so. The train is leaving the station, and I'm the engineer."

"This looks more like a limousine than a train. Do you always talk in management-speak metaphors?"

"Pretty much, yes. Yes, I do. Sorry. But hey, looks can be deceiving. Don't you feel the rockin' rhythm of steel wheels on steel rails?" He pantomimed lightly bouncing to a steady clickety-clack. "Wait a minute. Did you see that text crawl on the news? Somebody from Biontolics just died. Turn up the sound."

They listened to the news flash about Bertrand Lyon dying at a private hospital outside London. "Lyon was the CEO of Biontolics Holdings, a corporate conglomerate now under siege after revelations of irregularities and secret longevity treatments. Speaking off the record, because she was not authorized to address the public, a source at the clinic said the man's symptoms resembled those of the late Dr. Edgar Jabari Mbutsu, President-for-Life of the African nation of Busanyu. Unsubstantiated allegations posted anonymously on the Internet have claimed that Mbutsu had also been receiving treatment from medical personnel associated with Biontolics. The clinic, a re-search facility known to locals as Saint Sophia's because it had once been a teaching hospital, is owned by Sellian Atlantic, yet another part of the Biontolics empire.

"Now we switch to a live report from our affiliate, KOCA TV in Oakland, California. Reporter Sabrina Sadler is at the famed Quarry Ranch south of San Francisco where flamboyant billionaire Xander Quarry has called a surprise middle-of-the-night press conference. Xander Quarry has also been linked with the Biontolics firestorm that has swept through the Internet in recent hours. Bring us up-to-date, Sabrina."

"Yes. One-time playboy Xander Quarry, who has been implicated in the Internet imbroglio you mentioned, is said to be ready to confirm the allegations regarding Biontolics. A spokesperson for the London-based corporate giant has declined to comment except to say that Mr. Quarry is not authorized to speak for the company. As you can see behind me here at the luxurious Quarry Ranch, swarms of reporters and news crews are waiting for Mr. Quarry to appear. Ah, there he is now, looking uncharacteristically dapper in a suit and tie."

The camera panned away from the reporter and zoomed in on a grinning Xander Quarry standing with his arm around his daughter. He began without waiting for the buzz to die down. "Ladies and gentleman. My remarks will be brief, but I will take questions. My name is Alexander Roman Quarry, and this is my daughter, Nadia. She's here for moral support—and she knows how much my morals need support—and because she is soon to take over Quarry Industries. For the past forty-plus years, I have been an underwriter of the enterprise that came to be known as Biontolics Holdings International. Biontolics has kept me and a select group of people alive—and young—through an elaborate intervention scheme that its principals devised. God-awful expensive treatments, I should add. They have kept the technology to themselves for their select inner circle of mostly obscenely rich bastards like me.

"Well, if you've been following the news feeds or turned on cable in recent hours, you know that Biontolics is going down the toilet, which means all the turds with it." He looked down. "You can't see it, but Nadia just crushed my right instep. She doesn't approve of my coarse language, but in this case I think she's being a bit prudish, since I could have said that all the shits like me are going down, too.

"Whatever bullshit denials the company may make, I can confirm, in essence, most of what has been circulating on the Internet. To my old friends Douglas Dougherty and Andras Cass, I offer my apologies for joining in blowing the whistle, but there already was a flag on the play. And for those of you reporters who believe that journalism is more than just holding a mic and smiling into a camera, I can provide documentation from my own records to support all the allegations, including the work of paid assassins." He held up a neatly bound folder. "My people have hastily prepared a press kit that will be made available to all of you who made the trek out here in the middle of the night to help an old man, a very old man, come clean. Thank you."

The strafing of shouted questions from reporters began almost instantly.

Chapter 46

A light drizzle rattled on the roof of the car, and the air was heavy with the smell of moss, mud, and melting snow. Clinton opened the car door for Julia. "There's somebody I want you to meet."

"And we had to drive all the way to Canada to meet this someone?" She looked around. "There's nothing but dead trees and ugly rocks around here."

"We're not in Canada, at least not quite. I just hope I can retrace my steps. Otherwise, we're in for a very long meandering hike in the woods. Ah, here it is, I think. We go up this way, past that boulder."

"Which boulder? There's nothing but boulders all around. Are you now some sort of Boy Scout?"

He looked back at her and laughed. "Just follow me, and stay close."

As it turned out, he missed the shelter and ended up at a spring. He was about to head back downhill and start over again from the fire road when the sound of a shotgun being cocked behind them got his attention.

"My oh my, you two. I thought Clinton here was a noisy city kid, but together you are a regular traveling troupe of circus monkeys."

"Millie." He spun around with a wide smile.

"Clinton. And who is this you dragged into the woods with you?"

"This is Julia."

"Just Julia, no last name. Okay then, 'significant' Julia, we can surmise."

Julia turned and looked down at the shotgun. "Is this how you welcome friends?"

"Up here, it is. At least for people like me. I'm the no-name backwoods bug-and-bird lady. Now, that is. I use to be Millicent Geller, but she died in a fire in Falmouth in the fall."

"Wait a minute. You're Millicent Geller? You're the teacher who was killed."

"That's what I just said."

"But you're not dead."

"Apparently."

"So, you, like, faked it."

"Like."

Julia shook her head repeatedly. "You're as bad as Clinton."

"Or as good."

Julia threw her arms up in surrender as she looked from Millie to Clinton. "I love her. But I see where you picked up some of your annoying tics."

Millie put on a look of exaggerated puzzlement. "Annoying? Tics? What are you talking about? In any case, how about coming in for some hot tea before we all get soaked."

Millie led the way down a meandering path to her tiny cabin. Once inside, she apologized. "Only got the two chairs. You take them. While I get the kettle boiling, you can tell me what brings you to these parts."

"News, we're bringing news."

"I can't say there's much news that would interest me. I hear a little now and then when I hike into town for supplies, but what I hear is never that good."

"This is good. Biontolics bought it. The whole business is exposed; there are indictments here, in the UK, Switzerland; the CEO is dead, and the last time their head doctor was seen, he wasn't looking too good, either."

"And you call this good news? People dying, empires crumbling, humanity's hopes of immortality crushed? Doesn't sound very positive to me."

"But it means you can go home."

"I am home."

"I meant . . ."

"I know what you meant, but I'm content. Come summer, maybe I'll do some science programs for some of the farm kids, keep up my teaching chops. My research is going well. I have food and firewood. What else do I need?"

Clinton opened his mouth to speak but said nothing. Millie looked back at him as if to reaffirm his silence.

Julia filled the awkward gap. "You're a biologist. You might find it interesting what's going on with the Biontolics patients."

"I might."

"Basically, they were hoisted by their own petard. Their treatments meant that the genetic makeup of each patient kept getting more complicated and less manageable as the number of cell lines was multiplied."

Millie raised an index finger. "Let me guess. It's about the epigenetic effects of different cell lines each becoming part of the cellular environment of the other lines, everything impacting everything else in completely unpredictable ways. That's it, right? Particularly with regard to the oncogene expression that Janella Kai first found to be key in cell longevity."

"Yeah, at least that's sort of how I understand it, but I'm no scientist and not a doctor. Eventually, the treatments stop working, and there's no going back. This is one the scientists will be studying for decades, but I don't think there are going to be any more human subjects, not for a very long time. Biontolics is arguing that they have to continue treatments already underway or the patients will die the way your husband did. The news today said two of these people have committed suicide rather than face that."

"Oh, goody. More good news."

Julia lowered her head. "I'm sorry."

"Don't be. You succeeded where both Rosen and I failed. You brought this thing out into the daylight."

"Clinton and I did it, but you started it. If it weren't for the Millicent factor, we would never even have known the story."

"Can I ask a favor of you, Julia? I'm going to steal Clinton to help me bring some water back from the spring. Would you keep your eye on that kettle and use the poker to lift it away from the fire when it boils? Grab those buckets, Clinton, and let's hustle through the rain."

"Do you want me to make the tea once the water boils?" Julia asked.

"Sure. Pot's on the top shelf, tea's in the cupboard, tea ball is in the drawer . . . someplace. You'll find it. We'll be back."

Once outside, she took Clinton by the arm and steered him up the trail toward the spring. "Is this serious?" She nodded back toward the cabin.

"I guess so. Yeah, maybe."

"Real definitive, aren't you?"

"Yes, it's serious, but, well, she's my student . . . was . . . and she's, you know, a lot younger, and . . ."

"Those issues didn't seem so important to you last time you were here."

Clinton's ears started burning and his face flushed red. "I . . . I'm sorry . . . I . . ."

"Oh, Clinton, don't make too much of it, and don't be too hard on yourself. It was a lovely evening. You got to revisit a fantasy, and I got to feel flattered and young again. That was that." She brushed back the hood of her rain jacket. "Rain's letting up. In the old days this would have been another six inches of snow, but mid-winter rain is becoming more and more common. Okay, here we are. Let me show you how to fill the buckets without stirring up all the sediment at the bottom."

They filled the buckets and started back down the trail, with Clinton struggling not to slosh the water out. Between quiet curses, he restarted the conversation. "This whole one-on-one thing is hard for me. It's always been hard for me."

"You're a man. Males grow up more slowly."

"Do you think it matters, this age thing, the difference?"

"What do you think?"

"I don't have much experience to draw on. It hasn't been that long."

"What about a twenty-year crush on an older woman? Does it matter?"

"That's different. I mean does it matter in, well, marriage?"

"I don't know. It's real, but whether it matters, well, that depends on what matters to you. One thing that the biology part means is that you'll probably die before she does, maybe long before, since you belong to the biologically inferior sex. If you stay together, you'll both need to face that reality. It's a promise, not a guarantee, and Nature does not always keep its promises, but that's how things generally work. In some senses, you will also always be ahead of her. You already know what it's like to turn thirty; she's not there yet. On the other hand, you will never know what it's like to carry and give birth to a child, while that option is open to her. Probably."

"You and Dr. David never . . ."

"No, we didn't have children. I can't. But then again, I've helped raise a lot of kids. Look, whatever lies ahead for you two, don't focus on the things that separate you or get hung up on the social stereotypes about older men and younger women; other people will do enough of that without your help. Stick with what connects you. If it's right between you, it's right, however old or young you are.

"Rosen and I fell head-over-heels in love as college students; we were just kids. I have a teacher friend who found her soulmate when she was in her sixties. There is no right way to do life or love; it's chemistry and luck and hard work, with no formula for mixing the right ingredients in the right order."

"What do you think of her?"

"And now we get to the other agenda: looking for my approval and blessing. I just met her; I don't have much to think about except she obviously adores you. You are going to have challenges, though. That much is obvious."

"What are you talking about? You mean the age difference?"

"More than that. In case you hadn't noticed, you two are an interracial couple. Things are a hell of a lot better now than they were fifty years ago, but that doesn't mean it will be easy."

"Funny, in a very real sense, I hadn't noticed. I mean, it's not like I'm blind, but I think in my head I think of us as both being Portuguese-American."

"You think you think? You think in your head? You wax so eloquent, Clinton. You must be in love. Oxytocin tends to tangle the tongues of males."

"Oxytocin?"

"The bonding hormone. Heavy in the air between you two. Trust me, I'm a biologist; I know about these things."

With the rain stopping after they returned, Millie suggested they take their tea outside. "It's such a mild day. Bring the chairs out." In front of the cabin, Millie upended a log and sat on it. "Now, tell me more about the big news. I want to know how you actually did it, exposing Biontolics." She turned expectantly toward Clinton.

"Don't look at me," he said. "It was Julia who really pulled it off. She and her friends—"

"Your students," Julia interjected.

"—my students. They used social media to spread the word at the speed of the Internet. She helped set it all up in advance without consulting with me, even passed on a pilfered copy of my magnum opus for posting on the class blog—and everywhere else in the world, it seems."

"It wasn't pilfered," she said. "You gave it to me to edit, remember. I just passed on a copy of the final edit to Roger and the rest of his team."

"Right, but I never saw that final edit until it was posted online, and now I have to come up with another 20,000 words or so because the *Sacramento Bee* wants to publish the complete, full, unexpurgated story. They have their eyes on a Pulitzer, I think, and they expect me to deliver it for them."

Millie patted his knee. "Marvelous. I always knew you had it in you. You were one of my favorite students. It does a teacher's heart good to see a student finally coming into his own."

'Well, I couldn't have done it without Julia. Not only did she do a lot of the leg work, but she saved my skin—more than once." He reached for Julia's hand and gave it a squeeze.

"Okay, you two, none of that. Now I want a report: the full, blow-by-blow account of your travel adventures. Clinton told me you went to Africa together. Fill me in."

~ ~ ~

It was late afternoon before Clinton and Julia finally left. As the car bucked back down the rutted fire road, Julia was the first to speak. "I get what you saw in her. She is something else. Always teaching, even in casual conversation."

"Yeah, she's pretty special. But I hate leaving her alone up here in the woods."

"Oh, she can take care of herself. You, on the other hand, you wouldn't last a week up here, not without me, you wouldn't."

"Well, I guess I better hang on to you, then."

"I do hope you aren't thinking of doing the back-to-the-land scenario. Remember, I'm a California girl, and frankly, I am eager to get back to sunshine and surf."

"I have bad news for you. There's no surf in Sacramento."

'Details, details. I just want to get home. Well, with you, anyway."

Chapter 47

A landscaping crew was busy converting the front lawn at the nursing home to xeriscape, replacing water-wasting turf and shrubbery with rock gardens, succulents, and desert perennials. Julia took Clinton's hand and led him up the zig-zag path through the work-in-progress and to the main entrance.

"She's not going to remember me," he said. "She never does, and your being with me will only confuse her more."

"She's your mother. You're going to visit your mother. Do you understand?"

"Yes, ma'am, I understand. I'll just follow you, since you already know the way."

Julia frowned at him. "Don't you yes-ma'am me, mister, if you know what's good for you."

"Oh, that part I know. You're good for me."

"You got that right." She smiled broadly as she held the door open for him.

~ ~ ~

Sarah Toledano did not turn from the window when they entered her room. "Do you see that bird out there?" she said. "I am trying to remember what it's called. At first I thought it was a cat up there in the tree, but it wasn't. It was a bird. It must be a catbird, then. What do you think?" She turned abruptly and faced them. "Oh, you again."

"Yes, Mom, it's me again: Clinton."

"Oh, not you. I mean her, the pretty one. I think I know you." She stood up.

"You do. I'm Julia. Remember? I brought you the chocolates."

"Oh, I love sweets, so you must be sweet, too. Ha ha. But who is he?"

"He's your son, Clinton."

"Is that so? Then that man who keeps calling must be his father, but I don't remember his name."

Clinton shot an I-told-you-so glance at Julia. "Angelo," he said to his mother. "Your husband's name is Angelo, Mom, but it must be someone else who calls you."

"I had a husband, but I don't think his name was Angelo. Are you sure?"

"Yes, Mom, I'm sure."

There was an intermittent buzz from the direction of the night stand. It stopped after a while, then restarted. "I think something is buzzing in that drawer, Mom."

"Oh, that's him. He calls about this time every week. Or maybe it's every day; I wouldn't know."

"It's a phone? Are you going to answer it?"

"Oh, I can never figure out those things. It's not actually a phone. One of those—oh, I don't remember the word—like a phone but not. I always let the nurse do it."

The buzzing started up again. Julia opened the drawer "Here, let me take care of it."

"Are you a nurse? You have to be a nurse to do it, I think."

Julia held up a pink smartphone. "I think I can manage this, even without a nursing degree." She answered the call and switched to speakerphone. "Hello?"

"Is this Roberta? Can I speak with Sarah?"

"She's right here. Who is this?"

"It's Angelo. Who else would be calling on this phone? You don't sound like Roberta. Are you the new nurse Sarah told me about?"

"No, this is Julia. And Clinton is right beside me. How in hell . . . ? And where in hell are you?"

"Not in hell, thank you very much. Not in heaven either, that's damn clear. But I'm okay."

"How . . . ?"

"It always helps to have friends, especially friends with funds. Mine sprung me from the hospital. They can't spring me from this damn wheelchair, but they did set up an amazing wheelchair-accessible lab for me. I've been doing some great chemistry for them, and they treat me like a prince, although I'm pretty much confined to quarters. I guess I can't complain. It's a lot better than what your Biontolics buddies had in store for me." There was the sound of forced laughter. "Is my Sarah there?"

"She's right here, smiling."

"Hi, Sarah. It's me, Angelo. I love you."

"Well, I don't know any Angelo, but I suppose I probably love you, too. And you should see these two lovebirds visiting me. I don't know who they are, but they are such a cute couple."

Clinton feigned embarrassment. "She's learning to bake challah, Mom. It's pretty good."

Sarah's eyes and mouth opened suddenly with surprise and delight, as if someone had just turned the electricity back on in an empty house. "I remember making challah, kneading and braiding, that wonderful smell that would fill the kitchen as it baked before the start of Shabbos."

Clinton looked puzzled. "You never made challah, Mom."

"Silly boy, before you came along, when I was a girl. Momma taught me: your *bubbe*. You never knew her. She could be ... sometimes ..." Her voice faded and her face slackened. "What were we talking about?"

"Challah. Julia is learning to make challah."

"Clint, you should help her, help her learn."

"That's exactly what I'm doing, Mom, and she's teaching me how to make *feijoada*.

"And speak a little more Portuguese," Julia added.

Sarah reached for their hands. "You should see them, Angelo. You really should."

"I know, perhaps again someday."

"They look happy, happy and in love."

"That was us, too, Sarah. Once."

"I know, Angelo, I know."

Quiet recognition overtook them for a moment, then Julia whispered, "Alone, together, in the silent finite present."

Clinton looked at her. "What?"

"One of Hidalgo's poems, 'Internet Pause.' I saved it on my phone." She found it and started reading.

> *Bound by skeins of gossamer glass,*
> *Digital veins of captive sunbeams cast*
> > *across the seas,*
> *Bright bit-streams passed*
> > *between the rejoined absent:*

Alone, together,
in the silent finite present.

For that moment they were all there, all four, in the room, in the silent finite present.

~ ~ ~

~ ~ ~

Fiction by Lior Samson

The Homeland Connection
Bashert ~ The Dome ~ Web Games
Chipset ~ Gasline ~ Flight Track

The Rosen Singularity ~ The Millicent Factor

The Four-Color Puzzle

Requisite Variety: Collected Short Science Fiction

Acknowledgements

In addition to the crack editorial team I depend on for help with every book, I always turn to specialists: subject-matter experts who can steer me right on matters of technical detail where my own research may have failed me. For *The Rosen Singularity*, I turned to Mark Raizin, M.D., an amazing internist who actually spends time listening to his patients and who did his best to keep me from making boneheaded mistakes regarding modern medicine and medical practice. My friend and good university colleague, Jos van Leeuwen, a careful reader and my consultant on matters Dutch, suggested small but important changes.

For *The Millicent Factor*, I owe special thanks to biostatistician Tamar Sofer at the University of Washington, and to fire forensics expert Joseph LeFevre at Fox Valley Technical College, himself a writer. They not only helped me within their own areas of expertise, but made other suggestions that improved the story and its telling. I also want to thank Devan Lockwood for his pointed advice about contemporary social media. There were others, too, who declined to be named but whose contributions are no less appreciated.

I am also indebted to readers and reviewers who suffered through earlier versions of both novels and gave me the benefit of their intelligence and insight. Old friends and erstwhile debate partners were, more than once, pressed into service. For Rosen's story, Jim Hawkins, sailor and counselor extraordinaire, was helpful and supportive, and David Tutelman, friend and critic, told me straight out that my first draft simply failed. David told me enough about why and how I had missed the mark for me to correct my aim and zero in on the target.

A special note of deep appreciation goes to North Shore artist Dianna Daly for granting permission to use her painting "Passages" for the cover art. The watercolor—one of a series inspired by a photograph taken at the Crane Estate in Ipswich—was on temporary display at The Lone Gull, my favorite coffee shop in Gloucester. It seemed to fit, even before I knew the title and provenance, both so conmnected with these stories.

I am, as always, indebted to Lucy Lockwood, my wife and best friend, who infected me with the germ of an idea that launched both novels and then took time away from her graduate studies in marine biology to give me the benefit of her wise counsel and sharp editorial skills. And to Janet Lemnah, copy editor extraordinaire, who wields a red pencil with precision and panache, goes another round of my heartfelt applause.

I must also credit one person I have never met: the late Steve Jobs. His tenacity and untempered honesty, his blunt words while staring into the very face of Death itself, were another inspiration for this story. His words and his works live on.

About the Author

Lior Samson is the pen name of an emeritus academic who has won awards for both fiction and non-fiction writing as well as for his innovative work in interaction design. He is the author of more than two dozen books, including nine novels and a collection of short fiction. As a consultant and teacher, he has traveled the world and has served on the faculties of major international universities.

He lives in Massachusetts where he cooks creative fusion cuisine and composes serious choral music. He describes himself as a full-time novelist, part-time journalist, and full-time tech support and taxi driver for the three students in his family—and readily acknowledges that his time sheet doesn't add up.

He regards the readers who write with questions, kudos, and criticism as vital parts of the dialogue he hopes to spark through his writing. He enjoys hearing from readers and appreciates those who take the time to post reviews on Amazon and elsewhere. He can be reached by email at: lior@liorsamson.com

www.ingramcontent.com/pod-product-compliance
Lightning Source LLC
Chambersburg PA
CBHW030850030726
47495CB00005B/1453